My Sweet Vampire

by
ARABELLA HOLMES

CHAPTER ONE

Carly

C OFFEE REPUBLIC IS packed to the rafters. For a split-second, I stall by the entrance doors, drawing the shop's familiar air into my lungs. My head's telling me to turn back, that it's too crowded, that I'll never find a free table, but I'm a slave to my routine. Plus it's a Tuesday, and Tuesdays are always busy, especially at lunchtime in Central London. Forcing my feet to move, I enter the shop and shed the ice from my limbs like an unwanted coat. Delicious smells tease my nostrils: fresh bread, newly ground coffee.

It feels so good to be out of the cold.

Cheerfully, I approach the long serving counter and nod to the waitress. She flashes a warm smile.

"Hello, darling," I say. "A blueberry muffin—"

"…and a large white coffee in a takeout cup," she finishes. We both laugh.

It's an old joke between us. I come here every day for lunch, and every day I ask for the same thing. By now, this lady knows my order like the back of her hand.

"Okay, one coffee and a blueberry muffin coming up." She picks up a tong from the counter and moves toward the glass pastry case. My mouth waters as I watch her place the muffin on a plate. I imagine biting into it, the sponge soft and crumbly on my lips. I'm supposed to be on a diet, but I simply

1

can't resist a sweet treat every now and then.

"Do you have your loyalty card with you?" she asks.

"Oh, yes." I fumble through my pockets. "Mustn't forget that."

I flip open my wallet and slide the loyalty card across the counter. She brands it with the company logo and hands it back to me.

"Thanks." I'm now just two stamps away from a free beverage.

She turns away and begins drawing water from the coffee machine. I scan the shop for somewhere to sit. Finding a seat in this place is always a nightmare, but eventually, I spy a free table.

Hastily, I pay for my stuff and carry my tray through swathes of bodies to stake my claim before anyone else does. Once seated, I unbutton my coat and cast a critical eye over my surroundings. I see an old man arguing with his wife; two mums with their children, discussing life; a dark-haired student tapping away on his laptop. I am surrounded by people, yet for some reason I feel strangely cut off from everything.

I take a sip of my coffee and wince. *Hot, hot, hot.* Cringing, I put down the cup and glance at my *Kermit the Frog* wrist-watch.

One twenty-five.

Jesus, I still have thirty minutes to kill.

Tucking my hands under my elbows, I gaze out the window with a bemused expression. Fog as grey as slushy snow clings to Charlotte Street, and all of the buildings look as if they've been filtered through frosted glass. Even for early November, the weather's pretty grim. It's been like this all week: fog so thick you can barely see more than a few feet in front of you. Even so, I love the West End in winter. Charlotte Street is just a stone's throw from the bright lights of Soho, London's buzzing theatre district, and a mere five minutes from Oxford Street. Perfect if you fancy a spot of retail therapy after work (which I nearly always do).

Moistening my lips, I reach inside my bag and pull out a little compact mirror. I grimace at my reflection. Somehow, I've managed to get lipstick on my teeth (again), and my short, blonde hair is completely windswept. Goddammit, I look so washed out.

I really need to start going to bed earlier.

Closing the mirror, I peruse my bag in search of my phone. Obsessively, I study the battered handset like it's some sort of holy icon. To everyone else, it's nothing but a scuffed old Nokia, but to me it's a time capsule, a gift to be cherished.

For five years, I've nursed a broken heart. For five long years, I've studiously avoided an upgrade from the phone company and sacrificed all the perks of modern technology in the process. Old as this phone is, I can never part with it because it contains messages from Andrew, my ex-boyfriend. Sweet nothings. Little love notes. With painful tenderness, I scroll through his five-year-old messages, each word a dagger to my heart: *Morning angel, how R U today? I miss U so much. Remember I love you.*

Liar, liar, liar.

Loosening a great breath, I put the phone away and tell myself to fix up and get a grip. I switch on my iPod and listen to "A Whole New World" from Disney's *Aladdin*. Bathed in a symphony of enchantment, I imagine myself as Princess Jasmine, flying on a magic carpet through Agrabah—lost in a world of make-believe, so far removed from my reality. Most of the music on my iPod is from my childhood: songs from '80s movies and Disney films. Whenever I'm down, I find solace in the memories these soundtracks invoke. They take me back to a more innocent time, a time before the harsh realities of adulthood descended.

I peer down at my thirty-six-year-old hands and wonder where my life has gone. When did I stop being a child? When had the safety net been pulled so cruelly from under me? I ponder the speediness of our lives; how fast the months now seem to fly by. When I was a kid, I swear the days were longer than this, the summer holidays never-ending. If only time stood still. If only I could freeze this moment in a snow globe and stay forever in the present, with no past or future to worry about.

The *Aladdin* soundtrack comes to an end and fades into "Colours of the Wind" from *Pocahontas*. I blink a couple of times, realising I've been daydreaming for ages. Panicking, I check my watch and see that lunch ended five minutes ago. Hurriedly, I wolf down the rest of my muffin, take a few sips of coffee and make a swift exit.

As I step into the street, a harsh breeze stings my cheeks and I shiver despite my many layers of clothing. It's bitingly cold and I curse myself for leaving my gloves at home. Glancing left and right, I wait for the traffic lights to change, then scurry across the street toward my workplace. Based over five floors of a white Georgian building, Midas Media is a prestigious design company whose diverse client base includes the BBC and other prominent, multi-national organisations. I've worked there as receptionist for almost ten years and despite it not being my dream job, I've grown quite attached to it.

At first, it had just started out as something to do, a stop-gap between temping jobs before I embarked on what my mother called a 'proper' career. After leaving university, I'd initially toyed with the idea of working with children, maybe become a teaching assistant or something, but somehow this never happened and I ended up spending most of my twenties behind a reception desk. Not that I mind. Working gives me a reason to wake up in the mornings, and as far as jobs go, I could do a lot worse. Despite my cheerful exterior, I've always been a self-contained sort of person, happy in my own company, so being a receptionist suits me just fine. I mean sure, most mornings I'm constantly buzzing people in and out of the building, saying hi and handing out passes, but in the afternoon, there are great periods of solitude that I cherish. Periods that allow me time alone with my thoughts. I'm sociable enough when I want to be, but sometimes I just need silence.

A loud beep snaps me from my reverie.

I glance up in time to see a car skim through a puddle, and I narrowly miss being soaked. Startled, I step back from the curb and huddle in the doorway to my office, hugging my arms for warmth. Absently, I pat down my pockets in search of my treasured Marlboro Lights; I'm absolutely dying for a cigarette. With shaky fingers, I light one and take a few shallow puffs, closing my eyes as the nicotine whips through my system. My enjoyment doesn't last for very long; by the fourth puff, a voice inside is telling me that smoking's gonna give me lung cancer.

Great.

It was my New Year's resolution to quit, but here I am eleven months on, still battling a ten-a-day addiction. No matter what I do, I just can't seem to kick the habit. I've tried everything: chewing gum, Nicorette patches, but they've all come to a big fat nothing.

"Excuse me," says a voice from behind me. I whirl around to see a young man in a dirty tracksuit. "Sorry to bother you, but do you have a spare cigarette?"

"Of course." I offer him one. Then on a sudden impulse, I decide to give him the whole packet. "Here. You might as well have the rest."

"Really?" The man looks astonished. "Are you sure?"

"Positive. I'm trying to quit, so you'll be doing me a favour."

His eyes light up like a kid at Christmas. "Well, if you're sure … thanks! I really appreciate it."

When he's gone, I toss my lighter in the bin as a final act of defiance. *Okay. That's the last cigarette I'll ever smoke. As of today, I'm officially nicotine-free.*

Feeling like Superman, I step into the brightly lit reception of Midas Media. Everything about the place screams success: exotic potted plants, marbled floors, mirrored walls, and a five-grand chaise lounge.

Mark, the security guard, is sitting behind the reception desk, casually flipping through a copy of today's *Metro*. He's in his late fifties but could easily pass for forty, with a strong, athletic build, shaven head and a puckered little baby mouth.

He looks up from his paper and smiles at me. I smile back. We're greeting each other with the easy friendship of two people who have worked together for years.

"What time do you call this? I thought you'd been abducted by aliens."

"Very funny. Was I really gone that long?"

"You most certainly were, Carly Singleton. Honestly, what *are* we going to do with you?" He folds up his *Metro* and throws it down on the desk. "Now, on to more pressing matters. Did you remember to buy my M&M's?"

"Oh, yes, thanks for reminding me." I rummage through my bag and hand over the shiny, yellow packet.

"Merci beaucoup." He takes the M&M's and tears the wrapper open with his teeth. "How much do I owe you?"

"Forget about it. They were only a quid."

"You never let me pay for anything. I must owe you a bloody fortune." Tilting his head back, Mark demolishes half the packet in one gulp. Then he wipes his hands on his sweater. "Right, I'm off to the third floor. The women's toilet is broken again, and Tim wants me to reset the password."

"Wow, that's the fourth time in two weeks." I hang up my coat and take my place behind reception. Mark swipes his ID on the wall-mounted card reader and steps through the glass partition. As he heads toward the elevators, I shout, "Thanks for covering me, Mark. I really appreciate it."

"Anytime, sweetheart."

Within seconds, he's gone and I'm alone again. Straightening out my cardigan, I smooth back my hair in an effort to look more presentable. Then I crouch down and fumble through the cleaning box in search of the spray polish. When I find it, I wipe down the desk methodically. Just as I'm finishing up, Jill Hopkins, a senior designer who works on the second floor, enters reception. She looks immaculate as always, dressed in a smart tweed blazer with suede elbow patches and knee-length boots. She has a wonderfully horsey face: jutting chin, full lips with a slight overbite and thick, brown hair that comes down to her shoulders. I'm on first-name terms with most of the designers, but I have a particular liking for Jill. Right from the start, the two of us have got on like a house on fire, and I always make time to chat with her.

"Hey, honey, how was your weekend?"

"Great," I smile.

"Did you get up to anything nice?"

"Oh, you know me, forever the party animal ..." My voice trails off and I shift my weight awkwardly.

Jill's nostrils flare. Then she staggers back and covers her cheeks in mock horror. "Okay, hit me with it. What in the name of sanity are you wearing today?"

I snigger and start unbuttoning my cardigan. At work, my quirky dress sense is legendary, in particular my penchant for novelty clothing. It's become something of a running joke, and Jill is always clamouring to know what my T-shirt slogan will say today.

"Why...should I worry?" She squints at the writing on my chest, frowns, and shoots me a quizzical look. "What does that mean?"

"It's from *Oliver and Company*," I declare proudly.

Her frown deepens. "*Oliver and Company?*"

"You know, that song by Billy Joel? He voiced Dodger in the 1988 movie."

"Um, no. I'm not familiar with it." In an effort to pacify me, she adds, "That's a cool T-shirt, though. I love the font."

Deflated, I close my cardigan and remind myself that I'm a thirty-six-year-old woman with a geeky cartoon obsession. How can I possibly expect Jill to relate?

There's a short, uncomfortable silence. To change the subject, I ask her how her twins are doing.

"Oh, they're great," she enthuses. "Gavin and I took them to London Zoo at the weekend. We had so much fun. They particularly liked the gorillas, even though they were a little scared of them. Look, I'll show you some pictures ..." Proudly, she leans across the desk and flicks through her smartphone. "Aren't they just adorable?"

I take the phone and rest my gaze on a photo of two

gorgeous four-year-olds. "My goodness, they've grown so big!"

"I know. Crazy, isn't it?"

"They're absolutely beautiful." I flick though a couple more pictures, coo some more, then hand her back the phone. "I forgot to say, I've got a little present for you."

"Oh, no, you shouldn't have!"

Reaching beneath the desk, I retrieve a large carrier bag.

"What's this?" she asks, taking it from me.

"It's just a little something I made for the twins."

Excitedly, Jill rips it open and pulls out a pair of crocheted teddy bears. With a joyful squeal, she reaches over and gives me a clumsy one-armed hug. "Oh my gosh, Carly, these are absolutely gorgeous. Did you really make them yourself?"

"Uh-huh."

"Get out of here. I didn't know you were so talented."

I beam at the compliment, feeling suddenly bashful. "I-I just thought it would be nice to give them something special. Something nobody else has."

"Oh, honey, you're an angel. A perfect angel. Thank you. The twins are going to love them."

I'm smiling so hard my cheeks hurt. The teddies have gone down a treat, and I'm pleased my two weeks of non-stop crocheting has paid off. The glow in Jill's face has made it all worth it.

I love making people happy.

She tucks a hair behind her ear and clears her throat. "Hey listen, what are you doing this Saturday?"

"Saturday?" I wring my hands and start to get a sick feeling. I can guess where this conversation's heading. "Er, nothing. Why? Have you got something planned?"

"It's my fortieth birthday, and I'm having a little get-together. Nothing too fancy, just a few old friends I haven't seen in ages. I promise it won't be a late one. We'll probably just go for a meal in Nando's, then maybe on to a bar or something. I'd love it if you could come."

I grin insipidly. "Um, yeah, sounds great. What time on Saturday?"

"Shall we say seven o'clock? The girls have a loose plan to meet at London Bridge and take it from there." I nod vigorously. Jill pauses, her blue eyes scrutinising my face. "Are you sure you're definitely coming?"

"Of course! Wouldn't miss it for the world." I laugh but inside I'm crying. I don't have the heart to tell Jill her well-meaning invitation has ruined my whole week. How can I make her understand that I like my Saturdays to myself? That I need to be free to indulge my hobbies, namely crocheting, watching movies and trawling the Net for Disney memorabilia? How can I explain the mere thought of socialising turns my blood cold? That the idea of meeting new people and having to strike up conversations scares me to death.

"So, I'll see you Saturday?" Jill says hopefully.

I compress my lips. "Mmm."

"Definitely?"

"Of course! Wouldn't miss it for the world," I repeat. "Seriously, I can't wait."

"Fantastic." She fumbles through her pockets. "Sorry, honey, I seem to have forgotten my ID card. Could you let me in please?"

Smiling wanly, I buzz her through the partition and watch her vanish into the elevator.

As soon as she's gone, my shoulders sag and I release a pent-up sigh. *This is going to be a complete and utter nightmare. Why the hell did I say yes? Am I some sort of masochist?*

Privately, I console myself with the hope that I can always make up an excuse nearer the time to get out of it. Perhaps say I've had an emergency or something. I hate to let Jill down, especially as she's so lovely, but I feel I have no choice. She must have seen the presents as a sign that I wish to take our acquaintance further and hook up outside of work. Sadly, the thought of Saturday disturbs me so much I'm forced to sit down and have a glass of water. I'm completely panicking and know I won't have peace of mind until it's over. One way or another, I must find a way out of it. I have no intention of sacrificing my weekend to spend a night in the company of drunken strangers.

AT QUARTER PAST five, I pull on my coat, say goodbye to Mark and step out into the dark street. The fog has cleared but the wind is still as harsh as ever. Steeling myself, I turn onto the main road and begin marching in the direction of Regent Street. Hamley's, the world-famous toy shop, is twenty minutes from my office and the time passes quickly as I stride through hoards of late-night shoppers and tourists of every nationality. Even though it's still only November, I start to get a Christmassy feeling.

My heart soars as the bright lights of Hamley's finally come into view. The window display is calling out to me, making silent promises. Being here always makes me feel young again.

Excitedly, I enter the store and cast my eyes over dozens of colourful shelves jam-packed with gadgets and toys from every manufacturer imaginable. The place is absolutely teeming with people, and the queue for the checkouts stretches all the way around the shop. Undeterred, I head straight for the back shelves. I know exactly what I'm looking for. The only question is do they have it in stock?

For the past few months, I've been collecting Disney's limited edition designer dolls. So far, I've bought six, but I still need to get Ariel and Prince Eric to complete my collection. Squinting at the upper shelves, I spy a row of shiny blue boxes with *The Little Mermaid* logo on the front. I catch my breath. At a hundred quid apiece, they're certainly not cheap, but I simply have to have them.

Hurriedly, I move toward the display and attempt to pull down one of the boxes, but I'm too short to reach it. Helplessly, I beckon a young sales-assistant. "Hey, could you please get me down one of those dolls?"

"No problem. I'll get a stepladder."

Moments later, the boy returns from the stockroom looking a bit peeved. Forcing a smile, he wheels across the ladder and props it against the shelf to quickly fulfil his errand. As he hands me down a box, my face falls. "Oh. I'm sorry to be a pain, but could you get me another one? This one's got a huge dent in it."

"No problem." I detect a note of annoyance in his voice, but I'm not fazed. There's no way I'm paying one-hundred pounds for damaged goods. I like my dolls to be in pristine condition, and that includes the packaging. Stomping his feet, the boy climbs back up the ladder and selects me a different box. "Is this one okay?" he huffs.

"Yes, that's lovely. Thanks so much for your help."

Wiping his brow, he inquires if there's anything else he can do for me. I say no, so he leads me round the shop to the back of the queue for the checkout, telling me he's left my dolls behind the counter. Fifteen minutes later, I'm at the front of the queue, paying for my purchase by debit card.

As my receipt pumps through the till, the checkout girl gushes, "These new dolls are so awesome."

"Oh, yes," I enthuse; pleased I've found a kindred spirit. *"The Little Mermaid* is one of my all-time favourite movies."

"Mine, too! Ariel is so cool. When I was a kid, I wanted to be just like her, and I wanted to marry Eric."

"So did I! Oh, my God, that's exactly how I felt."

There's a short pause as the girl rips off my receipt and plops it in a Mickey Mouse gift bag. As she hands me my purchase, she adds, "So is this an early Christmas present for your daughter?"

"My daughter?" For a second, I'm confused, and then I laugh shrilly. "Oh, no. The dolls are for me, actually. I-I don't have any kids."

She frowns and then works her face into a smile. "Not to worry. I'm sure you'll have plenty of fun regardless." Glancing beyond me, she calls out for the next customer. I'm duly dismissed. Mortified, I leave the shop and head straight for the Tube station. I was planning to pick up a cheeseburger from McDonald's but I seem to have lost my appetite.

When I enter the Underground, I find a large crowd gathered at the ticket barriers, indicating delays to all lines, *again*. Grimacing, I pace around for a while, trying to shake off my embarrassment from earlier. Then finally, things start moving. I swipe my Oyster card and slowly follow the procession of disgruntled commuters through the ticket barriers. As I descend the escalator, I pass a poster for a theatre show called *Ghost Stories*. It looks interesting, and I make a mental note to check out ticket prices on the Internet. I haven't been to the theatre in ages, and this show is definitely one for the to-do list.

As I take my place on the crowded platform, I feel a headache coming and spend most of the journey clutching my temples. Before I know it, I'm back at Victoria and switching to the Overground to get a fast train to Clapham Junction. By six-thirty, I've arrived back in South London. Hurriedly, I head through the subway that leads to the southeast exit.

As I pass a newspaper stand, I catch a glimpse of the cigarettes display and feel a sudden urge to stop. My resolve is weakening and I'm torn in two. For short, agonizing moments, I wrestle with my conscience, deliberating what to do. Finally, I give into temptation. *Just one more smoke. One more and that's it. I can always quit tomorrow.*

I flash a sheepish grin at the shopkeeper. "Ten Marlboro Lights, please. Oh, and a box of matches."

After I've paid for them, I'm filled with deep self-loathing, but I simply cannot help myself. Smoking has become such a part of my daily routine, such a part of what keeps me stable, I'd feel lost without it.

The moon is high in the sky as I stroll down St John's Hill in the direction of my house. Puffing on a cigarette, with the wind blowing through my hair, I feel a bit better about things. Okay, I've broken my vow to quit smoking, but things will be different tomorrow. Tomorrow, I'll be stronger.

Five minutes later, I turn into a quiet residential street filled with rows of three-and-four-bedroomed semis. I stop outside the one with the blue door and a messy front garden and fumble for my house keys. It's nothing special to look at, just a three-bedroom semi like all the others, but to me it's a castle. My shelter from the storm. *The centre of my existence.*

As I approach the front door, I notice that all of the ground floor lights are on, meaning my dad's awake. With frozen hands, I let myself in, drop my bags and kick off my shoes in the hall. Then I head straight for the kitchen to pour myself a glass of water. As I down it greedily, I hear my father calling, so I finish up quick and go the living room.

Peering round the door, I find him slouching on the sofa with his laptop cradled between his knees. On the table sits a half-finished cup of tea with the bag still in it. The living room is big and bright, filled with dusty furniture and burgundy window drapes that haven't been touched since the 80s. The mantelpiece is teeming with replica Egyptian carvings and South American trinkets. All around, the sweet scent of patchouli permeates the air.

Dad takes off his glasses and grins, showing a row of wonky, discoloured teeth. He's tall and thin with high cheekbones, a nose like a beak and locks of lank, grey hair swept back in a ponytail. He's wearing his favourite ensemble: a paint-spattered *Rolling Stones* T-shirt with stonewashed jeans.

"Hello, my dear. Did you have a good day?"

"Yeah, it was okay." I crash out in the armchair opposite and ask him how the writing's going.

"Great! I've done two thousand words already."

"That's brilliant, Dad. You've finally gotten over your writer's block?"

"Yes, for the moment," he laughs. "Fingers crossed; if I keep this up, I'll have the first draft done by Christmas."

Now it's my turn to laugh. He's been on Chapter One since spring.

My father's Steve Singleton, a writer and something of a minor celebrity on the New Age book scene. In the mid-90s, he spent ten months in India, and on his return wrote the bestselling *Path to Enlightenment: Six Ways to Change Your Life*. This was followed by a succession of lacklustre sequels that have earned him a small but loyal fan base who ensure his twice-yearly royalty cheques keep coming.

"Something arrived for you from Amazon today," Dad says through pursed lips.

"Really?"

"Yeah. A big, brown parcel. I left it on your bed."

My face brightens; it must be the *Muppet Show* box set I ordered.

Dad sips his tea and winces when he realises it's stone cold.

I sniff the air. Beneath the scent of patchouli is a definite undercurrent of marijuana. I eye my father suspiciously. "Dad, have you been smoking pot again?"

"Of course not. Whatever gave you that idea?"

"I can smell it."

"Must be your imagination." I lean forward and he cowers back with a sheepish grin.

"Okay, okay," he admits. "I had one little joint at lunchtime, just to get my creative juices flowing. One joint, and that's it."

"Dad, you promised. Remember what we agreed? No more pot."

"I know, I know. It won't happen again." His shoulders sag. "Sometimes I just need that extra little kick to get me through my mental blockage. We writers have a history of working better under the influence. For God's sake, even Lewis Carroll was high as a kite when he wrote *Alice in Wonderland*."

"Lewis Carroll didn't have hypertension."

"He might have. Did you check historical records?"

"Dad, this isn't funny. You have to start taking what the doctor said seriously. I bet you didn't even remember to take your tablets."

"Oh, yes, I did. You think I'm stupid?"

My eyes narrow as I try to gauge if he's telling the truth.

"What?" he says innocently.

"Are you sure you definitely took them?"

"Cross my heart, Carly, I did."

"You better have." I sigh with exasperation; his flippancy drives me up the wall.

Eight months ago, my father was hospitalised due to his high blood pressure and the doctors told him to ditch the marijuana or face an early grave. Since then, he's been prescribed a combination of six tablets to take every day for the rest of his life to keep his condition stable. Frustratingly, he's somehow convinced himself he doesn't need conventional medicine and forever scours the Internet in search of alternative treatments to allow him to 'think himself' better. All well and fine, but why the hell take chances?

"Okay," I say, getting up, "I'm going upstairs to get changed and inspect this Amazon parcel. By the way, what's for dinner?"

"I've made chickpea curry and rice, or should I say *attempted* to. I'm warning you now, it's not the greatest. I think I may have used too much paprika, but it's edible. Your half just needs to be warmed up. I left it in the yellow pot on the stove."

"Thanks. I'm sure it'll be great."

And I mean it. Out of the two of us, Dad's the better cook by far. If it wasn't for his hit-and-miss 'experiments,' I'd probably be eating take-outs and Marks and Sparks ready meals every single night.

As soon as I get to my room, I tear open the parcel and scrutinise the box set meticulously to make sure it arrived in perfect condition. Then I collapse on the bed and take a few minutes to pull myself together. Looking around, it's like I've never seen the place before. Everything seems strange, twisted out of shape. Pink and pristine, my bedroom is a palace compared with the chaos downstairs. Nothing much has changed in twenty years. Stacks of books and DVDs line the walls, as do expensive display cabinets containing my precious Disney memorabilia. Stuffed toys from the *Muppet Show* dominate the bed. Judd Nelson and Molly Ringwald's eternally youthful faces gaze down at me from *The Breakfast Club* poster, along with images from all of my favourite movies: *The Goonies*, *Princess Bride*, *Labyrinth*, and *The Neverending Story*.

At last, I get up and cross to the window, throw it open and shiver as a blast of cold air filters in. I light a cigarette and exhale a couple of puffs into the dark night. Then I cough, and a wave of self-disgust washes through me.

This has to stop! I need to do something about this before it's too late.

Fired up, I crush out my half-finished cigarette and crumble the butt to shreds in the ashtray. Returning to the bed, I pick up my scuffed old laptop. Plugging in the charger, I flip up the lid and listen to the familiar hum as it boots up. The keyboard is covered with bits of chocolate and clumps of dust and I remind myself to find those bloody surface wipes to give the thing a damn good clean.

The laptop screen comes to life and I click on the Explorer icon to start the Internet. Within seconds, the Google homepage flashes up and I run a search for 'ways to quit smoking.' I've been here many times before, and for the first two or three results pages, I'm unimpressed with my options: chewing gum, Nicorette patches, everything that came to a big, fat nothing. Mentally, I tick each one off as a tried-and-tested failure. I'm about to give up when suddenly, one hyperlink catches my eye: *'Quit smoking for good at the London Hypnotherapy Clinic. We promise permanent results or your money back.'*

I arch an eyebrow. *Hypnotherapy?*

The term conjures up sepia-toned images of Victorian confidence tricksters bilking money from a theatre of gullible people. As treatments go, hypnotherapy sounds a little out there, but I decide it merits further investigation. Plus, what have I got to lose? I've tried everything else so ... *what the hell.*

With mounting curiosity, I click on the link and am taken to an expensive-looking website. The homepage features photos of a formerly obese reality TV star claiming she lost two stone through hypnosis. Her before and after shots are very impressive, but I'll need something more solid than that to be convinced. Doubtfully, I click the 'Featured' link and browse through various other testimonials from what I consider to be legitimate sources: sound bites from popular women's magazines such as *Closer* and *Cosmopolitan*.

Satisfied that this place is the real deal, I scroll to the 'About' page to find out more. *'...The London Hypnotherapy Clinic is the private practice of Dr Nick Craven, one of the country's leading hypnotherapists. Offering multiple fields of specialization, Dr Craven is proud to have personally treated some of the U.K's top politicians, CEOs and celebrities. Hypnotherapy is the most effective way to stop smoking for good, statistically five times more effective than all other methods. Book an appointment with Dr Craven today to beat your addiction permanently ...'*

There's no picture of Dr Craven, but his credentials certainly sound impressive. I navigate to the next page where Craven's short biography is followed by a bullet-pointed list of the health issues he treats, including stress, migraines, insomnia and depression. At the bottom of the list is a landline number next to the clinic's opening hours. I glance at my watch.

Seven twenty-five.

I've still got time. The clinic doesn't close until eight on a Tuesday, so I figure I may as well give the number a call. I'm not going to commit to anything yet, just get an idea of prices.

Carrying my phone to the window, I dial the number and wait for the call to connect.

"London Hypnotherapy Clinic, how can I help?" greets a female voice.

I stop the phone against my chest, and then raise it back to my ear. "Er, hello, I'm making inquiries about hypnosis for quitting smoking. I saw some stuff on your website but couldn't see a price list anywhere. I just wondered … well, I just wanted to know a bit more about the treatment."

"Certainly. Did you want me to give you the price for a single session or for the full treatment?"

"Er, just the single session, please."

She gives me the price and I stiffen. It's far more than I expected and certainly not something I can afford on my meagre salary. I'm about to make my excuses and hang up, when the lady does a U-turn and tells me they're running a limited fifty percent discount on the first session.

I think for a second. "All right, I'll book it. What's the earliest appointment available?"

The line goes quiet while she checks Dr Craven's schedule. "Someone just cancelled, so we've got a free slot this Friday at six-thirty."

"Perfect."

She takes down my name and telephone number and

before I know it, she's booked me in. As the call disconnects, I shake my head ruefully, overwhelmed by a mixture of excitement and unease. *Carly Singleton, what the hell are you doing? You know you can't afford this.*

Snapping the phone shut, I return to bed and rest the laptop on my knees. For a second-long eternity, I stare dumbly at the screen, wondering whether to open Pandora's Box. Then taking a deep breath, I log onto Facebook. I've never registered as myself, but a year ago I set up a dummy account under an alias to allow me access to Andrew's profile. I know it's sad to keep tabs on your ex, but I'm only human. I know it's self-destructive and wrong, know I'm setting myself up for heartbreak, but I just can't help it. *I need to know.*

I wait a moment as Facebook loads up.

My face crumples. Andrew's page pops up on screen. He's posted a new set of photos, and my pulse races as I realise they're all focused on the same girl. A girl dressed in white, a laughing, happy girl. A girl enjoying what should be the best day of her life. The setting of the photos is a chapel, somewhere tropical, possibly an island in the Caribbean.

And that's when I see a picture of Andrew standing next to the girl, looking all-debonair with his spiky brown hair and smart black suit. It takes a few seconds for the penny to drop, and when it does, I start to shake. This isn't just any blushing bride. Oh no, *this is Andrew's bride.* He's married someone else!

Numbly, I scroll through the rest of the photo album, each one a giant punch in the face. His parents, her parents; his friends, her friends. Everyone looks so happy and oblivious to the pain I'm suffering; it's almost like they're taunting me. Laughing at me.

The final straw comes when I notice the bride's baby

bump.

"No!" Flooded with despair, I slide from the bed to the floor, sobbing hysterically. I can't hold back anymore. I'm crying so much I start to get hiccups. I'm pleased for Andrew. Pleased he's living his dream, but at the same time, I'm devastated. "That could have been me," I whimper. "Oh, God, Andrew, where did it all go wrong? Why do I have to sabotage everything? We could have been so happy, but I never even gave us a chance …" I pound my knuckles against my head. "Stupid, stupid, stupid!"

Most times, my room is a source of comfort, a time capsule, a shelter from the snowstorm, but today it feels like a rose-tinted prison. I'm drowning in a sea of emotions, plagued by the blackest thoughts. I'm hit by extreme panic as I realise I'm hurtling toward my forties with absolutely nothing to show for my life.

They say you only get one chance. If that's true, then I've bloody well blown mine—living in fear, hating myself, loving the comfort of routine, but at the same time despising it. Time and again, I've said no to change, and as a result, I missed opportunities to improve my circumstances. Throughout my life, my fear of the unknown has prevented me from taking risks and now what have I got? A big, fat nothing. No partner, no children, no prospects, just a dead-end job and a stream of debts and miserable weekends stretching into eternity. And in the background of all this, looming over everything like a black cloud, is Jill's awful birthday gathering on Saturday. Why the hell did I ever agree to it? Oh, I know there are people far worse off than me in the world, people starving, people in war zones, but this does little to quell my misery.

"Carly, is everything all right up there?" My father's voice filters in from downstairs.

I stagger to my feet, wiping foundation and mascara from my face. "Yeah, Dad, everything's fine." I try to sound upbeat.

"Are you sure?"

"Yes, never been better." I smile maniacally through my tears.

CHAPTER TWO

First Session

I T'S RAINING CATS and dogs as I march through Oxford Street toward my Friday night appointment at the London Hypnotherapy Clinic. Through the sleeting rain, I race past H&M, take the second turning on the right through Holles Street then onto Cavendish Square. As I near my destination, a gust of wind inverts my umbrella and turns it into a big, yellow water basin. I have to fight to get it back in shape.

For goodness sake, why is British weather so bad?

Cursing under my breath, I soldier on determinedly.

The clinic is situated at 140 Harley Street, a road famous since Victorian times for its wide array of private specialists in medicine and surgery. It takes me ages to find the place because the house numbers don't add up. One minute they seem to run numerically, the next a random number pops up and I'm back to the old drawing board. After a lot of toing and froing, I stop outside a tall, grey building with a grand, pillared entrance.

140 Harley Street. *Thank God.*

Closing my umbrella, I skip up a short flight of steps and squint at the shiny plate by the door. The words engraved in brass confirm I've got the right place, so I ring the bell and wait. A moment later, a voice speaks through the intercom: "London Hypnotherapy Clinic."

"Hello, I've got a six-thirty appointment with Doctor Craven."

A buzzer sounds and I step into a spacious reception area. Everything's done up in white, black and gold, the décor an expensive '20s throwback. A crystal chandelier protrudes from the ceiling and a copy of Klimt's *Adele Bloch-Bauer I* hangs on the far wall.

I take a second to soak it all in.

Wow, this place is nice.

Then a beautifully groomed brunette smiles at me from behind the reception desk.

"Carly Singleton?"

"Yes, that's me."

"I'm Tara. We spoke on the phone. I'm the one who booked your appointment."

"Oh, yes," I nod, recognising her voice. "It's so nice to meet you."

"Likewise. If you want, you can put your umbrella over there." She points to a wicker basket in the corner.

"Thanks."

After I've disposed of my umbrella, she reaches beneath her desk and pulls out a questionnaire attached to a clipboard. "You're still a bit early, and Dr Craven is currently with another patient. Why don't you fill out this form while you're waiting?"

"Thanks." I take the clipboard and sit on one of the big, leather couches.

"Would you like a glass of water or something?"

"No, thank you."

"Coffee?"

I shake my head.

With a thin smile, Tara returns to her computer. I rest the

clipboard on my knees and start filling out the questionnaire. It's pretty standard stuff: name, address, date of birth, telephone number, prior medical history, etcetera, etcetera. It takes me less than five minutes to complete, and I'm just about to return the clipboard to Tara when a door opens and a stunning redhead steps out. I'm slack-jawed; she has the face of an angel and the body of a Hungarian catwalk model.

"Same time next week?" Tara beams.

The redhead tosses her hair and sighs. "Oh, yes, definitely. Doctor Craven's so fabulous. I've recommended him to all my friends."

Tara leans forward and squints at her monitor. "Let's see…next Friday will be the fifteenth. Is five-thirty okay with you?"

"Perfect," replies the redhead, looking at me. "All right Tara, I'm off. Goodnight."

"Night, Jess. Safe journey. Oh, and don't forget your umbrella."

Tara presses the release button under her desk and lets the redhead out. As she goes, she flashes me a warm smile and mouths, "Goodnight."

"Goodnight!" I squeak.

When she's gone, I wonder why such a perfect-looking woman needs to see a hypnotherapist. Surely, she can't have any hang-ups.

"You can go in now," Tara says as I give her back the questionnaire. "Just go through the arches and it's the first door to your left. No need to knock; just let yourself in. Dr Craven's expecting you."

"Thanks! See you later."

"Have fun."

I'm hit by a sudden pang of nerves as I follow Tara's

instructions. What if this is all a big mistake? What if I've wasted my money and get a big, fat nothing out of this? What if I can't quit smoking? What then?

Oh, well, too late to back out now.

I stop outside a door with Dr Craven's name on it. Smoothing down my skirt, I take a deep breath before turning the knob and entering. The room is completely quiet except for the rain slamming against the windows. The walls are stacked from ceiling to floor with books and the centre is dominated by two padded chairs facing each other. An Art Deco lamp stands by the window, and a large mahogany table at the back is littered with important-looking documents.

I lick my lips. So far, there's no sign of Dr Craven anywhere; I wonder if he's maybe popped to the bathroom or something. Meanwhile, the rain outside is growing more intense, harsh winds pummelling the glass like a gorilla trapped in a phone booth. I shiver inwardly; I'm glad I don't have to venture out again just yet.

Loosening my scarf, I step cautiously into the room to give things a closer inspection. On the edge of the table sits a Dictaphone and other recording equipment I suppose Dr Craven uses for hypnosis. Next to a stack of old cassette tapes is a well-thumbed copy of Dennis Wheatley's *The Devil Rides Out* and yesterday's *Telegraph*. I'm just about to touch the Dictaphone when—

"Carly Singleton?"

I freeze mid-motion. The male voice is soft and sexy with a huskiness that lingers, caressing every syllable of my name like a lover. My whole body tenses, and my skin rises into goose bumps that travel the length of my shoulders, neck and back.

I feel uneasy.

Out of tune with everything.

I'm aware of every one of my heightened senses. Slowly, I find the courage to turn around.

"Hello, Carly, I'm Dr Nick Craven." He slips his big, strong hand into mine and we exchange a greeting that seems to last forever. "I hope you haven't been waiting long?"

"No." I take an involuntary step back. "I-I haven't been waiting long at all." My pulse is going crazy and my heart is thudding like a machine gun. He releases my hand and a blast of heat shoots up my arm and licks me all over.

Holy fucking shit.

Nick Craven is tall, maybe 6'1" or 2" with broad shoulders and a nicely toned chest that tapers into slender hips. He's dressed in all black: fitted shirt, waistcoat, beautifully tailored trousers. I place him as being in his mid-to late-thirties, though I cannot be sure. His hair is thick and black, like his clothes, and he has a warm, olive complexion and lips that are slightly swollen. A nasty scar runs across his left cheek, giving him the appearance of a suave Bond villain. He is far from handsome, far from conventional-looking, yet there is something magnetic about him. Something I find *irresistible.*

"Good to meet you, Doctor Craven," I mumble.

"Please, call me Nick." Hazel eyes stare straight into mine, holding me prisoner, eyes that overwhelm, that shine with kindness, intelligence and serenity. "Can I take your coat?"

"No! I mean … yes, of course." I laugh nervously. I'm so agitated I can barely string coherent sentences. Suddenly, I'm paranoid about my appearance. Has the rain smudged my mascara? What about my hair? Do I look okay? And if I take off my coat, what will Nick make of my Mickey Mouse sweater, tasselled skirt and purple tights?

With trembling fingers, I start unbuttoning my coat, but before I've finished, Nick's behind me, hands on my shoulders, sliding my sleeves down with maddening ease. Momentarily, his breath burns a trail of fire on my neck, awakening a hunger within me I thought had died long ago. Just one touch and my crotch starts doing crazy things. Just one touch and he's got me jumping through hoops like a circus animal. No man has ever had this effect on me.

"You're wet," Nick murmurs.

My eyes widen. *Good God. He knows he's affecting me.*

"W-what?" I stutter.

"Your clothes ..." he smirks, carrying my coat to the rack. "They're absolutely drenched. Not a very pleasant day. Did you come by car?"

"No, I walked here." I sigh with relief. I must have got the wrong end of the stick.

Or have I?

With unnerving agility, Nick hangs up my coat, closes the door to his office then walks to the window and shuts the blinds. It all seems to happen simultaneously. "That's better. We don't want any distractions."

I couldn't agree more.

"Right, let's make a start." He gestures to one of the big, padded chairs in the middle of the room. "Please take a seat, Carly."

"Thanks." I love the way he says my name; love the way his dulcet tones play with my clit and make my stomach all jittery. With a voice like that, he could get me to do virtually anything.

I collapse in the padded seat, throat tight with anxiety. Nick takes the chair opposite and presses his fingertips together. For a moment, his eyes linger over my body, their slow, sensual progress sending a shiver down my spine. I clench my hands hard in my lap and pick a point on the floor to focus on. The intensity of his stare is making my head spin. Jesus, I'm reasonably attractive, but certainly not worth the once-over he's giving me.

"So Carly, tell me a bit about yourself."

"What do you want to know?" I ask timidly.

"Oh, just the basics: how old you are, where you grew up, that sort of thing."

"I already filled out the questionnaire at reception."

"This isn't an interview. I don't make notes, so nothing you say will be recorded. All I want is an informal chat with you. Before I start a course of treatment, I like to first build a picture of my patient: gauge your dreams, your fears, and your aspirations. In short, before I agree to take you on, I need to first clarify that we will be a suitable fit for each other."

"You mean you might not be able to help me?"

Nick laughs softly. "A popular misconception about hypnosis is that it works for everyone. The truth is some people are more susceptible to it than others. Though most of my patients can be successfully treated, there's a small percentage of people for whom it wouldn't work. Finding out more about you helps me determine which of the two categories you fall into." He smiles wryly, and for the first time, I catch a glimpse of his pearly-white teeth. "Does that answer your question?"

"Yes, it does."

"So, Carly...give me a brief history of *you*."

I stare at my hands, not knowing where else to look. His gaze is too raw, too intense. I clear my throat. "Um, well, I'm thirty-six years old. I grew up in Fulham but now I live in Battersea. I currently work as a receptionist for a media company in Charlotte Street."

He raises an eyebrow. "Charlotte Street? That's not far from here."

"Yes," I smile. "It's literally around the corner."

He hesitates, processing this information. Then he asks, "Are you married?"

"No, I live with my dad."

"Any children?"

"No." *For goodness sake, why does everyone keep asking me that?*

"And your mother?"

"My parents are divorced. My mother remarried and now lives in Purley with her new husband."

"How do you feel about that?"

I shrug. "I don't know. It happened such a long time ago, I'm pretty much over it."

Nick studies me closely, his eyes warm and inquisitive. He's trying to read me, work me out. "Tell me three of your favourite things."

"What?" The change in direction catches me off guard.

"Tell me three things you like."

I scratch the side of my neck. My mind has gone totally blank and all of my nerves are jangled. "Three things? Um … cream-coloured ponies and crisp apple strudels, doorbells and sleigh bells and schnitzel with noodles."

"*The Sound of Music*," Nick chuckles. "Great film. But I asked for three and you gave me five."

Heat creeps up my neck and colours my cheeks. "Sorry, I don't know where that came from. The song just popped into my head and I…that is, Julie Andrews—"

"Let's try that again," he interjects smoothly. "This time I want you to relax. I can tell you're nervous, but there's really no need to be. I don't bite, Carly. We have all the time in the world, so just take it easy, okay?"

"Okay." I giggle hysterically; for some reason, I'm behaving like a complete moron. I take a couple of breaths. "Right, three things I like are: fruit salads, Mickey Mouse and sunny days."

"And three things you hate?"

"Mushrooms, spiders, politicians."

"Do you like your job at the media company?"

"Yes."

"And why do you want to quit smoking?"

"Because I don't like it."

"Why don't you like it?"

"Because…because it's bad for me, and it makes my clothes stink and I think it will give me lung cancer. And…and it makes me feel weak."

"Do you like being in control?"

I blink at him with a stupefied expression. "What do you mean?"

"You said smoking makes you feel weak, so does that mean you like being in control?"

"Um, I suppose so. All I know is when I smoke a ciga-rette, I feel terrible afterward. I don't enjoy it and I've tried everything to quit but so far nothing has worked and there's something else, too. Eight months ago, my father was diagnosed with high blood pressure and the doctor told him to quit smoking or die. I've been trying to support him, but I feel like a bit of a hypocrite, given I can't even control my own addiction. I was thinking that maybe if I can do this for myself, quit smoking I mean, and then I'll be in a better position to help him, you know? That's another reason I'm here." I say the last part in a whisper.

There's a long, dark silence. I take in a lot of air to calm my racing heart.

Nick resumes, "When did you first start smoking? How old were you?"

"I don't remember."

"You must have some vague idea. Were you still at school? Did you sneak behind the bike shed for a clandestine smoke?"

"No, it was much later than that. I started smoking after I finished university, so I would have been in my early twenties."

"Interesting."

"Why?"

"Thought association," Nick says simply. "If I can take your subconscious back to the first time you smoked, it may help to kick the addiction. What is an addiction? Merely this: when you no longer feel you have the choice. During hypnosis, I will retrain your mind to disassociate from unwanted patterns of behaviour, helping you create new habits that enhance your wellbeing. No one ever enjoys their first cigarette, so getting you to experience those sensations is a technique I often use to combat it."

I smile apologetically. "I'm sorry, Nick, I don't remember the exact day I started."

"That's absolutely fine. There are still plenty of avenues for us to explore."

My face brightens. "Does that mean you've agreed to take me on?"

"What do you think?" When I fail to answer, he grins, "Yes, Carly. I believe you're an ideal candidate for me."

"Phew!" I wipe my brow. "Thank God for that."

We both laugh, and for a brief second, Nick's sultry gaze settles on my lips. My blood races and I squeeze my thighs tightly together.

I'm a complete and utter mess.

Nick's tone becomes serious. "Before we begin, do you have any other questions?"

"Yes. I won't do anything stupid, will I?"

"Of course not. Another popular myth is surrendering of your will. A lot of people think that when you go into trance, you lose your sense of self. This is completely untrue. When you undergo hypnosis with me, at all times, you will be in complete control of your behaviour, meaning you will not embarrass yourself, reveal secrets or do anything you wouldn't normally do in a waking state. Hypnosis is not about surrendering your free will. It is similar to a daydream and merely facilitates helping you learn to control unwanted behavioural patterns." He smiles thinly. "Does that put your mind at rest?"

"Yes. Thanks for explaining it so thoroughly."

"Good. Okay, let's get comfortable. Loosen up and relax." He pauses, and then as if suddenly inspired, says, "Take off your shoes."

"What?"

"Take off your shoes," he repeats.

Feeling slightly embarrassed, I stoop down and start to unlace my boots. My pulse skitters all over the place. I can't get my feet out and the blasted laces are tangled.

"Do you need any help?" There's a hint amusement in his voice.

I feel my face burning up. "No, no, I'm fine." At last, I manage to get the bloody boots off. Flustered, I lean back in my chair, run my fingers through my hair and flash a crooked grin. Why on Earth is the room suddenly so hot?

"Wiggle your toes," Nick whispers.

I smother a laugh. "Are you serious?"

"Try it. I think you'll find it relaxing."

Frowning and feeling kind of stupid, I follow his orders. Sinking my feet into the thick pile carpet, I flex my toes back and forth and find it strangely liberating.

Nick's right; I *do* feel more relaxed.

Our eyes lock and I see a flash of triumph on his face. I wonder how he got that awful scar. I wonder if he was glassed in a fight or if there was some kind of accident.

Nick leans forward, a half-smile tugging at his lips. He keeps stealing glances at my breasts, and the sexual tension is driving me crazy.

"That's right, Carly. Shake those toes. Doesn't that feel better?"

I nod vigorously. "Yes, but I do feel a bit silly."

"That's good. Feeling silly is good."

After a few seconds, I stop wiggling and sink back in my chair. Nick folds his arms and sits up straight. His expression is surprisingly tender. Covertly, I clock the delicious dip and swell of his biceps and fantasise what it would be like to run my hands all over them.

He moistens his lips and my nipples harden at the thought of him spreading my legs and sliding his tongue down my thighs.

"All right. Close your eyes and take a deep breath," he murmurs.

I follow his instructions and an instant wave of calm floods me. My muscles slacken, and I'm overwhelmed by a pleasing feeling of drowsiness. His voice drifts in and out of my awareness, travelling up my legs and into my thighs, permeating my whole body with a deep sense of relaxation.

"That's right, Carly," he purrs. "Empty your mind completely. Relax every part of your body, don't think about anything, just focus on my voice. Let all of your worries fade away to nothing, and just breathe. *Breathe.* Inhale deeply and exhale slowly through your mouth. That's right; you're falling deeper and deeper into trance. Deeper and deeper…"

Nick's words flutter through my head like fragments of a long-forgotten dream. I am barely aware of the subtle suggestions; barely conscious of the growing hold he has over me. At times, it feels like I've left my body, like I'm floating around the ceiling. At others, I'm aware of every flinch of muscle, every nerve ending.

For an interminable time, it feels like I'm falling down a rabbit hole. Down, down, down… And then I open my eyes and find I'm surrounded by never-ending blackness.

I hear the ticking of a grandfather clock: a pendulum swinging, counting down the seconds like a time bomb. Then I notice a weird, greenish glow that does not fade or flicker. I open my mouth to speak, but no sound comes out. A door materialises in front of me, a door with an ugly, Satanic knocker that seems to be leering. I hesitate before turning the knob and finding that it's locked.

I try again.

Still no joy.

"Where am I?" I yell. "For God's sake, someone tell me!"

My cries are met with a resounding silence, but I know someone is here with me. I can feel it, a dark presence creeping up my flesh like ivy. And then everything starts weaving around me and growing all dense and watery. I can't breathe, can't see properly.

Nick's voice echoes in the silence of my mind. Soft. Seductive. "When I will you to do a thing, it shall be done. From this moment on, my will is your will, and you shall cross land and sea to do my bidding. Do you understand?"

"Yes," I whisper.

I open my eyes again, blink a couple of times. Slowly, my surroundings come into focus. I'm lying in a steel-framed bed; antiseptic claws at my nostrils. The room around me is small and white, the bed-frame like prison bars. The only other furniture is a wooden hospital trolley. Tilting my head, I gaze out the window at blue skies and fields of green, rising and falling in a succession of glorious camel humps. Beyond, a glistening stream gives way to mighty slopes of forest that seem to go on forever.

The door opens and a nurse enters. "Your mother's here to see you, Carly."

I don't respond. Vacantly, I turn back to the window and focus on the sky.

"Shall I tell her to come in?"

I shake my head. "No. Tell her to go away. I don't want to see anyone yet; I'm not ready."

"Very well. I'll tell her you're not feeling up to it."

The nurse stares at me with a grim expression, her eyes dark and impenetrable.

Next thing I know, I'm flying through the sky, gazing down on a patchwork quilt of colours. My stomach lurches, the wind rushing through my hair and blasting my cheeks with a damp chill. I feel both frightened and exhilarated. I'm Superman, Peter Pan flying over Neverland.

Then Nick's voice cuts in: "Focus, Carly, focus. Deep down, we both know you're a strong woman. You have the discipline and self-control to do this. You know you can quit smoking anytime you want to. Breathe in deeply. Take a burst of fresh air into your sinuses, your lungs. That's right. Doesn't that feel good? Doesn't it feel great to finally be able to breathe properly without that horrible smoke stifling you? Now, hold for the count of five, four, three, two, one. And now you're awake."

I open my eyes and for a moment, it's like I'm seeing double. Slowly, I return to the current moment.

"How do you feel?" Nick's voice comes from somewhere behind me.

I spin my chair around and find him standing by the window with his back to me. The room is dark; the storm outside has calmed to a gentle murmur.

"How do you feel?" he asks again.

I hesitate before answering, "I feel … great."

And it's true.

My limbs feel light and my head is clear. For the first time in years, it's like a giant weight has been lifted off my shoulders. That omnipresent black cloud has, for the moment at least, gone. I wiggle my toes and find it a challenge to co-ordinate my movements. It's like I'm drunk, but in a good way.

Nick glances at his watch. "All right, I think we should call it a day. Overall, I'm very pleased with the progress we've made so far. If you continue responding in this way, this promises to be a very successful treatment."

Stooping down, I slip my boots back on. I can feel his eyes burning into me. Adjusting my sweater, I clear my throat and ask tentatively, "So, how many more sessions do you think I'll need?"

"Oh, four or five usually does it. Then again, it depends on the individual. But you've made a phenomenal start,

Carly, and I'm confident if we continue this way, we will definitely beat your addiction."

The kindness in his eyes, the sincerity of his words sparks a rush of colour to my cheeks. If only he knew what I'd like to do to him.

Silently, Nick pads over to the rack and takes down my coat. Straightening my skirt, I stand up and sling my bag over my shoulder. I'm disappointed the session's over so soon; it certainly doesn't feel like I've been here for an hour.

Nick comes up behind me and helps me on with my coat. Even through the thick material, the gentle brush of his fingers sends a shiver through me, and my body aches to be touched by him more intimately.

Once I'm presentable, Nick walks me to the office door. I stall with my hand on the knob, prolonging our time together for as long as possible. A brief hush falls between us. I wrack my brain for something sensible to say, but my mind has gone blank. We just stand there staring at each other, each lost in our private worlds. I'm obsessed with the sensual swell of his lips: the curve of them, the softness of them. I could spend forever ensconced in the warmth that seems to pour from them. This is crazy. We barely know each other, yet there seems to be a silent understanding between us; unspoken promises and a strange connection I cannot fathom.

Nick is the first to speak. "Well, Carly, it's been a pleasure. Shall we say the same time next week?"

"Yes, definitely," I reply, eyes shining.

"Excellent. See Tara on your way out and she'll book your next appointment. Have a safe journey home."

With a spring in my step, I bid him goodnight and stumble out of the room like a befuddled teenager. For a second I stand in the corridor, catching my breath, willing my heart to stop beating so fast.

Oh, my gosh, that was too intense.

Running my fingers down my nose, I smooth back my hair and head toward the reception.

Tara smiles magnanimously. "How did it go?"

"Brilliant!"

"Great! Do you want to pay by cash or card?"

My face drops. *Oh, yeah.* I'd forgotten about that. "Um, card …" I riffle through my bag in search of my wallet.

"Thanks." Tara takes my Visa Debit and runs it through a portable card reader.

As I wait for my bank to authorise the payment, I wonder what the hell I'm doing. Not only have I just paid the equivalent of half a week's wages for a hypnotherapy session, but also I've now committed myself to at least another four, which will end up costing me a small fortune. Still, in my crazy euphoric state, it seems a small price to pay for the chance to see Nick again.

Throughout the journey home, I'm lost in a blissful little fantasy world. Sitting in a packed train carriage, squashed between two overweight businessmen, I grin moronically at no one in particular. The people around me have miserable faces, hiding behind their newspapers and iPhones, in an attempt to pretend they don't see me. But I couldn't care less what they think. I'm too excited. I try to read the *Evening Standard* but the words swim before me in a haze of incoherence. It's no use. Thoughts of Nick Craven consume me, and I keep replaying the events of the night over and over again. Sure, I've had crushes before, but nothing like this. *Never like this.*

I think of Nick's laugh, his smile, his voice. The kindness in his eyes, those soft, swollen lips. The tightness of his shirt over his perfectly honed chest. I obsessively analyse what happened between us, picking apart our conversation in search of hidden meanings and double entendres. Maybe it's just wishful thinking, but I'm sure Nick was flirting with me. The way he looked at me...that couldn't have just been my imagination.

I shake my head dismissively.

No, it's definitely wishful thinking. Nick's a nice guy; he's probably nice to everyone. He's a professional, and this is what professionals get paid for: to make you feel special. Perhaps I'm misreading the signs. Perhaps he treats all of his patients like this. I tell myself I barely know the man, that I'm behaving like an excitable schoolgirl, not a thirty-something woman. Even so, my head is full of him and I love it.

Then I remember the gorgeous redhead and feel an unexpected pang of jealousy. I picture her flushed, excited face, and wonder what her session with Nick was like. Did he smile at her the way he smiled at me? Did he treat her with such gentle understanding? She was clearly besotted, so my guess is he gives all his patients the V.I.P. treatment.

I throw down the newspaper and fold my arms in a gesture of defiance.

Get a grip! You hardly know the man. Stop acting like a child.

THE NEXT DAY, I awake flooded with energy. I lie in bed staring up at the ceiling, my mind and body clear of all anxiety. *Bloody hell.* I've never felt so good. Miraculously, I'm still under the spell of Nick's hypnosis and feeling unusually optimistic about everything. Thanks to him, the world seems a brighter place, and I embrace the day with an enthusiasm I haven't felt in ages.

Throwing back the duvet, I jump out of bed and race over to the dresser. Opening the top drawer, I pull out a half-finished pack of Marlboros. For a while I study the cigarettes, reaching into my subconscious to decide if I still have the urge to smoke one. Has Nick's hypnosis really started to take effect?

Seconds pass.

With a sigh of relief, I put them back in the drawer and close it. Wow. This is great! I have no inclination to light up whatsoever. Yay! It looks like the treatment's working.

Grabbing a towel, I go to the en-suite bathroom and take a shower to wake myself up. As I clean my teeth at the sink, I decide that perhaps I *will* go to Jill's birthday after all. It's not often I'm in such good spirits and feel I should take advantage of it while it lasts.

Whistling a merry tune, I slip on my dressing gown and shuffle downstairs to make breakfast. In the kitchen, I put two slices of bread in the toaster and fill the kettle for tea. As the water boils, my father pops his head around the door. "You're in a suspiciously good mood today."

"Morning, Dad," I coo. "Sleep well?"

"Like a log. Why are you so happy?"

"Oh, no reason. Just happy to be alive, I guess. Do you want a cup of tea?"

"Love one."

Opening the kitchen cupboard, I take down another mug and place it on the sideboard. Then I tear open a packet of Tetley and plop the tea bags in. Neither of us takes sugar. As I pour the water, I make sure Dad doesn't see my guilty expression. I haven't had the heart to tell him about Nick because I know it will open a can of worms. He'll want to know how much I'm paying for it, and that's a discussion I don't really want to have. Dad's forever lecturing me about my bad money management. He thinks I need to grow up and stop indulging my hobbies. Each month, at least a quarter of my salary goes on film memorabilia, plus there's always those random purchases that take my fancy, like the time I wasted two-hundred pounds on a crate of powdered diet shakes I couldn't finish because they were so abysmal. And the time I bought a tooth-whitening kit that burned my gums and did no lightening whatsoever.

After I've added milk to the tea, I hand Dad his mug, and the two of us go into the living room to watch a morning cookery programme.

"Oi!" I shout as he cheekily swipes a piece of toast from my plate. "Make your own."

"We're family, and families are supposed to share." He cackles wickedly and takes a few chomps out the slice. "So, what are your plans for today? Got anything fun planned?"

"A friend from work is having a birthday get-together in London Bridge, so I'll probably drop by there later. Afterwards, I was thinking of meeting up with Ronan for a drink in Soho."

"Ronan?" Dad raises his eyebrows. "Now that's a name I haven't heard in a while. Nice lad. What's he up to these days?"

"Oh, nothing much. Just work and stuff."

"What does he do again?"

"Ronan's a visual merchandiser for Hackney Couture. He works at their flagship store in Westfield."

"What exactly is visual merchandising?"

"Basically, he creates store displays to attract customers to the shop. You know, arranging mannequins and stuff."

"So, it's really a posh term for a window dresser?"

"Dad, stop being so condescending."

"I am not!"

"Look, don't knock him, okay? He's out there doing his thing, getting to be creative, which is more than I do."

"Don't be like that. What about your crocheting?"

"Yeah, but it's not quite the same, is it? Crocheting's just a hobby for me. Ronan actually gets paid for what he does. He gets to be artistic in his day job."

"Well, send him my regards. I always thought he was a top bloke."

I couldn't agree more. Ronan Hewitt is my oldest and dearest friend. We've known each other since our early twenties and supported each other through numerous ups and downs. Nobody 'gets' me the way Ronan does. Nobody makes me laugh the way Ronan does. He's one in a million and over the years, I've found his friendship invaluable. Once upon a time, the two of us were inseparable, spending every weekend at the pub bemoaning our disastrous love lives. However, since turning thirty, our meetings have become less frequent, and we only occasionally speak on the phone. Still, he knows I love him to death, and no matter what happens, I know we have a bond that will never be broken.

"Another parcel arrived for you today," Dad says, rolling his eyes. "This one's from America."

"Where did you put it?"

"I left it in the hall for you. But, honestly, don't you think this is getting a bit tedious? You've got enough toys to fill three houses."

"They're not toys, Dad. They're limited edition designer figurines, and one day they'll be worth a fortune."

"That's what you keep saying. God only knows how

much you paid for them."

"Ask me no questions and I'll tell you no lies," I chuckle.

After breakfast, I go back upstairs to start my Saturday morning routine. I tidy up a little, dust down my display cabinets and sort through my DVDs to make sure each and every disc is in the correct box. Then I gather together all my odd socks and underwear to put in the wash.

About three o'clock, I grab a cup of coffee and an egg salad sandwich for lunch. Afterwards, I watch *Back to the Future* for a spot of escapism. By five o'clock, I start thinking about what to wear tonight. Ransacking my wardrobe, I look for something suitably glam but warm enough to brave the cold weather. It's Jill's birthday, so I want to make a special effort, especially as I don't go out much. There aren't many opportunities for me to really dress up, so I need to take full advantage. At a leisurely pace, I pick out a few sparkly tops and a selection of knee-length skirts. Then pulling off my dressing gown, I stand before the mirror and run a critical eye over my body.

Jesus.

All right, I don't look too bad but *damn*, I really need to start doing those sit-ups again. I pinch my stomach and suck it in to create the illusion of a flat tummy. Then I exhale and everything pops back out again. I sigh. I've never been comfortable with my body, and God knows there's a reason I don't wear sleeveless tops, even in summer. I hate how flabby my arms look. Vests with spaghetti straps are definitely off the cards tonight.

For the next thirty minutes, I try out different outfits until finally, I settle for a blue dress with polka-dot leggings and a pair of black pumps. With my blonde hair and brown eyes, the colours fit me perfectly. Make-up wise, I decide to be a little daring, opting for a bright red lipstick and, for the first time ever, false eyelashes. I have a devil of a time gluing them on, but I get there eventually.

At quarter to six, I grab my handbag and head out the door. "All right, Dad, I'm off."

"Have a good time."

"Thanks. I love you."

"Love you, too."

I step out the front door and drink the cool evening air into my lungs. The street is dark and silent under the November sky, the rows of semi-detached houses stretching as far as the eye can see. I get a sudden pang of nerves. Can I really endure a whole evening in the company of Jill's friends? What if they don't like me? Can I really make small talk and fake the facade of normality? I have no idea what the evening will bring, but I hope I'm not making a big mistake.

And then, with a sinking feeling, I realise something else.

I need a cigarette.

CHAPTER THREE

Nando's

B Y THE TIME I reach Nando's, I'm tired and pissed off. Despite leaving home in good time, delays to the Northern Line meant I missed the seven o'clock meeting with Jill at London Bridge Station. As a result, I had to go straight to the restaurant, which would have been fine if I knew where the heck it was. For a good fifteen minutes, I roamed around Bermondsey High Street asking passers-by who don't speak English for directions. Finally, after wandering through a myriad of cobbled lanes and back streets, I found the entrance to Nando's tucked beneath a railway arch.

Stalling at the glass doors, I glance in my make-up mirror to check I haven't got lipstick on my teeth. Then, taking a deep breath, I work my face into a smile, push open the doors and step inside.

A waitress rushes over. "Hiya. Table for one?"

"No, I'm here to meet some friends, actually. I think they're already seated."

Apprehensively, I glance beyond her into the busy restaurant and spy Jill waving frantically at me.

"Carly, over here!"

Smiling, I wave back and head uncertainly in the direction of her table. My heart lurches with unease as I approach and see six faces turn in my direction.

Oh, God, this is worse than I ever could have imagined.

Three couples. Three bloody couples. I have to take short, sharp breaths to control my anxiety. It looks like I'm going to spend the evening playing gooseberry again.

Story of my life.

"So glad you could make it, honey," Jill squeals.

"Hi, everyone," I beam, making exaggerated gestures to mask my terror. "So sorry I'm late, but it took me ages to find the place."

"Tell me about it," one of the men laughs. "I didn't even know there was a Nando's in London Bridge till today. It's very well-hidden."

There's an awkward pause. All eyes are on me—the women appraising my make-up and clothes with suspicion—the men evaluating my overall attractiveness on a scale of one to ten.

Jill pats the seat beside her. "Come and sit with me, honey."

I gratefully oblige, relieved I no longer have to stand around looking like a moron. "Happy birthday, darling," I say, handing her a bulging *Body Shop* bag.

"Oh, you shouldn't have! You already made the twins those adorable teddies. You didn't need to buy me anything else." She takes the bag and briefly peeks inside. "White Musk! My favourite."

Leaning over, she gives me a little hug, and then proceeds to introduce me to the rest of the table. "This is my hubby Gavin; I think the two of you have already met. And then there's Susan and Paul. We used to go to school together, and finally Bob and Louise, they've been our next-door neighbours since forever."

I nod like a solar-powered Buddha. "Lovely to meet you

all."

The men give me a very warm welcome, but I sense frosty vibes from Louise and Susan. No matter how hard I try, their faces remain cold and distant, like they're putting up barriers against the single woman; closing ranks to let me know their men are taken and not to get too friendly.

Jill hands me a menu. "I'm so sorry, Carly, but we couldn't wait so we've already ordered. Do you know what you want?"

I give the menu a cursory glance. "Um, I think I'll just have half a lemon chicken and chips."

"Good choice. You'd better hurry up and give the waitress your order or our food will arrive before yours. Ideally, I want us all to eat together."

"Sure. I'll go up now. Oh, while I'm there, does anyone else want anything? Are you guys all okay for drinks?" My voice is far too shrill and ricochets across the restaurant like a sonic boom. People at the next table stop eating and look at me.

Louise and Susan exchange glances.

Susan stifles a smirk. "No, Carly, I think we've got enough drinks, thanks."

"Okay, just checking," I giggle.

Feeling like a twit, I reach into the condiments basket, pick up the wooden chicken with our table number, and grapple my way to the counter to order my food. All throughout, I can feel Louise and Susan's eyes boring into the back of me. No doubt they're having a jolly good laugh at my expense. What exactly do they find so funny? My clothes? My social ineptitude? Dear Lord, have I got lipstick on my teeth again?

Oh, God, I just want this fucking night to be over.

When I've finished ordering, I return to my seat nursing a large glass of red wine. Instantly, Jill draws me into a debate about *Downton Abbey* but sadly, my knowledge of TV ended circa 2003 so she's completely lost me. Still, I do my best to humour her. As she chatters on, I take large gulps of wine to calm my nerves, but the effects are slow to kick in. *Damn.* All I want is to get smashed so this night will be over already.

About ten minutes later, our food arrives on a trio of oversized serving plates. For the next hour, I smile and grin, laughing at the appropriate times and pulling a serious face when the conversation inevitably turns to politics. Most of the time I remain silent, making no response unless it is asked for or seems urgently indicated. All the while, I'm clenching my fist under the table, driving my nails into my palms to stop myself from screaming. To be fair, Jill's been absolutely lovely and does everything she can to include me, but it's no use; I'm just not with it today. Plus, Louise and Susan keep whispering and snickering and I'm paranoid they're talking about me. It's complete and utter Hell. I'm operating on autopilot and all I want is to be at home, tucked beneath my duvet watching a DVD. I want to be anywhere but here.

Occasionally, Gavin reaches over and touches Jill's face; strokes her cheeks, her hair, and her nose. My heart aches with sadness. I wonder if anyone will ever touch me that way. I wonder if anyone will ever love me the way Gavin clearly loves his wife.

Am I destined to be alone forever?

Who will I be celebrating my fortieth birthday with? Will I still be a lonely singleton?

Oh, it's not that I'm envious of Jill, far from it. No, it's more an admiration; a yearning to *be* like her. To be loved. To be cuddled and kissed by someone. To be held. To be made to feel safe and protected. Hell, just to be normal and not feel like a freak all the time.

Glancing round the table at Jill's friends, I sense that this could never be me. I feel so isolated. The truth is, I've always felt like an outsider, a marked woman. I'm different some-how, like for some reason, peace of mind and happiness are off limits to me. Like each time I'm getting my life together, a dark entity casts a shadow over everything. Most of all, I still feel like a child, like being an adult is something unattainable. Something I am simply not capable of being.

By eight-thirty, I can bear it no longer.

"You'll have to excuse me. I need to go to the bathroom." I push back my chair so fast it's like I'm on fire.

"Honey, are you okay?" Jill puts her hand on my arm. "You've gone very pale. It's not food poisoning, is it?"

"No, I'm absolutely fine. I'll be back in just a sec."

When I get to the *Ladies*, I rush over to the sink and turn on the cold tap. Splashing water on my face, I glance in the mirror to inspect my reflection. I'm horrified to see one of my lashes has come unstuck and is hanging off my lid like a bedraggled spider. Cursing under my breath, I peel both lashes off and toss them in the bin. Taking a deep breath, I try to psych myself up.

Okay. Time to put my plan into action.

I pull out my phone. Before making the call, I check both cubicles to make certain there's no one there. Satisfied I'm definitely alone, I dial Ronan's number.

"Rescue me!" I hiss into the receiver.

"Is it really that bad?" he chuckles.

"Oh, my God, it's like my worst nightmare. Jill's friends are ghastly. They keep laughing at me and I don't have anything in common with anyone. And to top it off, I've had half a bottle of wine and it hasn't done anything. Not a thing! I'm still stone cold sober. You've got to get me out of here."

"Where are you?"

"Nando's in London Bridge. Where are you?"

"Bar Soho, having two-for-one cocktails with a very cute guy. Care to join us?"

"What do you think?"

Ronan laughs softly, and I picture him rolling his eyes, mouthing, "This girl's crazy."

"All right," he says. "Hang up the phone and I'll call you back in five minutes."

"Okay. And Ronan, please make sure it's no longer than five minutes. I'm absolutely dying here."

But the line has already gone dead. Hurriedly, I put the phone away and return to the restaurant.

"Is everything okay?" Gavin asks as I sit down.

"Oh, yes, everything's fine."

For the next few minutes, I sit on tenterhooks waiting for my phone to vibrate. As soon as it does, I make a point of checking the caller ID before answering. "Hey, Ronan, is that you? Wait, slow down..." All eyes are on me as I go through the motions. It's an old trick we've used countless times before to escape sticky situations. I hate to do this to Jill, but...

The conversation draws to a close. I bite my lip, frown, shake my head a little, then stand up. "Sorry, guys, I have to go. A friend of mine's had an emergency and I need to go see him. Thanks for the meal. It's been lovely."

"Oh, no, you're not leaving already?" Jill wails. "We haven't even had the cake yet."

"I know. I'd love to stay, really I would, but this is an emergency." I stoop down and kiss her lightly on the cheek. "Happy birthday."

"This isn't fair. You can't just up and leave. There's someone I wanted you to—"

Before she can finish, I pull on my coat, say my goodbyes and head for the door. Everything starts to go blurry, the room weaving and spinning around me in a kaleidoscope of colours. I feel on the verge of tears. Then I trip and fall headfirst into the arms of a strange man.

"Whoa, easy there!" he laughs.

"I'm so sorry," I mumble. "I wasn't looking where I was going."

The stranger holds me upright and stares directly into my face. He's boyishly handsome with a snub nose and eyes that crinkle at the corners. I place him as being in his early twenties, but he could be older. He's dressed in a scruffy tweed coat with a cluster of novelty badges on the pockets. This, together with his floppy brown hair combed to one side, give him the appearance of a messy art student. I like him immediately.

We grin stupidly at each other, and then Jill's high-pitched voice breaks the spell. "James, what time do you call this? You were supposed to be here two hours ago. Honestly!"

"Sorry, sis," the man grins, releasing me and turning his attention to Jill. "My train got delayed, and then I had to pop into Waitrose to buy you a present."

"Excuses, excuses." Jill's anger quickly evaporates to be replaced by a cunning smile. Clearly, she sees herself as a bit of a matchmaker. "Carly, I'd like you to meet my brother James. James, this is my friend from work. You know the one I'm always talking about?"

James blushes and I sense that his presence here is no accident. "Are you the one who knitted those toys for the twins?"

"Um, yes, that was me," I reply offhandedly.

There's a short pause. Then I remember Ronan's 'emergency' and start walking again. "I'm really sorry, but I have to go. It was nice meeting you, James."

"You, too. Maybe I'll see you again sometime."

As I pass through the doors to freedom, I can't help shaking my head. Was Jill really trying to set me up with her brother? If she was, then it was awfully sweet of her. Okay, so James is a bit young for me, but *still*. I can't help but be flattered.

One thing's for sure, the evening would have been infinitely more bearable if he'd arrived here sooner.

"It sounds as if your evening was even worse than mine," Ronan laughs, tapping cigarette ash on the pavement.

I feign innocence. "But I thought you said things were great with the cute guy and the two-for-one cocktails?"

"It was, until said cute guy proved to have the intelligence of a flea. All he talked about was Lady bloody Gaga, and then Donna Summer came on and he started doing this horribly camp dance to draw attention to himself. My God, it was so embarrassing." I snicker. "Don't laugh, Carly. The boy was a complete lunatic. Oh, and to top it all off, he tweaked my nipple."

"He tweaked your nipple?"

"Yep. That's a big deal-breaker in my book."

"But didn't some guy do that to you at G.A.Y. last week? Why does this keep happening to you?"

Ronan blows looping smoke circles in the air. "Search me. My life seems to be an endless medley of nipple tweaks and one-night stands."

I crack up. I've only been with Ronan ten minutes and already I feel better about everything. We're sitting under a big, striped umbrella outside a Soho coffee shop. It's bitterly cold but Ronan wants to smoke, so I'm braving the harsh weather for his sake. Ronan is short and slim but carries himself with the haughty assurance of a big man. Once upon a time, he possessed a mane of thick, dark hair so lush it drew favourable comments from everyone. Then an attack of alopecia in his twenties robbed him of his pride and joy, and he now hides his baldness under a succession of brightly coloured beanie hats.

"The problem is I feel old."

"Oh, come on, you're only thirty-six," I laugh. "You're not exactly on a Zimmer frame yet."

"Maybe not," Ronan agrees. "But clubbing just isn't fun anymore. When I go out, I don't feel that buzz. I don't have the stamina for it. By twelve o'clock, I'm knackered and all I want is my bed. Plus, all the bars in Soho are filled with teenagers, and with so much competition, old queens like me don't get a look in."

I reach across the table and pat his hand. "Now you're being melodramatic. You know you always get attention when we go out."

"Yes, but it's not the right kind of attention. For crying out loud, am I the only gay man in London who wants to be in a committed relationship? I'm sick of one-night stands. I'm sick of always sleeping on the wet patch. I want to live the dream: marriage, kids, the whole shebang. Is that too much to ask? All I need is Mr Right and wham! My whole life's sorted."

"Then perhaps you should stop cruising Soho."

"Why?"

"Well, you're hardly going to find Mr Right around here, are you? Maybe you should start hanging out at libraries or something."

"Very funny. The last time I read a book, Dr Hook was *Top of the Pops.*"

We both chuckle, and for a few seconds, the two of us sip our lattes, drinking in the unique atmosphere of Old Compton Street.

"Anyway, enough about me. How are you?"

"Oh, I'm all right. Just been working, sleeping, rinse and repeat. Nothing much to tell."

He gives me a look. "Come on, babe, I know that face. Something's up, I can feel it. It's time to spill the beans."

I hesitate, and then I blurt, "Andrew got married."

Ronan turns pale then clenches his jaw with irritation. "How did you find out?"

"I saw it on Facebook."

"Still stalking the ex, I see."

"It wasn't like that! I wasn't stalking him. I just, you know, wanted to see how he's doing."

"And why the hell would you care *what* that wanker's doing? Carly, it's been five years. You need to get over him."

"I *am* over him!"

"Then why were you on his Facebook page?"

I fall silent; he's right. I have no comeback.

Ronan glowers at me over the rim of his cup. When he speaks again, his tone is clipped and disapproving. "Babe, I love you to death, but you're seriously deluded if you think your relationship with Andrew was healthy. Your ability to rewrite history astounds me, but if you've forgotten what he put you through, allow me to refresh your memory. That bastard made you pay for everything. He never had a job the whole entire time you two were together."

"Yes, he did."

"Oh, really?"

"Yes, he was an actor."

"Psst! A jobbing actor is code-speak for 'I'm too lazy to work, so I'll sit on my backside and sponge off my girlfriend.'"

"It wasn't like that."

"Yes, it was. Remember how many credit cards you burned out? Remember the clothes and the holidays he got you to pay for? And don't let me get started on the car. For Christ's sake, Carly, you bought him a car! *A bloody car!*"

"It was only a second-hand Ford," I squeak.

"I don't care. No one on minimum wage should be buying their boyfriend a car. It's not right."

I shake my head. "But Andrew wanted us to move in together. He was ready to commit to me, but as always, I sabotaged it. It was my fault our relationship ended. He wanted to marry me, but I just wasn't ready."

"Babe, wake up and smell the coffee. Andrew only wanted to move in with you 'cos he was being evicted from his grotty bedsit in Hammersmith. It wasn't for love of you, I can promise you that. The guy's a total loser." Ronan drains his cup then pulls out his smartphone. "Right, what's his Facebook profile?"

"Why?"

"Duh! Why do you think? I want to see those stupid wedding photos."

Reluctantly, I tell him the profile name, and for the next few minutes, I watch his face change from confused to hysterical. "Some wedding. The groom's dressed in cast-offs from a Vanilla Ice video and the bride's a complete heifer."

"Don't be mean. She's pregnant."

"Whatever. The wedding looks tacky. And I bet the bride paid for everything. No way in Hell did Andrew put his hand in his pocket. I reckon you had a lucky escape."

I smile despite myself; Ronan always knows how to make me feel better.

He stumps out his cigarette and lights another. "Want one?" He offers me the packet.

For a moment, I'm strongly tempted. The way Ronan's lips wrap around the cigarette is giving me butterflies but, just in time, I hear Nick's voice like a distant melody.

"No, thanks, I've quit," I say quietly.

"Good for you." Ronan leans back in his chair and exhales a long plume of smoke through his nostrils. "On serious note, babe, you really need to stop obsessing about Andrew. You're too smart and beautiful to waste your life on that tosser. Trust me; Mr Right's waiting out there somewhere. You just haven't found him yet."

Defensively, I change the subject. "Oh, by the way. I made you something."

"A present? For moi?"

Rummaging through my bag, I pull out a small object wrapped in red tissue paper. Excitedly, Ronan tears it open to reveal a black-and-orange beanie.

"Aw, thanks, babe; I love it." Lowering his voice, he whispers conspiratorially, "Is anyone looking?"

I glance around quickly. "No. The coast's clear."

Swiftly, Ronan swaps his hat for my fluffy creation. "How does it look?"

"Fabulous!"

He grimaces. "I don't know. It kind of feels like I've got a massive bumble bee on my head."

ON MONDAY, THERE'S a Tube strike, which gives me an excuse not to go to work. I spend the morning at home, lounging around in my pyjamas, drinking copious cups of tea and eating Galaxy chocolate. Somewhere around twelve, I go down to the kitchen to wash the dirty dishes from last night's curry. Irritation grips me as I approach the sink and see a stack of food-encrusted plates Dad has been storing up for weeks in his bedroom.

Great, it's gonna take hours to get this crap off.

Rolling up my sleeves, I run the hot tap, add a dash of washing-up liquid and start to fill the sink. Honestly, if Dad had his way, we'd have no clean plates and be eating off the floor. When the sink's full, I turn off the tap and slide the plates in to soak. Then I switch on the kettle and take two mugs from the drying rack.

"Do you want a cup of tea, Dad?" I shout.

No answer.

When I passed the living room earlier, the door was shut and I could hear him typing away on his laptop. When the door's closed, it usually means he's working and doesn't want to be disturbed.

"Dad, can you hear me? I said do you want a cup of—"

I quit calling and decide to make him one anyway.

As I wait for the kettle to boil, I rest my head against the wall and relish the hot steam in my face. I close my eyes and immediately visions of Nick flash up. Since our meeting on Friday, I've been thinking about him constantly. I'm completely besotted and thoughts of him leave me in a perpetual state of arousal. I envisage his swollen lips, his warm, capable hands and my mind races with the possibilities:

him on me, me on him. Fantasies that fill me with both desire and disappointment. I wonder what it would be like to kiss those lips, to feel those soft fingers against my thighs. My attraction to Nick is all consuming, and the anticipation of seeing him again is what keeps me going. Even so, I'm still struggling to understand why a man I hardly know has had such an effect on me. Am I so desperate for male attention, so starved of sex that a kind smile and a few friendly words are all it takes to blindside me so completely?

A loud knock pulls me from my thoughts.

Blinking stupidly, I tighten the belt on my dressing gown and head through the hall to answer the door.

"Good afternoon. Is Mr Singleton at home?"

"Yes. Who shall I say is calling?"

"Robin Clarke from Latham & Co."

The man on the doorstep is a little over six foot, well-built but carrying a lot of excess weight around the middle. He addresses me tonelessly, his lips barely moving. Something about him scares me. Latham & Co is my father's bank. This must be serious if they have sent a representative to pay us a visit.

"What's this all about?" I ask defensively. "Why do you want to speak to my dad?"

"Unfortunately, it's a private matter that I'm not at liberty to discuss with you. Now, if you could just let Mr Singleton know I'm here, I'm sure we can resolve this amicably."

My father appears behind me and hastily ushers me away from the door. "Go inside, Carly. I'll deal with this."

"Dad, what's going on?"

"It's nothing. Please just go inside."

Cold fear pours through my veins as I hover in the hall, trying to catch snippets of their conversation. *What the hell is going on?*

After five agonising minutes, the front door closes and Dad returns inside, looking sick and shaky. Brushing past me, he shuffles into the living room. He paces about for a while then sits on the couch, wringing his hands. "Look, there's no easy way of saying this ..." He falters, takes a deep breath. "Okay, so basically, I've fallen behind with the mortgage. That man was from my bank's Income Recovery department. He came here to discuss what my options are."

There's a short, seething silence.

I hesitate, preparing for the worst. "Exactly how far behind are we?"

"Four months," he whispers.

"Four months! Oh, my God, I've been giving you money every month, Dad, money I thought you were paying toward the mortgage. This doesn't make any sense. If you haven't paid for four months, then what the hell have you done with my money?"

He doesn't answer; just gazes at something on the wall behind me. The fact that he can't meet my eye is worrying to say the least.

My heart sinks as I realise there's more, *much more.*

In a haze of confusion, I collapse on the sofa, clutching my temples. Part of me wants to hear this, but another part doesn't.

"It all started last summer," Dad begins softly. "I was having writer's block and needed something to take my mind off the manuscript." He swallows. "I-I started playing online Scrabble, just for a bit of fun. Then I moved to online Poker, and from there, I sort of got hooked."

"Jesus Christ!"

"I know it's a cliché. At first, it seemed like a bit of harmless fun. I played for small amounts then I upped the stakes and continued on a winning streak for a couple of months. Then the wins got smaller and the losses bigger. Inevitably, I was haemorrhaging more than I was able to put in, but by then, it was too late. I was hooked."

"Jesus Christ, Dad. Just how much money did you blow?"

He buries his face in his hands. "Since last summer, I reckon I've spent about five grand."

"Five grand! You've got to be kidding."

He shakes his head sadly. "I wish I was. I'm so sorry, my dear. I know I've let you down badly, and for that, I'll never forgive myself."

I rub my eye with one knuckle. I'm totally speechless. His deception feels like a betrayal of the highest order, and it takes all of my strength not to snap completely. When I speak again, my voice is calm and controlled. "So, all this time you were having a go at me for wasting money on 'toys,' you were going behind my back and gambling with our future. Do you realise the seriousness of this, Dad? Because of your stupidity, we could be made homeless."

"I know, I know! I'm so sorry…" He breaks off weeping, his whole body convulsing with emotion. I've only seen my dad cry twice in his life, so I know his remorse is genuine.

With a heavy sigh, I press the side of my face against his cheek and wrap my arms around him. "Please don't cry. I love you and I'm sorry. I didn't mean to shout. Somehow, we'll get through this, I just know we will."

"I love you, too. I can't tell you how sorry I am."

We both have a good cry then I pull him to arms' length and level with him. "Now listen, I've got just enough in my savings account to cover these arrears. I'll transfer the money over today and bring the mortgage up to date. Then we can draw a line under this whole sorry affair and start afresh. But there must be no more secrets between us, okay? And definitely no more online gambling."

"Oh, no!" Dad howls. "I don't want you using your savings. It isn't right. There must be another way."

"I'm sorry, but there isn't. My peace of mind is worth more to me than money. If we don't have a roof over our heads, then what have we got? We'll be out on the street, and I'm not willing to take that risk."

Reluctantly he agrees, and then I go to the kitchen and make us both a cup of tea to smooth things over. Afterwards, I go upstairs, boot up my laptop and transfer five grand from my savings account to Dad's current account. I feel sick as I watch the transaction complete. There goes my chance of ever seeing Nick again. Now that I'm completely wiped out financially, I simply can't justify paying for all those expensive hypnosis sessions. Not only that, I'll probably have to cut back on everything else, too. No more Disney designer dolls. No more *Muppet Show* box sets. As of today, it will all have to stop.

For Christ's sake, Dad, why did you do this?

I absolutely adore my father, but I can't help feeling resentment about the crazy situation he's put us in. Thanks to his carelessness, I now have to give up all the things that make my life enjoyable.

It's with a heavy heart that I dial the clinic's number to break the bad news. As I wait for the call to connect, my hands are shaking so much I have to sit down.

"London Hypnotherapy Clinic, how can I help?"

I clear my throat, embarrassed and at a loss. "Hey, Tara, it's Carly Singleton."

"Hello, Carly. How are you?"

"Oh, I'm fine. Actually … I'm not."

"What's the matter?"

My next words are spoken like a robot with brain damage. "Due to unforeseen circumstances, I won't be able to continue with my treatment. I won't be coming to this Friday's appointment or any after that. Sorry for the inconvenience."

Tara sounds genuinely upset. "Oh, I am sorry to hear that. I'll let Dr Craven know as soon as possible."

"Thanks." I hang up, too choked to continue. Everything is getting on top of me.

In despair, I roll onto my bed and stare up at the ceiling, dark thoughts marring my vision. I feel completely detached from everything, like this is happening to someone else and not me.

"Oh, Nick, I can't believe I'll never see you again," I whisper.

Closing my eyes, I try in vain to harden my heart against him. Try to tell myself that it was pointless dreaming, that he never liked me anyway and I never had a hope in Hell. Perhaps this is the wakeup call I need to stop obsessing about him.

"Silly little girl," I hiss, slapping my forehead. "Nick would never go for someone like me. I mean, why would he? What do I have to offer?" I bite the inside of my cheek, forcing back the tears that threaten to master me.

Changing positions, I try to take a nap, but it's no use. I'm too restless, too wound up to sleep. I roll over on my side and stare at the dresser, tears trickling down my cheeks onto the pillow.

And that's when my phone starts vibrating.

Wiping the damp hair from my face, I fish the phone out

from the side of the bed. Suspiciously, I scan the caller ID and see an unknown number calling.

Who the hell is this?

Tentatively, I answer. "Hello?"

"Carly, it's Nick Craven."

Holy shit!

Hearing his voice so unexpectedly ignites an explosion of fireworks inside me.

"Carly, are you there?"

"Y-yes, Nick, I'm here." My throat has gone all dry.

"Tara told me you don't want to continue with your treatment. May I ask why?"

"Um, there were unforeseen circumstances."

"Such as?"

His directness catches me off-guard, and I'm momentarily speechless. "I just, that is…"

"Is it for financial reasons?"

I hesitate then admit quietly, "Yes."

"I thought so. Now listen, I think we can come to an arrangement."

My heart soars. "W-what sort of arrangement?"

"In June, I'll be attending a hypnotherapy convention in Toronto. In the lead up, I plan to write a paper about the effects of hypnosis on smokers, and I will present my findings to the National Healthcare Trust. With your consent, I'd be happy to waive my fee if you'd agree to be my case study."

"You mean you'll treat me for free?"

"Exactly."

I'm smiling so hard my cheeks hurt. "Wow, I don't know what to say."

"Say yes."

"All right, *yes*. A thousand times, yes! And thank you.

Your kindness is overwhelming."

His silky-sweet chuckle flutters through every one of my nerve endings. "So, I'll see you this Friday, as arranged?"

"Yes. I'll be there."

He hangs up and for a moment, I'm shocked into silence.

Did that really happen?

CHAPTER FOUR

Caramel Latte

THE NEXT DAY, I arrive at work in a daze. I still can't believe Nick called me last night to offer his services for free. Things couldn't have worked out better, and I thank all that's holy for this second chance I've been given.

I spend the whole morning replaying our conversation over and over again, analysing every word, every detail, wondering if they betray hidden meanings. Does Nick genuinely want me for a case study, or is his offer a thinly veiled excuse to see me again?

God, I hope so.

"You're certainly looking very pleased with yourself." Mark grins, placing two coffees in a corrugated cup holder on my desk. "Is there something you want to tell me?"

"Mmm…no."

"Let me guess. You've won the lottery?"

"No."

"You're getting married?"

"Not likely."

"You've got through to Boot Camp on the *X-Factor*?"

"Not even close!"

Mark scratches his head. "Right, you've got me. Can't you just put me out of my misery and tell me why you've been grinning like the Cheshire Cat all morning?"

"I can't, it's a secret," I giggle.

"Come on, Carly, I just bought you a caramel latte. Doesn't that at least win me some Brownie points?"

"Hmm… maybe."

He eases his cup from the holder and takes an overzealous swig. "Now that's what I call a latte."

I smother a laugh; the coffee's left a huge, white moustache above his mouth.

"Mark, you've got some foam on your…"

"Oh!" Pursing his lips, he wipes his mouth with the back of his hand. "So, what's got you so excited? I'm guessing it's a bloke?"

I smile noncommittally. Much as I like Mark, I don't know if I'm ready to talk about Nick quite yet. Then again, Mark has always seemed trustworthy, and it *might* be nice to get a male perspective on things… Perhaps I can give him the basic scenario without being too specific.

As I open my mouth, the doorbell rings and I race to the intercom. "Hello, Midas Media."

A voice mutters something and, satisfied it's not a prank, I press the release button.

The doors open and a sour-faced man with a briefcase steps in reception. He makes an instant beeline for me. "I'm here to see Leon Phillips. We've got a two o'clock appointment."

"Of course," I beam. "Leon's based on the third floor. If you'll please just sign in the register, I can issue you a temporary pass."

"Make it quick, will you? I don't want to be late. This is a very important meeting."

With a strained smile, I hand the man a pen and the well-thumbed signing-in book. As he stoops over the desk to scribble his signature, I try to keep a straight face. Mark is sticking two fingers up behind his back and mouthing the word "Wanker! Wanker!" over and over.

After Hitler's finished signing in, I slide a visitor card into a plastic sheaf, hand it to him and give directions to Leon's office on the third floor. When he's gone, Mark and I burst out laughing.

"You are so bad!" I scold.

"Yeah, but you love it." Mark pauses. "So look, are you going to tell me about this bloke of yours or what?"

I stop laughing and resume my poker face. "There's not much to tell. Basically, I met a guy I really like, but I'm not sure how he feels about me. I think he might be giving me signals, but I could be reading it wrong. Men are so slippery."

"Why don't you make the first move?"

"What?"

"It's the twenty-first century, Carly. If you like this bloke as much as you say you do, then why don't you just ask him out on a date? You've got nothing to lose and everything to gain."

My face flushes. "Oh, no, I couldn't. It would be too embarrassing."

"Why? A lot of men like assertive women; I know I do. Look, if you're getting cold feet, you can always take the subtle approach. Ask him out to a gig or something. Tell him you've bought two tickets and your friend cancelled. You can make it sound casual, but trust me, he'll get the picture."

I fall silent, deliberating. Perhaps Mark's right. Perhaps, for the first time in my life, I should take control of my destiny and shoot for the stars.

"So, are you going to do it?" he presses.

"I'm still undecided."

"Don't spend too long deciding. Remember, I'm rooting for you, Carly. You only live once."

The rest of the afternoon flies by and come five o'clock, I'm starting to feel really fired up about everything. On a sudden impulse, I take a trip to John Lewis in Bond Street to pick up some wool and new crochet hooks. I've decided to make Nick a scarf as a little thank-you present for his generosity. Initially, I'd toyed with the idea of crocheting a hat, but as I only have three days until my next appointment, I figure a scarf is probably better. Plus, the weather's taken a turn for the worst, and Nick could certainly do with something nice to keep him warm.

Once I've finished in John Lewis, I run across to Marks & Spencer to pick up some ready meals and my favourite chocolate layer cake. Then I hop on the Tube and head for home.

"What's your word count, Dad?" I shout as I hang up my coat in the hall.

"Three thousand and fifty."

"Bloody hell. Sounds like you've really got your mojo back." I drop the bags on the floor and stick my head into the living room. Dad's huddled over his laptop with a satisfied grin on his face.

"Did you have a good day, my dear?" he asks.

"It was okay. Listen, did you manage to sort out that stuff with your bank?"

"Yes. The mortgage is up to date and I've reinstated my direct debit, so there shouldn't be any more problems."

I narrow my eyes. "Are you sure?"

"If you don't believe me, I can show you the bank statements."

"Okay, okay, I believe you. Right, I'll just drop these bags off and put the kettle on. Tea or coffee?"

"Coffee, please. Oh, by the way, your mother phoned to ask what we're doing for Christmas. She's invited us to spend it with her and Michael."

"Jesus," I grimace. "Is it Christmas again already? Where has the year gone?"

"Tell me about it. So, what shall I tell her?"

I run my fingers through my hair. "Umm …Tell her yes, we'll go, if that's what she wants."

"You don't sound too keen."

"No, it's fine. It will save us having to cook. Remember last year's fiasco?"

"I've done my best to blot it out."

I put away the shopping. When I'm done cramming everything in the fridge, I race upstairs to the bathroom to freshen up. I wet a washcloth and wipe off my foundation. As I turn off the taps, my eyes fall on the empty paper dispenser.

"Dad, what's going on? There's no toilet paper!"

"I know, we've run out. Sorry, I should have phoned you to buy some."

Or you should have got off your arse and gone to the shop yourself. Honestly, do I have to do everything in this house?

"DR CRAVEN WILL see you now," Tara says with a knowing smile.

Giddy with nerves, I glide through reception toward Nick's office, my movements slow and heavy like I'm wading through deep water. Stalling outside the office door, I smooth down my hair, straighten up my collar, take a deep breath and turn the knob. I've spent the whole week anticipating this moment, and my eagerness has now reached fever pitch.

Cautiously, I enter the room and find Nick shrouded in shadow, standing by the window with his back to me. Even before he turns around, he's penetrating my senses, causing a monumental swell of desire between my legs. I'm almost high with excitement as my gaze travels over his broad shoulders, slender waist and perfectly formed backside.

Good God, I need to touch him.

Dazed and breathless, I whisper hello. At the sound of my voice, Nick turns around and smiles disarmingly. "Hello, Carly. Good to see you again."

"It's good to see you, too." My crazy giggles erupt, and I want the ground to swallow me up. My nerves are shot to pieces. *Why does he always have this effect on me?*

With predatory grace, Nick walks toward me and asks for my coat. Without waiting for a reply, he twirls me around slowly, teasingly, his large hands cupping my shoulders as he slides down my sleeves, milking a small cry from my lips.

I give him a quick smile to hide my embarrassment. "Hey, I brought you something."

He returns from the coat rack with a quizzical expression. "Oh?"

Silently, I pass him a purple gift bag. He reaches inside and pulls out a neatly wrapped package. He frowns at me, and I grin goofily. Carefully, he tears off the tissue paper to reveal a grey-and-black scarf made from particularly fine wool. He studies it a moment, caresses the material gently with his fingers, and then fixes his gaze on me.

"Thank you," he whispers, eyes flickering with emotion. "It's been so long since anyone bought me a present." Something has stirred inside him, I can feel it. In some profound way, I know that I've touched him.

"I made it myself," I declare proudly.

"Wow, then that makes it even more special. I promise to cherish it always." He pauses, his eyes never leaving my face. "Who taught you to crochet?"

"My mother."

"How quaint. It's nice to know that the younger generation is still keeping the old pastimes alive."

I frown. *What an odd thing to say.*

"So," he continues, "I take it you like creating things."

"Oh, yes. Ever since I was little, I've loved making presents for people."

He laughs pleasantly. "What did you study at university?"

"Textile Design."

"So, you're a qualified designer?"

I make a noncommittal sound.

"Then shouldn't you be doing something that exploits your creativity? Why are you working as a receptionist and not following your dreams?"

"Because I never actually finished my degree."

"Oh. Why not?"

I look away, flustered. "I-I don't know…" There's an uncomfortable silence. He regards me steadily, searching my face for answers. I'm the first to speak. "Look, Nick, I'm sorry. That came out wrong. What I really meant was, I don't want to talk about it. It's kind of a long story, and not one I enjoy telling, if I'm honest."

"That's quite all right. If you don't feel comfortable talking about it, that's absolutely fine." Nick wraps the scarf around his neck and gestures to the padded chairs. "Shall we?"

Smiling, I take a seat opposite him and kick off my shoes, ready to begin the session.

"I think the treatment's working," I say brightly. "Since

last week, I haven't once craved a cigarette."

"Really? Not even once?" There's a hint of scepticism in his voice.

"Well…" I break off and laugh shrilly. "Okay, if I'm being completely honest, I *do* still have cravings, but something stops me from acting on them."

Nick scratches the side of his mouth. "Tell me your thought processes." I frown at him, but he continues: "Tell me what prevents you from smoking; what goes through your mind at the point of rejection."

I think for a second. "It's kind of weird. When I crave a cigarette, it's like I can hear your voice in my head, telling me not to. And then I can't go through with it. It's like you're inside of me." *Gosh, that came out wrong.*

"I think I know what you mean." Nick smiles mysteriously and leans back in his chair. "All right, Carly, close your eyes and take a deep breath. That's right…empty your mind completely. Relax every part of your body and just focus on my voice."

I close my eyes and swiftly drift into unconsciousness. Swirling images flitter through my head, fluttering like little pieces of paper, sucking me into a vortex of oblivion. There's no sense of time or space, just Nick's sweet, sultry voice, and then I'm flying outside of myself again. Flying over trees and fields and rivers. Flying over cars and houses and steeples. Then I'm falling into the dark tunnel again.

Down, down, down…

I open my eyes, blink a couple of times. Gradually, the mists of incoherence subside and my surroundings come into focus. I'm lying on an emerald-green hill with the sun blazing down on me. For a long time, I just lie there, relishing the fresh wind on my face, staring up at the clouds and the sky.

Presently, I spy a hot air balloon in the distance, its red and yellow fabric shimmering in the sunshine. I narrow my eyes and watch as it floats closer and closer to me.

I get to my feet and pull out a packet of Marlboros. Slowly, I walk up to the balloon and place the cigarettes in the gondola. Through hazy eyes, I watch the balloon rise higher and higher, until it's just a speck in the distance. I smile and wave goodbye; goodbye to the past, goodbye to my addiction.

A deep sense of peace floods me, and I breathe a sigh of relief.

It's finally over.

For a moment, I open and close my eyes. Now I'm in a brightly-lit hospital lounge with yellow wallpaper. Ronan and I are sitting in plastic bucket chairs arranged in a semi-circle. We're watching horse racing on TV with the sound down. Ronan still has a full head of hair and looks exactly the way he did when I first met him.

I turn around. To my right sits a hollow-faced girl with mousey, brown hair and eyes like glazed marbles. Next to her is a withered old man with his head tilted to one side, a thin trail of slobber oozing from his mouth. I have absolutely no idea what's going on so folding my arms, I turn back to the TV.

Suddenly, the doors fly open and a huge guy dressed in a dirty hospital gown appears. "They're trying to kill us!" he bellows.

"Who's trying to kill us?" Ronan frowns.

"Those bastard nurses. They're poisoning the fucking water."

Ronan shakes his head. "You've been saying that for two months. If they really were poisoning us, how come you're not dead already?"

"Because they're doing us one at a time. I'm telling you, these people are brutal. We're just pawns in their game. They don't give a shit about us."

I squeeze Ronan's knee and whisper, "Please don't wind him up. You'll only make it worse."

"He winds himself up, babe," Ronan grins. "Honestly, this place is like a cross between *Big Brother* and *One Flew Over the Cuckoo's Nest*. We'll all be bonkers by the time we're out of here."

The crazy guy gnashes his teeth, spittle trickling from his lips as he starts throwing chairs at the wall. There's a horrible cracking sound, wood splintering. Two male nurses arrive on the scene and grapple him to the floor, pinning his arms behind his back. His face turns purple and he bucks and screams like a wounded animal.

I shut my eyes and cover my ears to drown out the awful, braying noise.

"Make it stop!" I shout. "Make it stop, make it stop!"

Nick's voice cuts into the nightmare. "Enough. Now hold for the count of five, four, three, two, one. And now you're awake."

Gradually, I settle back into the current moment. My breath comes in short, ragged bursts; my hair is slick with sweat.

"It's not real," I murmur. "It's all in the past ... the past."

"Are you okay? You seem a little disorientated."

I look up at him, wide-eyed. "I-I'm fine. Wow, that was pretty intense." I force a smile.

"What happened while you were in trance?" he probes. "What did you see?"

I tell him about the green fields and the hot air balloon,

but I refuse point blank to talk about what happened in the hospital lounge.

"Is that definitely all you saw?" he pushes.

I nod vigorously. "There's nothing else. Only what I told you—the field, the hot air balloon, and that's it."

There's a tense silence. Nick's gaze never waivers, and I wonder where his thoughts have taken him. I bet he knows I'm lying.

Finally, he glances at his watch. "Right, that's about it for today. You've done very well, Carly. I think we're making real progress, and I feel privileged to be working with someone of your calibre. Your response to me has been phenomenal."

My blush deepens. "Thanks."

Adjusting my collar, I stand, clasp my hands, and then drop them to my sides nervously. I'm starting to get heart palpitations.

It's now or never.

"Listen, Nick …" I pause, picking words. "What are you doing tomorrow night?"

"Nothing. Why?"

"I just wondered …" I swallow hard and lick my lips. "Well, you see, it's like this: my friend was supposed to come to the theatre, but she's cancelled at the last minute, so I have this spare ticket going. I was wondering … I was wondering if you'd like to come?"

He doesn't say anything; just stares at me with a half-smile on his lips.

I cast my eyes downward, my pulse booming in my ears. "Of c-course, if it's against protocol, I understand. I-I know I'm your patient and that you might not want—"

"Carly, I'd *love* to."

I stop mid-sentence, stomach swirling with excitement. "What did you say?"

"I said yes. What time and where?"

"Oh, my gosh! Okay, well, the show starts at seven-thirty. It's at the Arts Theatre near Leicester Square, and the show's called *Ghost Stories*. I don't know much about it, but the poster looks good."

"Sounds great," Nick enthuses. "Would you like us to meet beforehand, maybe go for a coffee or something?"

"That would be wonderful!" I stoop down. My hands are trembling so much I can barely lace up my shoes. "Shall we say six o'clock tomorrow at Leicester Square station, Cambridge Circus exit?"

"Perfect. I'll be there."

On shaky legs, I finish putting on my shoes, and then we say our goodbyes and I stagger out of the office before I do something really stupid. When I'm safely outside the building, I punch the air in triumph. "Yes, yes. yes!"

I feel like singing. I feel like dancing. I feel like telling the whole of Harley Street I've scored a date with the sexiest guy on the planet.

Life doesn't get much better than this.

WHEN I GET home, first thing I do is search the Internet for tickets to tomorrow night's performance of *Ghost Stories*. Thankfully, there's still some available and I whack them on my credit card. I know I'm supposed to be cutting back on spending, but this is an absolute necessity.

Once I've received confirmation from the box office, I take a long, hot bath to get my head together. Tomorrow is going to be a big day for me. My whole future happiness depends on it, and I want everything to be perfect. My clothes, my hair, my demeanour; everything's got to be just right.

When I've finished bathing, I ransack my wardrobe in search of something to wear. I need to be sexy and alluring without appearing to overt or desperate; the last thing I want is to scare him off. Eventually, I narrow my options down to two outfits: a jumpsuit made of green chiffon and a hot-pink dress with black tights. For a whole hour, I play around in front of the mirror, critiquing myself from different angles until finally I settle on the hot-pink number. Yes, it's kind of short, but the tights balance it out, I think.

I go to bed with a huge smile on my face. I'm buzzing, excited. I haven't felt this way since I was a child. My nerves are all jangled with that kind of excitement you get before Christmas or a birthday. My mind is swamped by a sea of different scenarios, trying to predict how things will play out tomorrow; what I'll say, what I'll do, where this could all lead. It's like I've got my happily ever after all worked out in my head and it's just a question of making it a reality.

The next day is grey and blustery, dismal weather that makes you want to stay at home and curl up under your duvet. But I fight the urge to stay in my bed. Come rain or shine, it makes no difference; I would brave a tsunami, walk over hot coals, go to the ends of the earth to keep my date with Nick tonight.

The day passes quickly. In the morning, I go to the shops, pick up a few bits and pieces, then I make myself a coffee and a light Caesar salad for lunch. I don't want to eat anything too heavy so I don't feel bloated later. Around two, I huddle under my blankets and watch *The Breakfast Club* for the umpteenth time to soothe me and help keep my nerves in check.

At five o'clock, I slip on my leopard-print overcoat and head for the front door. "Bye, Dad. I'm going into town to meet a friend. I'll be back in a few hours."

"Okay, my dear. Have a good time."

I stall in the entry hall, patting down my pockets to check I haven't forgotten anything.

My heart skips a beat.

Where the hell is my phone?

Chewing my lip, I riffle through my bag and check both pockets again.

Nope. Definitely not there.

With a heavy sigh, I bolt back upstairs and search my room for the lost phone. I look everywhere: the dresser, the bed, the windowsill, even behind the TV. But there's no sign of it anywhere.

I grit my teeth in mental perplexity.

Come on, hold it together. The phone must be here somewhere. You just need to calm down and think. You saw it this morning so it's definitely here.

Racing back downstairs, I check the sideboard in the kitchen.

No.

I check the cupboards under the sink, the fridge, everywhere.

Nope. Not there either.

Now I'm really starting to panic. I need that phone because it's the only place I've got Nick's number stored. Technically, I could leave home without it, but if I take the chance and something goes wrong, say Nick's running late, or we can't find each other, how will I be able to contact him?

I stand in the middle of the kitchen, running my fingers down my face. *Why does nothing ever go right?*

Dad appears at the door, arms folded, watching me thoughtfully. "What's wrong, love?"

"Have you seen my phone anywhere?"

"No, I haven't."

In a blind panic, I continue my search, ploughing through every room of the house like a bull in a china shop. I'm on the verge of tears and ready to pull my hair out when fifty minutes later, I find the bloody thing tucked behind my CD rack. With shaky hands, I clutch the phone like a precious trophy.

Then, with a muffled sob, I dial Nick's number to let him know I'm running seriously late; his phone goes straight to voicemail. Cursing under my breath, I punch out a text to let him know I'm on my way. There's nothing for it now but to go to West End and just hope for the best.

"Are you okay?" Dad asks as I hurry through the hall. "You've got yourself into a right state. Who is this person you're meeting anyway?"

"It's no one you know," I snap. "Sorry, I've got to go."

Grabbing my bag, I peck him on the cheek and race out the house, half-running, half-skipping down the road toward the train station. I look a royal mess, but figure I can fix myself during the journey.

An hour later, I arrive at Leicester Square station feeling like I've been dragged through a hedge backwards. My hair is all over the place, my face hot and puffy from the packed commute. The evening's turned into a complete nightmare.

Frantically, I push through the crowds of Saturday-night revellers and clamber up the escalator, three steps at a time. Right now, every single second is critical and I won't let anything stand in my way. When I get to the top, I race through the ticket barriers and head straight for the Cambridge Circus exit.

Back in the open air, my stomach lurches with apprehension. Nick is nowhere to be seen. I glance left and right, scanning the dark streets.

Still no sign of him.

Did we definitely agree to meet at the Cambridge exit?

My head starts spinning. There are so many people coming and going, so many different faces, it's hard to tell who's who.

I look at my watch.

Seven-fifteen.

Bloody hell, I'm over an hour late. He probably thinks I've stood him up. Or perhaps he never showed in the first place. Maybe I'm the one who's been stood up. With trembling fingers, I dial his number, praying that this time he answers.

Once more, it goes through to voicemail.

Dammit.

I flip up my collar and step into a shop doorway. The air is cold and wet with strong winds that cling to your skin like a murky spider's web.

This night just couldn't get any worse.

In desperation, I pull out my phone again to try Nick's number. Before I get the chance, a powerful hand slips into mine and gives it a reassuring squeeze.

Startled, I glance up and see Nick towering over me like some kind of dark angel. My heart slams against my chest, and my pulse skitters all over the place. For a second, we stand in a timeless dimension of euphoria, just smiling at each other. I've never felt so happy to see someone.

"I'm so sorry I'm late," I stammer. "I lost my phone and then I—"

"Sssh…" he whispers. "You don't need to explain. All that matters is you're here now."

His grip tightens, sending a shockwave through me. I'm so starved of affection, so chronically untouched, I relish even the slightest contact. I smooth back a stand of hair that's fallen in my eye. "We'd better hurry. The show's due to start in ten minutes."

"Lead the way." Nick releases my hand.

My smile drops.

Oh. I was enjoying that.

He links his arm through mine and I start smiling again. We walk up the street at a steady pace, blending flawlessly with all the other couples out for Saturday night. I feel so proud to be on his arm. This is the first time a man has ever shown me affection in public. When I was dating Andrew, he refused to hold my hand and always walked a couple of feet ahead of me, like he was embarrassed to be seen with me.

Nick has no such hang-ups.

Cautiously, I study him from the corner of my eye. He's wearing an elegant, black coat with a high Mandarin collar and the scarf I made for him. My heart melts at the sight of it.

What a gent. Even if he's just humouring me, it's nice that he remembered.

"I still feel so bad for making you wait," I mumble. "I promise I'll make it up to you. Perhaps I can take you for a coffee after the theatre."

Nick smiles but doesn't say anything. There's real tenderness there, and—I hope I'm not misreading this—he seems delighted to be with me.

We reach a crossing and wait for the lights to change.

The Arts Theatre is located on Great Newport Street, sandwiched between a comic shop and a fancy-looking art gallery. As we approach, a small crowd is gathered outside and men in baseball caps are handing out flyers. We enter the foyer. To our left is a bar with a long queue of people waiting to buy refreshments, and to our right is the box office.

"I'll pick up our tickets," I say, pulling out the receipt I printed off the Internet.

Nick nudges his head toward the bar. "Fancy a drink?"

"Yes, but I don't think we have time. The show's due to start any minute."

I grab the tickets from the box office and we follow the ushers through to the auditorium. As we scramble to find our seats, a booming voice announces that the show is about to start. Then the lights go dim. Gently, Nick slips his fingers through mine.

"Do you like being frightened?" he whispers.

I giggle and shake my head. His warm breath is making my nipples stand to attention.

God, I want him.

And then the curtain rises and the show begins. Over the next two hours, the story that unfolds on stage is both terrifying and filled with surprises. On more than one occasion, I let out a little shriek, and each time this happens, Nick glances over at me, suppressing a chuckle. Clearly, he finds my cowardice amusing.

When the lights go on, the actors take their bows to rapturous applause from the audience. The show has been a huge success.

"That was bloody fantastic," I say.

"Pure genius," Nick agrees. "So many twists and turns, I never quite knew what was going to happen next. Thanks so much for bringing me; I haven't had this much fun in ages."

"Excuse me," shouts a lady further down the aisle. "Could the two of you please move along? We need to get out."

"I think that's our cue," Nick says, helping me to my feet. "Do you fancy going somewhere for a bite to eat?"

"Yes, please. I'm famished."

He takes me to the Corinthia, a fabulous hotel near Trafalgar Square. As we approach the grand marbled entrance, I catch my breath. The place is absolutely beautiful, and I can't believe we're going to be having dinner here. Andrew never took me anywhere this nice; in fact, I was lucky to be taken to McDonald's.

Taking my hand, Nick leads me into a vast lobby with high ceilings and Grey Marquino flooring. A massive Baccarat chandelier dominates the sweeping circular staircase and off to the left, glass doors lead to a maple-lined courtyard.

"Wow," I gasp.

Nick smiles. "Do you like it?"

"Like it? I *love* it!"

A concierge in a top hat takes us to the restaurant and settles us in. Then a waiter comes over and hands us two oversized menus.

"Anything to drink?" He directs the question at Nick.

Nick looks at me. "Would you like some wine, Carly?"

"Yes, that would be nice."

He turns to the waiter and without reading the wine list, requests a bottle of Château Begadan Cru Artisan Médoc.

He's obviously been here before, I think reproachfully. The idea of Nick bringing another girl here sparks an unexpected pang of jealousy.

For the next few minutes, the two of us sit in silence studying our menus. I'm considering having the white onion soup because it's the cheapest thing on the menu, partly because I plan to go Dutch on the bill, and partly because I don't want to appear a glutton.

"Have you decided what you want for a starter?" Nick inquires as the waiter fills our glasses from a bulb-shaped decanter. I tell him about the soup, and he doesn't look too impressed. "Are you sure that's definitely all you want? I thought you said you were famished?"

"I know, but I seem to have lost my appetite."

"Carly, humour me a little, eh? Have soup for starters, but eat something proper for your mains. I won't have you starving yourself to save me a few pennies."

I blush profusely. *Dammit, he's called my bluff.*

Discreetly, I lower my gaze to his sweater and marvel at the sensual curve of his biceps. I fantasise about touching them and have to take a large gulp of wine to cool my racing heart.

"How is it?"

"Huh?"

"The wine. Does it taste good?"

"Oh, yes, it's lovely. Very rich." My laugh is too loud, too excessive. He knows I'm lusting and clearly takes great pleasure from watching me act like a buffoon.

"By the way, Carly, I haven't told you how stunning you look tonight. That dress really compliments your figure."

My cheeks flame and I shrink down in my seat. "Oh, this old thing? Ha! It's just something I threw together at the last minute. But I'm glad you like it. You look really good, too. I-I love that shirt on you."

Wordlessly, Nick drinks deeply from his glass and shoots me a smouldering look that makes me want to roll over on the floor and submit to his every demand.

A short time later, the waiter comes back to take our order. Nick requests grilled native lobster with almond and herb butter, and I order a chicken club sandwich with dry cured bacon and lettuce.

"So, what made you want to be a hypnotherapist?" I ask, breaking a two-minute silence. "Was it something you always wanted to do?"

"Not at first," Nick replies. "I come from a long line of medical doctors. Before my father died, he enjoyed a distinguished career as a heart surgeon, so naturally, my family assumed I would follow in his footsteps. However," he adds, twirling the stem of his wine glass, "my interests have always leaned toward more sociological pursuits. The human mind fascinates me, and I've made it my mission to find out what makes people tick."

I nod eagerly. "Your website mentioned you've worked with lots of famous people. Anyone I might have heard of?"

"Sure, but confidentially prevents me from naming names. However, I will say that I once treated a Premiere League football player for a chronic gambling addiction that saw him blow half a million pounds in a single weekend. Then there was the TV chef with a sex addiction that tore his whole family apart. I'm pleased to say I cured both men and they're now living happy, fulfilled lives."

"That must be so satisfying for you," I smile. "To know that you're able to make a difference."

"It is. I wouldn't change what I do for the world. Helping people is a way of life. It really is a vocation for me, and I'm constantly humbled by all of the wonderful letters I receive from patients whose lives I've transformed. They are very uplifting." He takes a sip of wine and savours the taste. "So, tell me about your job at the media company."

I shrug. "There's nothing much to tell. What I do isn't very interesting."

"Let me be the judge of that."

"Er, well … what exactly do you want to know?"

"Tell me about the people you work with. Do you get along with them?"

"Oh, yes, everyone there is lovely. I have no complaints in that department."

"Do you socialise much?"

"Not really. But now that you mention it, I did go out the other day for my friend Jill's fortieth. It was a bit of a disaster."

"How so?"

I suppress a giggle. "Do you really want me to tell you?"

"Yes. I'm very intrigued."

I roll my eyes coquettishly. "Okay, I was wearing these false eyelashes—"

"False eyelashes?"

"Yes."

"Are you wearing them now?"

"No way; once was enough. But as I was saying, I wore these false eyelashes, and I didn't glue them on properly. So halfway through the meal, one of them came off and got stuck to my cheek, but I didn't notice till I went to the bathroom. And then, oh, my God, it was so embarrassing, I looked like I had a spider stuck to my face!"

Nick chuckles softly. "That's funny."

"No, wait, it gets worse," I continue. "On the way out the restaurant, I tripped over and fell into this guy. Actually, he was Jill's brother, but I didn't find that out till later. And then he…" I break off, realising my story's run out of steam. "So, um, yeah, it was really embarrassing. Not a night I want to repeat anytime soon."

He stares at me a second, his eyes flickering with amusement. "You're so funny."

"Funny? Funny in a good way, I hope?"

"Oh, yes. You're really quite beguiling."

He thinks I'm beguiling? Woo!

At that moment, our food arrives, and we drop the topic to focus on our plates. For a long while, we eat in silence, smiling every so often at each other across the table.

"So, Carly," Nick asks, crunching on a bread roll. "Is there anyone else in the picture?"

"What do you mean?"

With a knowing smirk, he lays down his bread and folds his arms. "Is there a secret boyfriend lurking around somewhere that I don't know about?"

"Oh, no," I laugh. "Trust me, I'm definitely single." *Gosh, that makes me sound so desperate. Play it cool, play it cool.*

Nick wipes his mouth on a napkin and then asks me outright: "Exactly how long have you been single?"

"Let's just say it's been a while," I reply diplomatically.

His eyes soak in every word coming out of my mouth. "It's been a while for me, too," he whispers, taking a bite from a celery stick.

Holy Mother of God. Is he coming on to me?

The waiter appears with dessert and the two of us tuck into a delicious chocolate and coconut mousse sprinkled with pineapples.

"This tastes so good," Nick says, scraping the last of the mousse from his bowl. "I could do with seconds." Slowly, teasingly, he withdraws the spoon from his mouth, turns it over and licks the metal clean.

Oh, my Lord, I want to be that spoon.

The waiter returns to clear away the plates, and Nick

politely asks for the bill. When it comes, he gives it the onceover and then places a platinum credit card on the table. Excitedly, I pull out my wallet and slide my Visa Debit toward him. "I'd like to pay for half. It's only fair."

He scoffs and slides it back at me. "Don't be silly, Carly. You've already paid for the theatre, so let this be my treat, okay?"

My mouth becomes a tight line. "Thanks. I don't know what to say."

The waiter brings over the portable card reader and takes Nick's payment. When he's gone and we're alone again, I can't stop grinning. *Wow.* What a gentleman. Andrew would never have turned down an offer to go Dutch on a meal.

"I've booked us a room," Nick says softly.

"Huh?" My mouth drops open.

"I said I've booked us a room."

"Oh." I suddenly get his meaning.

And then I laugh a big, hearty laugh and dab the corners of my eyes with a napkin. Maybe it's the wine getting to me, or maybe I'm going crazy. When I finally regain my composure, I say, "I think you're taking a hell of a lot for granted."

He arches an eyebrow. "Am I?"

I don't answer.

My expression tells him all he needs to know.

And then we both start laughing, and I can't look at him, because inside I'm feeling kind of sick. A part of me can't believe he's saying what I think he's saying.

Once the histrionics are over, Nick's face grows serious again. "So, are you up for it?"

"Yes. I'm up for it," I whisper.

CHAPTER FIVE

The Corinthia

OUR SUITE IS on the second floor of the hotel. As soon as we get inside, Nick switches on the lights, and I feel a flutter of apprehension. My legs are weak and it's a struggle to put one foot in front of the other. I'm also more turned-on than I've ever been in my life. I can't believe I'm about to do something I've dreamed of constantly since the first day we met. And yet, a part of me is petrified I'll end up disappointing him. It's been so long, and I'm so out of practice. What if this is all a big mistake?

Folding my arms across my chest, I step into the bedroom area of our suite. It's absolutely breath-taking, with a king-size bed, leather-panelled walls, a plasma-screen TV and a balcony with a panoramic view of the River Thames. By the window is a large cocktail cabinet, a gas fire and an ornately carved walk-in wardrobe. To my right, a glass partition slides back to reveal a spectacular bathroom with marbled walls, a huge stone bath and a gold-plated shower.

Suddenly, I start to panic; things are moving too fast.

"I'm sorry. I don't think I can do this." I turn to go, but before I reach the door, Nick's in front of me, barring my exit.

"Please, don't go," he begs, slipping his finger under my chin so he can see my eyes. "Nothing's going to happen if you don't want it to. We can just sit here and talk, or watch a movie. I don't want this night to be over. Please, stay. Is that too much to ask?" I stare up at him and for the first time, I see a desperation that almost matches my own. "Nothing's going to happen," he repeats. "Scout's honour, I promise to be on my best behaviour. I just want to spend some time with you, Carly."

My head is screaming for me to get out of there, but his eyes hold me entranced and my body is refusing to take instruction.

At last, I let out a sigh. "All right, I'll stay."

Bowing my head, I allow him to lead me over to the bed, and for what seems like forever, the two of us sit side by side, looking away from each other, the air thick with unspoken tension. My arms are still folded across my chest, putting up an invisible barrier between us. The screeching silence pulsates through the room like an electric current.

"So, do you come here often?" I ask, breaking the ice at last.

"You mean to this hotel?"

"Mmm."

"Yes, I stay here a couple of times a year. It's one of my favourite hotels."

I give a low whistle. "Sounds like you're a pretty busy guy."

"What's that supposed to mean?"

"Nothing."

"If you're implying that I bring women regularly to the Corinthia, I'm afraid you're very much mistaken. My business here is purely professional. Sometimes clients fly over from abroad, and I'm obliged to stay in the same hotel as a show of hospitality."

"How nice for you."

"Do I detect a note of sarcasm?"

"No," I laugh. "Definitely not."

There's another silence.

"By the way, Nick, I never asked you how old you are."

"How old do I look?"

"Oh, I don't know, thirty-five?"

"I'm one-hundred and fifty-five years old."

"Yeah, right. Pull the other one."

"I'm not pulling anything. It's true."

I decide to join in the fun. "Okay, I'll say this. If you really are over a century old, then you must use a bloody-good moisturiser. I must get the name of your supplier." We both chuckle and then I add, "No, but seriously Nick, how old are you *really*?"

"I just turned thirty-eight in September."

I smile in triumph. *I wasn't too far off.*

We go quiet again. I start getting heart palpitations; Nick's giving me long, lingering looks that make my body tingle. He's probing me deep, reading my face like my features are hieroglyphics.

Suddenly, he leans forward and whispers, "You're so beautiful. Can I touch you?"

I catch my breath then nod slowly.

Cautiously, he reaches out and tenderly caresses my cheek with the back of his hand. Then he gently strokes my hair and the dip and hollow of my ears, his fingers warm and slightly shaky. With a shock, I realise he's just as scared as I am, and this knowledge makes me feel a little less insecure.

Slowly, his hand travels down the side of my face, then down to my neck, and lightly caresses the sculpted base of my throat. As he works his way back up, tracing the outline of my veins, I marvel at the silky softness of his fingers.

"Shall I take off your jacket?" he breathes.

I swallow hard. "Y-yes."

With deliberate slowness, Nick eases off my coat and drops it to the floor. Then he takes off his own and I find myself becoming aroused as he fixes me with an expression so hungry, it's like he's got me paralysed. Desire spreads under my skin and burns me all over as he sits back down next to me. His sweet cologne is making my head spin.

"You're trembling," he observes.

I drop my hands into my lap. *Damn. He wasn't supposed to see that.*

"Don't be afraid..." He reaches out again and delicately touches my lips, my nose, my eyelids. I arch my back and moan softly as his strong hands slither down to my waist and pull me closer to him.

"Can I kiss you?"

I nod mutely.

Tentatively, Nick presses his lips against my cheek and breathes in my scent. Lightly, he kisses his way from the corner of my mouth to my neck and runs his hot tongue in and out of my ear hole. The heat from his breath makes me crazy and I utter a low groan of pleasure.

Goaded by my desire, he gently but firmly tilts my face toward him. His lips brush the periphery of my cupid's bow, teasing me into a frenzy that shoots straight to my crotch. With trembling hands, he cups my cheeks and takes my mouth in his, pulling on my lower lip with his teeth. I whimper as he kisses me hard and deep, his long, agile tongue plunging down my throat with reckless abandon, igniting an inferno of longing inside me. The force of his need leaves me breathless, his soft lips eating me out like he wants to consume every piece of me. No one has ever kissed me this way before, and the depth of his passion tips me to the brink of insanity.

For what seems forever, our tongues glide together in a flurry of unrelenting lust. Finally, we pause for air, and the room is quiet except for the sound of our heavy breathing. Nick stares down at me, his body shuddering in a way that indicates he's trying mighty hard not to act on a violent impulse.

Instinctively, I raise my fingers to my lips; they feel all puckered and bruised.

"It's been so long," he murmurs. "So very long..." His hand snakes around my back and starts to lower the zipper of my dress. I moan as he brings his face level with mine and whispers, "I promise I won't go too crazy."

His words send a shiver down my spine and I go from wet to soaking. I blink in stupefaction; I can't believe what's happening.

Nick guides me to my feet and helps me step out of my dress. With a gentle smile, he takes my wrist and slowly unbuckles my Kermit the Frog watch. Carefully, he lays it down on the table then he peels off my boots, leaving me standing in just my tights and underwear. I now feel completely exposed and start to fret about my stretch marks and less-than-perfect tummy. I suck in my stomach in a vain attempt to appear more toned.

"Take off your bra," Nick commands.

Self-consciously, I do as I'm told while he squats down in front of me and eases off my tights. The touch of his fingers triggers an explosion of juices that seep through my knickers and drizzle down my inner thighs.

Holy shit, I want him.

Once my tights are disposed of, Nick straightens up and

gently pushes me down onto the mattress. Not taking his eyes off me, he quickly sheds his clothes, leaving him standing in just a pair of boxer shorts.

My stomach turns somersaults at the sight of his beautifully toned body, and I moisten my lips in anticipation of touching and kissing it. Discreetly, my eyes flicker to the dark secrets below his waist. I almost have a seizure when I see the massive bulge in his underwear. The size of it makes my head swim, and I want him more than I've ever wanted anyone or anything before. And, *oh, my God, I need him inside me* now.

With a small, knowing smile, Nick peels down his boxers and drops them to the floor. My mouth gapes open. I am now faced with the full awesomeness of his arousal, and the sight of it renders me speechless.

Fixing his eyes steadily on me, he pads over to the bed and slides in. For a long moment, we face each other, listening to the steady rise and fall of our breathing. His gaze runs up and down my body, and the longing in his face makes my knees weak.

"You're absolutely perfect," he whispers.

"I don't believe you."

"You should start believing. I don't think you realise how gorgeous you are."

I bite my lip and lower my lashes; his compliments are making me blush.

Suddenly, Nick veers forward and rolls on top of me, his lips devouring mine in hot, sinful kisses that both beguile and bedevil me. My whole body is on fire, and I'm a slave to the crazy sensations whipping through my system. Moving his head lower, Nick trails his tongue from my neck to my collarbone, and then buries his entire face between my breasts. Coming up for air, he licks and sucks each nipple, while simultaneously squeezing my boobs together, making me growl with approval.

"I'll do anything," he murmurs, caressing me so gently I don't feel in the least bit afraid. "Just say the word and I'll do it."

"This feels … fine," I gasp. "I like what you're doing now."

He pauses, taking his time with me, making sure he leaves no curve unturned. "This is all I've ever wanted," he purrs. "From the first moment I laid eyes on you." With a long, delicious flick of his tongue, his lips circle my navel and continue working their way down.

As he slides off my knickers, I go rigid. I realise he's going to go down on me and I'm absolutely petrified. What if I don't taste good? I can count on one hand the amount of times Andrew went down on me during our relationship, and his evident reluctance did nothing for my self-esteem. It usually only lasted a couple of seconds, and then he'd always rush off to the bathroom to clean his teeth, making it abundantly clear he didn't enjoy giving head. As a result, I stopped asking for it and resigned myself to a love life free of foreplay.

"What's wrong?" Nick asks softly.

"I, that is, I don't feel comfortable."

"Why not?"

"I don't know."

He stares at me hard. Then he whispers, "Open up for me, darling. I need to taste your sweetness."

I chew my lip. I want to say no. I want this to stop, but it's like he's got me spellbound and all of my strength evaporates. Gently, he parts my legs and swirls his tongue up and down my thighs, sending little shockwaves of pleasure through me.

His kisses are soothingly persuasive; his lips eager to explore every last inch of me. Slowly, teasingly, his mouth edges closer to my special place, licking and sucking; covering my thighs with kisses that burn like a flame through rubber. He's taking his time, whetting my appetite, making me ache for him to taste my sweet spot.

Oh, Christ, please ...

I let out a high-pitched squeal as his teeth graze my skin.

"You're going to be doing a lot more screaming," he rasps.

Dizzy with excitement, I gasp as his large hands cup my bottom and raise my legs in the air, pushing my knees against my chest. Tentatively, he lowers his head again, licks all around my opening and then plunges his tongue deep inside my wet hole, flicking in and out like he's digging for buried treasure. I can't believe how good it feels. I have to bite my lip again to stop myself from screaming. Then he steps it up a gear and completely buries his face in my gushing slit, eating me out like he can't get enough, eating me out like it's the best meal he's ever tasted. I'm ready to explode; my senses are all over the place. He makes me feel loved and wanted in a way no one else ever has, and I can't believe he cares enough to do something so wonderful to me.

Suddenly, Nick stops licking and slides his index finger inside me.

I cry out.

Loudly.

"Shit, you're so wet for me," he breathes.

Slowly, he starts to fuck me with his finger as his tongue plays with my clit, taking me to seventh heaven.

"More," I whimper. "More, more!"

With a smouldering expression, Nick obeys my command

and adds another finger, pushing himself deeper with every thrust. My knees shake uncontrollably. I want to scream down the hotel. I have no sense of anything other than this glorious, glorious feeling.

"Holy shit, don't stop!" I cry.

Just as I'm about to explode, Nick withdraws his hand, puts his fingers in his mouth, and sucks off my juices, smacking his lips together like he's relishing the flavour. It looks like he enjoyed that even more than I did.

Pinning my legs back, he circles my clit with his tongue then, moving lower, he spreads my buttocks and licks up and down my crack.

"Do you like that?" he whispers.

I can't speak; my world has been smashed apart. Nothing I've felt can ever top this.

"Do you want me to continue?"

"Mmm."

"How much do you want it?"

"So much …"

A hungry smile plays on his lips. He's got me in the palm of his hand and he's absolutely loving it. Running his hands down my legs, he pushes me back a little, then spreads my cheeks and plunges deep inside my butthole, flicking his tongue in and out rapidly. I close my eyes and grit my teeth, forcing back silent groans. *Oh, my God. This is sooo good.* I'm in complete Heaven.

After Nick's finished sucking, licking and probing, he releases my legs and rests them back on the bed as he reaches down for his coat to get something. Fumbling through the pockets, he takes out an unopened packet of condoms.

I almost have heart failure when I realise that this is it. *He's going to fuck me.*

Oh my God.

Ripping open one of the foil packets with his teeth, he takes out a latex sheath and carefully rolls it onto his cock. There's a sharp popping sound. I look down and see the condom's burst. We both fall silent. Either Nick's not very good at putting them on or he's got one hell of a size problem.

"Lucky these things come in threes," he jokes. Cautiously, he opens another and this time it works a treat. Fixing me with sex-starved eyes, Nick guides me back onto the bed and spreads my legs wide. *Dear Lord, this is it.* I catch my breath as he rubs the head of his dick up and down my wet slit, coating it with my sticky juices.

"Do you want this cock inside you?" he murmurs.

"Yes."

"How deep do you want it?"

I whimper softly; I can't take much more of this teasing. "So goddamn deep."

Nick lowers himself between my legs and presses the tip of his dick against my pussy. I squeeze my eyes shut and let out a strangled gasp. His enormous size prevents him from getting very far, so he has to take it slow, easing in one inch at a time.

I yell out with pain, and he stops immediately.

"Am I moving too fast?" he pants.

"Please … don't stop."

Obediently, he pushes my legs further apart and plunges back inside, pummelling me with delicious strokes that stretch my pussy wider each time to accommodate his hugeness.

I cry.

I scream.

I swear.

Finally, he's all the way to the hilt and the thickness of him makes me want to pass out. Slowly, he withdraws until only his tip is inside, and then he plunges back in again, working his hips in an intense circular motion before demolishing me with huge, deliciously deep thrusts. I moan loudly and grab hold of his bottom, goading him to burrow deeper. His cock slams into me again and again, and I feel completely broken in two.

But I need more.

Much more.

He's being far too gentle with me. It's like he's released my dark side, turned me into a wild, untamed beast.

"Is that all you've got?" I wheeze.

Nick stops pounding and gazes down at me with a confused expression. "What did you say?"

I snarl at him like a cougar. "I want more. I need more. I want you to fuck me senseless."

A crazy fire burns in his eyes and I quake at the thought of what is to come. Wrapping my legs around his waist, Nick sweeps me off the bed with his cock still buried inside me and slams me up against the wardrobe. The wood is cold and cuts into my skin but I don't care. I feel alive, *so bloody alive.* With frightening strength, Nick fucks me hard and deep, banging me up against the wardrobe door until the wood starts to splinter. Banging me till the door completely breaks in.

But we don't care.

There's only him and me and this electrifying feeling.

At last, a fire ignites in my belly and a satisfying warmth ripples through me. Sensing I'm close to climaxing, Nick increases his thrusts, working me up into a crescendo of exploding fireworks. My pussy tightens around his dick as I finally come, but still he continues pounding till I feel an eruption of liquid in the condom.

Nick yells louder than me. He stops abruptly and carefully withdraws. My whole body feels numb, and I collapse to the floor like an abused rag doll. I'm hollowed-out; completely and totally spent. I didn't know how much frustration had been building up until he released it all.

I gaze in awe around the room; splintered wood and the smell of sex everywhere.

What the hell have we done?

Breathing heavily, Nick slips the condom off his throbbing penis and takes it to the bathroom to dispose of it. When he returns, he takes my hand and helps me back to my feet. His face is very serious and his eyes glimmer with repressed emotion. I wonder what he's thinking.

Wordlessly, he rotates my body to examine my shoulder.

"You're bleeding," he says quietly.

I tilt my head and see a small graze from where the wood cut through. "Oops! That doesn't look too good," I laugh.

A strange expression crosses Nicks face, but he quickly suppresses it. "I'll get you some cloths from the bathroom." Within seconds, he returns with a damp flannel and proceeds to wipe the blood from my graze. I close my eyes and relish the warmth of his touch against my skin. "I'm sorry I hurt you," he breathes. "I got carried away and didn't mean to be so rough. Will you forgive me?"

I laugh again in an attempt to make light of the situation. "Nick, there's nothing to forgive. I loved every minute of it." I hesitate. "But what are we going to do about the wardrobe? I don't think the hotel will be too pleased when they see what we've done. That furniture must cost a fortune to replace."

"Don't worry," he replies. "The manager is an old friend

of mine. I'll write him a cheque, and that will be the end of it."

"Are you sure?"

"Yes. Now please, stop worrying." Nick returns to cleaning my wound. When he's satisfied I've stopped bleeding, he looks me over very carefully from head to foot, taking his time about it. Slowly, sensuously, he grips my hand and kisses my fingers, warming them with his soft, supple lips. Keeping his eyes on me, he places my middle finger in his mouth and sucks on it deeply.

Shit.

He's completely skewering my senses. I close my eyes and feel a painful throb down below. I want him all over again. Without him inside me, I feel incomplete, like I've lost a body part.

"Are you sure you're okay?" he whispers.

"Yes. I've never felt better."

My heart flutters. *I'm really starting to fall for this guy.*

Holding me tightly, Nick leads me over to the bed, throws back the duvet, and guides me in. Plumping up the pillows, he helps me get comfortable, then switches off the lamp and plunges the room into darkness. I shiver with delight as he grabs me from behind and pulls me against his chest, wrapping me in a bear hug that makes me feel safe and protected. I love having his strong arms around me; love the feel of his firm chest pressed up against me. With a contented sigh, I snuggle into him and giggle as his cock brushes against my bottom.

I mouth silent gratitude to no one in particular.

I've never felt so at peace.

For long moments, I lie awake, blinking in the darkness, thanking Heaven and all the angels that I've met someone so wonderful. Things like this don't happen to people like me. None of it feels real and I still can't believe my good fortune. Yesterday I was living a lie; yesterday I was living in darkness. Now, it's like I've been reborn. Nick is the Mr Right I've waited for my whole life, and I vow never to let him go.

Till death do us part.

With a low murmur, Nick shifts positions and slowly runs his fingers through my hair over and over again until I fall asleep.

THE NEXT MORNING, I'm woken by the sound of running water. For a second, I forget where I am. Everything looks strange. And then I remember last night, and a playful smile tugs at my lips. Turning my head, I see the space beside me on the bed is empty. Sounds from the shower tell me Nick's in the bathroom.

Phew! He hasn't run out on me.

With a happy sigh, I roll onto my back and gaze up at the ceiling, my heart beating so fast I think it will explode. Every part of me aches from last night's physical exertions, and my nether regions are so sore it hurts whenever I move. But I wouldn't change a single thing; I absolutely *love it*.

The door to the bathroom opens and Nick appears, wrapped in a towel. His sleek, black hair falls about his face in little, soft ringlets and it's a struggle not to throw my arms around him.

"Morning, gorgeous. Sleep well?" he asks brightly.

"Yes. I don't think I've ever slept so soundly."

There's an awkward pause as I wrack my brain for something to say. I have a hundred questions but the sight of him has left me tongue-tied. Thankfully, a quiet knock at the door breaks the tension. Nick shoots me a look as he pads into the entry hall. For a few seconds, I hear him converse with an unknown woman, then the door closes and he returns pushing a trolley piled with food.

"Who was that?" I ask.

"The maid. She brought us breakfast. All part of the service, you know."

"How lovely." I yawn and then add, "By the way, what time is it?"

"Just after ten. We need to check out before eleven-thirty, so you'll need to eat this fast."

He wheels the trolley over to the bed and parks it in front of me. Gingerly, I lift the lid off one of the large serving dishes to reveal cinnamon porridge, smoked salmon and scrambled eggs. It looks delicious but for some reason, I don't feel particularly hungry.

"This is great," I say. "I hope you're going to help me eat it?"

"I'm sorry; I'm not really much of a breakfast person. I ordered it for you."

I force a smile. There's no way I'm going to be able to finish this, but I'll sure as hell take a crack at it. As I get stuck in, Nick returns to the bathroom to finish getting dressed. I can't understand why he doesn't just stay where I can see him so I can ogle him to my heart's content. I'd give anything to catch even a glimpse of what I enjoyed last night.

"So, what have you got planned for today?" I shout.

"I have a meeting with a client at one o'clock," he shouts back. "When we leave here, I'll be going straight to Shepherd's Bush."

"Oh." I feel a stab of disappointment. I'd been hoping we

could spend the rest of the day together, but it seems Nick has other plans.

Five minutes later, he slides back the bathroom door and steps out wearing the same clothes from yesterday. He looks great, but for some reason, my mood has soured. Adjusting his cufflinks, he asks me what I'm doing for the rest of the day.

I flounder. "Oh, I'll probably just go home. I've got lots to do, plus I don't fancy walking around West End in the same clothes from yesterday."

He laughs pleasantly. "That's true. Pity me then. I've got to get through a whole meeting before I can go home and get changed."

"Where do you live?"

"Pimlico."

"Very posh."

"Oh, not really. The best thing about it is the transport links. It's a doddle for me to get to work in the mornings."

There's an uncomfortable pause.

I down the last of my orange juice, and then I climb out of bed and make my way to the bathroom. I can feel his eyes on me; studying, probing, and all of my old body hang-ups come flooding back. I wonder just how bad I look in the cold light of day. Whatever's on his mind, I wish he'd say it already.

I race into the shower cubicle. As hot jets of water drum down around me, I close my eyes and reminisce about the mind-blowing sex from last night. It was the most wonderful, most perfect experience of my life and I can't stop thinking about it. The feel of his cock inside me. The heat from his lips. Oh, God, what I would give for him to come in here right now and have his wicked way with me again.

Right on cue, the bathroom door opens and Nick enters brandishing a pile of fresh towels and a fluffy, white dressing gown. He's nothing more than a silhouette against the steamed-up glass, but I know he's getting a good eyeful of my naked body. My blood races at the possibilities. For an interminable time, he hovers outside the cubicle, teasing me into a frenzy of excitement.

Then finally, he clears his throat. "Carly, I've brought you some fresh towels. I'll just leave them here on the rack, okay?"

"Thanks," I smile.

And then he's gone, and I'm left swallowing a bitter pill.

Damn it. I wanted him to ravish me.

When I've finished washing and dressing, I return to the bedroom to find him sitting on the bed, watching the highlights from a football game on TV.

"Are you ready to go, darling?" he asks sweetly.

"Yes, I think so."

Nick picks up the remote and switches off the TV. Shrugging on his coat, he takes one last look around the room. "Have we definitely got everything?"

I pat down my pockets. "I think so."

"Ah ha!" He snatches my watch from the dresser and dangles it before me. "We almost forgot this little treasure."

I laugh tonelessly.

Smiling warmly, Nick comes over and puts the watch back on my wrist. As he finishes strapping it up, our eyes meet and I silently plead with him to let me know what's going on. I need reassurance. I need to know that last night was more than just sex. *Please, don't let this be the end.*

He moistens his lips, and for a second, it looks as though he might say something.

But the moment passes, and his expression remains placid.

Silently, Nick turns away from me and gives our suite the final onceover before we close the door. Linking his arm through mine, he leads me out into the corridor and locks up. Then we take the elevator down to the lobby and drop off our keys at reception. As promised, Nick mentions the wardrobe to the concierge and a phone call is made. Minutes later, the manager appears and takes Nick to one side for a chat. In no time at all, an agreement is struck.

"So, I'll post you the cheque on Monday?"

"Yes, sir," the manager replies. "Whatever's most convenient for you."

Nick grins, shakes his hand, and leaves a big, fat tip for the concierge. Then, taking my arm, he leads me out of the building.

Wow. It seems Nick has friends in high places.

Feeling numb and a little spaced-out, I gaze around the wide West End streets in an attempt to get my bearings. A harsh breeze whips my cheeks, and I turn up my collar to fend off the morning chill. Instinctively, Nick reaches in his pocket and rolls out the scarf I made for him.

My heart swells at the sight of it.

Releasing my arm, he ties the scarf around his neck and looks into the middle distance. "Right, where do I need to take you? The nearest station is Charing Cross. Five minutes in that direction."

"Charing Cross will be fine," I shrug.

We start walking and in no time at all, we're standing at the entrance to the Underground.

"So, you'll be all right getting home?" Nick asks.

I nod stiffly. "Of course."

The silence stretches thin between us.

Taking a step forward, I wet my lips and ask in a strangled voice, "Aren't you getting the Tube, too? I thought you said you were going to Shepherd's Bush?"

"That's right, but I might have a browse of the shops first. I've still got some time to kill before the meeting."

I tuck a hair behind my ear and shift my weight awkwardly. *Why can't I go to the shops with him? Is he trying to get rid of me?*

As if sensing my thoughts, Nick snakes his arm around my waist and draws me close. Instantly, all of my misgivings fade away and I'm grinning like a happy five-year-old. Softly, he kisses my cheek. "Safe journey, darling. I'll call you when I get out of the meeting."

My face perks up. "Do you promise?"

"I promise."

With a shy smile, I add, "Thanks for a wonderful night. It was simply...*awesome*."

He doesn't reply, just gives me a final squeeze before letting me go. In a daze of euphoria, I wave goodbye and stand by the entrance to the Underground, watching his dark figure disappear down the street. With a blissful sigh, I turn around and make my way down into Charing Cross Tube station.

"A phone call would have been nice," Dad gripes as soon as I get home. "I've been mad with worry. I don't mind you staying out all night, but you could at least have had the decency to text me."

"Sorry," I reply sheepishly. "You're right; it was irresponsible of me. It won't happen again, I promise."

"So, what did you get up to? I take it you were out with a bloke?"

I nod feebly. "Yes. We went to the theatre and then dinner. It was a pretty good night." Hanging up my coat, I head swiftly through the entry hall toward the kitchen. "I could murder a coffee. Do you want a coffee? I'll make us one. Jesus, my head's absolutely killing me."

And that's the last we say on the subject. I know there's a lot more he wants to say, questions he wants to ask. But Dad knows better than to grill me about my love life. We've already been through this with Andrew, and of course I understand why he's worried, but the past is the past, and I can't go through life living in fear. At the end of the day, I'm not a teenager anymore and for this set-up to work, Dad needs to allow me some privacy.

After I've demolished a bacon sandwich and two cups of coffee, my hangover starts to diminish a little. In high spirits, I go upstairs and spend the rest of the afternoon watching Disney films. Every so often, I glance excitedly at my watch and wonder how Nick's day's going. I wonder how his meeting went and whether he enjoyed his browse around the shops. I wonder if he misses me as much as I miss him. I relive last night's events constantly, savouring every sweet moment, every sweet detail. I repeat aloud all of the lovely things he said to me. I may as well admit it. I'm irrevocably stuck on Nick Craven.

However, as night falls and there's still no call from him, my mood begins to dampen a little. I try to busy myself with random tasks that keep popping up one after another: getting my clothes ready for work tomorrow, organising my DVDs, but it's no use. Each little stir of enjoyment is short-lived and I'm constantly on edge; I can't relax no matter what I do. By nine o'clock, I'm really starting to panic. *Why hasn't Nick called?*

Pacing my room, I replay the events again from last night, analysing my behaviour, his behaviour; my reactions, his reactions, trying to see where it all went wrong. I must have done something to put him off, *but what?* Perhaps I appeared too desperate and he decided to jump ship before things got too intense.

Suddenly, I stop pacing and slap my hand across my forehead.

Oh, God. What if something bad happened to him? What if he got hit by a car? A hundred terrible images flash through my mind: the ambulance, flashing lights, Nick on a life-support machine.

Tears collect in my eyes, and I'm just about to lose it when I hear a low vibrating noise.

My phone's ringing!

In a frenzy of delight, I race around the room looking for it. Finally, with a sob of relief, I pounce on my handbag, wrestle out the phone and answer it without checking the ID.

"Nick?"

"No, darling, it's Mum. Who's Nick?"

I sink down on the bed and try to keep my voice steady. "Oh, he's just a friend. So, um, how are you, Mum?"

"I'm fine, sweetheart. How are you?"

"Great. I've quit smoking. Apart from that, nothing new to report." I try to sound cheerful but inside I'm dying.

Mum squeals with delight. "Oh, well done about the smoking. I'm so glad you're taking your health more seriously these days."

"Well, you know what they say: once you hit thirty, it's all downhill from there. I can't get away with what I used to."

"Whatever the reason, I'm just glad you quit. Smoking's a horrible, nasty habit."

I narrow my eyes. *It's no worse than your drink problem. At least I don't have Bloody Marys for breakfast.*

"Dad told me about Christmas," I say, trying to keep the atmosphere light. "So, it's all set. We're coming up to yours?"

"Yes, for Christmas and Boxing Day. I'm pulling out all the stops to make it our best ever."

"Great. Can't wait."

"Do you think I should make roast chicken or turkey this year?"

"Definitely turkey. It's more festive."

"Yes, but I've found a wonderful Heston Blumenthal recipe for chicken, so I'm sort of on the fence."

I press my fingers to my temples; this is starting to give me a headache. "Do whatever makes you happy, Mum. If you prefer the chicken, then that's fine with me. Whatever you do will taste wonderful, I'm sure."

She hesitates. "Darling, I have to admit I am a little cross with you."

"What have I done now?"

Her tone softens into a whine. "You don't call me like you used to. Oh, I know you're busy with work and stuff, but is a chat with your mother once a week really too much to ask? You're still my baby, and it hurts that you don't seem to have time for me."

I give a hollow laugh. "Oh, come on. You know I'm not really a phone person. You know I love you to bits, but I've just been so busy lately, I haven't had time to call anyone. It's nothing personal. I know that's no excuse, but..." I falter. "Look, I promise I'll make more time for you, okay? It will be one of my New Year's resolutions."

"Make sure that you do. And if you don't, I'll give you a bloody-good thrashing."

We both laugh and for a second, my mood temporarily lightens. We talk for a while about inconsequential stuff—items in the news, what her next-door neighbour's up to—before I make my excuses and go.

I'm nauseous, faint and on the verge of tears for the rest of the evening. I want so badly to call Nick, just to check that he's okay, but my pride prevents me. At the end of the day, it was he who said he'd call me, so as far as I'm concerned, the ball's in his court.

I pace up and down round my room for what seems like hours, standing outside myself, trying to assess the situation from every angle possible. Something's not right, I can feel it. I must have done something to scare him off, *but what?*

Finally, frustrated and at my wits' end, I decide to meet him halfway. I'll send a text. I figure it's not as pushy as a phone call and will serve as a gentle reminder of my existence. With a churning stomach, I grab my phone and punch out a message: *Hey, Nick, just wanted 2 say thanks again for a lovely time last night. Hope u got home safely. Carly xx*

Once I've pressed 'Send', I throw down the phone and sit rigidly on my bed, wondering if I've done the right thing.

This is getting interminable.

I wait five minutes.

Ten.

When there's still no response from him, I stumble to the mirrored wardrobe and gaze into the deep caverns of my eyes. "Oh, Nick, what the hell are you doing to me?"

CHAPTER SIX

Waiting Game

"**H**OW LONG WOULD you wait to call a girl after a date?" I ask Mark at work the next day.

"Let me guess. This is about your rendezvous with Lover Boy?"

"Bingo."

He scratches his chin. "That's a tricky one. If it was me, I guess I'd probably wait about three days before calling."

"Three days!" I almost spit out my coffee. "Why so long?"

"Men like to play it cool. 'Treat 'em mean, keep 'em keen', as they say. Phone a woman too soon after a date, and you'll come across as desperate. And no bloke likes to appear desperate. Leave 'em begging for more, that's what seems to work best."

"But we had such a good time," I bleat. "He knows how much I like him, so why must he play games with me?"

Mark shrugs. "Search me; it's just something men do. Look at it this way: either he's playing it cool, or he doesn't like you that much. But for the life of me, I can't see why. The guy would have to be crazy not to want to see you again."

I smile shyly. "Aw, that's sweet of you to say."

"Well, it's the truth. If I were only twenty years younger …"

"Ssh, stop embarrassing me," I giggle. For a moment, we

sip our coffees, each lost in our private thoughts. Then an idea hits me. "Hey, can I borrow your phone?"

"Why?"

"I want to phone his number, just to see if he picks up. I can't use mine because he'll see my name on the caller ID."

"Carly, this is getting silly. You're behaving like a soppy teenager."

"Please, Mark, do this for me. I only want to make sure he's okay. What if he's had an accident or something?"

"Trust me. He's okay. Like I said, he's probably just playing hard to get."

"Yes, but I need to know for sure. It won't stop bugging me till I do."

Rolling his eyes, Mark reluctantly passes me his phone and I copy Nick's number into his Contacts Directory.

"It's ringing," I say excitedly.

"Whoop de do."

Pacing up and down reception, I clamp the phone to my ear with a grim expression. It rings for a couple of seconds, and then the call cuts off. Frustrated, I dial again, but once more the same thing happens. A cold deadness sweeps through me. Does this confirm that something bad *has* happened to Nick?

"He's not picking up," I say, handing Mark back his phone.

"Give it time. I'm sure you'll hear from him soon. But try not to get too hysterical; you'll only end up looking desperate."

I nod vacantly.

At lunchtime, I try a different tack. Knowing I'm due another hypnosis session later this week, I decide to give the clinic a call to see if I can reach Nick there. Standing outside my office in the cold, I tentatively dial the number. My hands are shaking and my heart is beating like a drum as Tara picks up.

"London Hypnotherapy Clinic, how may I—"

"Tara, it's me, Carly."

"Who?"

"Carly Singleton."

I detect an air of frostiness in her voice. "Hello, Miss Singleton. What can I do for you?"

My brows furrow. *Miss Singleton?* She's never called me that before. What happened to plain old Carly? I find her aloofness strange but forge on nonetheless. "I just wanted to book my next appointment to see Dr Craven. Is this Friday available?"

The line goes quiet, and I hear the distant tapping of computer keys. Tara returns to the phone and says coldly, "I'm sorry, Miss Singleton, but there are no slots available this week. Dr Craven is fully booked."

"Oh. What about next week?"

"I'm afraid he's booked solid for the next two months."

My knees are about to give way, but somehow, I find the strength to speak. "But there must be some mistake. Dr Craven and I had an arrangement. He told me he needed to use me for a case study, so I'm sure I must be due at least two more hypnotherapy sessions. Please, could you let me speak to him so that we can sort this out?"

"I'm afraid that won't be possible, Miss Singleton. The doctor is with a patient right now and cannot be disturbed."

"Well, could you pass him a message and tell him to call me?"

"I don't think he has your number."

"Oh, my God, you're impossible!" Before Tara can respond, I hang up, feeling sick to my stomach. Frustration turns to anger as the full realisation of what he's done hits me.

That bastard!

Flooded with incredulity and rage, I immediately dial Nick's mobile number. I don't care if he knows it's me anymore. I don't care if he's busy with a patient. The gloves are off, and I won't rest until I've given him a piece of my mind. If it really is over between us, if he *really* was just using me, I guess I'll have to live with it. But the least he can do is grow some balls and tell me to my face.

Stalking up and down the street like a mad woman, I call Nick's phone again and again. Each time, the line goes dead after a few rings, but no problem, I just call him right back. Soon, the insanity of my behaviour fills me with an odd sense of elation and I become addicted to it. By five o'clock, I've dialled his number a grand total of sixty-eight times. Yes, I know I'm behaving like Glenn Close in heat, but right now, I'm beyond caring. Nick has completely destroyed me, and I won't let this drop without a fight.

On the way home, I'm so wrapped up in myself I nearly step in the path of a fast-moving taxi. I'm so lost, so utterly wretched, I've forgotten how to cross the bloody road. Shaken to the core, and with the taxi driver's abuse still ringing in my ears, I rush home and spend the rest of the evening in a detached bubble. I eat dinner, watch a movie, rearrange my dolls, tidy my room, keep busy, but inside I'm like a zombie, completely disassociated from everything—lost in a vacuum with a great lump of misery sitting in my belly.

The next day, I take half a day annual leave to visit my doctor. This feeling of hopelessness, this oppressive darkness has pushed me to the brink, and I need to get some professional advice to help keep me stable. At three-thirty I walk up to a modern, red-bricked building on Lavender Hill and pass through the automatic doors into a crisp, white reception. I glance from left and right. On one side is a waiting area; on the other a procession of booths assigned to different doctors' surgeries.

Taking a deep breath, I approach the first booth and tell the grey-haired lady behind the desk that I need to see my doctor urgently. She asks for my name, address and NHS card.

I tell her and slide the well-thumbed card across the desk. She takes it and continues tapping away at her keyboard. "What is your doctor's name?"

"Green."

"Hmm…" She squints at her computer screen. "Dr Green is off today, but you can see Dr Wong instead. I must warn you that it might be a bit of a wait as you haven't booked a prior appointment. Will that be okay?"

I nod eagerly. "Oh, yes, that's fine. I just really, really need to see someone. It's a bit of an emergency."

The old lady smiles kindly. "Okay, take a seat over there and wait for your name to be called. Hopefully, it shouldn't be too long."

"Thanks."

I shuffle over to the crowded waiting area and sit down. To kill time, I flick through a couple of old magazines, but the words swim before me in a whirlpool of confusion. I just can't seem to focus on anything right now; Nick has hijacked my brain. Roughly an hour later, my name is called, and I'm told to make my way to door five.

I enter the room and find a small, dark-haired woman seated at a table. She glances up from a stack of medical folders. "Please take a seat. I'll be with you in just a second."

"Thanks." I sit down opposite her and flash a weak smile.

Dr Wong looks about twenty with a beautiful face marred by too much foundation.

"You're Carly Singleton?" she asks.

"Yes."

"Good. At least I got your name right. Okay, what can I do for you today?"

I shift awkwardly in my seat. "I'm not feeling very well."

"How so?"

"I don't know… I guess I'm just feeling a bit hopeless again."

Dr Wong raises an eyebrow. "Hopeless?"

"Depressed," I clarify. "Down in the dumps. In the doldrums. Whatever you want to call it, I've got it."

Her voice adopts a soothing tone. "Have you ever been diagnosed with depression before?"

"Yes."

"How long ago?"

"I've had it on and off for the past fifteen years."

"Were you prescribed antidepressants?"

"Yes." I cross my legs.

"Which ones?"

I give her the name of my prescription.

Dr Wong nods in recognition, and then she begins scribbling something in my file. "I'm sorry, but I don't have your full medical history here, so I'm going to have to ask you a few more questions. Is that okay?"

I wet my lips. "Yes, that's fine."

She finishes scribbling, lays down her pen and looks at me. Her brown eyes are warm, compassionate. "Right, tell me, has anything happened to trigger this off?" I blink twice. She continues: "Has there been a particular incident that's upset you recently?"

Tears prick my eyes, and I can't speak for a couple of seconds. "I met a man. Someone I had a special connection with. I thought we had something really good going but he's...he's stopped talking to me, stopped taking my calls, and I miss him so much." My voice cracks. "I feel so empty inside, so dead... it's like I'm going mad."

The doctor falls silent, her delicate features etched with concern. "Go on," she says softly. "What else?"

I run my fingers through my hair. "I know this might sound crazy. I haven't known him very long, but... I think I'm in love with him."

Dr Wong pauses, choosing her words carefully. "And this wonderful man's refusal to commit has caused a reprisal of your symptoms?"

"Yes, I-I think so."

She scribbles something down in my file. Then, biting the end of her pen, she muses aloud: "Projection of hope."

I frown at her. "What does that mean?"

"Projection of hope," she repeats. "It's a term used to describe an attachment to someone upon whom your whole well-being relies. Even when that person cannot possibly live up to the ideals you project on them, they become the symbol of all your hopes for the future. In short, perhaps your 'love' for this man is merely a manifestation of your wish to be in a relationship, regardless of the suitability of the match."

"No," I say. "I'm not projecting anything. What I feel for Nick...I'm certain he felt it, too. It wasn't something I forced to happen."

The doctor maintains a dignified silence as she processes this information. "Do you ever have suicidal thoughts?"

I shake my head vehemently. "No, never. I love my family too much to ever hurt them in that way."

"Describe your typical day."

"Dark. Like everything's hopeless, like there's no point getting out of bed." I pause, biting my thumbnail. "Some days it's an effort just to wake up. To wash, to brush my teeth, to comb my hair. I burst into tears at the slightest provocation, and sometimes, just *sometimes*, I wonder what the point is."

"And yet you say you're not suicidal?"

"No, definitely not. I'm no use to anyone dead." I laugh bitterly. "Sometimes I feel I'm no use to anyone alive, either."

The doctor makes no comment, just writes more notes, then she gets up from her desk, walks slowly over to the window and opens the blinds to let some light into the room. Sitting back down, she opens a wall-mounted medicine cabinet and takes out two white boxes with green writing on. "I want to start you on these."

"What are they?" I ask.

"They're called Thurlax. They affect the neurotransmitter in the brain called Serotonin. It helps stop you from feeling depressed. I'm giving you one month's supply to see how you go. Take them twice a day, once in the morning, once in the afternoon, but don't ever have them on an empty stomach. Usually, the effects kick in within two weeks or thereabouts. Phone me to make another appointment before the month is up so we can see how you're doing, okay?"

"Okay."

She spends another five minutes going through the possible side effects of the tablets, then we say our goodbyes and I head home feeling slightly more upbeat about things. In the past, I haven't had much joy with antidepressants, and on the whole find them not to agree with me, but I'm hoping Thurlax might be the exception. The only snag is the time Dr

Wong says it takes for them to kick in. I'd been hoping for a quick fix to help numb the pain, but she says it could take up to two weeks. I pray I'll see results faster than she expected.

When I get home, I try to read a book, but my head just isn't with it. For a sweet distraction, I watch *The Princess Bride* for the umpteenth time, but once more find it hard to concentrate. Between seven and eight, I clean the kitchen: I wash and wipe down all the surfaces, mop the floor, even polish between the wall tiles. Then I make a sandwich and take my first dose of Thurlax, but I almost throw up at the first bite. My stomach can't seem to hold down any food, and in the end, I survive on endless cups of black coffee.

When I finally go to bed, I find it hard to sleep. My mind is buzzing too much and I feel unaccountably on edge. Also, my hands keep shaking and I worry that the new medication might not agree with me. After a long spell of relentless tossing and turning, I finally manage to nod off, only to be woken again in the early hours of the morning.

Something has disturbed me.

But what?

In the breathing dark of my bedroom, my eyes dart wildly around, trying to detect some hidden danger. There are shadowy corners everywhere, and all the places I look seem to be perfect dwelling for a monster. Everything is ominous; even my dolls look sinister. Eventually, my senses draw me toward the window. A trickle of soft moonlight is seeping in through the half-open curtains and at first, I cannot see what is so compelling.

Then, out of nowhere, I hear a gentle rapping noise. My brows furrow; surely someone can't be knocking on a second-storey window?

There it is again: a low thud, like knuckles hitting glass.

I stare at the window with morbid fascination. Gradually, a greyish-white mist reminiscent of dry ice from a smoke machine begins to cloud up the glass. I can't believe my eyes. It's like I'm hallucinating, but no, my senses are all in check; this is definitely happening. Rapidly, I slip into a pleasant trance-like state, somewhere between sleeping and waking. Gripped by some unknown force, I climb out of bed and stagger toward the window, my limbs guided by invisible puppet strings. The glass is now completely fogged by the mist and something shadowy is compelling me to open the window.

With a crazed smile, I throw back the curtains and loosen the latch, a bizarre thrill coursing through me like electricity. Cool air slaps my face, my nostrils, as I shift my gaze upwards. The mist is seeping into my bedroom in great billows of white, and in no time at all has consumed everything it touches.

From the depths of this hazy maelstrom, the silhouette of a man appears. I'm rooted to the spot, paralysed, afraid to confront the apparition unfolding before me.

And then a familiar voice calls out my name and my body freezes.

Nick Craven is standing in my bedroom.

He smiles at me, a warm, inviting smile.

I lick my lips and feel a delicious surge of longing as he walks toward me with an intensity that holds me both enthralled and wordless. For a long time, we gaze at each other, dual hearts beating as one. His smile broadens and his teeth glimmer brightly in the moonlight. A malevolent force is emanating from him like potent radiation; something dark and bewitching that coerces me to submit to him.

Slowly, Nick opens his arms and I step into a powerful

embrace that only lasts seconds but seems to last for years. His sweet breath fans my face as he presses his cheek to mine. "I never meant to hurt you," he whispers. "You've got to believe me. This wasn't supposed to happen."

I tilt my head to one side and emit a low whimper. Lost in his arms, I feel so safe and protected. Then softly, he starts to kiss me; first on the cheek, then full on the mouth. Hot, sweet kisses that make me giddy and send me slightly crazy. With a throaty groan, I grab his head and lock my fingers in his hair, goading him to kiss me more intensely. This is sweet, beautiful insanity, but I love every minute of it.

Tearing his mouth from my lips, Nick gently strokes my nightdress and traces the outline of my breasts through the flimsy material. His fingers are like magic wands casting a spell over me. As he works his way down, I moan and open my thighs to let his hands seek out the scorching-hot wetness there. He hitches up my dress and I gasp as his fingers tinker with my clit, caressing and teasing till I'm numb with delight.

"You feel exquisite," he breathes. "So warm, so alive."

Removing his hand, he works his way back up, planting slow, lingering kisses on my face and forehead that make my knees tremble. With a seductive smile, he pulls down one of my dress straps and softly grazes his lips over my bare shoulder. I close my eyes and whimper quietly; I can't take much more of this teasing.

Lowering his head again, Nick's lips pass below my mouth and chin and settle on my throat, caressing my skin with his poker-hot tongue. My pulse thuds in my ears. He appears to hesitate, like he's fighting the urge to completely devour me.

Silently, I will him to give in to his urges.

Take me. Oh, my God, take me now …

For a second-long eternity, the two of us remain frozen in an embrace, locked together as the hunter homes in on his prey.

His very willing prey.

Then finally, Nick pulls away. "No, I can't do it. You don't deserve this. I care too much about you to ever…" He falters, overcome with emotion. "Please forgive me." He steps back toward the window, a shower of mist engulfing him. "I relinquish my power over you."

And then he's gone.

With a loud scream, I sit up sharply. I feel confused, disorientated, my whole body shaking with fear. The bedroom is dark, the window is closed, and the curtains are drawn. Everything is as it should be, everything except the crazy pounding of my heart.

I glance at the clock on the dresser.

Five am.

Instinctively, I raise my hand to my throat and heave a huge sigh of relief. No teeth mark. It was a dream. *Only a dream.*

FOR THE NEXT two days, total unreality takes over. I eat, sleep, go to work, but continue to feel completely detached from everything. People come and go at the office, try to engage me in conversation, but it's like I can't hear them; like I'm swimming underwater with the volume turned down. I sit on park benches. I sit on train platforms. Nothing seems real. Each morning, I gaze out the window at another daybreak, and think, *I cannot do this anymore. I cannot live in a world with nothing to look forward to; a world with no love, no joy.*

I cannot live in a world without Nick.

I dial his number in the mornings; I dial his number in the evenings; I call him from work; I call him from home and find his silence strangely therapeutic. A couple of times, I'm even tempted to start smoking again, but something inside stops me: the last remnants of Nick's hypnosis, I guess. I think of him constantly as some distant, unattainable image of beauty: a chalice of sweet wine I'll never taste again. Like Icarus, I flew too close to the sun and got burned, but boy, was it a hell of a ride.

By Thursday morning, my desperation is at fever pitch and I realise the Thurlax has done nothing to improve the situation. Really, there is only one antidote; I simply must see him. Even if he refuses to speak to me, even if he's verbally abusive, that's a risk I'm willing to take. My need for answers far outweighs my fear of rejection, and I vow to do whatever it takes to get them.

So around seven pm on Thursday evening, I head to Harley Street to confront Nick outside the clinic. It's raining heavily, but this is no deterrent. Wild horses couldn't keep me away. My anger and indignation have given me the adrenaline boost I need to keep going. And I *will* keep going; nothing can stop me now.

For a whole hour, I stand across the road from the clinic, rain pelting down on my umbrella like a stone shower. I know I must look deranged, and a couple of people do double takes when they see me, but I'm past caring. They haven't walked a mile in my shoes. They haven't tasted paradise and had it cruelly snatched away from them. No, only I know what I feel. For a whole hour, I stand in the freezing cold, eyes glued to the clinic door, waiting with bated breath for Nick to emerge. At ten past eight, the lights finally go out in the building and he and Tara appear on the steps. For a second, they huddle together like rabbits, uncertain of their next move. Neither of them has an umbrella.

From where I'm standing, I can see Nick's wearing the scarf I made for him, and the sight of it fills me with hope. I read Nick's lips. He's laughing with Tara, making jokes about the bad weather, smiling like he doesn't have a care in the world. How can he act so normally when I'm out here suffering like this?

Eventually, the two of them say goodbye and part ways, Tara heading in the direction of Oxford Circus.

Time to make my move.

In crazed anticipation, I race across the street calling out Nick's name. He turns around and freezes. His expression is one of shock, but he quickly smooths it away with a smile. He can't, however, suppress the sickening guilt in his eyes.

"Carly! What are you doing here? You're absolutely soaked."

"I don't care, I need to speak to you. You won't take my calls, so what else am I supposed to do?" A heavy mist of rain brushes my eyes as I blink up at him. *Oh, my God. I never thought I'd ever be this close to him again.*

Nick glances around the street then lowers his voice. "All right, we'll talk, but not here. We'll both catch pneumonia if we stand in the rain. I'm parked just around the corner. Let's go."

"All right," I say, not taking my eyes off him. It's almost like I'm scared he'll run away.

Taking my umbrella so it shelters us both, he walks arm in arm with me till we reach a quiet, residential street. Releasing my hand, Nick takes out his car keys and presses a button on the chain to unlock the doors to a sleek, black

Jaguar. Closing my umbrella, I slip in the passenger side and wait nervously for him to join me. As he gets in the driver's seat, I squeeze my eyes shut to psych myself up. I can't let him know how much he's affecting me.

For a long time, we sit in silence, listening to the sound of our breathing and the rain pummelling the roof and windscreen.

"So…" Nick sighs. "What is it you wanted to talk about?"

"Why haven't you returned my calls?" I demand, trying to keep control of my voice. "Why are you treating me like this?" When he doesn't respond, I continue: "What you did was pretty low. Did you really have to get Tara involved to do your dirty work? What did you tell her? That I'm some kind of crazy stalker?"

"I admit I could have handled things better," he says quietly.

"That's the understatement of the century." I wipe the corners of my mouth. "I want an explanation, Nick. I need to know why you're treating me like this. What have I done wrong?"

He leans his head back and releases a heavy sigh. "All I can say is I'm sorry. You're right. I've behaved like a coward and what I've done is completely reprehensible, but you've got to believe, I didn't mean to hurt you."

I laugh mechanically. His words feel like a punch in the gut, but I manage not to show it. Right now, I hate him so much I think I'll die from it. Trembling, I drop my hands into my lap to curb the urge to touch him. Even with hot rage flowing through my veins, all I can think about is holding him and kissing his mouth—that soft mouth that only a few days ago was licking and sucking my clit.

"Why, Nick, why?" My voice cracks and I'm ready to

resort to begging if I have to. "Last Saturday was the best night of my life. To me, it wasn't just making love; it was like we had a real connection: something deep, something spiritual. Since that night, all I can think about is you. Talking to you, being near you, holding you ..." I break off, looking at him like a puppy trying to gauge its master's mood. "What I'm trying to say is, I don't want this to be over between us."

Nick loosens another sigh and focuses on the rain-speckled windscreen; he can't look at me. "I enjoyed Saturday, too," he says softly. "We had a lot of fun and I found it very entertaining, but I've taken this as far as I want it to go."

Tears claw at my nose and throat. "You planned this from the start, didn't you? You must get a sick thrill out of tormenting people. Is it just me, or do you sleep with all of your patients?"

"Now don't go too far, Carly, I'm warning you. Remember, it was you who asked me out. I didn't exactly put a gun to your head."

"And it was you who badgered me to take part in your bloody case study," I hiss. "You offered me free treatment. You booked us a hotel room. What was I supposed to think?"

There's a long, seething silence during which I concede that he's right. We both had a part to play in this mess. Silently, I start to cry, and once I've started, I can't stop. All the hurt, all the pain I've been bottling up comes crashing down, filling the car with a sad sea of despair. Yet Nick remains unmoved, motionless in his seat like a statue. It's like he's got a heart of stone.

"Why don't you want me?" I sob. "Wasn't I—wasn't I good?"

"It's not that," he replies evenly.

"Then what is it?"

Nick gestures, his hands suddenly awkward. "I just don't think it would be a good idea. We're simply not compatible, and it would only end in tears."

"Is there someone else?"

"No."

"Are you married?"

"No."

"Then what?"

He stares at me for a long time. Finally, he says, "This is insane. We barely know each other."

"How can you say that after what we did at the hotel?" I demand. "Sex isn't a handshake, Nick. It isn't something impersonal you can just erase like...like it never happened. People have feelings you know. I opened up to you, I gave you everything, we did the most intimate thing two people can do, and still you treat me like a stranger. What have I done to deserve this?" When he doesn't answer, I wipe mascara from my eyes and laugh bitterly. "I guess I only have myself to blame. I should have known this would happen. I won't bore you with the details, but let's just say my life up to this point hasn't been great. It's one big disappointment after another. But you know what's funny? Even after all that's happened, I always clung to the hope of a happy ending. I deluded myself that one day a person's luck can change for the better. Well, let me tell you something; you've completely destroyed even that one last shred of hope."

He looks away and chews the inside of his cheek. I can tell what I've said has affected him. Moistening my lips, I decide to try a different tack. "Listen, Nick, I understand if you don't want anything serious, but what about something casual?"

"What? You mean just sex?"

"Yes. Friends with benefits."

He frowns. "Would you really be happy with something casual?"

I swallow hard. "Y-yes. If it meant I still got to see you, then yes, I-I think I would."

"Too bad I'm not prepared to do that."

I rub my face with my hand. "Right, I give up. Why won't you give me a chance? Just tell me what your problem is."

"You really want to know?" he asks.

"Yes!"

"The problem is I'm in love with you, Carly. And I'm fucking scared. This wasn't supposed to happen."

I'm stunned into silence. The sudden passion of his words sends a tremor through me, and I stop breathing entirely.

He loves me?

Heart pounding, I look across at him and am shocked to see his face is deeply pained, contorted by some private torment I cannot fathom.

Nick loves me?

I've been dying to hear those words and yet his declaration leaves me both excited and confused. Why should loving me be the cause of such anguish?

Taking ragged breaths, he reaches down and locks his fingers through mine. Instantly, a bolt of heat shoots up my arm and licks me all over. His grip is slightly frightening. So tight it feels he could snap my wrist off.

He fixes me with burning eyes. "That feeling you described, that connection between us, I felt it from the first moment I saw you. I've never believed in love at first sight, but it's the only rational explanation." He pauses then speaks in a choked voice. "Last Saturday was insane. The second we

131

left the hotel and I said goodbye to you at the station, it felt like my life was going into freefall. I didn't want to let you go, but I knew I had to."

"Why?"

"Self-preservation," he says bitterly. "I knew if I didn't let you go then, I never would. And then there'd be no going back. I didn't want to fall in love with you. I tried so hard to fight it, tried so hard to keep things professional between us, but you've gotten to me in a way no one else ever has. Your kindness, your sweetness, it hits me right here." He takes my hand and presses it against his heart.

"But I don't understand," I whisper. "Why would you want to prevent yourself from being happy? Why is loving me so bad?"

He casts his eyes downwards. "Because I'm not right for you."

"What are you talking about? Nick, you're the best thing that's ever happened to me! Don't you think I should be allowed to decide what's right for me?"

He gives a small, weak smile, but his eyes remain stormy. I can sense there's a shadow hanging over him, something dark he's hiding, but for the life of me, I can't think what.

"I am not good enough, not worthy enough," he says. "I don't deserve you. There's so much you don't know about me."

"Yeah, and there's a lot you don't know about me," I counter. "I'm ready to swap notes whenever you are."

Nick laughs mirthlessly. "Your naivety is endearing."

I remain serious. "But isn't that how all relationships start? With neither person knowing much about the other? That's what makes it fun." He still looks dubious. The stress is now getting beyond endurance; it's time to lay my cards on the table. "I was living half a life before I met you," I whisper. "I was drifting through darkness, numb to everything. It wasn't a life; it was just existing, waiting for that day when the light is finally put out." My lips start to quiver; I've never spoken so candidly before. "And then I had that one night with you, that one perfect night, and everything brightened. Please, don't send me back to that dark place."

Nick bites his fist to stifle a sob. My words have deeply moved him and he's fighting back tears. I reach across and softly stroke the side of his face, caressing the raised bumps of his scar.

"Give me a chance," I whisper. "I know I can make you happy. Please, don't shut me out. If you let me in, I promise I won't put a foot wrong. Okay, so you've got secrets. Haven't we all? I don't care about that. All I care about is you, being with you; please … I just need to have you in my life."

"Are you sure this is definitely what you want?"

"Yes!"

He hesitates, prolonging the moment of suspense. Finally, he says with grim resignation, "Okay, if it's sure to make you happy, we'll give this relationship a chance. I can't bear to see you so upset and knowing I'm the cause tears me up inside."

Silently, he kisses my hand, then starts up the engine and steers the Jaguar onto the main road. Within seconds, we're moving through the rainy West London streets, heading toward an unknown destination. I ask no questions. I just keep my eyes on the road, watching the wipers dance back and forth across the windscreen.

"Put on your seatbelt," he instructs.

I hastily strap myself in.

With a sombre expression, he turns on the heater and a blast of warmth fills the car. I lean back, my skin prickling with nervous energy. Where we're going is anyone's guess, but right now, I'm game for anything. Nothing matters as long as I'm with him.

Through half-closed eyes, I steal glances at his bruised knuckles as he turns the steering wheel. The skin around the bone is red and punctured with teeth marks but there's no sign of blood.

"Are you okay?" he asks, catching me looking.

"Your poor hand. Oh, darling, I'm so sorry I made you do that. Do you need a plaster or something? I don't want it to get infected."

"I'm absolutely fine. It's only a little graze." He hesitates. "Apart from that, are you okay?"

"Uh-huh. Are you?"

"Yes."

"I hated seeing you cry."

"Same here. Let's make a pact never to make each other cry again, okay?"

"Deal."

We stall at a set of traffic lights. Nick turns on the stereo and randomly flips through radio stations to find something he likes. Briefly, an annoyingly hyperactive voice blasts from the speakers and my body tenses.

I know that voice. Oh, God. *How could I ever forget?*

"What's wrong?" Nick frowns. "Don't you like the radio?"

"Not really."

He turns it off and switches the stereo to CD. Immediately, a beautifully soulful voice permeates the car with a sexy version of *Fever*. I've always been familiar with Peggy Lee's version, but the male voice singing this adds a racier edge to it.

"Who is this?" I ask.

"Little Willie John," Nick replies, and then, as if reading my thoughts, adds, "He recorded the original version of *Fever*. Do you like it?"

"Yes, it's amazing."

He smiles and a deep thrill courses through me. His eyes are filled with rapacious need, a need I want so badly to satisfy.

A short while later, we arrive in Pimlico and I start to get butterflies as I realise he's taking me to his house. We swerve at a roundabout and then he guns the car into a wide square of three-storey houses plotted around a large, communal garden. Nick hits the brakes and pulls the Jaguar to the curb. Above looms a tall, Regency-style house with a white stucco facade and a black entrance door framed by two huge columns. The middle storey is dominated by an elegant, wrought-iron balcony with bow windows and pretty potted plants.

"Are you ready?" He kills the engine.

"Yes." Waves of excitement crash through me as I contemplate what he means by "ready." Unclipping my seatbelt, I clamber out the car and chase Nick through the sleeting rain to the steps of his house.

My breath catches.

He's lost his keys.

No, he hasn't.

I see his hands are shaking and realise he's just as anxious as I am. For what seems like forever, he fumbles with the lock till finally he gets it open and I follow him inside.

We don't make it past the entry hall.

CHAPTER SEVEN

Heat

A S SOON AS he kicks the door shut, Nick has me up against the wall, grinding his body against mine, hands tangled in my hair, lips devouring me with rough, hungry kisses that rob me of sanity.

"You make me so crazy," he growls against my mouth. "I haven't slept in days. All I could think about was you, the smell of you, the taste of you… It's been hell this last week. I wanted you all the time."

I moan as he thrusts his tongue back in and explores my mouth with ravenous urgency. My whole body is on fire. I have no sense of time or space, only a soul-destroying void that needs to be filled.

I can't believe this is happening.

It feels like a dream, a beautiful dream I never want to wake up from.

His hands are everywhere, mussing my hair, tearing at my clothes and breasts. Within seconds, both our coats are on the floor in an unceremonious heap. As Nick continues his sweet assault, I tear my mouth away and drop to my knees in front of him. The floor tiles are hard and slippery, but my desire to please him overrides the discomfort of my squatting position.

With painful need, Nick gasps as I unbuckle his belt and

slide down his trousers to reveal powerfully built thighs with an enormous erection nestled between them. I glance up at him, and our eyes lock with mutual longing. Slowly, I slip down his boxers to free his big, beautiful cock. The mushroom-shaped tip is already glistening with his juices, and my mouth waters at the prospect of licking and sucking it clean. I want every inch of him inside of me.

Flashing a sexy smile to let him know I'll do anything to please him, I lower my head and gently kiss and slurp his gleaming tip. He whimpers softly and leans his head against the wall, eyes closed in rapture. It's time to turn the tables; time to show him what he's been missing. I'll pleasure him so good he'll never think of leaving me again.

With considered slowness, I ease my fingers up and down his shaft, touching and teasing, giving him a little taste of what is to come. Then, still rubbing his dick, I lower my head and swirl my tongue around his swollen balls, relishing his bittersweet taste. Hungrily, I take each sack in my mouth, suckling them like oranges while simultaneously masturbating him.

"Don't stop," Nick breathes. "That feels fucking amazing."

He opens his eyes and looks down at me with awestruck tenderness. I can tell he enjoys seeing me on my knees, labouring so hard to please him. He loves the way my mouth wraps and folds around his dick, probing his little sensitive hole with my tongue. Greedily, I continue to kiss and suck him, licking and caressing every last remnant of tangy precum. Then, with great difficulty, I swamp my mouth around his entire shaft, forcing it down as deep as it will go, shoving it till it reaches the back of my throat. I'm now full to capacity and feel like gagging, but I can't stop. Won't stop. Nick's soft groans of approval turn me on so much I'm willing to risk choking to death to satisfy him.

Slowly, I withdraw, licking and suckling the underside of his cock with loving relish, then I grab hold of his buttocks and push him in so deep, it almost makes me pass out.

"Oh, my God, don't stop," Nick rasps, shovelling my throat so hard I can barely breathe. "Take it all the way." His words spur me to suck even harder. My jaw muscles ache but I don't care; I'm absolutely loving the power I have over him. I love hearing him whimper and moan.

After several frenzied minutes, Nick pulls away from me. "I can't take it anymore. I need to be inside you." His voice is thick with longing.

Dragging me to my feet, he turns my body to face the wall, like he's about to perform a strip search. Then he tears down my blouse, skirt and knickers with such ferocity, he rips the material.

"Leave the boots on," he commands.

I quake with delight at the dominance in his voice.

Silently, Nick steps out of his boxers, takes me by the hips and guides me down to the floor, forcing me to kneel with my back to him. Still gripping my hips, he licks me all the way from my neck to my crack, probing my virgin hole with his hot, hungry tongue. I bite back a scream; it feels so good to be licked out so thoroughly. When he's finished, he cups me to his sweat-drenched chest and murmurs, "What are we going to do? I don't know where the condoms are."

His words send a chill through me. Biting my lip, I push back against him and whisper, "I don't care. Just put it in."

Nick falls silent. After what seems an age, he asks me if I'm taking anything.

"Yes, I'm on the pill."

"Are you sure?"

"Yes, now, please...I'm dying here." Right now, I'm so turned on I'd tell him anything he wanted to hear. I'm so hungry for it I can't see past my need.

Nick's breathing grows shallow as he runs his large, strong hands down my spine and delicately massages my buttocks. I can tell he's beyond excited.

"I don't know if I should..." he whispers.

"Please, just do it!"

Cautiously, he rubs the tip of his dick up and down my wet slit, making my juices trickle down my thighs with frightening rapidity. He's playing with me, making me wait as he makes a final decision. The suspense is killing. I just want him to shove it in and fuck me senseless.

"Do you love me?" he breathes.

"You know I do."

"I want to hear you say it."

"Mmm... I love you."

"Tell me you're mine forever."

"I'm yours forever."

With trembling fingers, he parts my glistening pussy lips and dips the tip of his cock into my burning hole. I roll my shoulders and hiss like a cat. I want him to push it all the way in, but he's still stalling, making me wait, whipping me into a frenzy of half-crazed desire.

"Once you're mine, there's no going back," he whispers. "Tell me I own this body."

"You own my body," I rasp, pushing back against his cock in an attempt to invite him in.

"Spread your legs a little."

Giddy with anticipation, I do as I'm told and wait patiently as he positions himself on one knee behind me. Arching my back, I whimper excitedly as he grips hold of my buttocks and spreads them as far as they will go to help widen his point of entry. Gently, he rubs his dick up and down my pussy, and then pushes inside, moving his hips in slow, steady thrusts to help expand my tight hole. I scream as each delicious nudge buries him further in me, merging our two bodies into one. It feels so good having sex without a condom. Just when I thought it couldn't get any better, being skin to skin with him adds a new dimension of wonderful intimacy.

"Deeper," I moan. "Fuck me deeper."

Slowly, he extracts himself and then drives back into me like a red-hot nail, each thrust taking me an inch closer to oblivion. I bite back another scream. This is more than I can bear, but I love it. I love the feeling of being completely consumed by him.

Nick exhales loudly. "Fuck, you feel so hot and sweet. So alive. It's so good to be inside you properly...to feel your heavenly juices." To demonstrate the point, he flexes his hips and stretches me out even more, making me yelp with both pain and pleasure.

"Are you okay?" he whispers, stroking my hair out my face. "Do you want me to stop?"

"No," I gasp. "I just need a couple of seconds."

Obediently, he stops pounding and gives me time to cope with his size. My vision is blurry; I can't see straight. He's buried deeper than the Titanic, and I'm loving every single minute of it.

"All right, I'm ready to go again."

Gripping my shoulders, Nick pulls out and plunges back in again, slamming me so hard I forget who I am. *Oh, Lord, it hurts so fucking good*. Reaching down, I start rubbing my clit in time to his powerful thrusts to help me climax. Very soon, an explosive heat wells up inside me and I cry out loudly.

"No, don't come yet," he growls, pulling out immediately. "I need to see your face."

Lying on the floor, he orders me to switch positions. Submissively, I climb on top of him and carefully impale myself onto his throbbing shaft.

"Shit," he breathes as my scorching heat engulfs him. "I don't know how much longer I can last."

I straighten into a sitting position and slowly start to ride him. Sucking air through his teeth, Nick closes his eyes with an expression of complete ecstasy on his face. As my hip jerks increase momentum, he gazes up at me and begins massaging my breasts.

"My God, Carly, I could lie here forever watching you."

But 'forever' is short-lived as an earth-shattering wave of euphoria floods my system. This time, I can't hold back and let the full force of the orgasm consume me. Not wanting to miss out, Nick grips my waist and pounds into me as hard as he can, till he too is crying out with pleasure. We yell in unison, and he explodes inside me as we experience the mutual delirium of our orgasms.

It's over.

It's all…over.

Flushed and pouring with sweat, I slide off him and roll onto my back, taking huge gulps of air into my lungs to stabilise myself. I wince at the sudden coolness of the tiles. I'm shaking all over.

"That…was mind-blowing," Nick pants.

I nod mutely. I totally agree, but right now I'm incapable of speaking.

For a long time, we just lie on the hall floor, staring up at the ceiling, recovering. Eventually, he gets up and gently helps me to my feet. My legs are trembling and jolts of electricity are vibrating through me. I feel high and a little crazy. I'm still feeling the effects of the orgasm.

Nick sweeps me into a fireman's lift. "Let's go and clean up."

Effortlessly, he carries me over to the staircase and begins to ascend, two steps at a time. I shriek with delight; it's wonderful having his big strong arms around me. Within seconds, we're on the first-floor landing, surrounded by doors on either side. Kicking open the nearest one, Nick takes me into a lavish black bathroom with a large bath on a raised platform in the centre.

Setting me on the ground, he turns on the taps and proceeds to run water for our bath. As we wait, he holds me close and tells me he loves me. I nuzzle my head into his chest; I'm still too awestruck to speak. This feels so surreal, like a crazy dream. I can't believe I'm here with Nick, standing in his house, being held by him and spoken to so tenderly.

If this is a dream, I pray never to wake up.

When the bath's ready, Nick strips off his shirt and climbs in. He flashes a sexy grin.

"Aren't you going to join me?"

Smiling shyly, I peel off my boots and climb in, positioning myself between his thighs. The water glistens and ripples softly around us, and I start to enjoy the glorious sensations flowing through me; this is sheer bliss. With a contented sigh, I lean against his chest and submerge my hair in the water, making it fall about my shoulders in little golden ringlets. I watch the steady rise and fall of my breasts.

Nick reaches for a sponge and a bottle of shower gel and proceeds to gently soap me down, smearing my neck and back with cascades of rose-scented foam. I tilt my head to one side, moaning softly; it feels so good being pampered by him.

"I can't believe you're here," he whispers.

"Me neither."

"I missed you so much."

"Me, too."

I recline against his chest and sense the rapid beating of his heart. Tenderly, he starts to massage my shoulders, and I slip into a pleasant state of drowsiness.

"So, do you live here alone?" I ask, trying to keep awake.

"Uh-huh. Do you like it?"

"Yes, it's beautiful. Well, what I've seen of it anyway."

"Thanks. I inherited this house from my father. Been in the family for years. When you're ready, I'll give you a proper tour of the place."

"I'd really like that," I smile. There's a moment of loaded silence. "Nick, can I ask you something?"

"Sure."

"How did you get that horrible scar on your face?"

Abruptly, he stops rubbing and his whole body tenses.

"I'm sorry," I stammer. "I-I wish I hadn't said anything now. I hope I haven't offended you?"

"No, it's fine. It happened many years ago. I had a disagreement with someone and it ended badly."

"How terrible." I decide not to probe further as he's obviously not comfortable talking about it. Nick continues soaping and rubbing me but with less enthusiasm than before. I can sense my question has soured the mood a little.

Damn it, I'm such an insensitive fool.

"Does it bother you?" he asks finally.

"What?"

"My scar."

"Of course not. Nick, I only asked because I hate the idea

of anyone hurting you. I just wondered what had happened, that's all."

"Does it disgust you?"

"Oh, please, can we just drop it? Forget I ever said anything."

He goes quiet and I can tell he's brooding. Turning round to face him, I look him dead in the eye and repeat my apology. When he still doesn't respond, I lower my head and gently start to kiss and nibble his neck and chest. Tilting his head against the bath, Nick emits a low moan and I sense him melt beneath my touch.

"If I've been bad," I whisper, between kisses, "then you need to tell me what my punishment is…"

"Mmm, don't start something you can't finish," he groans.

"Who says I can't finish it?"

He grabs my head and pulls my face level with his. "Are you really ready for round two?"

I pull a lost-kitten face. "Actually," I say in a Scottish accent, "I'm still feeling a wee bit sore. I might need a bit longer to recharge."

Nick bursts out laughing. And then I start laughing, and all is forgiven. Smiling, I resume my former position, resting between his thighs, my head propped against his chest. Cupping a handful of water, he brushes my hair back and asks me if I want to spend the night.

"I'd love to, but my dad's expecting me home tonight. Plus, I've got work tomorrow."

"Does he keep you on a tight leash?"

My cheeks flush. "No, not at all. I just like to keep my promises."

"You sound like a model daughter."

"I try my best."

"And how is your mother?"

"My mother?"

"Yes, the one who lives in Purley with her new husband?"

I smile thinly. "She's fine. I got a bit of a bollocking from her the other day. She says I don't call her enough."

"How often do you speak to her?"

"Oh, about once a fortnight."

Nick rinses out the sponge and starts scrubbing my breasts with careful diligence. "Your mother's right," he says softly. "You don't call her enough."

I roll my eyes. "I know, but I'm working on it. Sometimes it isn't easy talking to her, though. She gets so sensitive about things, and it doesn't take much to set her off." I shut my eyes and momentarily immerse myself in Nick's warm, capable hands. "I'm dreading Christmas; Dad and I are supposed to be spending it with her in Purley."

"Is your relationship with her really that bad?"

"With my mother—*no*. The real problem is her husband, Michael. I still haven't forgiven him for breaking up my parents' marriage. He used to be Dad's best friend. They knew each other from school, did everything together. Then Michael's wife left him, and he had a nervous breakdown. My mother started going round to see him, you know, to comfort him and stuff. Next thing you know, they're an item. Can you imagine? It took my dad years to get over the betrayal."

"Sounds like there's a lot of bad blood between you," Nick murmurs. "But you can't let it ruin your relationship with your mum. Okay, so she messed up; it happens. She's only human. People fall in and out of love with each other all the time. Has your father forgiven her for the affair?"

"Yes."

"Then so should you. Remember, Carly, your parents won't be around forever.

Cherish them while you can. When they're gone, there will be no second chances. Every bad word you've ever said will come back and haunt you, and it's only then that you realise it just wasn't worth it."

"Do you have a good relationship with your mother?" I ask.

"I did when she was alive," he answers quietly.

"Oh, Nick, I'm sorry. I didn't know you'd lost both your parents. I feel like such a klutz." He doesn't respond, so I decide to switch to more pleasant things. "So, what do you have planned for Christmas?"

"To be honest, I don't really celebrate Christmas."

"You're not an atheist, are you?"

"No, I've just found that over the years Christmas has lost its sparkle for me. It's great when you're a kid, but when you're an adult...oh, I don't know how to put this. The excitement just sort of fizzles out."

"Darling," I pout. "You're breaking my heart here. I've got these crazy images of you sitting alone in this house on Christmas day, eating dinner for one."

He snickers. "Well, that's actually not too far from the truth. I *do* normally spend it alone. I don't have any close friends in London, and all of my siblings live abroad, so there's no one to spend it with."

"You have brothers and sisters?"

"Yeah, two brothers and one sister."

I hesitate. "Hey, listen: this year, why don't you spend Christmas with me and my family?"

"Oh, no. I wouldn't want to intrude."

"You wouldn't be intruding. My mother would love to

have you. The more the merrier."

"But she hasn't even met me yet."

"I know, but when she does, I just know she's gonna love you."

He's silent for a beat as he considers my offer. "I won't give you a definite answer yet," he says slowly. "It's still early days, so let's just see how things go. But you never know, I might take you up on your offer."

"Brilliant!" As long as there's a possibility he might come, then I'm happy. "Oh, by the way, I had a dream about you."

"Really? What was it about?"

"It was really weird. I dreamt that you came to my room in the middle of the night."

"That sounds sort of kinky. Did we have sex?"

"Not exactly. It was just really… *weird*. It felt so real, I could have sworn you were actually there with me."

Nick hesitates. Then he says, "Perhaps it's symbolic."

"Symbolic?"

"Of us finally getting it on."

I nod vacantly. *Perhaps…*

When we've finished bathing, Nick wraps me in a big towel and goes downstairs in search of my clothes. He's gone for ages and I wonder what on Earth's keeping him. Finally, he returns looking rather sheepish.

"What's wrong?" I ask.

He scratches the side of his mouth and suppresses a smirk. "I seem to have destroyed your clothes. I'm afraid we got a little too carried away again. Sorry, I promise it won't happen again."

I flash a mischievous grin. "Famous last words."

His smile widens. "Well, you certainly won't be able to wear them home, so I'll have to find you something of mine.

But for the life of me, I can't think what. I don't think I've got anything that will fit you."

My eyes dance with amusement. "Is this your not-so-subtle way of sabotaging my attempts to go home?"

Nick bursts out laughing and disappears again in search of something for me to wear. Five minutes later, he returns with an old T-shirt and a pair of purple tracksuit bottoms. They're kind of big, but I figure I can always use my coat to cover them.

When I've finished getting dressed, Nick takes me on a fleeting tour of the house. In addition to the bathroom, the first floor holds three bedrooms and a stairway leading to the attic. Nick's room is dark and Gothic, with a huge fireplace, black velvet drapes and a sumptuous four-poster bed. Downstairs has a huge kitchen, two receptions, a study lined with books and a conservatory that overlooks an immaculately pruned private garden. Every room is fitted out with Persian rugs and antique furniture; every available surface covered with priceless porcelains, urns and crystals vases. I'm very, very impressed. The contents of the house alone must be worth a cool couple of million.

As we sashay around, I recall the strange conversation we had in the car earlier: the one about Nick not being 'worthy' enough of me. Drunk in love as I am, I'm not as foolish as to dismiss his warning entirely, and my eagle eyes are constantly on the look-out for any sign of a female in residence. The optimist in me says Nick's reluctance to start a relationship was a simple commitment issue, but the pessimist still worries that there might be another woman lurking around in the background.

However, as we move from room to room, I see no obvious feminine touches. Sure the house is immaculately clean, and everything clearly has a place, but there are no signs of women's clothing or trinkets and the overall décor is decidedly male. In fact, I see no personal touches anywhere: no family photographs, no birthday or greeting cards to give the place a more intimate feel.

I breathe a sigh of relief. *So far, so good.*

Finally, Nick shows me the sitting room: an impressive living space with a marble-mantled fireplace, oak flooring, sash windows fitted with Venetian blinds and the same aristocratic furniture as the rest of the house. I'm completely blown away and make sure I let Nick know it.

"But I can't take all the credit," he says modestly. "The place is exactly the way my father left it. I've only made a few adjustments so really, this is his labour of love, not mine. Even so, I'm thrilled you like it. Hopefully, you'll be spending a lot more time here, and I want you to be comfortable." He takes my hand. "Darling, are you sure you definitely can't spend the night?"

"Honestly, I'd love to but…"

"Your father's expecting you."

"Um, yeah."

Nick laughs and leads me into the corridor. As he closes the door on the sitting room, something makes me do a double take.

That's odd.

At first glance, the walls appear to be blemish-free, but on closer inspection, I see faint rectangles of discolouration in places where pictures used to be. The numerous hooks still embedded in the plaster used to fasten the frames to the walls further support this. It looks as if this room was once filled with paintings but for some reason, Nick has removed them.

"Why did you take down your pictures?" I ask, pointing

to the white patches.

"Oh, *that*," he answers cheerfully. "I'm having this room repainted, so I've put them in storage. Some of my pictures are very old and very valuable, and I didn't want them damaged."

I nod approvingly. *That makes sense.*

"All right, shall we go?" Nick shrugs on his jacket. "It's getting late, and you'll want to get some sleep before work tomorrow."

Smiling, I button up my coat and follow Nick out the house into the dark, wet street. It's finally stopped raining and the air has a cool, crisp feel. Shivering a little, I walk up to the Jaguar and get in. Almost instantly, we're on the move, heading in the direction of Clapham Junction. My heart feels light. It's been such a wonderful evening, and I'm still on a high from all that's happened. I still can't believe Nick loves me.

"Let's have some music, shall we?" he grins, fiddling with the buttons on the stereo. He puts on a compilation of Little Willie John tracks and for the rest of the journey serenades me to a succession of slushy love ballads. His favourite is a song called "Talk to Me, Talk to Me", which he repeats over and over, like he simply can't get enough. As he mimes along with the lyrics, it feels as if they were written especially for me, and every time he does it, my stomach turns somersaults. He makes me feel seventeen again. I also make a mental note to download this album from iTunes to keep reliving our magical night.

Before I know it, Nick's steering the car into my road and I get a sudden pang of nerves. Compared with the grandeur of Pimlico, my street looks decidedly shabby, and I wonder what he'll think of my home. Following my directions to the letter, he parks across the road from my house. I snap my head up; the lights in the sitting room are on. Dad is still awake, probably working on his manuscript.

For a moment, we sit in semi-darkness, our faces illuminated by the green light from the dashboard.

"So…" Nick sighs.

"So…" I sigh. "I guess this is the part where we say goodbye."

"I hate goodbyes."

"Me, too."

"When do I get to see you again?"

"Anytime you like. Tomorrow?"

He nods vigorously. "Even that seems too far away."

Suddenly, I'm in his arms again and he's holding me close, holding me so tightly I can barely breathe. But I love it. I feel so protected in his embrace, so warm. Then his lips find mine and he's eating me out with that insane intensity that makes my head swim.

After what seems forever, he releases me. Tenderly, he strokes my cheek with his thumb, his gaze so penetrating I'm forced to avert my eyes.

"Don't…" I whisper.

"Don't what?"

"Look at me like that. It's embarrassing."

"But I need to look at you. I need to memorise your face so that when we're apart, I can recall your image in perfect detail."

I smother a grin. Never in my wildest dreams did I ever imagine someone saying something so romantic to me. It feels like a fairy tale, like I'm Belle or Cinderella, living the dream in one of my favourite Disney movies. I never want this to end.

After a final, lingering kiss, I unclip my seatbelt and reach out for the door. Then an idea hits me. "Hey, do you want to meet my dad?"

"I'd love to," he beams.

We get out the car and, gripping Nick's hand tightly, I lead him across the street to my house. Excitedly, I take out my keys, unlock the door and skip into the entry hall, expecting him to follow. It takes a second for me to realise he's still standing on the doorstep.

"Aren't you going to come in?" I frown.

Nick rocks back on his heels and looks away from me. "Is that a formal invitation?" he asks softly.

"Of course!" I find his sudden reticence a little strange but put it down to last-minute nerves about meeting my father.

Smiling, Nick trails after me and waits patiently in the hall as I go to the sitting room. "Hi, sorry to disturb you. There's someone I'd like you to meet."

Dad glances up from his laptop with an expectant expression. "You've got a visitor?"

"Uh-huh."

Placing his laptop in the charger, he slicks back his hair, tucks his shirt into his trousers and follows me to the hall.

"Dad, this is Nick Craven."

"Pleased to meet you," Nick grins. "Carly's told me so much about you."

"All good, I hope?" my father laughs. The two of them exchange a cordial handshake. Dad's a little guarded at first; I can see his eyes studying Nick, adding him up point by point, trying to work him out.

A throbbing silence descends, and Dad stares a little too hard at Nick's scar.

Finally, Nick clears his throat. "I can't tell you how great it is to meet you, Steve. I'm a huge fan of your work. In my opinion, *Path to Enlightenment* is one of the best books ever written on Transcendental Meditation. In fact, it's so good, I regularly recommend it to my patients who are seeking a safe alternative to Happy Pills."

My jaw literally drops.

Not only is Nick calling Dad by his first name, but he also seems to have thoroughly done his homework. I had no idea he even knew who my father was.

Dad raises his eyebrows in surprise. "Your patients?"

"I'm a hypnotherapist," Nick explains. "My offices are at Harley Street."

"I'll take that as a massive compliment, then." Dad smiles bashfully and suddenly, his whole demeanour changes. Clearly, he's flattered and, having appealed to his vanity, Nick has gotten my father right in the palm of his hand.

"I've got a massive favour to ask," Nick continues. "I've got a copy of your book in my car. I'd love it if you could sign it for me."

Dad looks at me. "I'd be glad to," he grins.

I laugh nervously. *Wow, yet another surprise.* But is he laying it on a bit thick, perhaps?

"Hold that thought." Nick races outside and returns a few minutes later brandishing a brand new copy of *Path to Enlightenment*. The three of us go into the sitting room, and Dad happily scrawls his signature across the first page. As we stand waiting for him to finish, Nick's eyes wander around the room, drinking in every last little detail. Then he rests his gaze on me, flashes a playful smile and winks; I suppress a smirk.

Dad hands the book back to him and they speak for a while about the benefits of Transcendental Meditation. It's at this point that I kind of switch off; once Dad gets started on this topic, there's no stopping him.

An interminable time later, Nick glances at his watch, makes his excuses and bids us both goodnight.

"I'll see you out," I say, following him into the entry hall. With Dad safely out of earshot, I whisper, "You're such a dark horse. How on Earth did you know about my father's books?"

Nick taps his nose conspiratorially. "When I fall for a gorgeous blonde with a penchant for Mickey Mouse T-shirts, I make it my business to find out everything I can about her. That includes background checks on her father."

I giggle and tuck a hair behind my ear. "That's so sweet. But really, how did you know?"

"Does it matter?"

"Yes! I'm really curious."

"I'm afraid I couldn't possibly divulge my sources. Plus, I think it's good to maintain an air of mystique. Keeps you on your toes."

Playfully, I agree to drop the subject but make a mental note to revisit this another time. There's no way he's getting off that easily. "So, what time are we meeting tomorrow?" I ask.

"I'll pick you up after work and we'll take it from there."

"I can't wait."

"Me neither."

There's a short beat. I desperately want to hug him, but I sense Dad hovering around in the background, so I settle for a smile and a wave. "All right, I'll see you tomorrow."

Turning on his heel, Nick jogs across the street to his car. I stand on the doorstep, watching the Jag reverse out of the parking space. He winds down the window, waves at me, and then he's gone.

With a happy sigh, I close the door and skip back into the

sitting room.

"So, what do you think?" I ask excitedly.

Dad takes off his glasses and rubs his eyes. "Yeah, he's great. I really like him. Bit of a posh boy, isn't he?"

"Do you really think Nick's posh?"

"Don't you?"

"I suppose he is well-spoken. But I kind of like that about him."

"Just as long as you're happy, that's all that matters to me."

I grin broadly. "Thanks for the support, Dad."

"So, how did the two of you meet?"

"I had a couple of sessions with him to help me quit smoking."

"And have you?"

"Have I what?"

"Quit smoking?"

"Yeah. Nick's treatment was very effective."

"Good." A shadow flits across Dad's face, and I wonder what he's really thinking.

A chill courses through me. I let out a huge sneeze and feel the onset of a nasty cold, no doubt the result of spending most of the evening in the rain. Rubbing my nose, I say goodnight and make my way upstairs. My footfalls are slow and heavy, like I'm wading through wet sand. As I collapse on my bed, it feels as if cold ice is pouring through my veins.

Something tells me I won't be going to work tomorrow.

CHAPTER EIGHT

Slow Burn

"ARE YOU SURE you're going to be okay?" Dad asks, tossing a packet of painkillers on my bed. "I don't like leaving you in this state. Are you sure you don't want me to call Dr Green?"

"No, I'll be fine. I just need to rest." I sneeze into a tissue and rub my nose for the umpteenth time. As predicted, the chill from last night has developed into a full-blown cold, and it looks as if I'm going to be spending the day in bed.

Dad's face is strained with concern. "I'd like to stay here and keep an eye on you, but I really have to go to this meeting with my publisher. Have you phoned your workplace to let them know you won't be coming in?"

"Yes, I've left Tim a voicemail. Now, please, you'd better hurry, I don't want you to be late." I falter, overcome by a fit of coughing. Grabbing a fresh handful of Kleenex, I dab my watery eyes.

Dad takes a step toward the bed, but I hold up my hands in protest. "Stay away from me. Honestly, Dad, you don't want to catch this bug; it's truly awful."

"Okay. Do you want me to bring you back anything? Cough mixture, perhaps?"

I nod and sneeze again. "Yeah, that would be wonderful."

Pulling on his jacket, he walks into the landing and starts

making his way downstairs. "Right," he shouts. "I'll be back in a couple of hours. Call me if anything happens, okay?"

"Okay. Love you."

"I love you, too, my dear."

I wait for the front door to slam. Then, reaching for the dresser, I grab a glass of water and gulp down two painkillers. With a low sigh, I sink back into the pillows, pulling the duvet up to my chin. It feels like I've got the mother of all hangovers and every part of my body is numb. To make matters worse, my period has started today, and I can feel those old, familiar cramps kicking in. Still, despite feeling so poorly, I'm in wonderful spirits. Nick has already sent three texts this morning, telling me how much he loves and misses me. He knows I'm not feeling well but regardless, I still plan to meet up with him tonight. There's no way I'm going to break our date. I'm hoping if I get a few hours' sleep, I'll be strong enough to leave the house later.

Some hope.

As the morning passes, my condition seems to be getting worse. I keep sneezing and my eyes are so watery I can barely see. At this rate, I won't be leaving this bed, let alone the house.

Then around midday, someone rings the doorbell.

I freeze. I haven't ordered anything recently, so I'm not expecting any deliveries. *Perhaps it's the Jehovah Witnesses or something.* Before I can react, my phone starts vibrating. Sitting on my elbows, I scour the room to see where I left it. Following the buzzing sound down the side of my bed, I wrestle the phone from under a magazine.

My mouth drops open when I see Nick's caller ID. "Hello?"

"Darling, I'm outside."

157

"Outside where?"

"Outside your house. Let me in."

I stop the phone against my chest. Nick's outside my house?

Excitedly, I clamber out of bed, throw off my dressing gown and pull on an old T-shirt and shorts. Then I race downstairs.

For a second, I forget to breathe.

Nick's standing on the doorstep looking all suave and debonair in a long, black overcoat and two-toned shoes. I grin goofily and lower my gaze; he's holding a shopping bag and a bunch of red roses.

"For you," he beams, handing me the flowers.

I inhale their glorious scent. "Thank you," I whisper, trying not to sneeze.

He raises his eyebrows. "Oh, darling, you're really not well, are you?" I shake my head. Peering beyond me into the house, he asks if my father is home.

"No, Dad's gone to a meeting in town and won't be back till this evening."

With a relieved smile, Nick follows me through to the kitchen, where I lay the roses on the sideboard. He places the shopping bag next to them and I peer inside. It contains a loaf of bread, a bottle of cough mixture and a carton of New Covent Garden Soup.

"What's all this?" I frown.

"Supplies to help you get better. I've come to look after you."

"Oh, my gosh, that's so sweet. But what about work? Don't you have patients to see today?"

"I did, but you're my number one priority. When I heard you were sick, I cleared my schedule for you."

My heart melts and I get a little choked up. "I can't believe you did that for me. I-I don't know what to say." I look up into his warm, hazel eyes and fall in love all over again. All that is kind, all that is good, radiates from him like a soft ray of sunshine.

Suddenly, I let out a massive sneeze that renders me momentarily deaf in one ear.

"Oh, my gosh, I'm so sorry." Hurriedly, I reach for some kitchen paper and dry my watery eyes. I'm beginning to feel very intimidated. Nick's towering over me, his face barely suppressing the intensity of his longing. I start to fret about my appearance. God, I must look such a state, what with my runny nose and everything.

Turning away, I mumble that I need to find a vase for the flowers.

Nick flings his arms wide. "Don't I at least get a hug?"

I shake my head and take a step back. "Please, don't get too close, darling. I don't want you to catch my germs. This thing I've got is really nasty and—"

Before I can finish, he catches me in his arms. "I don't care about your germs," he whispers. "You can give them all to me." Then he crushes his lips against mine and consumes me with a ferocity that makes my knees tremble. It's like he's starving; like he can't get enough of me. Lost in his embrace, I lose all sanity, all sense of self.

Feeling light-headed, I manage to pull away; I'm terrified I might have given him my cold.

"I-I need to find that vase," I murmur.

He slips his arm around my waist and guides me to the door. "Don't worry about the vase. Go and rest; I'll take care of everything."

Reluctantly, I return upstairs and dive under my quilt. As

I try to get comfortable, I hear sounds of cupboards opening and closing, the kettle boiling, the clatter of pots and pans.

Just what is he up to?

A short while later, Nick enters my room carrying a tray of cough mixture, bread, soup and tea. I smile indulgently; what a lovely surprise. As he rests the tray on my bedside cabinet, his eyes dart about the room with lively curiosity. My cheeks redden. I wonder what he makes of my dolls and posters, my cray-cray cartoon collection. I worry he'll think I'm a complete weirdo.

If he does, he certainly doesn't show it. After giving everything a thorough onceover, the only comment he makes is that I have eclectic taste. I choose to take that as a compliment. With a pleasant smile, he peruses my dresser and picks up a photograph of my mother and me.

"How old are you here?" he asks.

"About eight."

"Where was it taken?"

"Cornwall. It was one of our first family holidays."

"Your mother looks a lot like you."

"Really?" I raise my eyebrows. "Do you think so? Most people say I resemble my father more."

"No, I can definitely see your mother in you. What a beautiful little girl you were."

My blush deepens. "Thanks. Do you have any baby pictures? I'd love to see what you looked like. I bet you were really cute."

"Yes, I suppose I was. I don't really keep many pictures, but one day I'll fish out my old photo album to show you." Still smiling, he puts the photo back. Then he kicks off his shoes, removes his coat and hangs it up in my wardrobe. As he does so, he fumbles through the pockets and retrieves a small black jewellery box.

"I bought you a present," he grins.

Squealing with delight, I take the box from him and carefully open it.

I cup one hand over my mouth. Inside the box is a heart-shaped diamond pendant on a delicate silver chain.

"Oh, wow!" I gasp. "This is gorgeous."

"It belonged to my mother. Used to be one of her favourite pieces."

I shake my head incredulously. "Nick, I can't take this. It's much too nice for me. It wouldn't feel right."

"But I want you to have it. I want you to carry it with you always, as something to remind you of just how much you mean to me."

I hesitate, mulling it over. Finally, I accept. "Thank you. No one has ever been so good to me. I promise to treasure it forever."

He beams happily. "Here, let me put it on for you."

I feel slightly giddy as he comes to the bed and gently fastens the pendant around my neck.

"Perfect!" he exclaims.

I gaze down at his wonderful gift, twisting the silver chain between my fingers. It feels awfully heavy, but I love it. "Thank you," I repeat, looking at him. "This is the loveliest present anyone's ever given me."

"Glad you like it." Serenely, Nick crosses the room, pulls out the office-style chair from my desk and pushes it next to my bed. Sitting down, he unscrews the bottle of cough mixture and feeds me a spoonful. I lick my lips; it tastes sweet and tangy. Then he picks up one of the bread rolls, dips it in the soup and raises it to my lips. I hesitate, prolonging the moment far longer than is necessary. Finally, I take a bite.

Chewing methodically, I savour every last morsel.

Nick smiles lovingly as he continues feeding me. His eyes never leave mine for a second and I start to get hot under the collar. I note the firm broadness of his shoulders, the way his arms bulge as he feeds me, and reminisce about the explosive time we had last night.

I swallow dryly.

His gaze is fixed on my lips, watching me as I eat the bread, taking in every last chomp and chew. I have a pretty good idea what he's thinking. We're so absorbed in the sense of being close to each other that we do not begin talking for a while, the silence broken only by the gentle rise and fall of our breathing. It's so surreal having him in my bedroom, like my prince has stepped from the pages of a fairy tale into real life.

When I've finished eating, I ask him if he wants to watch a movie. Nick says he's happy to do whatever I want, so I suggest he slots *The Breakfast Club* into the DVD player.

He goes over to the glass shelving unit by the wall and peruses the coloured spines in search of my request. I ask him if he's ever seen *Breakfast Club*.

"No," he replies. "To be honest, I'm not much of a film man, but I'm always game for a good romance."

"Oh, it's not so much a romance, more a coming-of-age story, though there are some romantic elements. It was one of my favourite movies growing up."

"Sounds good. If you love it, then I'm sure I will, too. Watching it will be like getting to know a piece of your history."

My heart flutters. *What a lovely way of putting it.* Nick's such a sweetheart. When I was with Andrew, he never showed the slightest interest in my hobbies and constantly poked fun at what he called my 'kitsch' taste in films.

Once the DVD is in the player, Nick returns to the wardrobe, strips down to his boxers and hangs the rest of his clothes up neatly on hangers. Then, as the movie begins, he sits at the edge of the bed and pulls back the duvet to reveal my feet.

I squirm at his touch, fretting about my chipped nail polish.

He chuckles, as if sensing my thoughts. "Relax."

Taking my foot in both his hands, Nick gently walks his thumbs back and forth over the soles of my feet. I close my eyes and let out a small sigh; I can't begin to describe how good this feels.

"You have such pretty toes," he whispers, taking my other foot and working the pressure points with his thumbs. "Your skin is so soft."

Opening my eyes, I smile at him, roll my neck and force myself to focus back on the movie. With considerable skill, Nicks rotates my ankle clockwise and then anti-clockwise, rotating each toe the same way, before pulling gently on each.

"How does that feel?"

"Fantastic."

"Do you want it harder or softer?"

"Harder."

Obediently, Nick slides his hands up and down each foot, at the same time applying more pressure with his thumbs. Deep waves of relaxation wash through me. *Is there no end to this man's talents?*

When he's satisfied he's done a thorough job, he places my feet back on the mattress, slides up to the top of the bed and wraps his arms around me. I release a pent-up sigh; it's complete bliss being with him like this. I love his scent, the feel of his chest against my skin. Life just can't get any better.

For a long time, we stay frozen in the same position, pretending to watch the movie, but my mind is starting to wander. It's not easy being this close to him and not want to do things.

"You're supposed to be watching the movie," I scold, pointing to the TV.

"I'm trying to," he counters, "but it's difficult when there are so many sweet distractions."

I lower my lashes. "Please, concentrate."

But the order is more to me than him. It's obvious what we both want, but it can't happen. Not today, not with me in this state.

We try to settle down again, try to behave ourselves, but halfway through the movie, Nick moves in and starts kissing my neck. It feels so good that I put up no resistance; I love what he's doing and don't want it to stop. For a while I let it continue, then out of nowhere, he locks his fingers into my T-shirt and pulls it clean off. I gasp with surprise. There's a wild blaze in his eyes, a dark excitement that tells me a little too late I've been playing with fire.

"Nick, I'm not sure we should …"

But my protests die in my throat as he guides me back to the mattress and gently but firmly pins me down. I cannot move, cannot function; his touch has near paralysed me. Hungrily, he licks and kisses the underside of my right breast, rolling the nipple between his fingers and sucking it as he would my clit. Then he moves onto my left, taking my nipple in his teeth before blowing hot air over it. I moan lightly. Seconds pass. Minutes. A shiver shoots down my spine and I sneeze; he's not perturbed. Succumbing to my carnal urges, I allow his sweet assault to continue.

Softly, softly, he moves beneath the quilt, working his

wet lips from my breasts to my navel, tracing invisible shapes with his hot tongue. I whimper at how good it feels. It's only as his fingers grip my shorts and he starts to slide them down that I'm jolted back to reality.

"No, wait!" I hiss, grabbing his head.

"What is it?" Nick looks at me questioningly. "Don't you want me to taste you?"

"We can't do this. I'm on my period."

I see a peculiar glow in his eyes; a strange tightness to his face. Ignoring my pleas, he returns to my navel and continues kissing me, his hands easing down my shorts bit by bit.

I shut my eyes and try not to think about what's happening.

"Didn't you hear what I said?" I protest feebly. "We can't do this."

"Sssh… I'm going to make you feel so good."

Stroking my thighs with his palms, Nick slides off my knickers with the panty liner still intact and throws them to the floor. Fear grips me; I'm now completely at his mercy.

"Nick, please…"

He stares down at me, his features strained with a weird sort of desperation. "I need it," he rasps. "Since last night, it's all I can think about." He pauses, licks his lips. "Look me in the eyes and tell me you don't want it. Tell me you're not dying for me to taste you."

"I-I think that maybe—"

He gives me no chance to complete the sentence. Pulling me to the edge of the bed, he spreads my legs wide and buries his face between my thighs. Ravenously, he swirls his tongue around my clit, before moving deep inside my wet hole, slurping and savouring every last drop. My limbs go rigid, and my nerve endings are ablaze. At first, I'm scared and embarrassed he would do such a thing, but within moments, I can't believe how good it feels to have his tongue and lips exploring my darkest secrets. The truth is I *do* want this. Knowing how hungry he is for me, knowing that he will go to any lengths to please me, turns me on big time. It feels so taboo, so nasty, but dear Lord, it also feels fucking beautiful. Sparks of intense pleasure crash through my system as I finally surrender to the power of his need. It's so wrong and yet so right, so good I no longer put up a fight.

I blink a couple of times and stare up at the candyfloss ceiling. *Focus on inhaling and exhaling.* That's all I can do to keep myself from exploding.

"You've got the sweetest pussy I've ever tasted," Nick whispers from between my thighs. "I can't get enough."

I whine quietly as he slides his tongue back through my gushing slit, then up to my clit, making slow, circular motions that send electric shocks through me. I let out a gasp. Rapid waves of euphoria flood my body and I come harder than I ever have before. Nick halts what he's doing and gazes up at me with a mesmerizing expression.

"That's right, my darling," he pants. "Give it all to me."

My eyes widen. His face looks different somehow, younger, and his skin is glowing in a way it never has before. I assume it's a trick of the light, but...it's almost like he's been rejuvenated by me.

Releasing my legs, Nick gets up and steps out of his boxer shorts. I bite back a gasp at the sight of his throbbing arousal. I know that he wants to make love, but right now, I'm not sure I can handle it. Every fibre of my being feels so drained from the orgasm.

"I don't think I can take any more," I cough.

"Yes, you can," he breathes. "You've got to. I need to be

inside you, Carly. I need it now or I'll go crazy."

"But it's going to get messy. I'm going to be dripping everywhere."

Wordlessly, Nick pads over to the wardrobe and pulls out the lower drawers. Within seconds, he's found a fresh towel. Returning to the bed, he lays it down on the mattress and gently positions me on top of it. Bringing himself level with me, he tilts my body to the side so we're facing each other. Tenderly, he glides his hand down my thigh and wraps my leg over his hip. Pulling me forward, he folds his arms around me in a sidelong embrace and slowly starts to push his cock into me. We touch foreheads and I can feel his hot breath on my face. Our bodies are intertwined, soaked with sweat. Running his hand up my leg, he hitches me a little higher so he can fully penetrate me.

I groan loudly and take a few short breaths to help me cope with the pain.

"Am I moving too fast?" he asks anxiously. "Tell me how you like it."

"Don't stop," I murmur. "Just keep doing what you're doing."

With an appreciative growl, he slowly starts to fuck me, covering my face and lips with kisses as we rock back and forth in a waltz of mutual delirium. I adore this position; it feels so close, so intimate.

Nick gazes deeply into my eyes. "Oh, God, your pussy's so sweet and tight. I love stretching you out."

I grit my teeth. I'm struck dumb by the crazy sensations whipping through me.

And then he kisses me on the mouth, and I wince at the coppery taste of his lips. Blood. *My blood*. Sweet and sour. Sour sweet. With a sigh of pleasure, I drop my head onto his glistening chest as he pumps even deeper into me.

"Shit," I gasp. "Too fast, too fast."

"Okay…" he soothes. "We can take it as slow as you want." Then he's kissing me again, and my mind is all over the place. I'm lost in a beautiful netherworld from which there is no escape. Soon, we're both feeling the fireworks, me for the second time today.

With a loud groan, Nick releases me and the two of us roll onto our backs, gazing up at the ceiling, drawing our breath in ragged gulps. Reaching over, he grips hold of my hand, and for a second, we are connected: two hearts beating as one.

"I love you," he whispers.

"I love you, too."

"Do you promise you're mine forever?"

"Forever and ever."

Without looking, I can sense he's smiling. A rush of emotions swells in my chest; I never want this day to end.

Once he's come to his senses, Nick asks where the bathroom is so he can go clean up. Ten minutes later, he returns holding a jug of warm water and a flannel. Sitting beside me on the bed, he lovingly wipes down my body, paying special attention to the parts that are particularly sore.

"Did I please you?" he asks, dabbing the flannel between my thighs to dispel all traces of red.

"Yes," I reply. "So much."

Nick flashes a gentle smile.

When I'm satisfactorily clean, he helps me on with my clothes and puts back on his boxers. Then we snuggle up together under the duvet and lie peacefully in each other's arms, listening to the sound of rain hitting the window.

"You make me so happy," he sighs, stroking my hair.

"What you said yesterday about living in darkness ... that really touched me. I felt exactly the same before I met you. It's been years since I smiled. Years since I laughed. Then I met you, and you've bought such joy to my life. You make me feel young again. When I'm with you, I feel I hold the whole world in my embrace."

"Oh, Nick, what a beautiful thing to say." I drum my fingers on his chest.

"How much do you love me?" he whispers.

"So much."

"Really and truly?"

"You know I'd do anything for you, Nick. *Anything.*"

"What if I robbed a bank? Would you still love me then?"

"Of course! There's nothing you could do to stop me from loving you."

He hesitates, mulling this over. Then he kisses my forehead. "I've waited so long to find someone like you. I'm never letting you go, *ever.*"

Tears collect in the corners of my eyes. I can't believe, can't accept that he loves me as much as he says he does. Things like this just don't happen to people like me.

"Hey, I thought we said no more crying?" he laughs.

"I know, I know." I brush away a tear. "I'm not crying because I'm sad. I'm crying because I've never been so happy. I never knew life could be so wonderful."

He kisses me again and holds me tightly. For the next hour or so, we sleep soundly. Wrapped in his arms, I'm in complete Heaven, sheltered from the storm. Sometime around six, I'm woken by a harsh beeping sound. Squinting in the half-light, I tilt my head to find out where it's coming from.

"I think the phone's on your desk," Nick says. "Don't

worry; I'll get it for you." As he hands the mobile to me, he scans the caller ID. "It's your dad."

Taking the phone, I sit up and do my best to sound normal. "Hey Dad, how did the meeting go?"

"Oh, it went fantastically. My publisher wants me to sign a new book deal. You know what that means?"

"More money?

"Yes. Better still, it means I can pay you back what I owe you for the mortgage."

"Wow, that's fantastic news!"

"Isn't it? Things couldn't have gone better. It looks like my creative visualisation is finally working. Anyway, enough about me. How are you feeling, my dear? Is your cold any better?"

I rub my nose vigorously. "Um, yeah. Still feeling a bit groggy but I think I'm through the worst of it." I hesitate. "It's been a really good day, actually. Nick came around to keep me company."

"Nick's at the house? I didn't know you were planning to see him today."

I laugh nervously. "Me neither. He decided to surprise me."

Nick mouths "hello" at me and I pass the salutation to Dad.

"Tell him I said hi," my father replies. "Right, okay, I'm on my way back now. I should see you both in about an hour."

"Great."

He hangs up, and I chew the inside of my cheek.

"What did your dad say?" Nick asks, handing me a fresh wad of Kleenex to blow my nose on.

"He said he's on his way home."

"I suppose that means you want me to go?"

"No, darling, of course not. Stay as long as you want."

Nick nods mutely as he takes the phone from me to put back on the dresser. "What an old brick," he snickers, fiddling with the keypad. "I really should buy you a new phone. This one's positively prehistoric."

"Hey, don't take the piss. Perhaps I like living in the Stone Age."

We both laugh but, as he continues scrutinising the phone, I start to get a little apprehensive.

"Can I have my phone back, please?" I try to keep my voice calm. "Don't you know it's rude to go through other people's messages?"

Nick goes quiet, his eyes glued to something on the screen.

Desperately, I reach out and attempt to snatch it from him, but he's too quick for me. We tussle in a semi-humorous fashion, but I can sense his mood darkening.

"Who the hell is Andrew?" he demands.

Heat colours my cheeks.

"Who's Andrew?" he repeats, looking at me.

"No one," I whisper. "He's no one. Now please, can I have my phone back?"

"Come on, Carly, you've got dozens of messages here saying he loves you. Don't tell me he's no one."

"All right, all right! Andrew's my ex-boyfriend."

Nick stiffens. The hurts and vulnerability in his face breaks my heart. "He can't be an ex if he's still sending you these kinds of messages."

"Yes," I say, "but have you checked the date they were sent?"

Quietly, he scrolls through the phone. "Okay, so they're

five years old. But why do you still keep them? Are you in love with him or what?"

"Of course not."

He compresses his lips. "Is that why you keep this phone? To reminisce about the past?"

I pause, trying to find a way out, but he's got me. "Yeah, okay, I admit it. Before I met you, I was finding it hard to let go of the past. But that's all changed now. You're all I care about, Nick. Andrew doesn't mean a thing to me, I promise."

Nick's expression remains stormy. Moodily, he hands me back the phone, stalks over to the wardrobe and starts getting dressed.

"Darling, please!" I chase after him. "Don't let us part on bad terms." When he still doesn't respond, I start to panic. Hurriedly, I scroll through the phone and hover over the 'Delete All' button. "Look, look!" I say, holding up the screen. "Let me prove he doesn't mean anything."

"You don't have to prove anything."

"Yes, I do. I've upset you and I need to put things right."

Finally, this gets his attention. Smoothing down his shirt, Nick walks slowly back to me and scrutinises the phone as I press 'Delete.' Within seconds, five years of history is wiped away forever, and, rather than feel sorry, I find it strangely cathartic. This has been a long time coming and in a way, I'm glad this happened.

Nick's face softens. "Thank you. I know that can't have been easy for you."

"It was easier than you think," I say, hoping to be on his good side again. "You're right; it wasn't healthy for me to wallow in the past and…" The words peter out. I'm trying to be sincere, but I can still see the pain in his eyes.

"Who ended the relationship?" he asks.

"Does it matter?"

"Yes. To me it does."

I spread my hands. "I was the one who ended it. Happy?"

"Why did you end it?"

I hesitate, biting my thumbnail.

"Was Andrew unfaithful?" he presses.

"No. He wanted to marry me."

Nick laughs bitterly. "And that's a reason to end a relationship?"

"Yes, because it made me realise I didn't want to spend the rest of my life with him. Andrew never allowed me to be me. He hated my clothes, wanted me to wear black all the time. He said my voice was too loud, that I embarrassed him in public. He said I laughed too much. He hated cartoons, forced me to read Dostoyevsky and waffled endlessly about the Conservative Party. And once, when he got really mad, he threw me out of his car in the middle of nowhere and left me stranded."

"And you still keep this person's text messages?" Nick sounds incredulous.

I run my fingers through my hair. "I know it seems crazy, but I was afraid of being alone. Even though Andrew ill-treated me, I went along with it because I had no self-confidence. But one day, I just couldn't take it anymore; the mask slipped, and I had to end it."

"That still doesn't explain why you've kept his messages."

I take a few calming breaths and find a point on the floor to focus on. I've never spoken about this before. "After the break-up, I fell into a black depression," I explain softly. "With Andrew gone, I thought my life would get better, but it didn't, so I started to think that maybe things with him weren't so bad after all. Better the Devil you know, as they say. I thought perhaps I'd made a mistake and that we could have worked things out. But I was fooling myself. Nick, you've shown me what love is, what it truly means to care for someone. What I have with you, I never had with Andrew. He can't hold a candle to you."

Nick is silent for a long time. "Tell me about your depression," he whispers.

"No. Therapy is over. Why dig up the past?"

"Because I want to know everything about you, Carly. I want to know why you were so unhappy before you met me."

I shrug. "It was lots of things. Primarily, I didn't like myself very much. I beat myself up over every little thing: my inability to hold down a relationship, my bad money management, my weight, just about everything you can think of. That's why I stayed with Andrew for so long; I felt I couldn't do better."

"Are you sure that was all it was?"

"What else could it be?"

Nick slips his finger under my chin and tilts my face upwards. "Tell me what he was like."

My brows snap together. "What do you mean?"

"You *know* what I mean."

"In bed?"

"Yes."

I squirm; his gaze is too raw, too intense. "I don't want to talk about it."

"But I *need* to know."

"Can't we just drop it?"

Backing me against the wall, Nick puts his face very close to mine. Slowly, his lips part, his breath teasing the corners of my mouth.

"Tell me…" he murmurs. "Tell me everything."

"W-what exactly do you want to know?"

"Was he good?"

I swallow hard.

"Was Andrew good?" Nick repeats.

"He never made me come," I whisper.

He regards me steadily, his expression still serious. "Not even once?"

"Not even once."

"Thank you for being so honest."

"You're welcome. Anything else you want to know?"

"No. That will be all for today."

I smile weakly. "Please tell me that we're friends again?"

In answer, he pulls me into his arms and holds me tightly. I sigh happily and nuzzle my face into his chest; he smells so damn good.

"I'd better get going," he breathes, stroking my shoulders. "Your father will be home soon."

"Oh, no, do you really have to?"

"Yes. You need to rest. My being here is doing you no favours." I try to protest but he shushes me. Shrugging on his coat, he ushers me back to bed.

"When will I see you next?" I ask as he tucks me in. "Tomorrow?"

"It will probably have to be Tuesday or Wednesday. I'm going to Manchester for a conference on Monday."

"But tomorrow's only Saturday. Why can't we meet then?"

"Tempting as that is, I think you need to rest this weekend, darling. You need to get your strength back." He kisses me lightly on the forehead. "No more arguments. You're going to rest, and that's final."

"Spoilsport," I pout.

"Maybe so. But it's for your own good."

Walking to the bedroom door, he's about to leave when, on sudden impulse, he turns one final time to look at me. Smiling warmly, he blows me a kiss and I pretend to catch it.

We both laugh.

CHAPTER NINE

The Gallery

"**C**ARLY, YOU'RE BACK!" Jill squeals when I return to work on Wednesday morning. "How are you feeling? Mark told me you had a cold."

"Yes, I was in bed for most of the weekend, but I'm feeling much better now."

"Thank goodness for that. Everyone's missed you. It's not the same without your happy, smiling face here to greet us in the mornings."

I beam at the compliment. "What a lovely thing to say. I missed you, too."

Jill's gaze drops to my pendant. "What a gorgeous piece of jewellery. Can I touch it?"

"Sure."

Softly, she runs her fingers down the chain and holds the chunky diamond in her hand, covertly assessing its weight and quality. "Absolutely beautiful," she murmurs. "Where did you get it from?"

"My boyfriend gave it to me," I answer, a tad shyly. It still feels strange saying the word 'boyfriend,' but that's what Nick is, *my boyfriend*. Now that we're official, I want to declare it to the world.

Jill takes a step back and pulls a shocked expression. "Boyfriend? You certainly kept that one under your hat, Missy. I didn't know you were seeing anyone."

I shuffle nervously. "Uh, well, we've only been seeing each other for a short time. I'm not that big on... well, you know, broadcasting my business and stuff." I pause. "But so far, everything's going well. I'm really happy."

She claps her hands and shrieks with delight. "Oh how lovely for you. I'm so pleased, honey. It's about time you found someone nice. What's his name?"

"Nick."

"Well, Carly, do you fancy bringing Nick to the art exhibition this evening?"

"What art exhibition?"

"The one I texted you about."

I slap my hand across my forehead. *Sweet Jesus.* Yes, I do remember getting a generic text on Saturday about her brother James's exhibition in Whitechapel. At the time, I'd barely given it a second thought, assuming I'd probably find a way out of it.

"Sorry," I mumble. "It completely slipped my mind."

"But you *are* going to come, aren't you? So many people have cancelled already, and I don't think poor James is going to have a very good turnout."

I scratch the side of my mouth. "Of course, I'm coming. I'll phone Nick at lunch to see if he can make it, too."

"Fantastic! And then I'll get to meet this mystery man of yours."

"What time does the exhibition start?"

"Seven pm. But don't worry; we can grab a quick coffee after work and then travel up together. Nick can meet us there."

"Great," I smile, but inside I'm kicking myself. Why the hell couldn't I just make something up? It's been five days since I last saw Nick, and I've been missing him like crazy. We'd planned to go for a quiet meal tonight, but Jill's invitation has put a major spanner in the works. Still, if I play my cards right, perhaps we can show our faces and then find a way to slip off early …

"Right," Jill grins, snapping me from my reverie, "what in the name of sanity are you wearing today?"

Rolling my eyes, I unbutton my cardigan and show her my latest novelty T-shirt.

"Princess Aurora!" she laughs. "That's from *Sleeping Beauty*, right?"

"Yes," I nod. "The one and only."

She gives me a high-five. "Yay! I'm getting better at this."

At lunch, I call Nick to tell him about the change of plan; he's surprisingly unfazed.

"An art exhibition? That sounds fun."

"Really? So, you don't mind us going there for a bit?"

"Of course not, darling. It will be nice to meet some of your friends."

"Are you sure?"

"Positive."

"I promise we won't stay there too long."

"Darling, I don't care what we do as long as I'm with you. And anyway, you're spending the night at mine, so there will be plenty of time for us to be alone afterwards."

My heart flutters. Can he be any more perfect?

After work, I take Jill across the road to Coffee Republic. I nod at the waitress and order my usual: a blueberry muffin with a large white coffee.

"And for your friend?" she inquires, glancing at Jill.

"Just a skinny latte, please."

"Don't you at least want a muffin?" I frown.

"No, no, I'd better be good." Jill pats her impossibly flat stomach. "I'm supposed to be cutting down on the sweet stuff. You know, Christmas is just around the corner and I need to be able to fit back into my little black dress."

"Jill, you already look amazing. I'd kill to have a figure like yours. Surely you're allowed at least one little treat?"

"That's the problem. One treat with me leads to six in one sitting."

"Oh, come on; please get something. The blueberry muffins are amazing."

She pulls a face. "Oh, all right, you've twisted my arm."

We both laugh. While I pay for our food, she scans the shop for somewhere to sit. As always, finding a seat in this place is a nightmare, but eventually, Jill spots a free table. As soon as we're seated, she begins telling me about her problems with James. I'm surprised by her frankness, but grateful her non-stop chatter means I have very little to add to the conversation.

"The thing is," she says, licking the lid of her skinny latte, "my brother's the sweetest boy you could ever hope to meet, but he lacks drive. He's amazingly talented, but I think he gives up too easily. Ever since he left art college three years ago, he hasn't held down a stable job and so far, hasn't really made any money from his paintings. The art world is so hard to break into, but if he doesn't take a proper crack at it, he'll be left by the wayside."

"How old is James?" I ask.

"Twenty-seven," Jill replies brusquely. "Old enough to be living alone, don't you think? I mean, honestly, it's already a squeeze living with Gavin and the twins, but James in the spare bedroom makes things unbearable. He doesn't help around the house with anything, and he's always leaving dirty dishes and socks around the place. When I get home from work, I feel like I have to clean up after three children."

"Couldn't he get a place of his own?"

"Not unless by some miracle his paintings take off. Don't get me wrong, James has my every sympathy; it's not easy for young people to get on the property ladder these days, and rents in London are bloody astronomical. James says most of his friends from university are still living at home with their parents because they can't afford to go it alone."

I take a bite of my muffin and wipe crumbs off my jumper. "What about a flat share? Couldn't he split the rent with one of his friends?"

Jill sips her drink thoughtfully. "Perhaps I'll float the idea past him. I'm just praying this exhibition might be the start of something big. We've got so much riding on tonight, Carly. Gavin's paid a small fortune to hire out the venue, and I've sent invitations to everyone I know in the creative world. I've even invited a local journalist to see if we can generate a buzz."

"Sounds like you really love your brother," I say.

Her eyes grow misty. "Yes, I love him to bits. All I want is for James to start taking life seriously and make something of himself. He's wasted far too much time sitting at home on the Xbox."

I smile, remembering the cute, floppy-haired guy I'd briefly met at Nando's.

Everything Jill's told me resonates with my initial impression of a loveable, absent-minded student type. In a strange way, I'm quite looking forward to seeing him again.

We talk a little longer about work then, downing our drinks, we leave Coffee Republic behind and head for the Tube. Forty minutes later, we arrive at Aldgate East station and make our way through the diminishing light toward Whitechapel High Street. James's show is being held at an art gallery called the Chapel, a small, white building with oval-shaped entrance doors.

As soon as we enter, I'm surprised by how big it is. A myriad of sparse, white walls and high ceilings are designed to show off the artist's work in the best possible light, and the whole place has a wonderfully spacious feel. The first room contains images of voluptuous women painted in startlingly bright acrylics. With their large eyes and toothy smiles, they sort of remind me of X-rated Disney characters, and I instantly warm to James's style.

The second room is where it all seems to be happening. Thirty or so arty-looking people are huddled in small groups, sipping champagne flutes and chattering excitedly. When Jill and I enter, a few heads turn in our direction, then they resume their conversations as if we're not worth the effort. I'm not entirely sure I like the atmosphere. It all feels a bit cliquey, and I pray I won't have to be here for too long.

"Where's Gavin?" I ask, scanning the room.

"He's at home with the twins," Jill sighs. "He wanted to come tonight, but the babysitter pulled out at the last minute, so he had to stay behind."

"Ah. What a shame. It would have been nice to see him again."

James sidles up to us dressed in the same tweed coat he wore to Nando's. He is, however, still just as disarmingly handsome.

"Sis, you made it!" he beams, embracing Jill in a bear hug. "So good to see you."

"How's everything going?" she whispers. "What's the feedback been like so far? Have you sold any paintings?"

"Steady on. The exhibition only started twenty minutes ago. Let's give it some time, huh?"

Jill turns to me. "James, do you remember Carly?"

"Of course, how could I forget?" He shakes my hand warmly. "The last time we met, I seem to remember us ending up in a bit of a tangle."

"God, don't remind me," I laugh. "I cringe every time I think about it."

"Thanks so much for coming," he continues. "I really appreciate your support."

"Oh, it's no trouble at all. But I have to say, James, I really love your paintings. They're so beautiful and vibrant. They sort of remind me of an animated film."

His cheeks flush. "Cheers. Glad you like them. Which one did you like best?"

"So far, I'd say the blue one with the peacocks, but that may change as I haven't seen them all yet."

"Well, make sure you give me your final verdict before you go, okay? I need as much feedback as possible."

"Oh, I will, I will."

"Any sign of your boyfriend, Carly?" Jill interjects. "I don't see any tall, dark strangers anywhere."

"Er, no. Nick doesn't finish work till seven, so he might not be here for a while."

At the mention of the word 'boyfriend' James's enthusiasm cools visibly. There's a moment of silence then he clears his throat. "Hey, can I get either of you ladies a drink? We've got Pimm's, champagne or orange juice."

Jill gives him a sharp look. "Champagne sounds great, but after you've bought us our drinks, please make sure you do plenty of mingling. You need to sell yourself, James. Tonight is all about making connections, so you need to start networking. Let your personality shine. And remember that guy from the newspaper is gonna be here soon and he'll probably want to take pictures."

"Yes, Your Majesty." James gives a low bow and flutters his hands regally. "Two champagnes coming up, and then I'll leave you both to have a girly chat." Like a man with a purpose, he marches across the room to a table covered with snacks and bottles of alcohol.

Jill turns to me. "So, what job does Nick do?"

"He's one of the country's leading hypnotherapists," I declare proudly.

She claps her hands. "Ooh, how exciting. Last Christmas, Gavin bought me a weight loss book by that Paul what's-his-name."

"McKenna?"

"Yes, that's right, Paul McKenna. It was great. I lost over a stone following his diet plan. What sort of stuff does Nick treat?"

"Oh, everything, really. Smoking, obesity… He's person-ally treated some of the U.K's top politicians and celebrities."

"Wow."

"You know that girl from the *Essex Show* on Channel Four who's just had a baby, the one who's always in *Heat* magazine?"

"Becky Bullock?"

"Yeah, that's the one. Nick helped her lose two stone."

"He never!" Jill squeals. "Oh, my God, where do I sign up? This man sounds like the answer to my prayers. He can help me lose this jelly belly before Christmas."

I smile indulgently. I'm not usually one to brag, but I just can't resist talking Nick up. I'm so proud of everything he's achieved. It feels so good to finally be in a proper adult relationship with a man who earns his own living and doesn't have to rely on me. For the first time in my life, I truly feel part of a team.

For the next hour or so, I roam around the gallery, trying to look important, gazing stoically at James's paintings and scarpering anytime somebody approaches to strike up a conversation. Naturally, Jill must be left to her own devices. She has her friends to catch up with and paintings to sell, so I couldn't possibly stay glued to her side all evening. It just wouldn't be fair. Every so often, I catch James stealing admiring glances in my direction. He knows I'm in a relationship but doesn't let that stop him perusing the sweet shop. I find his attention very flattering but do hope he tones it down before Nick gets here; I wouldn't want to cause a scene.

Occasionally, I check my phone to track Nick's progress. The last text he sent me was at seven-fifteen, stating that he was getting in his car. Now it's well gone nine pm; I expect he should be here any minute.

Moistening my lips, I make my way toward the snack table. Apart from the muffin earlier, I haven't eaten anything today and champagne on an empty stomach tends not to agree with me. As I approach the table, my breathing quickens. Louise and Susan are standing there, sipping Pimm's and fussing over cheese chunks and cocktail sausages.

Rolling my eyes, I brace myself for yet another awkward exchange.

"Hi!" Susan trills. "Fancy seeing you here. You're Carly, right?" I nod stiffly. She continues, "So, how are you?"

"I'm fine. How are you?"

"We're great," Louise chimes in. "James's painting are spellbinding."

"Yes, they're wonderful," I say flatly.

Susan squints at me. "By the way, how's that friend of yours?"

My face goes blank. "My friend?"

"Yes. Remember, you had to leave Jill's birthday early because you said your friend had a big emergency. I just wondered if you managed to sort that out."

I laugh nervously; God, I'd forgotten about my little white lie. "Oh, yes, everything's fine now. It was my friend Ronan. He, um, had to go to hospital …" My voice trails off. "That's a lovely dress, Louise," I gush. "I really love that colour on you."

"Thanks. It's Karen Millen."

There's a short, uncomfortable silence. None of us know where to look.

"Sorry, could I access the table? That food looks scrumptious." Moving past them, I pick up a paper plate and proceed to stock up on sandwiches and cocktail sausages. I can feel Louise's eyes on me, studying, probing, no doubt assessing how much my shoes cost or something equally banal. For Pete's sake, why do women have to behave this way toward each other?

As I pile up my plate, I continue to hear snippets of their conversation: "Fucking hell, Louise. Have you seen what just walked in?"

"Who am I supposed to be looking at?"

"That guy by the door. Can you see him? The one dressed in black…"

"Holy shit!"

My shoulders tense. Even before I turn around, I can already sense his presence. Covertly, I glance toward the entrance doors and draw in a sharp breath. Nick's standing there, looking all dapper in a beautifully tailored suit and the grey-and-black scarf I made for him. Seeing him again gives me monumental whiplash; I'm high as a kite and grinning like a happy schoolgirl.

Peering round the gallery, I notice it's not just Louise and Susan who are obsessed. Dozens of curious eyes are frozen in his direction and for the first time, I fully appreciate the overpowering effect he has on people. It's the same feeling I had that first time we met, that crazy magnetism that appears to be felt by everyone.

"Jesus Christ!" Louise hisses.

"I know, I know," Susan laughs, fanning herself. "Give me a second to cool down." She takes a huge gulp of Pimm's. "Have you ever seen anyone with that kind of…" She falters, shakes her head. "I don't quite know how to describe it. I sort of want to pounce on him."

"I feel exactly the same," Louise agrees. "But what is it about him? Jeez, I think I need another drink."

The two of them titter before Susan resumes: "His face isn't the greatest. In fact, he's really rather ugly, but my God, what I would give to get under that."

"That makes two of us!" Louise sniggers.

Susan continues fanning herself. "I'm so glad my husband isn't here to spoil the fun. It means we can drool from a distance without feeling like wanton slappers."

They both snort with laughter.

Hot rage boils inside me. *How dare they call Nick ugly?* I've a good mind to confront them, but I check myself. Do I really want to cause a scene and ruin James's big day? Plus, some of what they said could be taken as a backhanded compliment. Even so, they've got a bloody cheek passing judgment on my boyfriend. Just who the hell do they think they are?

Slowly counting to ten, I focus on my breathing and try to push my anger back down inside. Then, working my face into a smile, I race across the room to hug Nick. All eyes are on us as we embrace, and I'm swamped by a sea of emotions. Holding Nick in my arms again feels like a dream, and I can't get enough of his warmth, his touch, his smell. Five days apart has only intensified my hunger for him and if I had my way, we'd ditch this place immediately.

"I'm so glad to see you," I whisper.

He gazes deep into my eyes. "Are you okay? You seem a bit agitated. Has something happened?"

"No, no, everything's fine. I just couldn't wait to see you, that's all." I struggle to control my excitement.

Beaming, he kisses me on the nose and wraps his arm protectively around my waist. We turn to face the crowd of onlookers. "Do you want to introduce me to your friends?" he purrs.

Before I can respond, Jill lunges forward with an out-stretched hand. "Hi there! I'm Jill. You must be Nick. Lovely to meet you. Carly's told me so much about you."

"Ditto." They exchange a genial handshake.

"You're a very lucky man," she continues. "Carly's a perfect angel. Heart of gold. Everyone at work adores her; she's like a ray of sunshine."

"Oh, believe me; I'm fully aware of how lucky I am."

"Make sure you take good care of her."

"I will."

Blushing profusely, I steer Nick away and introduce him to James. "Darling, this is Jill's brother."

"So, you're the artist?" Nick gestures to the canvasses on the walls.

"Well, I'm trying to be," James replies modestly. "This is

my first exhibition. It's not exactly the Tate, but we've all got to start somewhere."

"I'm sure it won't be your last. From what I can see, you have a very unique talent."

"Cheers."

I smother a giggle. Nick's laying on the charm again, just like he did with Dad, and he's already got James eating out the palm of his hand.

"Would you like a drink?" Jill asks Nick. "There's champagne or Pimm's."

"Champagne would be fantastic."

"Come on, Carly; let's go and get your boyfriend a drink."

Throwing me a look, she drags me away and ushers me toward the snack table, where Louise and Susan give us a wide berth. Obviously, they realise I heard every single word they said about Nick, and the embarrassment on their faces is priceless. *Good.* Serves them right.

"Where on earth did you find him?" Jill hisses as soon as we're alone. "Good gracious, the man's astonishing."

"Do you really think so?"

"May I speak frankly?"

"Please do."

"Nick has an aura about him; something intangibly special. He's like a magnet and sort of pulls people to him, if that makes any sense. I'm not surprised he's such a successful hypnotist. I mean, just look around you. He has this whole place mesmerised." To demonstrate the point, she nudges her head toward the large group of people crowded around him. My mouth gapes; I'm in complete awe of his ability to strike up conversations with total strangers.

"How did the two of you meet?" she pushes.

"I went to him for hypnosis to help me quit smoking. His

offices are based in Harley Street."

"Ooh, very swanky. Well, at least you'll have an interesting story to tell your grandchildren."

I burst out laughing. "Grandchildren? Whoa, I think you might be getting a bit ahead of yourself. It's only been a few weeks."

"Weeks, years, who cares? I think the two of you make a fabulous couple, and I can tell from the way he looks at you that he worships the ground you walk on. This one's definitely a keeper."

"Aw, thanks, Jill. That's so sweet of you." I turn away before I get too emotional and pick up a champagne flute for Nick. Suddenly, I freeze. *Shit.* I've forgotten to take my second Thurlax tablet. To compound matters further, I can't remember what Dr Wong said about mixing alcohol with medication. Could there be any nasty side effects? Oh, God, just how many glasses of champagne have I had?

"Are you okay?" Jill asks, touching my arm. "You just went a bit white."

"I-I'm fine. Let's take the drinks over to the guys."

When we return, we find Nick and James chatting away like old friends. There's a lot of back slapping, a lot of laughter, and I wonder what on earth they're so happy about.

"Guess what?" James grins. "Nick says he wants to buy two of my paintings."

"Wow, that's fantastic news!" Jill beams. "Which ones have taken your fancy?"

Nick tells her and I watch her face transform from pleased to ecstatic. I have no idea how much the paintings cost, but from her reaction, I'd say they must be pretty expensive.

"Thank you," she says with sincerity. "Your support means so much to us."

"Oh, don't thank me," Nick grins. "I'm the one who should thank you. This kid is going places, so I've got to get in there early and grab a bargain while I can."

"Are you a big art collector then?"

"I dabble a little from time to time. I'm more into antiques, but once in a while, I'll pick up a nice piece of modern art."

Brother and sister exchange silent smiles. It looks as if Nick has really made their night.

We hang around the gallery another thirty minutes or so, then make our excuses and head outside to the Jag.

"You were magnificent," I say as we climb in. "Everybody loved you. You're such a people person, Nick. Thank you for making this night bearable; I don't know what I would have done if you hadn't been there."

He laughs gently. "Darling, it was no trouble at all; I enjoyed every minute. Plus, it was nice to get to meet your friends." He performs a three-point turn and steers the car back onto the high street. "Are you cold?"

"A little."

He switches on the heater. In a warm haze, I lean against the headrest and stare out the window at shop fronts, people, twinkling lights. Tentatively, I ask him how much he paid for James's paintings.

Nick smiles mysteriously. "Why do you want to know?"

"I'm just curious."

"Take a guess."

"I have absolutely no idea."

"I paid two grand apiece."

"What!"

He winces. "Do you think that's too much?"

"I don't know much about art, but...wow. That's more

than I earn in a whole month. You must have really liked them to buy on impulse like that."

"I do. I genuinely think James has got talent."

"When will you pick up the paintings?"

"The gallery said they will organise a delivery in the next couple of days. It's all worked out rather well, I think. I needed some new paintings for the living room, and those ones will do nicely." Nick takes his eyes off the road just a second to meet my gaze. "James is really smitten with you, isn't he?"

"You noticed?"

"I notice everything."

My cheeks redden. "Sorry, I hope it doesn't bother you."

"Why would it bother me? Another man acknowledges how gorgeous my girlfriend is, I can't think of a bigger compliment."

"You had your own fair share of admirers," I counter. "All the women there were practically drooling over you. I thought I had a big fight on my hands."

"Were you ready to fight for me?"

"You bet your life I was."

"Proper fisticuffs?"

"Yes. Pull hair. Scratch eyes out. The whole works."

"That makes me feel all warm inside." We both chuckle. I can't keep my eyes off his lips; I'm so hungry for them I'm finding it hard to think straight.

"Did you bring your overnight bag?" he asks.

"Yes," I grin. "I even remembered to bring my toothbrush. Oh, and get this, I bought two pairs of tights this time, so I'll have a replacement if you decide to destroy them again."

"How very sensible of you."

Snickering, I peer out the window and watch as we speed past office blocks, warehouses, restaurants, rows and rows of houses. I have no idea where we are but figure we've still got a long way to go before we reach Pimlico. I don't know if I can hold out that long; I want him so bad it hurts.

We stall at a set of lights.

Nick glances at me. "By the way, have you checked the back seat?"

"No. Should I?"

"Yes, I think you'll like what you see."

Cautiously, I reach down the back and retrieve a bulky Selfridges bag. "What's this?" I ask suspiciously.

"Open it and you'll find out."

Excitedly, I look inside and find a medium-sized box embossed with the Apple logo. I flip it over and see an image of the latest iPhone.

"Oh, my gosh! Is this for me?"

"Uh-huh. I thought you could do with a replacement."

"Wow, this is amazing. Thanks so much, my darling." I lean across and peck him on the cheek. He's so kind and thoughtful it makes me want to weep.

The lights change and Nick guns the car forward. For a long time, we drive in silence, basking in the sheer joy of each other's company. Then he asks if I still want to go to a restaurant.

I pat my stomach and laugh. "I'm actually pretty stuffed after all those sandwiches I ate at the gallery. If it's all right with you, I think we should just head straight back."

"My sentiments exactly."

For a second, we hold each other's gaze.

"Are you still on your period?" he asks softly.

"No…"

Relief washes over his face, then his eyes slowly drop to my lips. "I can't wait to get you home. The whole evening, all I could think about was licking you out and making you come…again and again and again."

I slouch down in my seat, jaw tight. My nipples harden; I love it when he talks dirty. His silky voice, the way he enunciates the words gives me an indescribable thrill, and I have to squeeze my legs together to stem the flow of juices. He turns me on so much.

"I'm going to fuck you all night," he whispers. "Is that what you want?"

"Y-yes."

"How many times do you want to come?"

I catch my breath. "W-what?"

"Pick a number."

"Three?"

"Your wish is my command."

By the time we get back to Pimlico, it's well past eleven at night. As we enter the house, my stomach starts doing flip-flops and I can barely contain myself. It's so exciting to be back, and as I throw off my shoes and follow him through the darkened hall, I can't help reminiscing about all the things we got up to the last time.

"Come here," Nick growls, sweeping me off my feet and carrying me toward the staircase. As we ascend, desire hot as a wave of lava bursts over me, and my knees go weak at the thought of what is to come. We reach the first-floor landing, he kicks open his bedroom door and carries me in.

With frightening strength, he throws me down on the bed and hungrily consumes my face with hot, passionate kisses. His hands are everywhere; tearing at my clothes, pawing at my skin. Within seconds, the two of us are completely naked, rolling, writhing, like a pair of animals locked in a carnal embrace. He sucks my lips, licks my eyelids, my cheeks, my hairline, everywhere. Lost in a whirlwind of desire, we thrash about on the bed, devouring each other like our lives depend on it. Finally, I tear my mouth away and whisper, "Slow down. I want to taste you."

He freezes and looks me dead in the eye, an expression of surprise on his face. He's not used to me being so forthright, and it takes him a second to soak it up. Then, with a sexy smile, he slides off me and rolls onto his back.

"I'm in your hands." He closes his eyes, exhales softly.

Trembling with joy and longing, I gaze down at his firm, muscled chest and get a crazy rush of adrenaline. I can't believe he's given me carte blanche to do whatever I want and *finally* I'm in control, free to unleash the full force of my desire on him.

"Turn over," I command.

Obediently, he rolls onto his front and I get an eyeful of his beautifully sculpted back. Admiringly, my eyes travel down the length of his body, openly salivating at the delectable feast on display. His bottom is smooth and supple as a peach, and it sticks out in a way that makes me want to sink my teeth into it. But I manage to control myself. I want to do it, want it so badly I can almost taste it, but I need to take my time with him, show him just how good I can make him feel.

Gently, I slide onto Nick's sweat-soaked back and softly rub my breasts up and down his spine, making him quiver with excitement. I work his body slowly, giving him a sensual massage, he'll never forget.

"Oh, God, you're killing me," he rasps. "That feels so damn good."

I continue rubbing my breasts on him, whipping him into a frenzy. Then I slowly start to kiss and lick his neck and shoulders, milking quiet groans of approval from his lips. It feels so good knowing I'm the one causing those sounds. Hearing him moan like that makes me feel in control. Powerful.

Working my way down, Nick hisses as I run my tongue over his spine, tracing the letters of the alphabet on his silky-smooth skin. Skipping his delectable bottom, I softly lick and suck the backs of his thighs, his calves, his feet, then I gradually work my way back up. I walk my fingers over his shoulders, lightly scratching the surface of his skin with my nails; he shudders with delight.

Then I kiss and lick him some more, each touch of my lips breaking down his barriers. When I finally return to his bottom, I hesitate, prolonging the moment of suspense, making him wait as I deliberate what to do. I want so badly to give Nick that same exquisite pleasure he's given me, but I'm scared. I've never done this before and wonder what it will be like. I wonder if I'll do it right, but I'm determined to try and show him just how adventurous I can be. Right now, I'm pretty much game for anything.

"Are you okay?" he murmurs.

"Uh-huh."

"Then why did you stop?"

I push my hair behind my ear. "No reason."

"Please, continue what you were doing. It felt so good." Turned on by the desire in his voice, I bend down and gently swirl my tongue around each buttock, taking my time to savour the salty-sweet taste of his skin.

"Don't stop," he groans. "That feels fucking amazing." Tentatively, I lower my face further, spread his buttocks and lick a long, slow stroke up and down his crack. Nick's gasping moans grow suddenly more frantic, and I know then that I've hit his sweet spot. "Fuck, don't stop..."

At last, I release all of my inhibitions and really put my back into it, licking him out like I'm licking an ice-cream cone. He shivers at each fervent stroke of my tongue, crying out like I'm sending him crazy. I reach down and rub my clit, *shit, I'm getting wet just hearing how excited he is.* It feels wonderful being so intimate, so at one with him.

At last, I come up for air. "Turn around," I breathe.

Dutifully, he does as he's told and, sitting astride him, I pause for a second, staring down into his gorgeous hazel eyes: so warm, so intense, so full of love. We smile at each other. Slowly, sensuously, I lick a trail from his neck to his abdomen, causing him to whimper quietly. Teasingly, I blow hot air over his dick, swamping every delectable inch of him with my sweet heat.

"God, I love you, Carly. No one has ever made me feel ..."

I cut him short. Hungrily, I lap his balls, sucking his forbidden fruit into my mouth like a starving wolf. My jaw muscles ache but I hardly notice the pain; white-hot lust has numbed me to everything but the taste of this big, beautiful cock.

I stop to catch my breath. My hair is all in my face; my skin slick and shiny with sweat. Biting my lower lip, I lovingly stroke my fingers up and down his pulsating shaft then, throwing caution to the wind, I decide to push the boundaries even further. Seductively, I suck on my index finger to lubricate it, and then gently slide it into his butthole.

Nick's body tenses and he draws in a sharp breath. For a second, I worry that maybe I've gone too far and hastily withdraw my finger. "I-I'm sorry. I didn't mean to—"

"Don't stop," he gasps. "That was fucking beautiful."

"Are you sure?"

"Yes!"

With a sexy grin, I slide my finger back in and tongue the underside of his cock, my lips making soft suction noises as I devour every last piece of him. Nick's cries grow more and more heated, more desperate, and I sing inwardly, knowing that I've finally got him where I want him. I love the expression of ecstasy on his face; love knowing that I have this hold over him. Joining my hand and mouth together, I jerk up and down his penis in a slow, steady rhythm while at the same time pushing my finger deeper into his warm, tight hole. This role reversal feels amazing and for once, I love being in the dominant position; adore the feeling of omnificence it gives me.

Bobbing my head up and down, I suck more vigorously, desperate to taste his salty cum in my mouth. I've pushed him to the brink and sense that he's going to come, but just as I'm about to bring him to the point of no return, he pulls away from me.

"Why… are we stopping?" I pant. "You were about to come."

"I know," he replies, "but I need to satisfy you first. I've been longing to taste you all night. Bring that sweet pussy here."

I need no further encouragement. Shaking irrepressibly, I lower myself into a sixty-nine position and straddle his face. Forcing down the urge to climax immediately, I gasp as his hot tongue plunges deep inside my soaking-wet hole. I shut my eyes and grit my teeth. Jesus, I need a few seconds. *Shit, shit, shit, this feels too good.* Moistening my lips, I bend down and take his cock in my mouth again, swallowing him all the way to the hilt, almost choking myself. But I can't stop now. I love the taste of him and can't get enough of his tangy flavour.

Suddenly, I stop sucking and throw my head back, crying out as waves of intense pleasure crash through me and I experience my first orgasm of the night.

"That's right," Nick whispers from between my thighs. "Give it all to me. Let that river flow."

With a loud gasp, I lurch forward onto his stomach, my whole body bucking and twitching with sparks of electricity. I'm completely and utterly spent, but Nick's only just getting warmed up. Gripping my hips, he guides me down and carefully lowers me onto his rock-hard dick. I clench my teeth to force back a silent scream as he impales me and stretches me out with slow, delicious thrusts. Still with my back to him, I push myself up and down, grinding my clit into his pelvis each time I reach the hilt. I can feel his cock stiffening with every bump and jerk. He groans in rapture, his grip tightening around my waist like a vice. I whimper as he pounds into me again and again, hitting my G-spot every time. The room spins around me and I can't think straight, can't see straight. The smell of sex is everywhere. I scream as his thrusts grow so intense, it's like he's splitting me in two.

"I-I don't think... I can take any more," I wheeze.

"Yes, you can. You're killing me with this view. I love watching you take every single inch of me."

Spurred on by his words, I reach back my arms and spread my buttocks, opening myself up so he can get a full view of his cock penetrating me.

"Shit," he whispers. "I've never seen anything so beautiful."

At last, an incredible warmth ripples through me and an

explosion of fireworks erupts in my belly. My pussy tightens around his cock and I come for the second time, but still he continues thrusting into me, pushing through the tightness, sending me beyond the point of no return.

With a loud moan, Nick finally pulls out and drags me to the edge of the bed to enter me again from behind. My hands are shaking; every single part of me is totally numb. Taking the rear entry, he plunges back inside my burning hole. I feel so weak, so sore, but I'm powerless to resist. I asked for this, and I know he won't quit till we've reached that lucky number three. Rolling his hips, Nick penetrates me deeper than he ever has before. I shut my eyes and lose myself in the intensity of the pleasure. I try to breathe, try to focus on keeping conscious. Jesus, it hurts so good I think I might pass out.

Suddenly, he does something I'm not expecting. Still pulverising me from behind, he sweeps me clean off the bed and suspends my body in mid-air to give him more leverage. I yelp in surprise as the blood rushes to my head. He's taking me further than he ever has before, and the strength of him both excites and terrifies me.

"That's just how you like it, huh?" he whispers. "Rough and deep."

"Yes, oh, yes… harder. *Harder!*" I puff air through my mouth, bringing each out-breath from my belly, my diaphragm contracting in time to the force of the explosions surging from my abdomen to my upper body. We could have been doing this for minutes. We could have been doing this for hours. I have no sense of time or space. My head goes dizzy as an indescribable blast of euphoria sweeps through me for the third time, and every part of me shakes convulsively. There's a final eruption, and then the world goes dark around me.

CHAPTER TEN

Naughty

"**I**T'S SIX O'CLOCK, time to get up." The robotic voice sounds cold, unfriendly. Squeezing my eyes shut, I try to block out the annoying noise, but it seems to be getting louder. Mingled with the command is the sound of heavy rain hitting the window, an unpleasant combination that serves only to push me further under the duvet.

"It's six o'clock, time to get up," the tinny voice repeats.

Nick emits a groan, and I nuzzle my face deeper into his chest. His arms feel so strong and warm around me, so comforting; I never want him to let me go. Our naked bodies fit together so well, like two pieces of hot clay melded together. I could spend forever like this, but as the screeching voice from the alarm continues to bash us, he gently eases out of my embrace.

"You heard the lady. Time to get up, gorgeous." He reaches for the dresser and turns off the clock.

"Do we have to?" I murmur. "I was having such a great dream."

"That's funny. So was I."

"Really? Was I in it?"

"Of course."

"Was it a naughty dream?"

"Yes. A very, very naughty one."

"Mmm. Tell me all the details."

"I'd much rather give you a demonstration, but if we go down that road, neither of us will be going to work today." He kisses my forehead then throws back the covers and races to the bathroom to take a pee. With a satisfied smile, I bury my face in his pillow and breathe in his sweet scent. The bed feels so empty without him, and I'm already craving his heat again. Suddenly, images from last night flash through my mind and I get a rush of butterflies. What a night. What a crazy, crazy night. What mad, passionate sex we had.

Heat colours my cheeks and I chuckle to myself as more images flash up: Nick suspending me in mid-air. Me coming three times, the third one so intense it caused me to black out. My blush deepens and I shake my head incredulously. Right now, at this very moment, life is the best it has ever been.

For a few heartbeats, I lie on my back, listening to the sound of hard rain pelting the window. Harsh winds. A tree branch banging against the glass. Doors opening and closing outside on the landing. Creaking floorboards. Taps turning. The rush of water as Nick steps in the shower. God, I really don't want to go to work today. I want to stay here, warm and cosy with the man I love, sheltered forever from the pressures of the world.

Pulling up the duvet, I snuggle back down and try to get a bit more shut eye, but the odds are against me. Within seconds, Nick's standing over me with an angelic smile on his lips; his eyes glisten with adoration. Reaching out, he softly runs his fingers down my cheek. "Last night was mind-blowing," he whispers. "I've never known anything like it. What you did to me, the way you loved me so completely … it was the most wonderful experience of my life. You've brought me back from the brink, Carly. Made me feel I have the right to walk in the land of the living once more."

I blink up at him and smile, showing all my teeth. There's a lot I want to say, but the words won't come, so I just keep smiling, hoping all I'm thinking can be communicated with a look.

"Darling, I've run you a bath," he continues. "And I'm fixing us breakfast. So, whenever you're ready ..." He glances pointedly at a chair stacked with fresh towels and a black-silk dressing gown. "I don't want you to be late for work."

I laugh good-humouredly. "Okay, I'm going, I'm going."

Gently, Nick helps me into the dressing gown and after securing the belt, ushers me to the bathroom where he leaves me to finish getting ready.

When he's gone, I climb into the tub and allow the water to completely submerge me, every muscle and nerve growing calm. This is just what I need to wake me up. When I've finished bathing, I towel myself down, brush my teeth and return to the bedroom, where I find all my work clothes laid out on the bed. Cutting short my morning make-up ritual, I dress in a hurry, apply only a bit of lippy and mascara, then make my way downstairs.

As I enter the kitchen, my nostrils are greeted by the glorious scent of bacon and freshly-ground coffee.

"I hope you're feeling hungry," Nick smiles. "I wasn't sure what you'd like, so I made you a bit of everything." He takes a pan off the cooker and shakes the steaming contents onto a plate. "Did you have a nice bath?"

"Yes, it was lovely. Wow, that food smells delicious. You really are spoiling me; I don't feel worthy."

He laughs softly as he takes a second plate from the drying rack and lays it on the sideboard. Smoothing down my bright-pink cardigan, I covertly survey the room. It's wonderfully old-fashioned and sort of reminds me of a rustic farmhouse. In the centre sits an island made of solid oak, above which hangs an array of pots and pans suspended from a metal ceiling rack. A traditional red kettle stands on the stove, whistling merrily as the water is boiled. I glance behind me; no sign of a dishwasher or microwave anywhere. Clearly, Nick likes to keep things Old School and conjures up everything from scratch.

My mouth starts to water. It looks as if he's cooked us up a real feast: French toast with bacon, scrambled eggs, fruit salad and coffee.

"That looks so good," I murmur.

Smiling sweetly, Nick dishes out the food, and then we sit beside each other at the island, perched on chrome-plated stools. We don't talk a whole lot, just focus on clearing our plates. I eat and eat, this time not caring if he thinks I'm a glutton. This food is too good to tackle delicately; it needs to be devoured and appreciated the way it deserves to be.

"What?" I ask, wiping my mouth with the back of my hand.

"Nothing," he smirks. "I just love watching you eat. Does the food taste okay?"

"Absolutely scrumptious."

"You're so cute."

"Cute? What happened to sexy?"

"That goes without saying."

I grin broadly. For a moment, I dare to dream of a life of domestic bliss with him. I imagine it being like this every day, us living together, waking up every morning together. How great would that be?

I shake the thought from my head. *One step at a time. The idea of moving in together so soon is absurd, so don't even think about it.*

When we've finished breakfast, Nick clears away the dishes, and I help him; he doesn't want me to, but I do anyway. I wipe and he washes. Then we lock up and head out to the Jag. It's still raining heavily, but Nick gallantly shelters me in the folds of his long, black coat as we make a run for it.

I climb in the car and place my bag and new iPhone on the back seat. Nick sets the Jag in motion, and the sudden jerk throws me against him.

"Sorry, darling; I pulled out too quickly. You're not hurt, are you?"

"No, I'm fine," I laugh, strapping on my seatbelt. "No cuts or bruises to report."

He reaches out and runs his hand tenderly over my cheek. "You sure?"

"Positive. It takes more than a bit of whiplash to floor me."

Carefully, Nick reverses out of the parking space and smoothly steers us onto the main road. Humming to himself, he turns on the stereo and cranks up the volume on James Brown's "I Want You So Bad".

For the next half hour, we say very little, soaking up the music and the serenity of the moment. Words are not necessary; we're completely comfortable in each other's company, so the frequent gaps in conversation don't feel awkward. Around a quarter to nine, Nick turns into Charlotte Street and surveys the Resident Permit Holder's spaces in search of somewhere to park.

"You can drop me at the curb," I say. "Parking round here's a nightmare, and I don't want you getting a ticket. Those attendants are always on the prowl."

Wordlessly, Nick pulls up to the curb and stops briefly for

me to get out. Unclipping my seatbelt, I lean across and lightly kiss his cheek before reaching for the door.

"Wait," he says. "When do I see you again?"

"Tonight?"

"I'm working late tonight, but if you're willing to hang around, we could grab a bite to eat somewhere and then I can drive you home."

"Perfect! Can't wait." I kiss him again, this time on the lips. "I'll phone you at lunch."

The car behind starts beeping and somebody shouts: "Get a move on, will ya?"

"I think that's our cue," I grin. "Thanks again for a wonderful night. I love you."

"Love you, too."

I blow him a final, lingering kiss and he pretends to catch it. Laughing, I open the door and exit onto the sidewalk. Waving goodbye, I turn and race toward my office. My heart swells with joy; it feels like I'm walking on air.

When I enter reception, I find Mark sitting behind the desk, deeply engrossed in today's *Metro*. We lock eyes and he flashes a wry smile. "What time do you call this, young lady? I thought you'd been kidnapped by terrorists."

"Oh, Mark, I'm so sorry. I got a lift to work and there was so much traffic I didn't realise how long it would take."

"Aw, save your breath sweetheart," he chuckles. "The question is, how do you plan to make it up to me?"

"A caramel latte?"

"Throw in a super-size packet of M&M's and we'll call it quits."

We both laugh. As I hang up my coat, Mark waves the newspaper at me. "Jesus, did you read this story? I honestly don't know what the world's coming to."

"What story?"

He passes me the *Metro* and all the colour drains from my face. *"Ex-beauty queen found murdered,"* screams the headline. Beneath is a photograph of a stunning young woman, a woman I instantly recognise as the redhead I met at Nick's office on my first visit.

"What's wrong?" Mark frowns. "You've gone as white as a sheet."

"Oh, my God, I think I know her."

"What! Are you sure?"

I nod and get a sickish feeling in my throat, like I've swallowed something heavy. Thunderstruck, I scan the first couple of paragraphs: *"A former Miss Great Britain and part-time actress, who had bit parts on Doctor Who and Holby City, has been found murdered in her London home. Police say a bloodless corpse found in Knightsbridge, West London, is that of missing actress Jessica Kemp-Barton, who has not been seen by her family since last Tuesday. Detectives believe she was murdered after attending the premiere of a new play in nearby Kensington.*

Detective Superintendent John Hudson, who is leading the investigation, said: "It is important that we piece together Jessica's movements from Tuesday until the discovery in Knightsbridge yesterday. We also urge anyone with significant information about this case to contact us as soon as possible. In particular, we would like to hear from anyone who may have seen any suspicious activity around her home address or has reason to believe someone would wish her harm."

The discovery came after officers expressed concern for Jessica's welfare and searches were organised by her brothers Thomas and Peter Kemp-Barton. Post-mortem examinations have so far failed to determine a cause of death, although detectives are puzzled by the loss of almost 1.2 gallons (4.7 litres) of blood from her body. A spokesman for the Metropolitan police said: "Early post-mortem results suggest that the victim's blood was somehow drained, despite there being no obvious marks or incisions on the body. In addition, the lack of blood in the room where the victim was found would suggest that the murder may have taken place elsewhere. Further tests will be carried out shortly, and we hope to establish a definite cause of death soon." Police are releasing images of Jessica in the Knightsbridge area in the run-up to her death in the hope that witnesses will come forward. She is survived by her partner, set designer Benedict Lewis, and her four-year-old daughter Molly."

I drop the newspaper on the desk. There's no doubt about it: Jessica Kemp-Barton is definitely the woman I saw at Nick's office. I never forget a face, plus I distinctly remember Tara referring to her as "Jess."

Dear Lord. That poor woman. I can't begin to imagine what her final hours must have been like, the pain her family must be going through. And, oh, my goodness, she had a four-year-old daughter who will now grow up without a mother. What a terrible, terrible thing to happen. I just hope and pray the police find her killer soon.

"How do you know her?" Mark probes. "Was she a good friend of yours?"

I shake my head. "No. She was just someone I crossed paths with. Gosh, this is so awful. How the hell can someone do that to another human being? It's despicable."

"Tell me about it. And did you read the part about the body being drained of blood? I mean, how sick is that? I bet it was one of those Gothic, Satan-worshipping weirdoes. They're all into that crazy blood-sacrifice stuff. Either that, or there's a vampire on the loose."

I freeze at the word 'vampire.' The idea is totally preposterous, but for some reason, the thought sends a dark chill through me.

"Vampires don't exist," I say firmly. "It's humans that are sick in the head. I just hope the police find out who murdered Jessica before they do it again."

Mark raises his eyebrows. "What makes you think it's a serial killer? It could have been a crime of passion. Perhaps an ex-boyfriend or something."

"That's true. Oh, I don't know. It's just so terrible, isn't it?"

He opens his mouth to reply but is cut dead by the phone ringing. Hastily, I race to the wall and answer it.

"Hello, reception desk, Carly speaking. Uh-huh. Yes, he's here." I stop the phone against my chest. "Mark, it's Tim. He says the women's toilet is broken again, and he wants you to reset the password."

Mark rolls his eyes theatrically. "Off we go to the third floor again. Honestly, this is really starting to do my head in. I'm a security guard, not a janitor, for Christ's sake."

Placing the receiver back in the cradle, I press the buzzer and watch him disappear into the elevator. As soon as he's gone, I pick up the newspaper again and scrutinise the story in more detail. My heart races. Poor Nick. I wonder if he knows what's happened yet. I have no idea how well he knew Jessica or how long he'd been treating her, but I'm certain this will hit him hard. She *was* one of his patients, after all.

I spend the rest of the morning in a fever of agitation, trying to unravel everything. Jessica's death has brought me back to Earth with a bump, and the magic from last night seems to have soured a little. I feel unaccountably nervous and on edge, my mind racing at the possible implications. Will the police want to involve Nick with their enquiries? As her hypnotherapist and possible confidante, he might hold important information that could help the detectives with their case.

Glancing down at my beloved pendant, I twirl the chain between my fingers and sigh miserably. Why can't my life ever go smoothly? Why does my fairy tale always get shattered by something dark?

By lunchtime, I'm bursting to escape the building and speak to Nick. In a numb haze, I cross the street to Coffee Republic to get some privacy. The sky is swollen and streaked with storm clouds; thankfully, the rain has stopped but the air still retains an icy chill. Shivering, I stand outside the coffee shop with my phone clamped to my ear, waiting impatiently for the call to connect.

I punch the air when he answers.

"Darling, are you all right?" I ask breathlessly. "I read about what happened. I'm so terribly sorry."

"What are you talking about?"

"Your patient, Jessica Kemp-Barton. The story about her murder was in today's *Metro*. What happened to her is truly awful …" My voice trails off and the line goes silent. "Nick, are you still there?"

"Yes," he replies coolly. "I'm still here."

"Didn't you hear what I said?"

"Yes, Tara told me. She read it in the *Guardian* this morning. It's absolutely horrific. Such a sweet girl. What a waste of a young life." He hesitates. "How did you know Jessica was one of my patients?"

"That first day I came to your office, I saw her in the waiting room. She had the appointment just before mine."

"Ah, yes, I remember. You've got a very good memory." His voice sounds oddly distant.

There's an awkward pause. "Did you know her well?" I ask.

"No, not really. I think I saw Jessica a total of three times, but we weren't really making much progress, so she decided to cancel her treatment early."

"What was wrong with her?"

"BDD."

"What's that?"

"Body Dysmorphic Disorder."

"Right…" I'm familiar with it: an anxiety disorder that causes sufferers to spend a lot of time worrying about their appearance.

I run my fingers through my hair. "So, do you think the police will want to speak to you?"

"Why on earth should they? I wasn't part of her inner circle. I barely knew her."

"Yes, but I just thought that maybe…" I break off, feeling slightly stupid.

His tone softens a little, almost like he's humouring me. "I think it's highly unlikely, but if the police do decide to contact me, I'm ready to answer any questions they throw at me. But I don't see how anything I say could help the investigation. Apart from the obvious, Jessica seemed a perfectly normal, well-adjusted young woman. I knew nothing of her personal life. To get a proper insight, the police would be far better off speaking to her family, her friends, her boyfriend. Not someone who spent less than three hours in her company."

"Yes, I suppose you're right." We talk for a few minutes more, and I keep saying how terrible it all is, and he keeps saying what a nice young woman Jessica was. Finally, he draws the conversation to a close.

"Darling, I have to go. I've got a patient arriving in five minutes, and I need to do some prep work. Just to check, are we still on for tonight?"

"You mean going to a restaurant?"

"Yes."

"Of course. I wouldn't miss it for the world."

"Brilliant. I can't wait to see you. And Carly?"

"Yes?"

"Please, don't fret too much about this whole business with Jessica. What happened to her is tragic, but we need to put things in perspective. The world can be a cruel and terrible place, with light and dark in equal measure. Always has, always will be, and we can't do a damn thing to change it." He pauses. "What I'm trying to say is, don't let this ruin your day. I know how stressed you get about things, and I don't want this to become another issue for you to worry about. This is my problem, not yours, so if and when the police decide to contact me, I'll deal with it. Okay?"

"Okay."

"Good. I love you. Now, go and get some lunch. Relax and listen to some music. I'll see you tonight."

He tells me again that he loves me, then hangs up, and it takes me a second to soak it all in. Nick's right, of course. There are bad stories in the news every day—murders, rapes, kidnappings—and we're so desensitised to it, most days we barely give it a second thought. We read the morning paper on the commute to work, poring over all the evil on display, then calmly switch off and order ourselves a Starbucks coffee or a McChicken sandwich. Tunnel vision is a coping mechanism vital to humanity's survival; the ability to filter life's joys and miseries into neat little compartments that we view on a 'need to know' basis. Jessica's murder is truly terrible, but is it any worse than the dozens of atrocities committed around the world on a daily basis?

Probably not. But I still can't stop my hands from shaking, not least because it has stirred up memories buried deep in my own subconscious. For a second, I'm back in the brightly-lit hospital lounge with the yellow wallpaper. Ronan and I are sitting in orange bucket chairs arranged in a semi-circle. The horse race is playing on TV …

No! I shake my head. *Stay strong, stay strong.*

In a trance, I push open the door to Coffee Republic and amble through the swathes of bodies to the serving counter. I smile at the waitress, place my order and take my tray to a secluded spot by the window. Absently, I chew my muffin, but the taste doesn't register.

I tell myself to calm down, not to get so worked up. I tell myself that Nick's right: I *do* stress too much about things. Why the hell am I letting this bother me so much? I didn't even know her.

I take a sip of coffee.

Uh-uh. No matter which way I turn it, something just doesn't sit right with me. My gut's telling me that something's off, *but what?* Why can't I get Jessica's face out of my head? Why can't I forget how excited she'd been that day she came out of Nick's office? The way her eyes sparkled, the way she tossed her hair and gushed about how fabulous he was?

And that's when it hits me.

Nick said Jessica cancelled her treatment because she wasn't happy with their progress. Fair enough. But this doesn't fit with the way she'd behaved the night I saw her. She'd seemed giddy, elated, and had even said she'd recommend Nick to her friends; not the actions of someone ready to throw in the towel. Add to this Nick's charisma, his incredible sex appeal, and ability to turn most women's heads, and I very much doubt she would have been the one to end their association.

No. Either Nick's playing down his involvement to spare my feelings, or he's lying for some other reason. True, I don't have a whole lot to go on, just a woman's intuition, but it's never failed me in the past.

I take another sip of coffee and chew the inside of my cheek.

I keep telling myself to get a grip, to stop being so negative about things. This is self-sabotage, pure and simple. What right do I have to pass judgment on Nick's response to the tragedy? Okay, so I find his coolness a little disconcerting, but he's still the kindest, sweetest guy I know. And he loves me. *I know he loves me.* So what if he's being a little economical with the truth? So what if he seems a little detached? I'm sure he has my best interests at heart, so he must be behaving this way for a reason. Perhaps he's privately grieving for Jessica. Perhaps he doesn't want to show his true feelings and is putting on a brave face for my sake.

Reaching in my bag, I pull out a packet of Thurlax and take my second tablet of the day. Then my phone beeps. Flipping it open, I see a text from Ronan inviting me for drinks in Soho after work. I'm about to decline when suddenly, I check myself. What am I doing? Maybe some time with my friend is just what I need to loosen up and help gain some perspective on things. Plus, there's plenty of time to kill before Nick finishes work, so hooking up with Ronan slots into my agenda perfectly.

I message him back, tell him where to meet, then finish my coffee and head back to the office, feeling slightly less agitated.

CHAPTER ELEVEN

Doubt

"**S**O, BASICALLY," RONAN says through a cloud of smoke, "my new manager's a complete bastard. Walks around like he's got a pineapple stuck up his arse. He's had it in for me right from the word go, and since his arrival, I can do nothing right."

"Why don't you take out a grievance against him?" I suggest.

Ronan shakes his head. "It's not that simple. A lot of what he does is subtle. I'll give you an example. Last week, he said it was okay for me to come to work late on Fridays. Then at the staff meeting, he has a right go at me in front of everyone for coming in late! When I reminded him of our conversation, he pretended it never happened, making me look a complete fool."

"Gosh, he sounds terrible. You should start keeping a diary of everything that happens, just so you've got yourself covered if it ever goes to a tribunal."

"Damn right, I will. I'll even tape record the bugger if I have to. Carly, I've given that company six years of my life. *Six years!* I'm telling you, I won't go down without a fight. If they want me out, fine, but they'd better have a big, fat redundancy cheque waiting for me."

I nod silently, but I'm only partially listening. Images of

Jessica keep popping into my head, and I'm finding it very difficult to remain calm. I'm trying to engage in the present moment; trying to keep focused on bright things, happy things, but she just won't let me be.

We're sitting outside our favourite Soho coffee shop, sipping lattes in the gathering twilight. Ronan lights another cigarette, the glow from the match illuminating his face like a Jack o' Lantern. He cocks his head back and blows smoke toward me.

"Want one?" he asks, proffering the packet.

I hold up my hands defensively. "No, thanks. I told you, I've quit."

"Well done, you. To be honest, babe, I didn't think you'd stick it out, but it looks like I was wrong."

"Thanks." I hesitate, stirring the spoon in my latte. "Actually, I've got something to tell you. I've met someone."

His brows lift questioningly. "You've met someone?"

"Uh-huh. I mean, like as in a boyfriend."

Ronan mouths a silent "O." Then he grins mischievously. "So, tell me something I don't know."

I blink at him. "You knew?"

"Of course."

"How?"

"Your whole aura's changed. The light is back in your eyes. It's like I've got the old Carly back, and I knew, I just *knew* it had to be a man. Plus, you haven't mentioned Andrew once, which is nothing short of a miracle."

"Are you angry I didn't tell you sooner?"

"Babe, of course not. Better late than never, eh? So, what's he like and where did you meet him?"

I tell him all about Nick: the hypnosis, our first date, the visit to James's art exhibition. Ronan doesn't say much, just sits there and listens attentively, smiling and nodding like a proud parent. When I finally pause for breath, he says, "Nick sounds fantastic, but what I want to know is are you happy?"

"Yes," I reply softly. "I don't think I've ever been so happy in my life. For the first time in years, I look forward to getting up in the mornings. The black cloud has gone, and it's all because of him."

Ronan reaches across the table and pats my hand. "Babe, this is amazing. I'm so fucking pleased for you. I mean, seriously, this guy has worked wonders. When do I get to meet him?"

A shadow falls across the table.

My head snaps up. "Nick!"

"Hello, darling, so sorry I'm late. My last appointment ran a bit over, but I came here as fast as I could." Stooping down, he lightly kisses the top of my head. Then he nods to Ronan, pulls out a chair from the adjacent table and sits with us. "Are you guys okay for drinks? What are you both having?"

"We're fine," I say. "But you should get something." I slide a menu to him. "Try one of their fruit smoothies; the strawberry ones are fantastic."

"It's a bit cold for a smoothie," Nick smiles, "but I might have an espresso." He signals the waitress and places his order. Then he flicks a glance at Ronan, who's been trying mighty hard not to look at him. "And you are …?"

"Ronan."

"It's good to meet you. I'm Nick."

"Yes, Carly's just been telling me how you swept her off her feet."

Nick chuckles softly. "Quite the reverse, actually. It was *she* who swept me off my feet."

They both laugh.

Discreetly, Ronan's eyes rove over Nick's body, checking out every inch of him and taking his time about it. Then he looks at me and gives a half-amused, half-embarrassed smirk.

My lips make a tight smile.

For a while, the three of us talk about inconsequential things: Nick's job, Ronan's job, how bad the weather is. Then, as the waitress returns with Nick's espresso, he asks, "So, have you two been friends for a long time?"

"Yes," I say. "Ronan and I have known each other for close on twelve years."

Nick sips his espresso, his gaze fixed on Ronan. "Wow, that's great. Where did the two of you meet?"

Ronan and I exchange glances.

"Um, we…" he begins. My eyes plead with him to keep this simple. "We, er, that is to say…"

"We used to work together," I interject. "At a little clothes shop in High Street Kensington. We just hit it off and stayed friends ever since."

Nick eyes me shrewdly. "Was that before or after you left university?"

"After," Ronan says quickly. "Definitely after."

There's an uncomfortable silence.

Nick swallows the last of his coffee and glances at his watch. "Well, darling, it's ten to nine. Do you think we should start thinking about heading home?"

"Okay," I say, thankful the grilling's over. I stand up and smooth down my jacket. "It's been so nice seeing you, Ronan. We need to do this again soon."

"Definitely," he grins. "Same time next week?"

I nod vacantly. "Yes, definitely. I'll text you." I walk around to his side of the table and give him a big hug. "Take care."

"How are you getting home, Ronan?" Nick asks. "My car's parked just around the corner. If you need us to drop you somewhere…"

"Oh, no, I'm fine," Ronan laughs. "I think I might stick around here a bit longer. A friend of mine works across the street in Bar Soho, so I might go there for a while."

"Okay. Well, if you change your mind, the offer's there."

Nick takes my hand and, waving goodbye to Ronan, we head up the street in the direction of the car.

"Darling, your hands are freezing," he whispers. "What happened to your gloves?"

"I think I lost them somewhere."

He squeezes my hand to help warm my fingers. I sigh; his skin feels so soft. "I've missed you so much. I couldn't wait to get you away."

I smile up at him. I don't need words; my expression says it all.

"Ronan seems very nice," he continues softly. "I can tell he cares a great deal about you."

"Yes, he does. He's absolutely lovely. We've been through so many ups and downs together over the years and he's always been there for me."

"That's good. I'm so happy you have such a wonderful friend to look out for you."

"Yes, I'm very lucky."

The conversation dies, and I wonder where his thoughts have taken him. I suspect he knows there's more to the story about how Ronan and I met, but right now, that's not a conversation I want to have.

We pick up the Jag from Greek Street and head toward South London. After we've been driving for a few minutes, Nick tells me he spoke to Jessica's mother.

I stiffen. "You did?"

"Yes. I phoned her to send the family my condolences. I've also arranged for flowers to be sent to their home in time for the funeral." He steals a quick glance at me and then returns his gaze to the traffic. "It just seemed the right thing to do, you know? To reach out to them. Losing a child like that... I can't imagine what they must be going through." He hesitates, and then checks himself. "No, actually I can. Having lost both of my parents, I know all too well the pain of losing someone you love. The feeling is excruciating."

"Oh, Nick!" I reach out and squeeze his knee. "We don't have to talk about this if you don't want to."

He wets his lips, appearing to weigh up his words. "I must apologise for how I behaved earlier. My attitude may have seemed a tad mercenary, given the circumstances, but you must understand that I'm not always good at conveying emotion. When I first heard the news about Jessica, I was in total shock, and I didn't quite know how to react. You must forgive me." Briefly, a streetlight illuminates his face, then drops it back into darkness. I wait for him to continue, but he just stares straight ahead, his face the picture of disquietude. It seems he's said all he wants to, and I decide not to push it.

"Do you still want to get something to eat?" I ask, trying to brighten the atmosphere.

"Sure. What do you fancy?"

"I don't really know. You choose somewhere."

"No, you choose. I think the lady should always decide."

I work my face into a smile. *Such a gentleman.*

In the end, we drop by a Lebanese restaurant in Old Street and grab two take-out Shawarmas to eat in the car. It's not the most comfortable set-up. We get our fingers dirty and the onions stink to high Heaven, but at least it gives us something to do.

Then we're on the move again, and before I know it, we're pulling back into my street. Nick kills the engine and looks at me uneasily. "Oh, I forgot to mention, I'm going to be away for a couple of days. I leave for Cambridge first thing tomorrow. There's some important business I need to attend to."

"Oh." I try not to show my disappointment. "When will you... when will you be back?"

"Next Saturday."

"Oh, my God! That's a whole week without you."

"I'm so sorry, darling. I know I should have mentioned it before but, with everything that's been happening, it sort of slipped my mind."

I stare at him, frowning. "What about the paintings?" I ask suspiciously.

"Paintings?"

"Yes, James's paintings. The ones you bought yesterday. You said the gallery was supposed to have them delivered to your house in the next couple of days. If you're going away, who will be there to pick them up?"

"Ah. That's a very good point." He pauses. "I guess I'll phone the gallery and get them to put off the delivery till I get back."

I continue to stare at him. Panic sets in. "I wasn't born yesterday."

"What are you talking about?"

"This is all so random, and I won't be fobbed off. Do you seriously expect me to believe you're going to Cambridge for a business trip? What about your patients? I mean, *come on*."

"Honest to God, it's the truth."

I shake my head, my voice starting to break. "Is this because of Jessica?"

"No, of course not."

"Then have I done something to upset you? Is that why you want to get away from me? Please, Nick, if I'm to blame, you must tell me so I can—"

"Sssh…" He takes my hand and kisses it. "I love you more than life itself. *You know that.* Please, stop all this crazy talk. Of course, I want to be with you. *Of course!* If I could somehow get out of this trip, I would, but I can't. I promise I'll phone you every single day, and I'll be back before you know it. We'll do something extra special when I return to make it up to you, okay?"

I make a non-committal sound; I'm still not convinced.

"I would die for you," he whispers. Passionately, he sucks each of my fingers in turn, licking the tips in a way that makes me throb painfully below. I close my eyes. He's completely skewering my senses again. Releasing my hand, he tenderly caresses my cheek and then gently strokes my hair and ears, his fingers warm and slightly clammy. My stomach tightens and I'm consumed by uncontrollable longing. My God, I want him so much. He knows exactly what buttons to push and is milking it for all it's worth.

I feel the painful throb again. My pulse is all over the place. Finally, he releases me and I place my hand over my jaw to compose myself.

"I can always cancel," he says softly. I raise my eyebrows. He continues: "Seriously, I won't go on this trip if you don't want me to. If it really bothers you that much, then I can cancel. No big deal."

I release a heavy sigh. "No, darling, it's okay. I'm sorry for my outburst; I was just being childish. Of course, you must go. I don't want to get in the way of your work. It's only a week. Okay, it's going to be difficult, and I'll miss you terribly, but I'll survive."

"Of course you will." He kisses my nose, my forehead, and then takes me in his arms. When he tries to loosen his grip, I continue to cling to him, not wanting to let go.

Gently, he pulls away and kisses my forehead again. When our eyes meet, his appear to sparkle with tears. "You'd better go inside now and get some sleep, darling. I'll phone you tomorrow."

"Okay." We hug each other one last time, then I get out the car and wave goodbye to the man I love.

As soon as I get in the house, I stand with my back to the door, catching my breath. I can hear the tap of computer keys coming from the living room; Dad is still awake, working on his manuscript. He calls out to me, asks me how my day has been, and I tell him yeah, everything's great. Then I go to the kitchen and drink two cups of espresso, one after the other, and think about smoking; I can almost taste the tobacco. But in the end I don't, because whatever Nick's done to me has worked. Shaking my head, I go up to my bedroom and lock the door. I need time to think.

Sitting on the edge of the bed, I kick off my shoes and rub my temples. Taking a few breaths, I loosen up a little and start to see straight again. I glance around my room. It's like I've never seen the place before. Everything seems strange with nothing familiar to hang onto. For something to do, I play around with my new iPhone and try to figure out how to work the thing. Eventually, I give up, realising it needs my full concentration, and right now, my head just isn't with it.

I take out my laptop and plug it in the wall socket. Cradling it between my knees, I wait impatiently for the screen to boot up so I can surf the Net for more updates on the Jessica story. Once I'm in, I scroll through every major newspaper to see if the police have made any progress finding the killer; so far, no joy. They all seem to be running pretty much the same story as earlier. However, the *Daily Mail* goes into more detail about Jessica's background, her bit parts and theatrical achievements. A lump forms in my throat as I study a photo of her aged twelve. Her eyes sparkle with excitement, like she's got her whole life to look forward to; a life that has now been so cruelly cut short.

Staring into Jessica's innocent young face has a profound effect on me, gets me thinking about my own life. At twenty-five, Jessica was eleven years younger than me, yet she'd achieved so much. From the numerous anecdotes given by her family and friends, it seems she lived her life to the fullest: travelled the world, starred in numerous plays and in between partied constantly, making the most of her short time on the planet.

As I continue to peruse the different pictures chronicling Jessica's history, I have a sudden epiphany. I think about my own life and wonder if I died tomorrow, what would my legacy be? Would I go to my grave with regrets about all the things I didn't do?

And then I get to thinking about Nick: the strength of my feelings for him, how devastating it would be if I ever lost him, and wonder what the hell I'm waiting for. This is the man I love, the man I want to be with forever. Why should we waste time going through the motions before making a serious commitment to each other? Time waits for no man, and life's too short to delay my future happiness. I'm tired of waiting for things to happen of their own accord; tired of always being sensible and living in fear of taking risks. What if I died tomorrow? Would my time on the planet have been well spent?

And then I get the craziest idea. *The craziest, craziest idea ever.*

I decide I'm going to ask Nick to marry me.

Closing my laptop, I reach down to my bedside cabinet and pull out the bottom drawer where I keep all my important documents. Sifting through a stack of crumpled paperwork, I quickly find what I'm looking for: a recent letter from my bank confirming they've increased my overdraft limit.

I gaze up at the ceiling, jaw tight. I take in a lot of air to calm my racing heart. Am I really planning to blow the last of my money on an engagement ring for Nick? I know it's a stupid, insane thing to do, but I figure it'll be worth it if he accepts my marriage proposal. Maybe it's the Thurlax finally starting to work its magic, I don't know. All I know is right now, I feel on top of the world. Invincible. It's time to take a risk and actually start *living.* There are no second chances and in a strange way, I see Jessica's death as the catalyst to a new, dynamic me.

CHAPTER TWELVE

Fate

"WHAT KIND OF image are you going for?" the make-up girl asks as she blends foundation into my cheek.

"Something to give me a smaller nose," I chuckle. "And bigger lips and high cheekbones. Sprinkle me with your fairy dust and make me as chiselled as possible."

She laughs. "Okay, tilt your head back and look at me." I obey. She chews her bottom lip, focusing intently on my face. "Right...I'm going to show you the power of contouring. That's what it's all about. Contouring, contouring. All of the celebrities do it. It's kind of like a mini-facelift."

I shut my eyes and let her work her magic. I sigh happily; there's something so soothing about the gentle brush strokes on my face, moulding and sculpting me into a better version of myself.

It's Saturday afternoon and I'm sitting at one of the cosmetics counters in John Lewis, having a makeover in preparation for tonight. Nick's due back from Cambridge today, and the plan is for me to take him out to dinner before making my proposal. I'm determined to look my best; tonight is the night I stake my claim on the man I love.

I've spent the whole week in a whirlwind of excitement, getting everything ready, planning it all in meticulous detail.

I've been so busy buying the engagement ring, finding the perfect venue, picking out the right clothes, I haven't had a moment to think about poor Jessica. Between my daily dose of Thurlax and a strict ban on the news and TV, I've managed to block it all out, and in so doing, pushed down those nagging doubts to help preserve my fairy tale. In my fragile bubble, there is no murder, there is no darkness. There is only Nick, the man I adore; the man I miss so much I spend every day counting down the seconds till I can hold him in my arms again.

In my head, I've got it all worked out. Tonight is going to be the most romantic, most perfect night ever. We'll have dinner, Nick will accept my proposal and then we'll ride off into the sunset and live happily ever after.

"What do you think?" The make-up girl's husky voice pulls me back to Earth. I blink into the mirror she's holding up for me to check out her handiwork.

"Oh, wow, that looks fantastic!" I gasp, touching my face. My skin is positively glowing: a perfect blend of lights and shades that make me look airbrushed. Playfully, I run my fingers through my newly-cropped hair and laugh at how young and fresh I look. For the first time in ages, I'm truly happy with my appearance and can't wait to show Nick the transformation.

"All right, I'll take it all," I beam.

The girl looks shocked. "Really? Even the tinted moisturiser?"

"Yep. I want everything."

"Wicked! Come over to the counter and I'll throw in some free perfume samples, too."

Having spent a small fortune on cosmetics, I leave John Lewis and move onto Ted Baker where I purchase a pair of round-toed ankle boots to go with the pink mini-dress I'm wearing tonight. As I'm paying for them, I spy a gorgeous dove clutch bag and throw that in, too. I know I'm being a terrible spendthrift, but my credit card's already damned to hell, so I figure I may as well run with it.

By ten past five, I'm back home and anxiously counting down the minutes till Nick arrives to pick me up. My nerves are shot to shreds. What if Nick turns down my marriage proposal? What if this is all a big mistake?

Standing at the kitchen sink, I take a second dose of Thurlax to calm myself. Then I go to the living room in search of Dad. I find him sprawled on the couch, sipping tea and eating a sandwich. He looks up at me through bleary eyes and flashes a crooked smile. I sniff the air; I'm sure there's a faint hint of marijuana but decide to push it aside for the moment. Tonight, nothing's going to spoil my good mood.

"Are you hungry?" he asks between mouthfuls. "I bought some duck pate from Sainsbury's. It's terrific in a rye bread sandwich."

"Tempting, but I'll have to pass. I'm eating out tonight."

Dad chews his bread thoughtfully. "So that's why you're all dolled up. Is Nick taking you somewhere nice?"

"Yes," I nod. "We're going to a new steakhouse near Liverpool Street. It's had loads of good reviews in *Time Out*…" My voice falters. I'd love to tell him my plans, but I know he'd only try to stop me. Asking Nick to marry me so soon into our relationship is just about the craziest thing I'll ever do, and I know it won't go down well with my father. Of course, he has good reason to be protective of me, but the past is the past. Tonight, nothing is going to stop me. Nobody is going to rain on my parade, and I won't stop until I've got what I want.

"Are things all right between you two?" Dad probes. "I haven't heard you mention his name in a while."

"Oh, everything's great. Nick's just been away in Cambridge on a business trip, but he's back now."

"Hmm. Well, send him my regards."

"I will. Actually, you'll probably see him tonight. He's picking me up at six-thirty."

Dad glances at his watch and gives a low whistle. "Six-thirty? You'd better get a move on. I know how long it takes for you to get ready."

Laughing, I cross the room and kiss his cheek. "Love you."

"I love you, too. Sure you don't want a duck pate sandwich?"

I raise my eyes Heavenward; Dad is incorrigible.

"All right, I'm going to get ready. See you later." I head back upstairs, take a shower, and get dressed. Once I've finished my ablutions, I reapply my new make-up using the techniques the lady showed me at John Lewis. The result isn't perfect, but for a first attempt, I think I've done a pretty good job.

Humming a merry tune, I pop in my stud earrings and play my Disney CD on repeat. Spinning round a couple of times, I'm in high spirits singing along with "Once Upon a Dream" from *Sleeping Beauty*. I imagine myself as Princess Aurora, dancing with her Prince Charming. Tonight, my fairy tale is going to come true. It's just got to.

At six-thirty, I receive a text from Nick telling me he's parked outside. I get a rush of butterflies as I apply my lipstick. Hurriedly, I pat down my hair, check that I've got everything, then race downstairs to the hall. Shouting goodbye to Dad, I unlock the front door and step out into the cool evening air.

With a thudding heart, I stall on the drive, surveying the panorama of semi-detached houses in search of Nick's Jag.

I start to panic. I can't see him anywhere.

Then I hear a loud beep and start smiling; now I see him. Swallowing hard, I glance left and right, then cross the street and walk toward the car.

When I get in, I let out an audible sigh. He blinks at me a second.

For a moment, neither of us says a word. James Brown is crooning softly from the stereo. I can't believe I'm really here, sitting next to him again.

"I've missed you so much," I breathe.

Nick doesn't answer. He just stares at me, eyes wandering from my face to my dress and then back again, taking in every last detail.

"Wow," he murmurs, touching the side of my face. "You look absolutely stunning."

I nod eagerly, too excited to speak. He continues to stroke my cheek, milking a small sigh from my lips. I'm so starved of his love that just one touch makes my head swim.

Reaching down, he gently threads his fingers through mine. With his other hand, he steers us out of my street and onto the main road in the direction of East London. As he drives, his eyes keep flickering back to my legs, a roguish smirk on his lips. I grin broadly, secretly loving all the attention. Being next to him like this, knowing how much he wants me, is the best feeling in the world and I never want it to end. Inwardly, I'm singing; the night is off to a cracking start.

Around a quarter to eight, we reach the Spitalfields Steakhouse on Commercial Street, an inconspicuous building that from outside looks like a disused warehouse. Inside, however, the restaurant is vast and sumptuous, with low ceilings and old-fashioned lamps lining the walls to provide light in the absence of windows.

As soon as we enter, a smartly dressed waiter checks my reservation, and then leads us through the crowded restaurant to our table at the back. So far, I'm impressed. The Spitalfields Steakhouse has lived up to its prestigious reputation.

"Wow, what a fabulous place," Nick comments as we get seated. "What a wonderful surprise. Thanks so much for bringing me here."

"I'm so glad you like it, darling," I say. "I wanted everything to be perfect."

"It's always perfect when I'm with you."

We smile warmly at each other.

The waiter hands us two fancy-looking menus and asks for our drinks order. Without missing a beat, I request a bottle of Château Begadan Cru Artisan Médoc.

"Wow, I'm really getting spoiled tonight," Nick laughs. "I wonder what other surprises you have in store."

I smile mysteriously. Averting my eyes, I study the menu. "So, how was Cambridge? I want to hear all about what happened there."

"Do we really have to? I'd much rather talk about you."

"There isn't much to tell."

"Oh, come on. Humour me."

I release a sigh. "I just spent every day missing you, waiting for you to get back. It's been too long."

"I know," he agrees. "Each second I was apart from you was agony." He reaches over, touches my face and I feel myself melting. I take a massive gulp of water to calm my racing heart.

At that moment, the waiter returns with the wine and

takes down our food order. Nick has Tamworth pork ribs for starters and a lobster for mains. I have blue cheese soup followed by steak with new potatoes. For dessert, we order chocolate fudge sundaes.

"How's your food?" Nick asks as I plough through my second course.

I close my eyes in rapture. "Tastes divine. How's yours?"

"Delicious. Why don't you try some?"

I nod eagerly, and he feeds me a forkful. "Mmm, I wish I'd got that now," I grin.

We talk for a while about his trip to Cambridge. Apparently, he'd had to meet some people to organise the convention he's attending in Toronto next June. Meanwhile, I cheerfully update him on the comings and goings at my office: Jill's gushing appraisal of him, Mark's argument with Tim, a lost dog we found in the street.

As the waiter takes away our dishes, he gives me a convert wink and my cheeks flush with excitement. That's our secret code to confirm that everything I agreed with the staff is on track. It's time to set the wheels in motion and I get a sudden pang of nerves, terrified that something will go wrong.

"Carly, are you okay?" Nick asks. "You look a little agitated."

"No, I'm fine."

At that precise moment, the waiter returns with our desserts, and the music changes from soft, tinkling jazz to "Talk to Me, Talk to Me" by Little Willie John, Nick's favourite song.

He shoots me a look, and I realise then that I've been rumbled. He knows I set this whole thing up for him; the song is too obscure to have been randomly selected by the restaurant. Before he can speak, I reach across the table, slip my hand over his and gaze deeply into his eyes. My fingers are shaking, but I know there's no turning back now. I just have to go through with it. I have to let him know what I'm feeling.

"Nick, listen, there's something I need to tell you."

"Go on," he says gently.

I take a deep breath. "I was living half a life before I met you. I was drifting through darkness, numb to everything; it wasn't a life, it was just existing. Then you came along and saved me. Brought light and love to everything." I pause as a signal to the waiter. Obediently, he places a chocolate layer cake before Nick emblazoned with the words: *Will you marry me?*

Nick gawps at it.

Clenching my jaw, I reach in my bag and pull out a small, crocheted pouch. Wordlessly, I slide it across the table. Nick's lips begin to tremble. Slowly, he opens the pouch and takes out a court-shaped engagement ring, rounded below and on the top. He stares at it a second, then he lifts his eyes, and they look strangely seared; not the reaction I'm expecting. Nonetheless, I persevere.

Taking his hand again, I whisper, "Darling, will you marry me?"

He opens his mouth and moves his lips silently, helplessly. Then he gives up completely. I've put him on the spot, and he hasn't a clue what to do.

My heart is thudding like a machine gun. Scratching the side of my neck, I glance nervously around the restaurant. Dozens of eyes are on us. Clearly, we've caught the attention of the other diners, and Nick's stillness is starting to get embarrassing. Jesus, I just wish he'd say something, instead of leaving me hanging like this.

I swallow painfully, trying to assess the situation. It's difficult to tell what he's thinking. Is he pleased or angry with me? Finally, his smile warms up and begins to look a little more natural. He takes the ring out of the pouch, tries it on a couple of fingers before settling for the one next to his pinkie on his left hand. Then with a low sigh, he looks up at me, eyes shimmering with tears.

"I'm completely speechless," he whispers. "Are you sure this is definitely what you want?"

"You know it is."

"I-I don't know what to say."

"Say yes. Make me the happiest woman alive. All it takes is one word, Nick. Please, I want to spend the rest of my life with you."

He remains silent, his face tight as a corpse.

A lady at the next table sits on tenterhooks awaiting his decision.

"Nick…" My eyes plead with him. "Say something."

He licks his lips and gives a small, wan smile. "If it's certain to make you happy, then yes, I'll marry you."

The waiter's shoulders sag with relief, and the whole room breathes a collective sigh. Then the other diners start clapping, cheering, and stamping their feet. Nick gets up, comes around to my side of the table and hugs me. Now I'm crying, too; I've never been so happy. I can't believe this is really happening.

When the entire furore is over, we return to our seats and finish our desserts. I pour Nick another drink.

"Does the ring fit all right?" I ask anxiously. "The jeweller said we can have another size made if it doesn't."

"No need, it fits perfectly," Nick grins. "Like a glove. You know me so well." He pauses. "Aren't you going to have any wine? You've been on water all night."

"I know. I'd love to join you, but I'm on medication at the moment, so alcohol is strictly off-limits."

He raises an eyebrow. "What medication?"

"Oh, just some antibiotics prescribed by my doctor. You know, for that flu I had?"

"I thought you were all better now?"

"I am, but I've still got to take the full course regardless. You know how it is."

Nick nods and drops the subject.

I'm relieved. I don't fancy talking about my depression or my increasing dependency on Thurlax.

When the bill comes, I give it the onceover and place my card on the table. Nick bats it away and fumbles for his wallet, but this time I stand my ground. Tonight is all about my wonderful husband-to-be, and no expense will be spared. Reluctantly, Nick accepts my generosity but insists he must make it up to me tomorrow by taking me somewhere equally as swanky. As we finish our drinks, he asks me if I'm going to tell my father about our engagement.

"Of course," I smile. "I'm going to tell everybody. I want the whole world to know."

He nods serenely, but his face seems troubled.

"What about you?" I ask brightly. "Are you going to tell your family about us? Your brothers, your sister?"

He puts down his glass and suddenly looks uncomfortable. "Yes, I suppose I should call them to share our wonderful news. They're travelling across Europe at the moment, but I'm sure they'll be happy to cut their excursions short."

"What about Tara? Are you going to tell her?"

"Of course. She can be one of our bridesmaids."

I squeal with delight. "Oh, Nick, it's going to be amazing, isn't it? We've got so much planning to do. I want us to get married as soon as possible. It doesn't have to be anything too fancy. Just a couple of people and—"

"Whoa, slow down," he laughs. "What's the hurry?"

I make a face. "What do you mean? I thought you'd want us to tie the knot as soon as possible. What's holding us back?"

"Nothing. I just meant there's no harm in taking our time to do things properly. I want everything to be absolutely perfect. I want us to plan things properly, make it the best day of our lives. I mean, who knows? We might even want to get married abroad. How does a spring wedding in Italy grab you? I know a beautiful village in Tuscany. Sprawling vineyards. Old-world charm. You'd love it."

I reach across the table and hold his hand. "Italy? Oh, my gosh, that sounds so romantic."

WE ARRIVE BACK in Pimlico around midnight. As we step out the car, I sigh happily at the star-scattered sky, privately wishing this night would last forever. It's been a truly magical evening, and it all still feels a bit unreal. I can't believe Nick's agreed to be my husband. It's like a wonderful dream I never want to wake up from.

Taking my hand, Nick locks the car and leads me into the house. He switches on the lights, then goes to the kitchen and fetches a bottle of wine from under the sink. Back in the living room, we sit on the couch and he pours himself a drink. Wearily, I kick off my shoes and flex my toes. I'm so glad to be out of those goddamn heels; they've been pinching my feet all night.

For a moment, I sit perched on the sofa, staring at the floor, thinking. Then I glance out of the corner of my eye and catch Nick watching me. His face is filled with love.

"What?" I smile.

He doesn't answer. Setting down his drink, he pulls me onto his lap and kisses me with an urgency that takes my breath away. Grabbing the back of his head, I pull his face into mine and moan softly as our tongues dance together in a tango of lust. There is nothing else on this planet, only him and me and the rapid beating of my heart.

At last, I come up for air, breathing pretty hard. "Mmm, that was nice," I whisper, half-closing my eyes. "We're going to be so happy, aren't we?"

He responds by devouring my lips again, eating me out like he can't get enough. His hands move to my dress zipper.

"Wait," I say, pulling back. "I forgot to tell you. I got you another engagement present."

"What?" He gives me a reproachful look. "Carly, you've got to stop spoiling me. Don't you think you've spent enough already? I dread to think how much all this has cost you."

"Who cares? It's only money. My love for you is priceless." Tenderly, I plant a kiss on his forehead, then climbing off him, I fumble through my bag in search of the gift I bought from the jewellers. "Okay, close your eyes."

With a playful smirk, Nick screws his eyes shut.

"No peeking now," I scold. "Hold out your hand…"

He obliges and I place a sterling silver crucifix into his palm. Instantly, he starts screaming and races out of the room like he's on fire. Shock rattles through me.

What in the hell?

Scarcely daring to breathe, I follow Nick into the kitchen

and find him huddled over the sink, running the cold tap over his hands. He's got his back to me, so I can't see his face, but there's a horrible sense of foreboding in the air; a sense that I'm in the presence of something abnormal.

"Darling, what's wrong? Are you okay?" My voice is barely a whisper.

He doesn't answer.

I stand in the doorway. Tense. Waiting. A smothering stillness descends over us.

The tap continues to run. Nervously, I take a step forward and join him at the sink. "Nick, what's going on?"

He still doesn't say anything, and I shiver. All of a sudden, the room seems to have gotten cold. I stare at his shoulders. He's shaking uncontrollably. *What on Earth's the matter with him?*

Gently, I touch his arm and glance down at his hands. My temperature drops to zero. *Fuck!* I'm coming apart inside. The crucifix has burned a deep imprint in his palm, the heat so scorching I can actually see smoke rising from the incision. And then I look up at his face and a crippling fear seeps through every pore of my soul.

Nick's face has lost all trace of humanity. His head is swollen and misshapen; his skin as white as chalk, his eyes sunk back in his head with bloated pouches beneath. His lips are the most frightening: cracked and twisted in a grimace that reveal razor-sharp upper incisor teeth.

Sweet Jesus.

I dare not move, dare not breathe or blink as I watch what the man I love has become.

And then he stares at me with those awful, red eyes, and I feel powerless to do anything. I'm frozen; transfixed on him like a blind woman who has suddenly regained her sight.

"I'm s-sorry…" he rasps. "Please…"

A cold paralysis creeps up my neck and my back. It's like a gate has been thrown open, letting in a flood of images I've refused to look at until now. Little dark pieces of a jigsaw coming together to create the most horrendous picture: Jessica's murder, the strange dream, flashes of Nick making love to me. Somehow, everything culminates in one horrific conclusion …

With an anguished cry, I bolt out the kitchen and scramble upstairs to the bathroom. Locking the door, I collapse on the floor, my whole body trembling with fear. "Jesus!" I rock back and forth, screaming and crying. "Jesus, Jesus!"

This can't be real; I must be hallucinating. Perhaps I finally *have* lost my mind. Yes, that's it; it must be the Thurlax making me see things. No way in Hell can this really be happening. I don't believe in …

No.

I won't even allow myself to think it.

And then there's a quiet knock at the door. I shriek with terror.

"Darling, let me in." Nick's voice is a soft and soothing lullaby, slinky as a box of chocolates. Somehow, this makes everything all the more horrific.

"Go away!" I shout. "I-I don't want to see you."

"Carly, baby, please open the door. I need to talk to you."

"No!"

"Darling, I love you. If you'll just let me explain—"

"You're a vampire. A f-fucking vampire, a v-vampire …"

There.

I've said it. The man I love is a vampire. A bloodsucker. A creature of the night. But even as I say it, I'm overcome with a deep sense of incredulity. What the hell am I babbling?

Vampires aren't real. They only exist in books and movies, a figment of Bram Stoker's overactive imagination. This is real life, for Christ's sake. I have a job, a family, I go to the shopping mall, I do normal things. My world is so friggin' mundane, vampires just don't figure.

"My God, this is driving me crazy," Nick shouts. "I want you so much, Carly. I worship the ground you walk on. I need to hold you, to be with you. If I don't, I'm going to do something stupid."

"You're a monster!" I cry. "Y-you killed Jessica."

There's a long, black silence. I say it again. "Y-you killed Jessica. You sucked her f-fucking blood."

"No, I didn't. Please, you've got to believe me. I didn't kill anyone."

"Yes, you did! You k-killed her, and now you're going to kill me."

He slams his fist against the door, causing me to cower back against the bath. My stomach lurches, and I fight the urge to throw up. I need as much distance between us as possible. Then I hear him sobbing, crying like his whole world has ended, and my heart breaks a little.

"I could never hurt you," he chokes. "I love you more than anything. You know that."

"You lied to me, Nick! You lied to me about everything. All this time, you've been hiding the truth from me. I thought you were perfect, but you're a vampire and a murderer and, oh, Jesus… I can't believe I'm saying this. Either this is some sort of nightmare, or I must be going crazy. This can't be real."

Nick continues to cry, the full weight of his body pressed against the door. "So, is this how it ends?" he sobs. "You're going to just leave me standing here? What happened to forever, Carly? What happened to all those promises you made? You said you'd love me no matter what. You said you wanted to marry me."

"I-I did. But that was before... oh, God, I can't take this." And then I start crying, too.

Nick scrapes his fingernails down the door. "Please, let me in. Let me hold you, darling. I promise I can take all the pain away."

"No..." I wipe my nose on my sleeve. "I can't ever open this door."

He slams his fists again. "I warned you, Carly. Right from the start, I told you I was no good. I told you to stay away from me, but you wouldn't listen. I never wanted to bring you into this, but you made me fall in love with you. What the hell was I supposed to do? You were so damned persistent."

I get a hold of myself, partly. "Did you kill Jessica?"

"No!"

"Then who did?"

He falls silent.

Minutes pass. On the other side of the door, I can hear him breathing. *A monster breathing.* I think about my next move, ways to escape, but my brain has gone into meltdown. The four walls of the bathroom have suddenly become a prison, and I'm starting to feel hemmed in. *Like a caged animal.*

Blinking back tears, I imagine Jessica sprawled on a bed, her pale face twisted and caked with blood. My inner compass is telling me that deep down, I've always known what Nick is. That weird instinct that drew me to buy the crucifix was telling me something. At the time, I couldn't understand the attraction, but now I see that a higher power was leading me to the truth.

My God.

Glancing down at Nick's pendant, my resolve starts to weaken. The diamond weighs heavy on my chest as a constant reminder of the love we once shared, a bond I thought could never be broken. I think of the wonderful, caring man I fell in love with and find it hard to reconcile this with the horrendous apparition standing behind this door. *This has got to be a hallucination.*

"I can't do this, Nick," I breathe. "I-I can't hate you. I know I should, but I can't." Covering my eyes, I muffle another sob, mascara streaming all down my cheeks. This is too much to bear. I still love him, and no matter how hard I try, these feelings just won't go away. But how can I continue loving a monster? A despicable creature that may well have murdered an innocent young woman?

Wiping my face, I drag myself across the floor and press my cheek against the door. "Tell me everything," I whisper. "I need to know the truth. Tell me I'm not crazy. What I saw in the kitchen...that was real, wasn't it? I didn't imagine it."

There's a short beat. Then he replies, "No, you didn't."

"Fucking hell." I lubricate my throat. "So, that time you came to my bedroom, and I thought it was a dream... When you came through my window, that wasn't a fantasy, was it? You really came to see me and you almost... Jesus!"

"I'm so sorry, darling. It was never my intention to hurt you." He sucks air through his teeth. "I wish to God you'd heeded my warning and stayed away from me. We could have avoided all this pain, and you could have continued living in blissful ignorance. But now, it's too late."

"Too late? What do you mean?"

"You're part of me now, Carly. I love you too much to ever let you go."

I make no response. My voice has deserted me. I just sit against the door, staring into space, staring at nothing. Gradually, I return to my senses. "I-I want to know what happened with Jessica. Did you visit her at night like you did me? Did you go to her house?"

"Stop this! I told you, I never touched her."

"Then who did? Tell me that, Nick. I want so much to believe you, but can't you see my predicament? Can't you understand how difficult this is for …" I break down again.

"Easy there," he soothes. "Everything's going to be all right. There's nothing to fear, my darling. You know I love you. You know I would never hurt you. We can get through this. I just know we can. Take your time, relax, close your eyes…"

Reluctantly, I follow his instructions and shudder as a wave of calm floods through me. His voice drifts in and out of my awareness, travelling up my legs and into my thighs, infusing my body with a deep sense of relaxation. I'm completely spellbound. His hold on me is as strong as ever, and it takes all my strength to keep my eyes open.

"That's right…" he purrs. "Empty your mind completely. Relax every part of your body. Don't think about anything, just focus on my voice. Let all your worries fade away to nothing, and just breathe, baby. *Breathe.*"

My eyelids droop. When I open them again, I'm lying in a small, white room with the heavy smell of antiseptic all around me. The door opens and a nurse enters. "Your mother's here to see you, Carly. Shall I tell her to come in?"

"No, tell her to go away. I don't want to see anyone. You know I'm still not ready."

My life flashes before my eyes. It all feels completely hopeless. I cover my face with my hands, shaking uncontrollably. It's all too much, the fear, the terror. Everything I've been bottling up comes crashing down. I have no sense of time or space. No sense of who I am or *where* I am; just a swirling vortex of misery.

Then I'm flying through cornflower skies and fields of green, dipping and swaying at breath-taking speed. Looking straight down, I yelp as blood rushes to my head. Gaining altitude, my stomach plummets. Slowly, I start to descend, and then I hear a funny popping sound in my ears that makes my throat all dry. Next thing I know I'm back on solid ground, my head so woozy I can barely see straight. When the fog clears, I'm lying on an emerald-green hill with the sun blazing down on me. I shut my eyes, relishing the heat on my skin as a gentle breeze blows tendrils of hair in my face. Dreamily, I gaze up at the sky, an endless canvass of shimmering blue. Suddenly, an old-fashioned hot air balloon appears in the distance, floating closer and closer until it's almost level with me. Smiling, I get to my feet and take Nick's engagement ring out of my pocket. Slowly, I walk up to the balloon, place the ring in the gondola and watch it drift away to nothing.

Free.

I am finally free.

Then everything starts weaving and swirling around me and I find myself in a vast, shadowy hall with a bearskin rug stretched before a flickering fireplace. The room appears to be empty, the ceilings so high my neck hurts trying to look up. In the far distance, I can see a trio of arched doors that I presume lead to other parts of the building.

For a few heartbeats, I gaze up at the enormous sloped windows, their glass blacked out so it's impossible to tell whether it's night or day. I don't like this room; it feels warm and grand yet somehow curiously devoid of life. All around…silence. An icy, dead silence broken only by the spit and crackle from the fireplace.

Cautiously, I cross the hall and head toward the first of the large, heavily engraved doors. It's locked, so I try the second. Still no joy, so I try the third. This time, I'm in luck.

Pushing open the door, I enter a small, white room. In the centre sits a big stone platform surrounded by candles with a picture of the Virgin Mary at the head. A black-velvet shroud covers the entire surface, and for some reason, the sight of it fills me with dread. I want to run, want to look away, but it's like I'm bound by an invisible force. Something ominous is calling out to me, drawing me irrepressibly forward.

Hesitantly, I approach the shroud and pull it back to reveal an eight-cornered coffin. With trembling fingers, I slip my hands beneath the lid and open it. My heart thuds in my ears, every nerve ending tingles.

There's a corpse inside the coffin, a corpse with *my face*. Ghostly white. Lips as red as blood. Sockets of coal for eyes.

I cup one hand over my mouth. "Oh, my God!"

Then I sense that I'm being watched; a horrible feeling, like icy fingers stroking my skin. Touching me. Caressing me. I am not alone.

I can feel it.

Consumed with terror, I spin around expecting to be dealt a blow, expecting to see someone or *something* behind me.

What I see is far worse than I ever could have imagined.

With a loud gasp, I pop open my eyes and settle back to the current moment. My breath comes in ragged bursts, and my hair is plastered to my face. I shake my head, desperately battling Nick's hold over me. I cannot, *will not*, allow him to manipulate me like this. Gritting my teeth, I focus hard and manage to throw off his influence like an unwanted cloak, digging my way back from the pit to come up fighting on the other side.

Unsteadily, I get to my feet and slide onto the edge of the bathtub. For a while, I'm lost in a strange world, a world filled with vampires and werewolves and just about every kind of monster imaginable. But no matter how terrifying that world is, no matter how strange, nothing beats the insanity of the world outside this bathroom.

Finally, I snap out of it and stumble over to the sink, careering to and fro like a drunk. With a cold deadness in my heart, I gaze at my reflection and flinch. I look so worn, so haggard; like I've aged about ten years in the last hour.

I guess that's what shock does to a person.

Turning on both taps, I wet my face, pat it dry with a towel, then take a long drink of water. Wiping my mouth, I put down the cup and frame some words in my mind, but nothing makes sense. I stand for what seems like hours, listening to the wind in the trees and the silence of the house. Behind the locked door, Nick has stopped speaking, stopped breathing; he hasn't made a peep in ages.

I start to feel claustrophobic again. The room seems to be getting smaller; the walls closing in on me like some crazy optical illusion. I clutch my throat and gag. It's like there's an invisible rope pulling tighter and tighter, strangling all the air from my lungs.

My mind is made up.

Vampire or no, I can't stay locked in this bathroom forever.

Taking a deep breath, I raise my eyes Heavenward and

pray for protection. Perhaps these will be my final seconds on Earth. Perhaps the moment I open that door, Nick will pounce on me and it will all be over. Who knows? All I know is I can't spend another minute in this stifling prison. Bracing myself for the worst, I jerk forward and force my feet to move. I stall for a moment, remembering Nick's horribly deformed face, the deranged look in his eyes, his razor-sharp teeth and lose my nerve temporarily. *Hold it together. Hold it together.* I shut my eyes, calling forth every ounce of courage I can muster. *Come on. You can do this.*

Slowly, I turn the lock and step out into the landing.

CHAPTER THIRTEEN

Fear in the Night

T HE HOUSE IS silent as the grave. Cautiously, I step out of the bathroom into the landing, eyes shut, preparing to meet with my maker. I stand in the doorway for what seems forever, heart slamming against my chest, dutifully waiting for the axe to fall; waiting patiently for the man I love to put me out of my misery.

Minutes pass.

Slowly, I open my eyes and survey the panorama of the first-floor landing. No sign of Nick anywhere. With doors on either side, there's now only one direction to go. Tentatively, I edge toward the banister, my knees weak with apprehension. Soundlessly, I make my way downstairs one step at a time, hoping and praying that the wood doesn't creak.

Shit.

This is the longest walk I've ever taken.

Slowly, slowly, I continue to descend until finally, I touch back down in the hallway. I breathe a sigh of relief. So far, so good. The floor tiles feel cool against my feet and I vaguely remember leaving my boots somewhere in the living room, along with my bag and phone.

Dammit.

I need them, but now is not the time to go searching for lost shoes. No sir, I'm not out of the woods yet. There are so many places for Nick to hide; so many shadowy corners, he could be lurking virtually anywhere, waiting to pounce on me.

Right now, all I must focus on is getting out of here. *My very life depends on it.*

Pressing my back against the wall, I slide cautiously toward the front door, my movements slow and timid as a mouse. Bit by bit, inch by inch, I ease myself closer to freedom. *Oh God, please don't let anything go wrong. Please!*

Finally, I reach my destination.

With trembling fingers, I turn the latch, push open the door and step out into the night. For a brief second, I stand at the entrance to Nick's house, unable to believe I've actually made it out of there alive. It feels so surreal. Snapping from my stupor, I stumble down the steps into the street.

My eyes dart about wildly. I'm still not convinced I'm safe. Glancing left and right, I survey the semi-circle of white regency houses with their blacked-out windows. The place seems eerily deserted; not a single light is on and for a moment, it's like I'm the only person left on the planet. I get a sick feeling as the full horror of my predicament dawns on me. It's the middle of the night and I'm stuck in a strange area, alone and afraid, in my bare feet and a flimsy pink mini dress. Worse still, the man I love is a …

No.

I won't even allow myself to think it.

Mustering all my strength, I stagger across the road, taking care to avoid stones and pieces of broken glass. Somehow, someway, I've got to find a way out of this nightmare. Tilting my head, I scrutinise the empty street again. No sign of a bus stop anywhere and I haven't a clue how to get to the train station. Where I am is anybody's guess, but I have to keep going. With renewed determination, I start walking again, only to stop abruptly as something sharp presses into my heel. Screaming silently, I raise my foot and find a metal pull tab from a Coke can has lodged itself in my skin.

Hastily, I brush it off and flinch. *No bleeding, thank God.*

Painfully, I hobble on the sides of my heels to the end of the street in the hope of flagging down a passing car. For an interminable time, I stand on the sidewalk, waving frantically to every vehicle that passes, but nobody seems interested in my plight. Can I really blame them? I know I must look deranged, what with my panda eyes and tangled hair, but surely someone cares enough to at least pull over and check that I'm okay? What has the world come to? Are people really that insensitive?

Every so often, I glance furtively back at Nick's house, hoping against hope that he doesn't follow me outside. If I ever have to see his face again, the way he looked in the kitchen …

Oh God.

The low growl of an engine pulls me from my thoughts. Squinting through the darkness, I spy a taxi pulling up to the curb opposite; a large, bald-headed man is beckoning me to come over.

Is he for real?

Wiping sweat from my brow, I stagger up to the half-open passenger side window.

"Where to, love?" the cabbie asks.

"Battersea. And p-please make it quick."

He nods and hits a switch on the armrest to unlock the door. Sobbing with relief, I jump in, unable to believe my good fortune. Almost immediately, we're on the move. He yanks the wheel from left to right and keeps on driving until the darkness has consumed all traces of the nightmare I've endured.

For a few heartbeats, I sit rigidly in the back seat, hugging my arms tightly for protection. Tears wet my cheeks. I'm coming apart inside and my nerves are shot to shreds. I keep talking to myself; babbling a load of disjointed sentences that make no sense.

I reckon the cabbie must think I'm either drunk, crazy, or both.

Probably both.

"This can't be happening," I mutter under my breath. "Vampires don't exist. This is a fucking hallucination. It's got to be!"

"Had a rough night?" the cabbie asks. When I don't respond, he turns his head and steals a quick glance at me. "Here look, are you sure you're all right back there? Do you need me to take you to the hospital or something?"

"No."

"The police station?"

"No, I'm fine."

"You don't look it, love. To be honest, I think you look pretty terrible. Have you been in a fight?"

"No, like I said I—"

"And what happened to your shoes? Why are you walking around in bare feet?"

"I must have lost them somewhere. Thanks for your concern, but you needn't worry. I've just had a little too much to drink. It was my friend's birthday, you see…" My voice trails off. I'm so weak, so drained, it's a struggle for me to form coherent sentences.

"Are you definitely sure you're okay?"

"Yes!"

Finally, he takes the hint and focuses back on the road. *Thank goodness.*

Turning my head, I gaze out the window at the cold West London streets. It's started to rain again, transforming everything into a coloured mosaic. As the taxi rolls along, I relive the evening's shocking events, trying to convince myself that it isn't true. How can Nick Craven, the man I love, the man I wanted to marry only a few short hours ago, be a bloodsucking vampire? It's utterly inconceivable.

Every time I close my eyes, I see him; I can't shake him off, no matter what I do. In the air, his silky voice follows me around like a distant melody. I feel the softness of his fingers against my skin, stroking me, caressing me. He's so close I can almost taste him.

Nick made me love him more than anything in the world, and now he's completely destroyed me. If what I saw tonight was real, if that horrific apparition in the kitchen really *was* a vampire, then I really don't know where to go from here. I remember his chalk-white skin, red sunken eyes and razor-sharp teeth; the murderous expression on his face as he held the burning crucifix. How could that have been real? How could my perfect husband-to-be have turned into a monster before my very eyes? It *has* to have been a hallucination—a weird delusion caused by the Thurlax or the wine I don't remember drinking.

"We're not far from Battersea now." The cabbie's deep voice brings me back to my senses. "Where do you live? Do you have the postcode and house number?"

I tell him the address and he programs it into his Sat Nav.

A little after four am, we pull back into my street. The rain has stopped, but the air retains an ominous chill.

"Okey-dokey, that will be fifteen twenty, but let's call it fifteen," the cabbie says as he parks up.

For a moment, I sit silently, my hands folded in my lap. "What did you say?"

"I said, that will be fifteen pounds, please."

I stare dumbly at him. Then I suddenly get his meaning. *Shit!* How am I going to pay the fare? Absently, I reach for my handbag and freeze when I remember that I left it back at Nick's house, along with my phone.

I slap my hand across my forehead. "I'm so sorry, but could you hold on a second? I just need to run inside and get some money."

He nods stiffly. Clearly, he's getting a little hacked off with me.

Throwing open the door, I race across the street toward my house. As I march up the gravel drive, I notice that all of the ground floor lights are off. *Great.* My dad's asleep and certainly won't appreciate being woken up in the middle of the night, but what choice do I have? My keys are in the bag I left at Nick's.

Bracing myself for a barrage of questions, I ring the doorbell and wait.

A minute passes.

Two.

I ring the bell again, and this time hold my finger down on the buzzer. No reply. *That's strange.* I call through the letterbox. "Hey Dad! It's me, Carly. Can you let me in, please?"

Still no response.

Chewing my bottom lip, I glance back at the taxi. The cabbie rolls his eyes and shakes his head. Crouching down, I look through the letterbox and gasp when I see my father slumped on the hall floor, his arms contorted at a weird angle.

Fuck!

"Dad!" I yell. "Wake up, wake up!"

His body remains rigid.

"What's the matter?" the cabbie shouts. "Are you okay?"

"Something's happened to my dad!" I shout back. "We need to call an ambulance."

CHAPTER FOURTEEN

Panic

I RUB MY eye with one knuckle and blink a couple of times. My vision is blurry and it's a struggle for me to keep awake. Unsteadily, I take another swig of lukewarm coffee, wipe my mouth with the back of my hand, and place the cup on the table. I glance at my *Kermit the Frog* watch.

Nine twenty-five am.

Jesus, I don't know how much longer I can keep going without any sleep.

I'm sitting in a small green waiting room in the Hyper Acute Stroke Unit at Queen Victoria Hospital in Tooting. I've been here for well over three hours, drinking endless cups of coffee and praying that my father is going to make it. The paramedics say he's had a stroke, the severity of which is still being determined. No one yet knows what the long-lasting effects will be—if he's paralysed, if he's got brain damage—it's still too early to say. They can't say with certainty what caused the stroke, but won't rule out Dad's pot smoking, or his reluctance to take his blood pressure pills on time. No one can put my mind at rest, so right now, all I can do is wait for an update.

I press my fingers to my temples and shake my head ruefully. These past few hours have been a complete nightmare. After the taxi driver called for an ambulance, we were hit with yet another hurdle when the paramedics arrived and said they were not authorised to break the door down to get my father out. As a result, we were forced to wait another twenty minutes for the police to arrive. Thankfully, one of the officers managed to access the property through a back window, saving them having to kick the door in.

After, I spent the whole journey to the hospital hating myself for not getting there sooner, tearfully imagining a future without my dear old dad. The Queen Victoria in Tooting was not our nearest hospital, but the ambulance brought us here because it's the only one in South London that provides comprehensive aftercare for patients with neurorehabilitation needs. Its recent refurbishment and state-of-the-art equipment mean my father is in the best possible place to pull through. I just hope to God he makes it. I don't know what I'll do if he dies and I never got to say goodbye; never got to tell him just how much I love him, or how much he means to me.

Shivering, I wrap my dressing gown more tightly around my shoulders, and wonder if the nurses could turn up the heating. The ward is freezing and I dread to think what this could be doing to the elderly, more vulnerable patients. With conditions like this, is it any wonder people catch pneumonia? Despite this, I have to admit that most of the staff have been lovely.

When I first stepped out of the ambulance in my skimpy mini dress, someone immediately found me a pair of slippers to wear. There have also been non-stop offers of tea and biscuits, which I certainly can't complain about. My only gripe is the lack of communication regarding my father's condition. Since the initial assessment made by the paramedics on the way down to the hospital, no one has been able to give me a solid diagnosis or tell me the name of Dad's doctor. I appreciate staff at the NHS are run off their feet, but really, three hours with no updates is simply not acceptable.

Gritting my teeth, I try to stay calm and hold it together. Every fibre of my being wants to sleep and I'm constantly on the verge of losing it, but somehow I keep going. I don't know how, but I do. I need to stay strong for my father. *He needs me more than anything.*

Faint vestiges of the horror from earlier still linger on my mind, but I try to shake them off; try to block out those dark, nagging doubts that threaten to master me. For the sake of my sanity, I have decided that what happened at Nick's house must have been a powerful hallucination—or I must have dreamed the entire episode. It's the only rational explanation.

I mean, how can Nick possibly be a vampire? He walks around in daylight and certainly doesn't sleep in a coffin. He's one of the country's leading hypnotherapists! He's got friends in high places, has treated CEOs and Premiere League football players; he's helped Becky Bullock off the *Essex Show* lose two stone. Oh, and he enjoys a glass of wine and going out to eat at expensive restaurants. If Nick is a vampire with a chronic blood dependency, then surely someone else would have noticed by now?

That's what I tell myself, anyway.

"Hi, are you Steve Singleton's next of kin?"

I glance up and see a tall, dark-haired man standing in the doorway of the waiting room. He's holding a clipboard and dressed in a white laboratory-style coat with a stethoscope around his neck. He's got a nice, friendly face and sort of reminds me of Tom Selleck.

"Are you Steve Singleton's next of kin?" he repeats.

"Y-yes," I stammer, getting to my feet. "I'm his daughter,

Carly."

The man steps forward and shakes my hand. "Pleased to meet you, Carly. I'm Dr Richard Noble, the Consultant Stroke Physician. I've been assigned to your father."

"Great!" My smile begins to warm up. Now we're getting somewhere. "Has my dad regained consciousness?"

"Yes. I'm pleased to say he's making very good progress. You should be able to go in and see him in a minute, but I just need you to complete this form and discuss a couple of things with you. As his next of kin, we'll need your contact details plus your authorisation to go ahead with further tests."

"Tests? What sort of tests?"

"Perhaps you'd better sit down." Obediently, I allow him to guide back to my seat. He pulls up a chair opposite and hands me a pen and a clipboard. "Now listen, there's no easy way of saying this, but your father's stroke may have quite serious long-term implications."

"Oh my God, but he's going to live? Please tell me he's going to live."

The doctor pauses and lets his breath out slowly. "Yes, I'm confident he will live. So far, he's responded well to treatment, but there are a few things you should know. Firstly, the stroke has left the whole right side of his body completely paralysed and at the moment, he has no feeling in his arm. The stroke has also affected his vision, so he's seeing double and finds it very hard to co-ordinate his movements."

"Jesus Christ! Are you saying he'll never walk again? He's paralysed for life?"

"No, that's not what I'm saying. Please calm down. The symptoms I've described are actually quite common in stroke patients and part of our rehabilitation programme will involve trying to help him regain his mobility. But we can't make any promises. It's far too early to predict the extent to which his brain has been affected or what the long term effects on his quality of life will be. Your father's stroke was caused by a massive clot which has impaired the arteries supplying blood to the brain. To treat this, we're giving him aspirin along with a combination of other drugs to help thin his blood and hopefully dissolve the blockage. Remember every stroke is different and we have to treat each patient on a case-by-case basis. But for now, I'm pleased to report that your father seems coherent and I am hopeful he will make a full recovery."

I bury my hands in my knees to stop them from shaking. I can't believe what I'm hearing. My father's condition sounds far worse than I imagined, and it takes all of my strength not to break down in front of the doctor.

"When can I see him?" I whisper.

"As soon as you fill out this form," Dr Noble replies. "We need your consent to run an MRI scan on him to help us determine the level of damage to the brain. Afterwards we'll be able to give you a better picture of the way forward in terms of his treatment."

I force a smile. "Okay."

The doctor stands and heads for the door. "Right, I'll leave you to complete the form, then I'll send a nurse to fetch you and take you to see your father. Would you like a glass of water while you're waiting?"

"No, thanks. I've already had about six cups of coffee."

He laughs. The door closes and I'm alone again. Jesus, I wish Nick was here to cuddle me and tell me everything's going to be all right. It feels like I'm carrying the weight of the world on my shoulders, with no one to help lighten the load. I don't even have my phone to call my mother and let her know what's going on. My brain is like a sieve when it comes to memorising numbers, so I'll have to wait till I get home and go through Dad's old phone book.

Miserably, I fill out the consent form. My stomach is in knots. Despite Dr Noble's cheerful exterior, I sense that there's a lot he's not telling me. Is he really as confident about my dad's chances of survival as he's making out? And what the hell is this MRI scan? It all sounds so bloody morbid.

Five minutes later, a nurse called Issey arrives and takes me up to Churchill Ward on the third floor. The place is absolutely teeming with people and there's a constant sense of urgency in the air. Nervously, I follow Issey down the long, winding corridor to a small side room where I find my father lying in a bed with tubes coming out of his body. He's dressed in a flimsy blue hospital gown which makes his arms and legs look frighteningly emaciated.

I am in shock. I can't believe I haven't notice how skinny he is. With his penchant for baggy tops and hipster jeans, Dad's managed to hide the true extent of his deteriorating health, and this realisation cuts me to the core. Why, oh why didn't I try harder to get him to take his medication and quit smoking those damn joints?

In a numb haze, I stare down at my beloved father, my throat clogged with tears. He looks so weak and frail, I am in no doubt how close to death he is. *My God, I really think I'm going to lose him.*

"I'll leave the two of you alone," Issey says softly.

For long moments, I continue to stand there frozen. Finally, he opens his eyes and blinks at me a couple of times. His lids are red and swollen, his skin an ashy-grey colour. He doesn't move, doesn't speak, just smiles a weak, lopsided smile. I can see it hurts him to do it so I tell him to stop.

Reaching down, I gently take his hand in mine and finally, I start to crack. My tears fall slowly, bitterly. Grief turns to anger as the full seriousness of the situation hits me, and I realise just how easily this could have been avoided. Why the hell couldn't Dad have listened to what the doctor told him? Why couldn't he have just taken those damn blood pressure pills? Thanks to his carelessness, my father now faces the possibility of life in a wheelchair and for what? Getting a few cheap highs? Was it really worth all this pain and suffering?

There's so much I want to say to him; so much I want to get off my chest, but now is not the right time. In this delicate state, he wouldn't be able to handle it, and God knows the last thing he needs is more stress to bring on another stroke. No, for the sake of peace, I must keep my mouth shut and offer only my love and support. After all, who knows how much time we have left together? The doctor says Dad will make a full recovery, but what if he doesn't?

CHAPTER FIFTEEN

Frozen

FOR THE NEXT twenty minutes, I stay by Dad's bedside, soothing him and telling him everything's going to be okay. I let him know that Dr Noble is very optimistic and that he just needs to focus on getting better. Then, with a heavy heart, I say goodbye and pick up a taxi to take me home. I hate to leave my father in this state, but I simply must get some sleep. If not, I won't be able to do the things that need doing; now is not the time to have a breakdown. I need to hold it together for Dad's sake.

A little after eleven, I'm back in Battersea.

"Could you hold on a minute?" I say, unclipping my seatbelt. "I just need to run inside and get the money."

"No problem," the cabbie smiles.

Jumping out the car, I race across the street, braving the morning chill in my dressing gown and slippers. With frozen hands, I let myself in using Dad's front door keys, race to his bedroom and retrieve a wad of twenty-pound notes from the dresser. Then I head straight back outside and settle the fare.

When the taxi's gone, I return to the house feeling totally empty inside. I'm a zombie working on autopilot, lost in a nightmare I can't wake up from. I'm still having trouble processing what's happened.

In a daze, I stumble up to the bathroom. Approaching the

sink, I run the cold tap and splash some water on my face. I glance at my reflection. My eyes are swollen from crying and my cheeks are streaked with mascara. I bathe my face a second time and beg my fingers to stop trembling. I peek back at my reflection.

Damn it.

The mascara stains don't want to go. Cupping a handful of water, I aggressively rub the skin under my eyes, but this only makes it worse. Now it looks like I've been punched in the face.

Finally, I give up, pat my skin dry and return downstairs. I want so badly to sleep, but first I need to phone my mother to break the news about Dad. As I pass through the hall to the living room, something stops me in my tracks and makes me do a double-take. Frowning, I walk toward the shoe rack by the door, my eyes as wide as saucers. On the bottom shelf sits a pair of round-toed ankle boots—the same ones I wore to the restaurant last night and left at Nick's house.

Oh my God! What does this mean?

Incredulously, I crouch down to examine them more closely. Yes, no doubt about it, those are definitely the same boots. There's even mud still on the heels. Biting my thumbnail, I go to the kitchen and survey all of the work surfaces. Then I go to the living room and almost have a heart attack.

My dove clutch bag is lying on the coffee table.

Fuck!

I lunge on it and empty the entire contents onto the floor. Everything is present and accounted for: my phone, my purse, my make-up, my house keys.

Shit. Nick has been in the house today, but how did he get in? I'm certain the front and back doors were locked, and the police officer made sure all of the windows were closed before we left in the ambulance. I chew my lip perplexedly. Fleetingly, my mind races back to the strange dream I had a few weeks ago, the one where Nick came through my bedroom window in a billowing white mist.

Holy Mother of God. Is this proof that he *does* have supernatural abilities after all?

Rigidly, I continue to crouch on the floor, thinking about the whole situation. The idea of Nick being a vampire is beyond crazy, but what other explanation can there be? Standing up, I return to the front door and double check that it's definitely locked, then I inspect every window of every room of the house. When I'm satisfied that I'm definitely alone, I go back to the living room to try and figure it out.

Just how the hell did Nick access the property?

And then it hits me, and I give a crazy laugh, because the answer is so obvious, I can't believe I didn't see it before. *Nick used my keys to let himself in.* Of course! No mystery, no intrigue, no supernatural abilities. He must have driven to my house while I was at the hospital and dropped off my stuff. When he rang the bell and found no one was at home, he did the next best thing by letting himself in and leaving the bag in the sitting room.

With this puzzle finally solved, I start to breathe more easily. The fact that there's such a simple explanation gives me hope that the whole vampire theory might be equally redundant.

Picking my mobile up from the floor, I examine the screen and realise the battery's dead. Hurriedly, I go to my bedroom and attach it to the phone charger. With a heavy heart, I dial my mother's number. It rings a couple of times before she picks up.

"Carly! What a lovely surprise. It's so nice to hear your—"

"Mum, I've got something to tell you."

"What is it? Darling, you sound hysterical."

"Dad's had a stroke," I blurt. The line goes silent. "Mum, did you hear me?"

"Oh my God! When?"

"Last night."

"Oh my God, oh my God." The line goes quiet again, and I can hear her husband Michael in the background, asking what's going on. She quickly fills him in, then returns to the phone. "Right, sweetheart, we're coming down. Which hospital is your father in? Are you there now?"

"He's at the Queen Victoria in Tooting, but don't come yet, Mum. I've only just got home and I'm completely shattered. I need to sleep or I won't be able to function. Also, morning visiting hours are over. The nurses said we can't go back again until after four. I think we should—"

"For goodness sake," she interjects. "Why didn't you call me as soon as this happened? We could have come down ages ago. I don't like the thought of you having to deal with this on your own."

"I know, and I'm sorry. So much has happened, I just wasn't thinking; plus, I didn't have my phone on me." Hastily, I fill her in on everything else: what Dr Noble said, his hopes for Dad's recovery and the upcoming MRI scan.

"What ward is your father in?" Mum asks when I've finished. "I'm going to call the hospital now to check how he's doing. Then as soon as you're ready, Michael and I will come down and get you, and we can go there together this evening. How much sleep do you think you'll need?"

"Give it a few hours. Shall we say six o'clock?"

"Okay my darling. We'll see you then. I love you."

"Love you more." I hang up and stand by the window a second, taking time to soak it all in. Now that I've told my mother, it feels like a great weight has been lifted. Knowing I've got her and Michael's support makes me feel so much better about things. I am no longer alone; I now have other people to share the burden with.

Tossing the phone on the bed, I glance down at my beloved pendant and twirl the delicate chain between my fingers. Nick said it had once belonged to his late mother, and when he first gave it to me, I thought it was the most perfect, most romantic gesture ever; a symbol of a bond which could never be broken. Then I picture the demented expression on his face in the kitchen and remember the burning imprint left in his palm by the crucifix.

No! I shake my head. *I can't think about that.*

Sluggishly, I cross to the dresser and pick up my laptop. Taking it to the bed, I flip open the lid and boot up the Internet. As I wait for Explorer to load, I wonder if I'm doing the right thing. Really, I should be sleeping, but I simply can't resist opening Pandora's Box.

The Google homepage appears. Running my fingers down the keyboard, I type in the words 'Nick Craven vampire hypnotist.'

I hold my breath as the results page loads. Then I release a sigh.

Of course, nothing remotely supernatural comes up; just a bunch of hyperlinks and testimonials from The London Hypnotherapy Clinic website. Undeterred, I run a general search on the word 'vampire.' This time I get hundreds of results, everything from *Twilight* to Bram Stoker to Bat Boy from the now defunct *Weekly World*.

I rake my fingers through my hair in frustration. Of

course, I shouldn't be surprised. I mean what the hell was I expecting? A Wikipedia bio with a photo of Nick dressed in a bat cape and drooling fangs? I click on a website called *bloodsuckers.com* and read some of the most common facts about vampires. Mentally, I tick each one off as preposterous:

1. *Vampires are afraid of sunlight.* No, this definitely does not apply to Nick. I've seen him out in the daytime on more than one occasion.

2. *Vampires hate garlic.* Hmm. Now that's a tricky one. I've never put it to the test, but we've eaten at several restaurants and I don't remember Nick ever mentioning an aversion to garlic seasoning.

3. *Vampires sleep in coffins.* Ridiculous! Nick sleeps in a regular bed just like everyone else.

However, the hairs on my neck stand up when I come to bullet point number four:

Crossing the threshold. My eyes widen as I read the first few paragraphs. *'Evil cannot enter a man's home unless it is invited. Such myths apply to vampyres. Romanian folklore states that a vampyre cannot enter a person's house unless expressly invited by the occupant.'*

My mind races back to the first time Nick came to my house. He'd acted so strangely, refusing to come in until I'd formally invited him. At the time, it hadn't made much sense, but now …

I pound my knuckles against my head. "Stupid, stupid, stupid!"

What the hell am I doing? I shouldn't be wasting my energy on this crap. The only thing I should be focusing on is my father. He's the one who needs me. Reading all this

Hocus Pocus will only make me more paranoid and the last thing I want is to lose the plot completely.

In despair, I switch off my laptop and pad over to the dresser. Opening the top drawer, I pull out a pack of Marlboros; I almost tear the box to shreds trying to get them open. With shaky fingers, I light one and take a few shallow puffs, closing my eyes as the nicotine whips through my system. I take another puff and realise that I don't feel bad at all; in fact, I feel *exhilarated*. In my head, I can hear Nick's voice telling me not to, but I manage to blot it out. This is one battle he won't win.

"Your treatment doesn't work, Nick!" I shout at the ceiling. "Look, I'm smoking again. Ha, ha! You hear that? You're not in my head anymore and I can do whatever I want." I pause and take another drag. Laughing maniacally, I raise the cigarette in the air and wave it around like a royal sceptre. I'm on an imaginary stage, performing for an imaginary audience. "Yes Nick, your hypnosis was a flop and I want all of my money back. I'm going to tell everybody you're a fake and a fraud and your treatment doesn't work. I'm smoking again and you know what? It feels fucking great."

Taking a final drag, I stub the butt out and roll onto the bed, my body weak with exhaustion. I feel completely drained and detached from everything, like this is happening to someone else and not me. As soon as my head hits the pillow, I'm out cold.

CHAPTER SIXTEEN

Mother

AT PRECISELY SIX o'clock, I step into the back of Michael's shiny blue Range Rover. As I fasten my seatbelt, my mother peers anxiously at me from the passenger seat. She has short brown hair, warm blue eyes and a smile that makes you feel good. Dressed in a maroon Burberry jacket and Jimmy Choo heels, she oozes class and sophistication—a sharp contrast to Michael's dishevelled windcheater and scruffy combat boots. As always, my mother looks a million dollars, which I always find funny. Years ago, before she divorced my father, she clothed herself from charity shops and virtually lived in baggy shirts and gypsy skirts. Then she married Michael, a successful businessman, and got used to the high life very quickly. No more shopping in Primark for her; no more cut-price shoes from eBay. Now only the best will do.

"Darling, you look absolutely dreadful."

"And hello to you too," I reply sarcastically.

"Katherine," Michael warns. "Is that any way to greet your daughter?"

"But it's true, Mike. Carly looks terrible. This thing with Steve has really taken its toll. I told you she wouldn't be able to cope."

Michael shushes her and steers the car onto the main road

to join the town-bound traffic. After we've been driving for a few minutes, he asks how I'm doing and I tell him yeah, I'm doing okay, all things considered. Then he asks me exactly what happened to my father, and I give him a blow-by-blow account, even though Mum's already told him.

Afterwards, Michael tells me a story about his cousin from New Zealand who had a stroke at thirty and made a full recovery. He says I should stay positive because he's certain my dad's going to be okay. Then he turns up the radio and we listen to a political debate on LBC for the rest of the journey, which suits me fine, as I have very little else to say. Every so often, Mum twists round in her seat and throws me a pitying glance. I smile and assure her I'm okay; Dad's the one we should really be worrying about.

At quarter to seven, Michael guns the Rover into the hospital car park. After he's locked up, we walk briskly through the night and enter Queen Victoria through one of the back entrances. We spend the next twenty minutes going round in circles, trying to find the elusive Churchill Ward; very few of the staff speak English and those who do seem incapable of giving coherent directions. After much toing and froing, we finally reach the third floor and I start to recognise my surroundings. Then Nurse Issey passes us in the corridor and I ask her if I can see my father. Cheerfully, she leads us to his room.

"Oh my God!" Mum gasps when she sees how frail he is. "My poor darling. How are you feeling?"

"Good," Dad croaks. "The n-nurses have b-been ... w-wonderful."

I wince. His voice sounds so strange. He's slurring his words and his tone has risen up an octave; one of the effects of the stroke, I presume.

Mum smiles and takes hold of his hand. For a second, I see real love there. A decade on from the divorce, my parents still have a heart connection, and the sight of it warms me immeasurably.

"Hey, how you doing, big fella?" Michael grins, taking Dad's other hand. "Enjoying your stay at this five-star luxury hotel? I hear the food here is really something."

Dad chuckles, then has to stop abruptly. He makes a horrible gurgling sound in his throat. Then he starts coughing, so I tell him not to talk for a while. Soothingly, I reach down and stroke the side of his cheek. He beams at me and I start getting emotional, thinking about how devastating it would be if I ever lost him.

Dear God, please let my dad survive this. I'll do anything you want, even start going to church again, just please, please let him live.

For the next hour or so, the three of us stand around the hospital bed, making jokes, trying to keep the mood light, but I'm only partially engaged. Images of Nick keep popping into my head and I'm finding it very difficult to concentrate.

I'm trying to engage in the current moment; trying to keep focused on Dad's recovery, but my brain won't let me be. I keep thinking about last night and doubt any of those events could actually have taken place. I figure I must have dreamed the entire episode. And yet...and yet, if that's the case, why am I so reluctant to contact Nick? Why do I have no urge to call him? In fact, come to think of it, why hasn't *he* called me? If I really did imagine everything, then surely, he would at least have tried to make contact by now?

There's a quiet knock at the door and Issey enters. "I'm sorry to disturb you guys, but visiting hours are over. I'm afraid you'll need to say your goodbyes."

"Okay," Mum says. "But first, I'd like to speak with Dr Noble. My daughter tells me he's the Consultant Stroke Physician and the best placed person to give us an update on Steve's condition. It's about time someone gave us a full run-down of what we're dealing with. For example, I'd like to know more about this MRI scan. I hope it doesn't contain radiation."

Issey smiles thinly. "I'm sorry, Dr Noble finished work at five. You'll have to pass by the ward tomorrow during the day if you wish to speak with him."

"But I want to speak to someone now. Look, who's your supervisor?"

"Her name's Annie, but she's gone home too. Like I said, if you want to speak with someone, you'll have to—"

"That is really not good enough!" Mum explodes. "How can your organisation function without a supervisor? I'm telling you, I won't be fobbed off. There must be someone in charge who we can—"

"Calm down, Katherine," Michael says, squeezing her arm. "Don't bite the poor girl's head off. She's doing the best she can. It's not her fault the hospital is under-staffed. Don't blame the nurses, blame the Government. Having a pop isn't going to help the situation." Then, turning to Issey, he apologises for Mum's behaviour and asks for some pamphlets about Dad's condition.

"Certainly," Issey replies coolly. "You can find some literature on the table near the exit doors."

"Thank you."

Muttering silent curses, my mother kisses Dad goodbye and follows Michael into the corridor. Rolling her eyes, Issey trails after them.

For a moment, I hesitate in front of the bed, my heart

aching with sadness. I hate leaving my father like this.

"Sorry about that, Dad," I whisper. "You know how Mum is. It doesn't take much to set her off, but it's only because she cares."

"I-I know my dear," he wheezes. "I-I know."

Tucking a hair behind my ear, I lean over the bed and kiss him lightly on the cheek. "I love you."

"Love y-you too."

"I'll be back tomorrow, I promise. Now get some sleep. You'll be out of here before you know it."

When I get outside, Mum is still ranting about the unfairness of it all. I can smell alcohol on her breath, and I wonder how many whiskies she had before she left her house. An old lady in a wheelchair is gawping at her and two male nurses giggling at some private joke. In an effort to calm the situation, Michael suggests we go for a coffee before heading back. I readily agree.

We take the elevator down to the ground floor and go to the hospital cafeteria. As we approach the serving counter, I see all the nice food on display and realise that I haven't eaten since last night. I don't feel particularly hungry, but decide to get something small to keep my strength up. Taking a tray from the steel trolley, I peruse the assortment of cakes on offer, before settling for a large piece of chocolate gateau. At the checkout, I order a medium white coffee in a take-out cup, then join Mum and Michael at a table by the window.

As we sip our drinks, she continues to bemoan the ineptitude of the NHS and says she's planning to make a formal complaint. It's at this point that I switch off. I agree with some of what she's saying, but at the end of the day, these people just saved my father's life, so I have very little to complain about.

Picking up my fork, I break off a chunk of gateau and lift it towards my mouth. Just as I'm about to take a bite, my mother says, "Is that really such a good idea?"

Frowning, I put down my fork and glare at her. "What do you mean?"

"I mean, should you be stuffing your face with that cake? You've put on an awful lot of weight recently and I can't help thinking you've started comfort eating again. Honestly sweetheart, you could do with shedding a few pounds. You've got such a beautiful face but your weight lets you down. Take my advice and—"

"Oh will you be quiet, Mum!" I snap. "I know I've put on weight, but do I need constant reminding? Right now, joining a gym isn't exactly my top priority. With my father at death's door, do you really think I give a shit about my calorie intake? I've had the worst day of my life and all you can think is to slate me for eating a piece of cake. For Christ's sake, you should hear yourself! You have no tact whatsoever." I slam my fists on the table. A couple of other diners look over. "I'm sorry I'm such a disappointment; I'm sorry I'll never be as pretty, or as slim, or as clever as you, but I can't change who I am, Mum. And you know what? I don't want to!"

"Sweetheart, please," she coos. "You're taking this far too seriously. I didn't mean it to come across like—"

"Like what, Mum?" She doesn't answer. There's plenty more I want to say, plenty I *could* say, but I don't have the energy or the inclination. Right now, the last thing I need is a major bust-up.

Pushing back my chair, I storm out of the cafeteria and march to the front of the building. Trembling with rage, I pat down my pockets and dig out a crumpled packet of Marlboros. As I cup my hands around a match, Michael appears beside me. Through bleary eyes, I give him the onceover. With his five o'clock shadow and tastefully grey hair, his face still bears the ghost of a ruggedly handsome man. I can certainly see why my mother was attracted to him all those years ago.

"I thought you'd quit smoking?" he laughs.

"So did I."

"Do you have one to spare?"

Wordlessly, I pass him my freshly lit cigarette and fumble through my pockets for another. For a while, the two of us stand side-by-side, smoking and watching the comings and goings of the hospital. Then Michael breaks the ice: "Please don't be mad at your mother, Carly. She really can't help herself, you know."

"Yeah, well perhaps she should try," I say bitterly. "Look, Michael, I know you mean well, but I'm tired of people making excuses for her; she's old enough to know better. For crying out loud, my dad's just had a stroke; he almost died. How can she be so insensitive?"

Michael jerks his head a little, nodding. "I totally agree with you, but perhaps this is her way of dealing with the situation. This thing with Steve has hit her hard, and maybe she's just letting off steam."

"No, she isn't; she's just a bloody attention seeker. She always has to make everything about her. Even when it's Dad in hospital, she still needs to be the centre of attention. I'm telling you Michael, I'm sick to death of it. She has no right to treat me the way she does. Doesn't she think I'm stressed enough already?"

He regards me steadily. "Are you sure that's all it is?"

"What do you mean?" I blow smoke through my nostrils.

His eyes stray from mine. "I'm just concerned about you,

that's all. You don't seem yourself, Carly. Is there something else going on in your life that we don't know about?"

My boyfriend's a vampire.

No, I don't say it, but I want to. For a split-second, I actually toy with the idea of blurting it out, just to get it off but chest, but decide against it. I mean, with my medical history, if I start babbling about vampires, the hospital will probably have me sectioned.

"Are you definitely sure you're okay?" Michael repeats. "Is anything else bothering you?"

I shake my head slowly. "No, there's nothing else; just my dad. That's all I care about."

We stay out there a while longer, smoking and talking, then we go back to the cafeteria to find my mother. She apologises for what she said and I apologise for shouting and we hug and all is forgiven. Then we leave the hospital and Michael drops me back to Battersea.

As soon as I get home, I take a long hot bath. Then I swallow my second dose of Thurlux, make myself some coffee and a sandwich, but they don't taste of anything. I feel so restless and uneasy, it's difficult to hold anything in my stomach. I pace around constantly, moving from room to room, checking all the windows to make sure that they are securely locked. I keep looking through the curtains too, squinting through the darkness to see any signs of Nick's Jag. I'm paranoid he might be out there somewhere spying on me. After all, he *did* come by the house earlier, so who knows when he'll next pay a surprise visit?

Once I'm satisfied Nick's definitely not stalking me, I return to my bedroom and watch *The Lion King* for a spot of escapism. I try not to think too much and focus on the current moment. Sometime around eleven-thirty, I finally fall asleep.

CHAPTER SEVENTEEN

Lost

FOR THE NEXT four days, I give a performance Meryl Streep would be proud of. Every morning I go to work and slap a smile on my face. I put on my make-up and a fresh novelty T-shirt and fake the facade of normality. I grin continuously; laugh whenever Mark tells a bad joke and act like everything's great and wonderful.

Most of all, I remember to keep my mouth shut. I don't tell a soul about Dad's stroke, or my fears for my sanity. I don't say a word to anyone—not Mark, not Jill, not even Ronan. I can't bear to have anyone fuss over me.

In the evenings, I visit Dad in hospital; I bring him flowers and fruit and freshly washed clothing. I talk to him softly, tell him funny stories and pray for his speedy recovery. I put in the hours, stick rigidly to a routine, and manage to just about hold it together, because it's the only thing I've got; the only thing that keeps me stable. I'm also back to smoking with a vengeance, demolishing at least two packs of Marlboro a day. I don't particularly enjoy it, but what the hell, it's something to do. I constantly need to stay busy and not think too much, because when I think too much, that's when there's trouble. I just have to keep going, because it's the only thing I *can* do.

Still, I'd be lying if I said it was easy. On Tuesday, I get a call from a guy at the jewellers, asking if Nick's engagement ring fits properly. I almost break down as I take the call, but manage to keep composed as I tell him yeah, the ring fits great, and then I confirm that it's okay for the jewellers to go ahead with the monthly direct debit I set to pay for it. I don't have the heart to cancel.

I'm trying so hard to be cool, but every now and then, the mask slips. It's worst at nights, when I'm alone in my silent house; that's when I fall apart completely. I miss Nick and crave his touch like a junkie craves heroin.

Every time I close my eyes, I think about the mind-blowing sex we had; the most wonderful, perfect sex of my life. I think about his cock inside me, the heat of his lips, and then I feel guilty for having such perverse thoughts. Without Nick in my life, I feel incomplete, like I've lost a body part, and mourn him like he really is dead. My fingers are constantly itching to call him, but whatever happened to me that night—whether a dream or drunken hallucination—has left such a powerful impression, I'm incapable of acting on my impulses. Now whenever I get the urge to call him, I only have to remember what happened with the crucifix, and that he could have murdered Jessica, and my desire quickly withers.

"You don't seem yourself," Jill comments at work on Friday afternoon, as she passes through reception to lunch.

I close the signing-in book. "Don't I?"

"No," she says, scrutinising my face. "I sense something's up. Are you sure you're all right?"

"Of course. Don't I look happy?"

"You do, but I sense an undercurrent." Jill hesitates. "How's Nick?"

My laugh is too loud, too excessive. "Oh, he's fine," I grin.

"You guys haven't had an argument or anything?"

"No, everything's great between us. Life's never been better."

"Well, if you're sure, honey. I still think something's up, but you can't knock a girl for trying, huh? I just want you to know that you can talk to me anytime, okay?"

"Okay, thanks Jill. But you needn't worry, like I said, everything's fine."

She glances at her watch. "Hey, shouldn't you be getting off for lunch round about now? It's past one."

I look at my watch. "Oh my gosh, you're right."

"Come on then. Get Mark to cover you on reception and we'll nip across the road for a coffee."

Reluctantly, I phone upstairs, and Mark agrees to come down in five minutes. Then I grab my coat and bag and follow Jill out of the building. I don't fancy a further interrogation and hope she finds something other than my wellbeing to talk about. When we get to Coffee Republic, I order my usual blueberry muffin and large white coffee. Jill orders a mint smoothie and then we find a table by the window.

"How's James?" I ask as we sit down.

"Very well indeed," Jill replies brightly. "His artwork has really started to take off. Since that Whitechapel exhibition, he's sold another six paintings and had two private commissions. Isn't that great? If he keeps this up, he'll have enough money to put a deposit on a flat after Christmas."

"Wow, that's wonderful news."

"I know. Gavin and I are over the moon for him. Oh, that reminds me; we simply must have you and Nick around for dinner one day next week. I won't take no for an answer, Carly. It will be our little thank you present."

I smile tightly and take a swig of coffee to calm my nerves. As I put down the cup, some of it spills on the table.

"Oppsy daisy!" Jill laughs, passing me a napkin to clear it up. "Those lids aren't very secure, are they?"

"W-what do you need to thank us for?" I stammer.

"For supporting James and helping his career to take off. Honestly, Nick buying those paintings at the exhibition was a total godsend. It really helped give James a boost, especially in front of that journalist from the local paper. In fact, the guy was so impressed, he gave James a whole two-page spread in the colour magazine last Sunday. He also gave the show a great write-up."

"Wow, it sounds like James is really going places," I beam.

"Yes," Jill agrees. "If you hold on a minute, I think I've got a copy of the article here with me somewhere." Diving into her handbag, she fishes out a shiny magazine with well-thumbed pages. Flipping to the centre, she slides the glossy across the table. "Look, here it is…"

I pick it up and study a photo of James standing beside one of his canvasses. The headline reads: 'East End Boy Makes Good.' I smile warmly as I scan the first couple of paragraphs. The journalist has given James a glowing appraisal and predicts he will heading for great things. My smile widens. Despite all the dark events in my life, I'm happy his career is taking off.

When I've finished reading the article, I cast my eyes over some of the other photographs that were taken at the gallery. There's one of Louise and Susan grinning like Cheshire Cats, holding champagne glasses and looking the worse for wear; another showing a group of elderly men gazing stoically at one of James's naked Barbie doll paintings.

"This is great," I say. "I'm so pleased for him."

Just as I'm about to close the magazine, something odd catches my eye. Frowning, I home in on a photo in the left-hand corner of the page. At first glance, there's nothing remarkable about it; just a small, distant shot of the gallery hall and all the attendees laughing and talking. However, when I scrutinise all the different faces, I recognise myself standing beside James's peacock painting. My face is tilted upwards, my eyes gazing adoringly at Nick. Only problem is, Nick isn't there. In the place where he should be standing is a blank white spot.

I gasp and drop the magazine on the table.

"What's wrong?" Jill frowns. "You look like you've seen a ghost."

My hands are shaking. "I-I'm fine. Listen, is it okay if I keep this magazine? Do you have other copies?"

"Of course, you can, honey. Gav bought six so we can afford to lose one."

"Thanks." Hastily, I fold it up and put it in my bag. "So, are you and Gavin all set for Christmas?"

Jill rolls her eyes. "Don't get me started …"

For the rest of lunch, she tells me stories of Gavin's ghastly mother and the nightmarish Christmas they had last year; but I'm only partially listening. I can't stop thinking about that photograph. Why is there a white spot? Could it be a corruption on the original negative? Is it a trick of the light or is there something more sinister at play? Mentally, I tick off all the things I know about vampires. Along with an aversion to stakes and sunlight, apparently they cast no reflection. Perhaps Nick isn't showing up in the picture because the dead cannot be photographed. So is this evidence *finally* that he is indeed a supernatural?

Once more I start to question my sanity, so much so that after lunch, I feign a headache and leave work early to pay my doctor a visit. All throughout the train journey, I study the photograph obsessively. I tell myself this is a mistake, yet another hallucination, but my gut instinct is telling me it isn't. There's something ominous about that white spot.

At quarter to four, I arrive at Lavender Hill Health Centre.

"I'd like to see Dr Wong," I tell the lady behind reception. "I know I don't have an appointment, but it's an emergency. I'm on the verge of a breakdown and I have some serious concerns about the medication she prescribed me."

The receptionist smiles and asks for my name and address. I tell her and she checks Dr Wong's appointments calendar on the computer. "Hmm. We don't have any slots available today but if it's an emergency, she just might be able to squeeze you in before closing time. I can't make any promises, though."

I nod eagerly. "That's fine. I don't care how long it takes; I just need to see her today."

"Okay, take a seat over there and wait for your name to be called."

"Thank you."

I shuffle over to a bench in the waiting area and sit down. Riffling through my handbag, I pull out the magazine again and spend the next hour transfixed on the photograph. People are looking at me. I'm a bag of nerves and I can't stop fidgeting. Finally, at half five, my name is called on the loudspeaker and I'm told to make my way to Dr Wong's office.

CHAPTER EIGHTEEN

Dr Wong

I ENTER THE room and find Dr Wong finishing up her notes from the last patient. "Hello, Carly," she smiles. "Good to see you again. Please take a seat. I won't be a minute."

"Thanks." I sit down opposite her and find a point on the floor to focus on.

"So, how are we doing with the Thurlax?"

I clench my jaw. "Great."

"Have you noticed any improvement?"

"Yes, quite a bit." I shift awkwardly. "Actually, I do have a couple of questions."

"Fire away."

"I don't know where to start."

Dr Wong looks at me. Her eyes shine with warmth and integrity. "Are you okay?" she asks softly.

"No, not really. I-I feel like everything's getting on top of me again." Tears stream down my cheeks. Dr Wong passes me a box of Kleenex. "Thank you." I blow my nose. "I'm sorry for blubbering like this."

"No worries; take as long as you need." As I struggle to compose myself, Dr Wong's voice adopts a more soothing tone. "So...do you want to talk about it?"

I wet my lips. "It's lots of things. Basically, I've lost control of my life. My father had a stroke and I've been living in a nightmare ever since. I've been going up and down to the hospital every day, and the stress is killing me. I keep wondering if he's going to make it."

"I'm very sorry to hear that. It can't be easy for you. Have you been getting any support from your family?"

"Yes, my mother and her husband have been great. But it's still a lot for me to carry." I blow my nose again.

"And what about your boyfriend?"

"My boyfriend?"

"Yes, the man you told me about on your last visit."

"Oh, you mean Nick ..."

"Has he been very supportive?"

"Um, he doesn't actually know. We haven't spoken since Saturday."

"Why is that?"

Because he's a vampire who may or may not have murdered an innocent woman.

No, I don't say that, but I want to. Right now, I'd love nothing more than to open up to Dr Wong and just tell her the truth about everything. But I can't, because I know she'll think I'm nuts. And, quite honestly, I no longer know what the truth is myself. Do I seriously believe Nick's a vampire? Even thinking it seems crazy.

Dr Wong continues to stare at me, awaiting my response. In the end, I just shrug and look at the floor. "We had a bit of an argument, that's all."

She begins scribbling something in her notebook. Then she lays down her pen, pulls out a large grey medical folder and spends .a few moments leafing through various documents. Then she scratches the side of her mouth and says, "Okay, Carly, I'll tell you where I am. Since your last appointment, I've managed to get full access to your medical records. Having read through them, I'm now in a better position to help, but first I just need to clarify some things." She pauses. "It says here that between September 2004 and April 2005, you were a patient at St Ann's Psychiatric Hospital. Is that true?"

"Yes," I reply.

"And you were treated for a post-traumatic stress disorder?"

"Yes, that's right." I close my eyes. For a second, I'm back in the brightly lit hospital lounge with yellow wallpaper. Ronan and I are sitting in plastic bucket chairs arranged in a semi-circle. We're watching horse racing on TV with the sound down. Suddenly, the doors open, and a huge guy dressed in a dirty hospital gown appears. "They're trying to kill us!" he bellows.

"Who's trying to kill us?" Ronan frowns.

"Those bastard nurses. They're poisoning the fucking water!"

Grimacing, I shake the memory away. *No, I can't allow the past to consume me.*

And then, other memories come flooding back. I see myself at eighteen years old, on my first day at university. I was so carefree back then; so happy and excited to be living away from home for the first time and making new friends in my halls of residence. One guy in particular, Dylan, was especially friendly. He was popular and good-looking and I felt so flattered by all of the attention he showed me. I only saw him as mate, nothing more. He wasn't really my type, but he made me laugh and helped me to settle into student life by introducing me to his crowd. For three months, uni was great—the best time of my life.

And then one night, walking back to my halls of residence, feeling slightly drunk from the SU bar, Dylan offered to escort me home safely. Looking back, I was so naive, with no real experience of men or how to fend off unwanted attention. I knew Dylan fancied me, but I never allowed it to threaten our friendship. I couldn't see the signs that were staring me in the face.

When we got back to my room, Dylan made a heavy pass at me. He pinned me down on the bed, smothering me with drunken, sloppy kisses, trying to hitch up my skirt. Terrified, I begged him to stop, begged him to get off of me, but this only made him mad. And then he started to get violent. He knocked me about, punched and kicked me, told me I was a whore and this was what I deserved for leading him on. In the end, I managed to fight him off. I clubbed him over the head with a lamp and finally—*finally*—the bastard got the message that I wasn't interested.

Dylan never forgave me for spurning his advances. Shaking with rage, he left my room, and the very next day, started spreading false rumours about me all over uni. He told everyone I was a slapper, an easy lay, and that I was stalking him after a one-night-stand (that never happened). My so-called female friends all began shunning me and everywhere I went on campus, people pointed and laughed.

For a few weeks, I tried to put on a brave face, attending lectures as normal, pretending everything was fine, but inside I was falling apart. In the end, I couldn't take it anymore, and had a complete mental breakdown. Tearfully, I phoned my dad and begged him to pick me up and take me home.

And I never went back. Ever. I dropped out of uni completely and hid myself away in my bedroom, surrounded by the happy childhood memories of life before Dylan. Before the attempted rape. To block out the past, I sought solace in everything that helped me to forget that painful period in my life. Those wonderful Disney movies. My dolls. Living with my father. It was a coping mechanism. And it's worked. I barely think about Dylan now. Except for when I hear his fucking voice on the radio.

Dr Wong's gentle voice pulls me back to Earth. "So, how did you find your time at St Ann's? Do you think your treatment there was successful?"

"Yes," I say. "My anxiety attacks stopped and I started to sleep better…" My voice trails off. *The flashbacks never stopped, though.*

She chooses her next words carefully. "After you were discharged from St Ann's, were you ever offered any counselling for the … ordeal you went through?"

"Yes, I attended regular therapy sessions until about three years ago."

"May I ask why you stopped attending?"

I shrug. "I didn't feel I needed them anymore. We weren't making much progress and anyway, as I said, the anxiety attacks had stopped so I thought I was okay."

Dr Wong writes some more notes. Then, chewing the end of her pen, she asks me if I would ever consider going back into therapy.

I shake my head. "Not at the moment. I don't think I'm quite ready to take that step."

"Okay. If you do change your mind, let me know." Closing her folder, Dr Wong reaches to a wall-mounted medicine cabinet and takes out two green boxes.

"What's that?" I ask.

"Another two months supply of Thurlax."

"I don't think I want them."

"Why not?"

I remain silent.

"But I thought you said they were working? You said you'd seen an improvement."

I hesitate. "Can Thurlax cause hallucinations?"

"No, not that I know of. Why?"

"Are you sure?"

"Positive. Have you been having hallucinations?"

"I-I don't know. Maybe…"

"What sort of things do you see?"

"Scary things. Things that make me question my sanity."

Dr Wong knits her brows. "Such as?"

"Vampires."

"Vampires?"

"Yes. I know it sounds mad, but please hear me out." I run my fingers through my hair. "Something bad happened to me on Saturday. The craziest thing ever. I thought my fiancé…" The sentence dies. What am I doing? As if she's going to believe me.

"Go on," Dr Wong says softly. "Your fiancé…?"

I change the subject. "Do you think the walking dead can be photographed?"

"I'm not sure what you mean by 'walking dead.' Are we talking about zombies?"

"Maybe. Oh, I don't know. Look, forget I ever said anything. My head's all over the place and I'm not thinking straight."

"Carly, I'm very worried about you. You're behaving erratically."

"I know, but I haven't lost the plot, honestly. No need to call the men in white coats." I laugh shrilly and drop my gaze to the floor. "It's just all this stuff with my dad. It's getting to me, but once I've had some Thurlax and some sleep, I'll be fine."

"Well, if you're sure…" Dr Wong places the Thurlax in a paper bag and hands it to me. "Take these and see how you go. Remember, it can take a good few weeks before the effects start to kick in, so why don't we give it till Christmas? Then, if you aren't seeing a major improvement, we can explore other treatments. But Carly, please do think about what I said."

"Huh?"

"About getting some counselling. It's definitely something for you to consider."

"Oh, I will." Smoothing down my skirt, I stand up and sling my bag over my shoulder. "Thanks. Talking to you has made me feel so much better about things."

Dr Wong shakes my hand and wishes my father a speedy recovery. She also tells me to phone her if I have any more questions.

On shaky legs, I leave the office and stand in the corridor, catching my breath. I pound my knuckles against my head. *Idiot!* I can't believe I almost told her about Nick.

As soon as I get outside the building, I dump the bag of Thurlax in the trash. My mind is made up: *no more antidepressants*. Despite what she said about giving them time to take effect, deep down I know they do nothing for me.

CHAPTER NINETEEN

Saturday

ON SATURDAY EVENING, I arrive at the hospital to find my father in a terrible state. According to him, the nurses haven't changed his incontinence pad for five hours and the bed sheets are soiled. He also doesn't appear to have been fed since morning. Angrily, I stomp to reception and demand to speak with someone in charge.

"I'm afraid Dr Noble isn't working over the weekend," the nurse replies. "And most of the staff here are from a temping agency."

"Well, isn't there someone else?" I shout. "This is totally unacceptable. My father has been left lying in his own faeces for more than five hours and in all that time, no one thought to go and check on him. I mean, is that acceptable to you? If it was your father, would you be happy?" I run my fingers down my nose and lower my voice. "Look, I know you're busy, but for God's sake, couldn't someone at least—"

She holds up her hands. "Don't worry, I'll send someone to change him right away."

"Thank you, but can you see where I'm coming from?"

"Yes, I can."

"What guarantee do I have this won't happen again? How can I leave here tonight knowing that he's not being looked after properly?"

"But we're doing the best we can."

"I'm telling you, it's not good enough. Listen; put me onto your supervisor, this Annie person."

"Certainly." In a fluster, the nurse scurries off to find her supervisor. Five minutes later, she and a male colleague go into my father's room to carry out the necessary ablutions. While I'm waiting in the corridor, a large blonde lady in her fifties waddles over to me. She's carrying a brown medical file and her ID badge tells me her name's Annie Daniels.

"Hello there," she trills. "Nisha said you wanted to speak to me about your father, Steve Singleton."

"Yes, are you the nurse in charge of this ward?"

"Yes, I am."

"Good. Well, first, I just wanted to say I'm not happy that my dad was left wearing the same pad for five hours. It's completely unacceptable."

She nods her head serenely. "My sincere apologies. I can assure you, it won't happen again."

"Secondly," I continue, "I'd like an update on his condition. He had his MRI scan on Tuesday and so far, no one has come back to me with the results."

"Not a problem, I have all of Steve's notes here." Putting on her reading glasses, Annie flicks through the medical file. Then she quietly tells me to step into her office so that we can have a bit of privacy.

I take a seat at her desk and wait nervously as she double checks the doctor's notes. Taking off her glasses, she looks me squarely in the eye. "Okay, so we've got the results back from your father's scan…"

"And?"

"I'm afraid the news is not good."

I get a sickish feeling in my throat, like I've swallowed

something heavy. "Go on."

Annie chews the inside of her cheek and drops her gaze to the table. "Since Steve was admitted, he's had two more mini strokes."

"Jesus Christ!"

"This is actually quite common. Once a person has suffered a stroke, it opens the floodgates for more, so we have to tread very carefully. However, so far, they don't seem to have caused any major damage to the brain, but we've had to increase his aspirin dosage to help keep him stable."

I bury my face in my hands. This is all too much. Everything's getting on top of me again.

"I'm afraid there's more," Annie sighs.

"Oh God, how much more can I take?"

"Please try to stay calm. Would you like a glass of water?"

"No, I just want you to be straight with me and stop prolonging this agony."

"Okay." She pauses. "I'm afraid it's unlikely Steve will ever walk again."

"What!"

"I'm so sorry. The whole lower part of his body from the waist down is paralysed. He is also unlikely to ever get back the feeling in his right arm."

"But how can this be? Dr Noble said …"

"Dr Noble made a provisional assessment, but now that we have the results of the MRI back, we can conclude that the stroke will have a life changing effect on your father."

"Jesus!" I wipe my hand across my cheek. "Does my dad know? Have you told him?"

"Not yet," Annie says quietly. "And for the moment, I suggest you don't say anything either. Steve needs as much positivity around him as possible. Do you understand?"

"Yes," I whisper.

She turns to her computer and types up some notes about our conversation. Then she looks at me from under her fringe and smiles sympathetically. "Okay, well, that's all I have for you at the moment. If anything changes, I'll let you know. Before you go, do have any more questions?"

"No. You've been extremely helpful. Thank you."

Numbly, I stagger out of Annie's office and return to see my father. As I enter the room, I feel completely empty. I have expended so much emotional energy on this nightmare, cried so many tears, I am now incapable of being demonstrative. I am spent; totally spent.

Dad looks up at me like an expectant child and it breaks my heart all over again. I think about what Nurse Annie just told me and hate the fact that I have to lie to him. When he learns the truth, I know it will totally destroy him.

"How are you feeling?" I croak. "Did the nurses clean you up properly?"

Dad nods stiffly. Clearly, he's too weak to talk.

Brushing a hair out of his face, I reach down and gently stroke his cheek. His skin feels warm and soft. I want so much to cry but the tears refuse to come. After a while, I release his hand, pull up a chair and sit by his bedside. Resting my head in my hands, I murmur silent prayers.

Dear God, or whoever is out there listening, I know I'm not perfect. I know I'm as guilty as the next person for only calling on you in my time of need, but please, if you can hear me, let my father be okay. I'll do anything, just please grant me this wish.

Closing my eyes, I clasp and unclasp my hands, trying in vain to make contact with the astral plane. For a while, it all feels completely hopeless, like I'm talking to myself and no one is listening. Then I pop open my eyes and settle back to the current moment. Instantly, I sense that I am not alone.

Even before I turn around, he's penetrating my senses, making my skin rise into goose bumps that travel the length of my shoulders, neck and back. I draw in a sharp breath. My whole body tenses. Slowly, I find the courage to turn around.

Holy fucking shit.

Nick Craven is standing in the doorway. He's wearing an elegant black overcoat with a high Mandarin collar and the grey-and-black scarf I made for him. He looks what I can only describe as magnificent. With his warm, olive complexion and irresistibly full lips, he's back to his breath-taking best, and all memory of the creature I saw in the kitchen swiftly evaporates. This is the real Nick; the man I fell in love with, the man I wanted to marry.

With predatory grace, he strides across the room toward my father's bed, his movements smooth and slinky as a tiger. He makes no eye-contact with me; his only focus is my dad. Hastily, I get to my feet and back away. I need to keep as much distance between us as possible.

For a second, Nick hovers over the bed. My father gazes up at him with a serene expression. It's like they have a secret understanding between them. Then Nick pulls his hand from his pocket and I stifle a scream. On the index finger of his right hand is what can only be described as a metal claw with flexible joints. Attached to the tip is a long, stainless steel blade that extends upward in a poised, ready-to-strike position.

The sight of it makes me queasy. I want to intervene, want to call for help, but I'm rooted to the spot like a statue.

Slowly, Nick raises his left hand and pricks one of his fingers with the blade. Then he gazes deeply into my father's eyes and tells him quietly to part his lips. Obediently, Dad does as he's told, and Nick pushes his bleeding finger into his mouth.

"That's right," Nick murmurs. "Take it all in; drink from my blood eternal." After a few seconds, he retracts his hand. "When you awake, you shall remember nothing." Then, without looking at me, he sweeps out of the room.

My shoulders sag and I start breathing again. *Did that really happen?*

Hesitantly, I walk over to the bed and gaze down at my father. His eyes are closed, and his face looks the picture of peace. Faint traces of blood stain his lips. I stare and stare at him, trying to fathom what the hell I just witnessed. And then I see the colour return to his cheeks, and a dewy sheen washes over his skin like a magic wand, making him look about ten years younger.

I let out a loud gasp. *Fuck! What has Nick done to him?*

Slowly, my father opens his eyes and blinks up at the ceiling a couple of times. Then he turns his head and looks at me, a broad grin slapped across his face. "My dear, what on Earth's the matter? Why are you crying?"

I bite my fist to stifle a sob. Words have deserted me. I can't believe it—his voice has returned to normal. It's like the stroke never happened.

"Where am I?" He sits up on his elbows, his hair all matted and dishevelled.

"Don't you remember?" I whisper through my fingers.

"No. What is this place?"

"Queen Victoria Hospital."

He lifts his brow questioningly. "What am I doing here?" When I don't reply, he pushes back the blankets and tries to climb out of bed, but the tubes in his arms prevent him. "For goodness sake, what is all of this?"

"Jesus, Dad, don't you remember? You've had a stroke."

My father frowns at me and wags his head from side to side. "What stroke? I've never felt better in my life."

"Think hard, Dad. You've been in hospital for a week. Don't you remember what happened before the ambulance came? Before I got home and found you?"

"No. All I remember is going out to water the plants, then, after that, everything is blurry."

"But you collapsed, Dad. We had to bring you here in an ambulance and everything. Think hard."

"I told you, it's all a blur."

Unbelieving, I race out into the corridor and shout for help. Within seconds, Annie and a male nurse arrive on the scene. They're both shocked at the transformation in my father: not only is he sitting up and smiling, but he looks about forty-five.

The male nurse hurries over and tries to coax him back down onto the mattress.

"Get your hands off me!" Dad bellows. "You can't keep me here against my will. I want to go home."

"What is going on?" Annie turns to me. "Carly, can you explain?"

"I-I don't know. He just woke up and started talking, and then he tried to climb out of bed."

"But his face…" Annie breaks off, her eyes wide and incredulous. "Something's happened to his face. He doesn't look the way he did earlier. His skin is so … young. How can this be?"

I chew my thumbnail. "I can't answer that. All I know is, you said he was paralysed; you said he'd never walk again but see…he's moving his arms and I think he can walk. I'm sure of it."

"I've never seen anything like it," the male nurse murmurs. "It's a miracle."

"Miracle? We'll see about that." There's a touch of bitterness in Annie's voice. Then she clears her throat and addresses my father: "Listen Steve, I understand why you're perplexed, and believe me, we're just as mystified, but causing a scene isn't going to help the situation. I simply cannot allow you to leave this hospital until Dr Noble has had a chance to examine you. At the very least, you'll need to stay here overnight for observation."

My dad nods and reluctantly allows the nurse to tuck him back in. "I don't understand any of this," he grumbles. "I don't understand why you would want to keep me here against my will. I'm telling you, I'm fit as a fiddle."

"Dad," I say gently. "Please do as Annie says. I know it's hard, but to be honest, I agree with her. I think you should stay here tonight and if everything's okay, I'll pick you up tomorrow and take you home. Deal?"

"But I'm absolutely fine, Carly!"

"I know, but just to be on the safe side. Please do it for me. I mean, what if you leave here and something happens? What then? Please just let them run their tests."

"This is crazy. I absolutely detest hospitals."

We argue some more, but eventually, he gives in and agrees to stay the night. And it's not just his safety I'm thinking about; I'll also need time to get my own head together. I'm still reeling from the shock of seeing Nick again and the miraculous effect he's had on my father. I don't fully understand what I just witnessed, but I intend to get answers—*tonight*.

CHAPTER TWENTY

Confrontations

A s SOON AS I leave the hospital, I call a cab and head straight for Pimlico. I can't remember the name of Nick's street or the precise location but figure I'll cross that bridge when I come to it. Besides, Pimlico covers a relatively small area of London so I'm sure I'll have no trouble retracing my steps.

As we drive through the dark, wet streets, a violent storm erupts. Torrents of rain pelt the windscreen like a hail of bullets and as we stall at traffic lights, a flash of lightning illuminates the sky. I wonder if this is Nature's way of telling me to turn back. Then there's another flash, and another, followed by a rumble of thunder, and I lose my nerve temporarily.

Hugging my arms tightly, I ignore the voice in my head telling me to end this insanity and go home before it's too late. My emotions are all over the place but I'm on a roll and can't stop now. I question if I'm really ready to face Nick again so soon after what happened. What if he really *is* a vampire? What then? There are a thousand reasons to turn around and go home, but my curiosity has reached fever pitch and my need for answers outweigh any of my misgivings.

At last we reach Nick's street, and the cabbie hits the brakes and pulls the car to the curb.

"This is great, thank you. You can just drop me here." I fumble for my wallet and hurriedly settle the fare. Steeling myself, I step out of the car onto the pavement. Instantly, a huge gust of wind blows my umbrella inside out and I struggle to keep my balance.

As the taxi disappears, I get a rush of butterflies. This feels wrong, so dreadfully wrong, but it's like I'm in the grip of an invisible force. I need to know the truth if it kills me. Cautiously, I cross the deserted street and head briskly toward a row of tall white houses with large columns and black entrance doors.

Just as I reach the steps to Nick's building, another gust of wind knocks me to the ground. Staggering to my feet, I wipe down my skirt, pick up my umbrella, and soldier on determinedly. My knee is grazed from the fall, but I can't stop now, I just have to keep going. Nothing can stop me.

On wobbly legs, I clamber to the top of the steps and ring the doorbell. A minute passes. A heavy mist of rain brushes my eyes as I peer up at the front of the house. The lights are off in every room. I glance behind me nervously. How do I even know Nick's at home? When he left the hospital, I assumed he must have gone straight back to Pimlico, but in reality, he could be anywhere.

I ring the bell again and start to get a sinking feeling. *Perhaps this has all been a big waste of time.*

Then, as if by magic, the door swings open. My mouth gapes. Like Aladdin, I stand on the steps to the cave of wonders, wondering whether or not to enter. *Is this really such a good idea?* I stand for what seems forever, staring into the dark hall, until finally, I muster enough courage to go inside.

Almost instantly, the door slams shut behind me. My fate is now sealed.

Trembling with nerves, I timidly call out Nick's name.

No answer.

I get a bad feeling about this...

Up ahead, I spy a faint glimmer of light coming from a half open door. Bracing myself, I walk quietly through the hall toward the light source. Catching my breath, I push back the door and step into the kitchen. My eyes dart from left to right. The lights are on but the room is completely empty. There's no sign of Nick anywhere.

Everything is just as I remember: the red kettle on the stove, the oak kitchen island in the middle; pots and pans suspended from the ceiling. Not long ago, this room held such happy memories for me. Not anymore.

"Carly..."

I drop my umbrella on the floor. Whirling around, I find Nick standing behind me. He looks sexy as hell dressed in a white silk shirt unbuttoned to the navel, revealing his impressive washboard stomach. His damp hair falls loosely about his face in little black ringlets.

He flings his arms wide and moves forward to embrace me. "Oh my darling, my darling, you've come to me. I knew that you would."

I raise my arms as if to block a punch. "Stay back!"

Nick's smile quickly fades and is replaced by a look of anguish. "So I'm not allowed to touch you? Is that how it is?"

"I-I'm sorry, but I can't have you near me right now."

There's a short, throbbing silence. Slowly, I drop my arms to my sides and start to breathe again. My heart is thudding in my ears. For a moment, we stare at each other, the air heavy with unspoken tension. Briefly, Nick's eyes slip over my body and his face burns with repressed longing.

"Why must you torture me?" he whispers. "You know

how much I worship you."

I drop my gaze to the floor, not knowing where else to look. His stare is too raw, too intense. I run my fingers through my hair.

"What did you do to my father?" I ask softly.

He hesitates before replying, "I gave him a fresh lease of life."

"What exactly does that mean?"

"I have a very unique blood type," he explains. "It has certain... healing qualities. When it entered your father's bloodstream, it reversed all of the damage caused by the stroke."

"You mean...?"

"I saved your father's life." For a second, the words hang there. I can't believe what I'm hearing. Before I can say anything else, he continues: "Each day, I sat in that hospital car park, watching you go to see Steve. I saw the devastation on your face, the tears in your eyes, and I wanted so much to help, but after what happened last Saturday, I was scared to approach you. But I knew, I just *knew* I had to do something to take your pain away."

There's a short beat as I process this information. At last, I lift my head and look at him. "I hope you haven't made him like you."

"Like me?"

"Yes. By sharing your blood with my dad, I hope you haven't turned him into a..." I falter, unable to complete the sentence.

Nick smiles slightly, but his eyes are hard. "No, your father isn't going to turn into a vampire, if that's what you're thinking. He'll be buzzing for a while, feel on top of the world, but that's about it."

I cover my mouth with my hand. It's the first time Nick has ever openly said the word 'vampire.' I can't believe it. Finally, he's addressed the elephant in the room and the admission sends me reeling. "Jesus! Then you really are…"

"Yes," he confirms quietly. "But it doesn't change anything. I'm still the same person you fell in love with; the same person you want to spend the rest of your life with."

"Oh my God, what are you?" I whisper. "You say you're a vampire, but what does that even mean? Are you alive or dead?"

"Neither. I am the *undead*."

"Jesus!" I take another step back, my stomach lurching with fear. "But where do you come from? I mean, how did you become what you are? Were you ever a normal person?"

"Yes, of course I was. Once upon a time. A very long time ago."

I hesitate, trying to soak it all in. "So is it like in the movies? You … you feed on blood?" My voice shakes as I say the words.

"Yes," he replies calmly. "Human blood to be precise."

"But I don't understand. I've seen you eat normal food loads of times. When we went out to restaurants, you drank wine, you ate beef…"

"All a charade. To blend into normal society, I am capable of appearing to eat like everybody else, and I do it happily, but it doesn't taste of anything, and it certainly doesn't provide me with the nourishment I need to survive."

I look away from him. This is starting to get scary. "So how does this work exactly?"

"What do you mean?"

"Where does the…*blood* come from? I mean, how do you select who you are going to feed on?"

"That's a very good question."

Images of Jessica pop into my head, but I try to force them away. "I want to know everything. How do you select your victims and what exactly do you do to them?"

"I don't like to use the word 'victims.'"

"Well, isn't that what they are? What other word would you like me to use? Your targets? Your prey?"

"Okay, okay. Look, I only take what I need. I never harm any of them. You've got to believe me, Carly."

"I'm not saying that you do, but, Nick...you've got to help me to understand."

He hesitates, looking faintly embarrassed.

"Well?" I press.

"I use the clinic as my initial point of contact. My extensive client list provides me with an unlimited source of...possibilities."

My mouth gapes. "My God, you mean you feed off your patients?"

He scratches the side of his mouth. "Well, yes. But I'm very discerning with my selections. For instance, I would never dream of targeting someone with children. If something went wrong and I wasn't able to control myself, it wouldn't be right to leave a child without a parent. If that happened, I wouldn't be able to live with myself."

"Oh, how very noble of you," I say bitterly. "So, was I fair game then? What with me being a childless spinster and all?"

"Stop it. You know it wasn't like that."

"Then tell me what it was like. Help me to understand this insanity."

CHAPTER TWENTY-ONE

Insanity

IT'S A LONG time before either of us says anything. Nick is the first to speak. "Look, I don't expect you to understand, but I'll try." He sucks air through his teeth. "I have a craving inside of me; a thirst that must be quenched at least once a month. Whenever I... *feed* on someone, I make certain to adhere to a strict code of conduct. For one, I never drink from the same person twice. When I feed, I only take the bare minimum I need to survive, resulting in such a small blood loss, the person doesn't experience any unwanted side effects. It means they are able to continue with their lives unhampered, never knowing our paths crossed in such a way."

I silently process this information. "What would happen if you broke that rule?"

He raises an eyebrow. "How do you mean?"

"If you fed on the same victim twice... what would happen?"

"I probably wouldn't be able to control myself," he admits. "Once I get a taste for someone, if I keep going back for more, it gets harder to not want to drain them completely. Blood is like a drug to me, an addiction I'm constantly having to control, so by limiting my intake, I'm able to reduce the chances of harming someone."

A dark chill courses through me as I remember the time

Nick went down on me during my period. *Oh God*. So he's already had his first taste of me. So what would happen if...

I shake the thought from my mind. It's too much to comprehend.

"You make it all sound so simple," I say.

"Oh believe me, it's anything but. You can't begin to know the anguish I endure because of this. Most of the time, I absolutely despise myself. That's why I never allowed anyone to get close to me. The complexities of my situation are not something that I would inflict lightly on someone." He checks himself. "That was... *until I met you*."

He waves his engagement ring at me. "This is all I've had to hold onto; the only thing that's helped keep me sane this past week. When I was at my lowest ebb, mourning your absence like a lost child, this ring was my only source of comfort." He hesitates, his voice choked with emotion. "I am completely obsessed with you, Carly. Before I met you, I was living in darkness; each day was like a life sentence, and I prayed for the end to come swiftly. I felt I had no right to walk this Earth. Then I met you, and you brought such joy to my existence. No one has ever touched me the way you touched me. The way you loved me so completely, the way you make love to me... I'll never get enough of it."

I squeeze my eyes shut and exhale sharply. *This is too much to handle*. I take a step back to get more distance between us.

"Why are you so afraid of me?" he demands. "For Christ's sake, I saved your father's life!"

"I-I know, and I'm very grateful to you for that. Words can't begin to describe just how grateful. But Nick, this is insane. How can you expect me *not* to be afraid of you? You're a vampire. You drink people's blood!"

He flexes his shoulders and takes a few breaths. His expression is stormy. When he speaks again, his voice is worryingly calm. "Okay, so my eating habits disgust you. I get that. But ask yourself this: why, when there was still an opportunity to get out, didn't you take it? Why didn't you run? I told you right from the start to stay away from me; you knew I was trouble, but still you pursued me relentlessly. You gave me a taste of the sweetest love I've ever had, and now I'm addicted to you. You're like a drug to me, completely vital to my existence. Because of that you've got to at least take some responsibility for the position you now find yourself in." He pauses and looks me dead in the eye. "Why, when I'm at my most vulnerable, are you incapable of loving me the way I need to be loved?"

"I-I don't know," I mumble. "I don't know what you expect me to say."

"I love you. Please come back to me. A week ago you wanted to marry me. You said you wanted to spend the rest of your life with me. You can't just switch your emotions off that quickly."

"But that was before…" I break off. "Dammit, I can't think straight. I'm so confused about everything."

"Since you ran out on me, I haven't been able to sleep, haven't been able to do a single thing. All I can think about is you." He licks his lips. "What happened to forever? I thought you were in this for the long haul, but it seems I was wrong. If you really and truly loved me, it shouldn't matter to you what I am."

"But you can't just expect me to—" I falter. This is crazy. Totally fucking crazy. Why am I talking so calmly to a vampire? Why do I have to defend not wanting to love a creature that feeds on human blood and could well be planning to make me his next victim? I've got to hand it to him though. He's succeeded in turning the tables and made me feel like I owe *him* an apology.

"You know how good we are together," Nick whispers. "You know how perfect we are for each other, but you're not listening to your heart. You're letting your fear of the unknown and your prejudice blind you to what you truly feel. No matter how many times you reject me, no matter how many times you beat me down, I'm never going to stop wanting you; I'll follow you to the ends of the Earth if I have to. My desire for you will never be sated."

I swallow painfully. An inferno of longing burns between my legs as I imagine him fucking me hard on the kitchen floor; fucking me raw, taking me from behind, banging me up against the wall. The first trickles of juice soak through my knickers and coat my inner thighs. Desperately, I try to push the thoughts from my head, but it isn't easy. His voice is like an aphrodisiac; sweet as a box of chocolates, coercing me to submit to my basic instincts.

"I-I have to go," I murmur. "I can't stay here."

"Yes you can. You've got to. I need you."

"But I can't! This feels wrong. I want to be brave; I want to be all of these things you're telling me to be, but I can't. I have too many reservations."

"Such as?"

"Well for one, I still don't know if you killed Jessica."

"I told you, I never laid a finger on her. I'll admit I've done a lot of things in my time I'm not proud of, but murdering Jessica isn't one of them."

"Then who did? Tell me that. Her body was drained of blood; she was one of your patients; you acted strangely when I first told you about her death. It was almost like you'd been expecting it, like you had inside information. You've got to admit that's pretty incriminating."

"I agree, but I still tell you, I didn't do it."

"But how do I know for sure?"

"You don't, so you'll just have to trust me. But know this: I wouldn't lie to you about something like this. And besides, Jessica had a daughter."

"What has that to do with it?"

"I told you, I never target people with children. It's unethical."

"I'm sorry, but it's one coincidence too many. She was drained of blood, Nick. Are you telling me there are two vampires on the loose in London killing people?" When he remains silent, I start to get a sick feeling. "Fuck! I've hit the nail on the head. I'm right, aren't I? There *are* more of you."

He refuses to answer the question. I'm struck dumb, unable to get my head around the enormity of this revelation and what it means in the bigger scheme of things. It's too much to comprehend, too much to even think about.

Turning away from him, I hurry over to the sink. "I-I need a drink." Taking a glass from the rack, I run the cold tap and take a long drink of water. Wiping my mouth, I put down the glass and try to hold it together. Suddenly, Nick's behind me, so close I can feel his breath on my neck. We're almost touching, but I refuse to turn around and face him. I'm afraid if I do, I won't be able to control myself.

"Why must you deny your feelings?" he purrs. "I want you, and I think you want me too. In fact, I'm sure of it."

"I-I don't know what you're talking about," I stammer.

"Oh, I think you do..." Gently, he reaches out and runs his fingers through my wet hair. I shiver. His hands are warm and soothingly persuasive, travelling up and down my head, gathering my hair into clumps, before stroking their way back to my temples.

"Does that feel good, baby?" he breathes. "Am I making you feel good?"

"Mmmmm."

He starts to apply more pressure, the sensation growing more intense with every caress. I feel completely intoxicated. Tilting my head back, I lose control and emit a low groan.

"That's right baby, let out all that tension. Your body knows what she wants, so stop trying to fight it." Slowly, his hands drop to my shoulders and in one fell swoop, he eases off my coat and throws it to the floor. I am now standing in just my blouse and skirt. Smoothly, his fingers travel down my spine to the small of my back, before working their way up again. Even through my ruffled blouse, the heat from his fingers scorches me, sending jolts of longing straight to my crotch. I squeeze my thighs together to stem the flow of juices.

Dear Lord. What am I doing? This man is a vampire. Why am I letting him touch me so intimately?

Because you like it.

"Please, stop," I whine. "Nick, please!"

With deliberate slowness, he slides his fingers down the sides of my shoulders, rests his hands on my hips and leans into me, his sweet breath disturbing the hairs on my neck. I gasp. I can feel his huge erection pressing against me.

"Do you feel that?" His voice is a whisper. "Do you feel how hard I am for you?"

"Mmmm."

"This is what you do to me, Carly. This is the reason I'm on the brink of insanity."

Cautiously, he reaches out again, pulls back my hair and

gently strokes the side of my cheek, the heat from his fingertips cutting through the cold like a knife. Then his hand travels down my cheek to my jaw and rests at the edge of my chin. I hear him catch his breath.

"My God, you make me so crazy," he rasps. "Here's some advice, baby. If you wanted me out of your life, then you shouldn't have let me fuck you. Because once I fucked you and got a taste of that pussy...the sweetest pussy I've ever tasted, there was no going back for me. I need it all the time now." I yelp as he presses his mouth to my ear and grips my lobe in his teeth. "Do you want me to fuck you? Is that what you want? Want to get fucked by a vampire?"

I hesitate. My throat has gone all dry. My heart is beating rapidly and I feel so vulnerable. By rights I should be terrified, but my legs are weak from lust and refusing to take instruction. It's like I'm rooted to the spot, spellbound by the seductiveness of his voice. He's right. I *do* want to get fucked—in the worst possible way.

Slowly, Nick peels himself from my body and drops down to his knees. Crouching at my feet, he carefully helps me out of my shoes and tosses them across the room. Then he moves his hands along the bottom of my thighs, touching and caressing, before working his way up my buttocks and into my skirt. I moan loudly as his fingers hook into the waistband. Slowly, he peels down my skirt, gathering the material in a heap around my ankles. Then, gripping the top of my sheer-coloured tights, he pulls them down as well. I bite my lip. My legs are now completely bare and the cut on my knee is starting to sting a little.

Softly, soothingly, Nick starts to kiss the backs of my thighs, his warm, supple lips sending a trail of goosebumps up my skin. I wince. This is more than I can bear. I'm completely breathless with ecstasy. I need those lips to be kissing me somewhere else.

"My God, you smell delicious," he growls.

His words send a quiver up my spine and I go from wet to soaking. I'm crying silently for more. *Fuck, what have I gotten myself into?*

"Don't be afraid," he murmurs. "I promise I'll be gentle as a kitten."

I nod mutely.

Moving higher, he softly strokes the cheeks of my buttocks with his fingertips, then presses his lips to my left rump. I stop breathing. *Shit, this feels too good.* Slowly, he kisses a trail from my left buttock to my right, exploring up and down the crease, before sinking his teeth into my knickers and pulling them down slowly. My pussy gets hot as he continues to drag the knickers down, past my thighs, past my ankles, before tossing them on the floor. I'm now stark naked from the bottom down.

Suddenly, I come to my senses. *What the hell am I doing?*

Panicking, I peer down at Nick. He's still crouching at my feet, his cheek pressed against my leg, eyes shut tightly in rapture. In that split-second, my mind is made up. *I've got to get out of here.* Taking advantage of his vulnerable position, I quickly step over him and scramble for the door.

CHAPTER TWENTY-TWO

Prey

B EFORE I CAN reach the door, Nick catches me in his arms,
spins me around and drags me kicking and screaming to
the oak kitchen island. Holding my waist with one arm, he
uses his other to sweep all of the plates and silverware onto
the floor. Having cleared a space, he throws me down in the
centre of the island. Each time I try to sit up, he forces me
back down, blocking every one of my badly aimed punches.
The strength of him is frightening, but still, I continue to fight.

"Let go of me!" I scream. "Let go, let go!"

"Hit me if it makes you feel better," he pants. "Go on, hit
me!" I slap his face, and then I hit him again, and again, trying
to cause as much damage as possible, but it doesn't make
even the slightest impact. "That's right. Let it all out. My God,
you're beautiful when you're angry."

I continue to thrash about, but I know I'm fighting a
losing battle. There's no way I'll ever get the better of him.

"One kiss," Nick breathes. "That's all I'm asking. One
kiss, and then you're free to go."

"I'm not kissing you!" I shout. "Get off me!" We tussle
some more, but eventually, my rage fades and the fight ceases
to matter. "Okay, one kiss … and that's it."

Loosening his grip, Nick runs his hands up my thighs, and
then lifts my legs and pushes my knees against my chest.

Slowly, his eyes rove along the bottom of my thighs to my buttocks before settling on the wet, welcoming slit between my legs. The hunger on his face is both thrilling and terrifying.

"One kiss," I remind him sternly. "That's what you said."

"Yes," he agrees. "But I didn't specify where I would kiss you."

A tremor rattles through me. *Jesus, he turns me on so much.*

Lowering his head, Nick crushes his lips against my right knee, covering my bleeding graze with sweet, sensual kisses. I close my eyes and focus on my breathing. *Fuck, this feels so good.* I whimper quietly as he licks long circles around the wound, before savouring every last drop of my blood. For a second his mouth quivers, his body shuddering in a way that says he's trying hard not to act on a violent impulse. Finally, he raises his head and fixes me with smouldering eyes. We both know that one kiss will never be enough... *for either of us.*

Savagely, he tears open my blouse and buries his face between my breasts, licking and sucking my nipples as he would my clit. Then, teasingly, Nick kisses a trail from my boobs to my abdomen, before parting my legs and lightly grazing his teeth over the sensitive skin of my inner thighs. I shiver with delight. This is a very dangerous game we're playing, but in a crazy way, I love it. Knowing that he could sink his teeth into me at any time and suck me dry turns me on big time. Dicing with death has never been so sexy.

Running his hands up my calves, Nick pushes me back a little, then spreads my legs and buries his face deep inside my wet hole. *Oh my God.* I have to bite my lip to stop myself from screaming. I can't believe how good it feels. Hungrily, he licks a long, slow stoke through my glistening pussy lips, then works his way to my clit, consuming me with a ferocity that

313

makes my knees tremble. It's like he's starving; like he can't get enough of me. Lost in the moment, I lose all sanity, all sense of self.

At last Nick comes up for air, his mouth shiny from my juices. "Shit, Carly, you taste even better than I remembered."

Sensuously, he licks his lips and closes his eyes, relishing the flavour like it's the best meal he's ever had. Then, unbuckling his trousers, he quickly sheds his boxers and frees his huge throbbing cock. The sight of it makes my head spin and my nipples harden at the thought of it entering me.

Pushing my knees against my chest, he lowers himself between my legs and slides the head of his dick up and down my gushing slit.

"Do you want this dick inside you?" he asks, his voice twisted with longing.

"Y-yes."

"How much do you want it?"

"Please, Nick, I don't want to play games ... just fuck me."

Silently, he continues to slide his cock up and down my burning hole, whipping me into a frenzy of half-mad desire. I want him to push it all the way in, but he's stalling, making me wait as he whets my appetite.

"Tell me that you love me," he whispers. "Tell me you can't live without me."

"Nick, please...don't torture me like this."

"I need to hear you say it."

"I love you. For Christ's sake, you know I do. Now please just..."

Gently, he presses his cock against my tight hole and finally, *finally*, he grants my wish and enters. *Oh shit, it hurts so good.* I moisten my lips; moan silently. Moving his hips in slow, steady thrusts, Nick hisses and then exhales as each delicious nudge of his shaft buries him further in, stretching me out with his hugeness.

"I'm back to where I belong," he gasps. "Deep at the heart of your sweetness. You feel so fucking good, Carly. You belong to me. Every single fucking piece of you." Slowly, he eases out until only his tip is inside, then he goes back in full throttle, fucking me like a man possessed.

The wood beneath us shakes and creaks to the pounding of flesh against flesh. I have relinquished control and it feels wonderful. Breathing raggedly, I open my eyes and see my creamy breasts bouncing up and down, rippling in time to Nick's powerful thrusts, as he pushes ever deeper into me. His cock slams into me again and again, hitting my womb every time. *Holy shit, it hurts so fucking good.*

Just as a fire ignites in my belly, Nick pulls out of me abruptly, leaving me tense and confused.

"Why are we stopping?" I gasp. "Please, Nick, I'm dying here."

Wordlessly, he rubs his dick up and down my pussy, coating it in a thick layer of wetness. Then, without warning, he slides his cock past my burning hole, spreads my buttocks and lingers on my butthole.

I draw in a sharp breath. *Dear Lord.*

"Nick, what are you ..."

"I promise I'll be gentle," he says softly. "If you give me the chance, I promise to show you the most exquisite pleasure imaginable."

I lie still, my heart riddled with indecision. A part of me wants to be daring and try something new, but another part of me is terrified. What if it hurts? What if I don't like it?

"Do you trust me?" he whispers.

I hesitate before answering, "Yes."

For a second, our eyes lock and my fate is once again sealed.

With trembling hands, Nick parts my buttocks and with one swift thrust, pushes his cock into me. For a second, I'm paralysed; then, as he slowly eases himself in, I start to get used to the sensation. Little by little, inch by inch, Nick's enormous shaft burrows deeper and deeper into my butthole, infusing me with feelings of both shame and desire.

"Shit," I gasp. "Too fast, too fast."

"Okay…" he soothes. "We can take it as slow as you want."

As I surrender to the force of his need, I realise I have never felt so vulnerable, so utterly taken, but I love it. I love giving it up to him.

As Nick's soft grunts of lust gain momentum, I reach down and finger my clit. Then I wrap my legs around his waist, goading him to push even deeper.

"Fuck, you're so sweet and tight," he gasps. "I don't know how much longer I can last."

Finally, he's all the way to the hilt, and the pain is so excruciating, I almost pass out. Gradually, I return to my senses and have to take deep breaths to keep steady. Nick reaches down and tenderly strokes my cheek with his thumb. "Are you okay, darling? I'm not hurting you too much, am I?"

"No, please…don't stop."

Slowly, he extracts himself and continues to fuck through the tightness, his hips slamming into me with a savagery that renders me breathless. Very soon, a crescendo of fireworks erupts inside me and I yell as I come harder than I ever have before.

"You're mine," Nick pants. "All mine. I'm never letting

you go. Not ever."

I nod mutely. Right now, I'm incapable of speaking.

After a few seconds, he pulls out of me and continues to rub his dick vigorously. He's still rock-hard and I'm disappointed I didn't make him come.

"Oh, darling, do you want me to…?"

"No, it's fine," he says. "We can have round two later."

With a gentle smile, he takes my hand and helps me back to my feet. I'm dripping with sweat and tiny jolts of electricity threaten to floor me. I'm light-headed and every single part of my body is on fire.

Dizzy from a mixture of pain and euphoria, I stumble toward a chair, but Nick catches me before I fall over.

"Are you okay, baby?"

I nod stiffly, unable to speak.

Sweeping me into his arms, Nick carries me up to the bathroom. Kicking open the door, he sets me on the ground and proceeds to run water for a bath. As we wait for the large marble basin to fill, I press my cheek to his chest and breathe in his glorious scent as I listen to his whispered promises and earnest declarations of love.

I'm drifting in and out of consciousness, buzzing from a high I fear can never be replicated. The sex tonight was so mind-blowingly intense that everything else leading up to it feels like ancient history. Right now, in my head, there are no vampires, no dark clouds on the horizon; there is only Nick and me and the merging of two hearts as one. In the back of my mind, I have a million unanswered questions, a million reasons to run, but I don't want to. *This* is where I belong—in the arms of the man I love.

When the bath is ready, Nick gently helps me in, then sheds the rest of his clothes and climbs in opposite me. As soon as I hit the water, every muscle and nerve grows calm, and my soreness starts to subside. For the next half hour, we both say very little, soaking up the serenity of the moment. Nick doesn't once take his eyes off me. It's like he's keeping watch; making sure I'm never out of his sight for even a second.

When we've finished bathing, he towels me down and carries me into his bedroom. Carefully laying my body on the bed, he starts to cover me with sweet kisses. Sweet kisses that make my head swim and send me slightly crazy. I moan as he sucks my lips, licks my eyelids, my cheeks, my hairline, everywhere. A warm fire crackles in the fireplace, filling the air with the scent of burning wood. Outside, I can hear the sound of heavy rain hitting the window. When Nick's finished devouring me, he pads over to an antique chest of drawers and returns carrying a bottle of sweet smelling liquid.

Gently, he rolls me onto my front, then beginning at my shoulders, he applies lavish quantities of oil to my body. I whimper as his large, strong hands rub along my spine and up toward the sides of my breasts. Gradually, he works his way down the backs of thighs, and then to my calves. Moving back up, his fingers start to knead my shoulders, giving me the most perfect massage I've ever experienced. Pretty soon, my body is crying out for even further exploration. As if reading my mind, Nick begins stroking along my buttocks; exploring up and down the crease; moving from my right cheek to my left.

"Do you like that?" he whispers. "Does that feel good?"

"Uh-huh. So good."

"I can't get enough of you. Your skin is so soft."

With a sigh of pleasure, I drop my face into the black-silk pillows. His hands are everywhere, massaging every single inch of me, from my feet to my toes, to the tips of my fingers. It's such an intimate, divine, almost spiritual feeling. I have never experienced anything quite like it.

The fire continues to spread its warmth through the room, and I start to get drowsy. Soon, it's very difficult to keep my eyes open. Abruptly, Nick stops the massage and guides me under the duvet covers. Then he takes me in his arms and slowly runs his fingers through my hair, over and over again.

"I'm so scared about what the future holds for us," I whisper.

Nick plants a kiss on my forehead. "Don't be. I promise I'll take care of you."

I sigh. Being in his arms feels like coming home, and I can't believe I've lasted seven whole days without him. Somehow, someway, despite all the darkness, we will find a way to make this work.

CHAPTER TWENTY-THREE

Dark Proposal

PATCHES OF SUNLIGHT filter in through the curtains, highlighting the intricate wood carvings on the bedpost. The room is warm and cosy and remnants of a fire still burn in the hearth. For a moment, I stare at the black-silk sheets, trying to remember what happened and how I came to be here. Then, with a sexy smile, I roll over and bury my face in Nick's pillow, greedily savouring his sweet aroma. The bed feels so empty without him, and I'm desperately craving his heat. Without him inside me, I feel incomplete, like I've lost a part of me.

Suddenly, images from last night flash through my mind and I get a rush of butterflies. *Oh my gosh, did that really happen?* I'm still having trouble believing any of it was real.

My boyfriend is a vampire. My boyfriend is a vampire.

Once I get over the initial shock, I start to calm down a little, and what once seemed hopelessly bleak, now has a strange appeal that fills me with a deep sense of excitement. Yesterday, I was a total wreck, but today my mood is somewhat more philosophical.

Yes, Nick Craven, the man I love, is a vampire, but he also just happens to have saved my father's life, and for that I will be eternally grateful. He's also brought unimaginable joy to my life and made me happier than I ever dreamed I could be. For those two reasons, I'm determined to make this relationship work.

Smiling, I turn onto my back and gaze up at the ceiling. Every part of my body aches, and my nether regions are so sore it hurts whenever I move; but I wouldn't change a single thing. Last night was amazing. Nick took me to levels of ecstasy I didn't think possible and I'm literally salivating at the prospect of what else he has in store. In my giddy, lust-filled state, I feel totally invincible; ready to take on the world. It's like I'm in the endless throes of a rolling orgasm.

I run my fingers down my face, grinning like a perpetually happy five-year-old. *Last night I made love to a vampire! Oh my God. This is insane; totally insane.* In the space of just a few hours, my humdrum existence has been shaken to the core and nothing will ever be the same again. It's like I've stepped into the pages of a romance novel and got the excitement I've always craved.

Before Nick, my world was a narrative of sorrow and broken dreams—now when I wake up, I look forward to the future, and it's all because of him. For years I'd dreamed of finding my Prince Charming; always dreamed that out there, somewhere, witches and magic and fairies really do exist. Well, this is not quite a fairy tale, but what I've found is pretty damn close, and I cannot, *will not* give it up.

The bedroom door opens and Nick appears. His short black hair is damp from a recent shower and he's wearing a red dressing gown with gold embroidery. Under his arm, he carries a stack of fluffy towels.

"Morning, gorgeous," he grins. "Did you have a good sleep?"

"Mmm. The best ever." I shift into a sitting position. "What time is it?"

"Just past twelve. No, don't get up. There's no rush darling; you can take your time." He smiles angelically and his eyes glisten with love.

"Where have you been?" I pout. "When I woke up and found you weren't there, I was distraught."

He snickers. "I was downstairs doing a little spring cleaning. I was also fixing your breakfast."

"Aww, how lovely. You're much too good to me."

"Don't be silly; it's the least I can do for my beautiful bride-to-be."

I stiffen. "You still want us to get married?"

"Of course. Don't you?"

"Yes, but how can we?" I falter. "I mean, that is, you're... you're dead."

Laughing, Nick places the towels on a chair and walks over to the bed. Taking my hand, he presses my palm firmly against his chest. "Does this feel dead to you?" he whispers.

I close my eyes. He's right. His heart is beating so fast it feels like it will explode.

"It wasn't always like this," he continues. "I'll let you into a little secret. For over sixty years, my heart had ceased to function; my whole body had shut down and I'd lost the will to live. Then came the day you walked into my office, and the instant I laid eyes on you, my heart came back to life, and it hasn't stopped beating since. Your love is like oxygen to me."

A deep thrill courses through me; he's so romantic it makes me want to weep.

Nick releases my hand and I find my voice again. "But I still don't see how we can get married. Aren't there other things for us to consider?"

"Such as?"

"Well, for one, I thought churches would be off limits. I

mean, after what happened to you with the crucifix…"

"Ah, but who needs a church?" he smiles. "This is the 21st century, Carly. We live in a secular society, so we can get married anywhere we choose. We can write our own vows, seal our commitment to each other in any way we please. People do it all the time." He chuckles. "I mean, we could even tie the knot and then go bungee jumping, if that's what took our fancy. There are so many different options, so many choices; that's the beauty of the modern world."

I bite my lip. "Yes, I guess you're right, but…" The sentence dies. Of course I want to be Nick's wife more than anything else in the world, but how on Earth could it work? There are so many unanswered questions, so many obstacles for us to overcome, it hurts my head thinking about it.

"Don't look so serious," Nick laughs. "I'm only pulling your leg. Well, partly—about the bungee jumping, anyway. But on a serious note, I do want to marry you and *soon*. I want to make our love official and give you the kind of life you deserve. No expense will be spared. I promise I'll make an honest woman of you if it kills me." Still smiling, he reaches out and softly runs his fingers down my cheek. "Are you feeling sore from last night?" he asks sweetly.

My cheeks flame. "Yes, a little; but it's a nice kind of sore."

"I'm sorry if it hurt but… I just *had* to have you, Carly. Every single part of you. You must understand; I just *had* to."

"I know," I whisper. "There's no need to apologise. I enjoyed every minute."

Gently, he continues stroking my hair and the dip and hollow of my ears, his fingers warm and slightly shaky. Then he moves down to my neck, and lightly caresses my throat in a way that makes me throb painfully below. "God, I love you.

I feel so at peace in your presence."

I squeeze my eyes shut. He's completely skewering my senses and I'm consumed by uncontrollable longing. *Dear Lord, I want him so much.*

Opening my eyes, I gaze up at him adoringly. I don't even notice his scar anymore; I accept it as part of what makes him beautiful. When I look into his perfectly imperfect face, I know that he is good, and believe he's being truthful when he says he didn't harm Jessica.

For a few heartbeats, the two of us stare at each other, lost in a timeless dimension of euphoria. Then, playfully, I take his hand and open up his palm. The crucifix burn has vanished and his skin is now as smooth and blemish-free as a child's. Softly, I kiss his hand and tell him how sorry I am for hurting him. Jokingly, he accepts my apology and tells me not to even think about spiking his coffee with holy water.

Silently, he plants a kiss on my forehead. Then he looks me over very carefully. A shadow flits across his face. "You're not wearing the pendant I gave you."

I redden. "No, I-I'm sorry Nick, it's at home. I took it off because I was scared."

"Don't worry, I completely understand."

"As soon as I get home, I promise I'll put it back on. I know how much it means to you. I promise I'll never take it off again."

He shrugs. "It's fine. Only wear it if you want to."

"Of course I want to." I press his hand to my cheek. "I love you. Everything you give me is precious."

"I love you too." Resuming his smile, Nick releases my hand, throws back the covers, helps me out of bed and wraps me in one of the big fluffy towels. Then he ushers me into the bathroom. As he pushes open the door, I'm greeted by a blast of steamy air and the heavenly scent of fresh flowers. To my delight, I find he's filled the tub with hot water and scattered little rose petals along the surface. Scented candles adorn every shelf, bathing the room in a warm orange glow.

I cover my mouth with my hand. "Oh wow, this is beautiful! You're spoiling me far too much."

He pecks me on the cheek. "Enjoy. I'm going back downstairs to finish making breakfast. Come down when you're ready."

When he's gone, I climb into the tub and allow the water to completely submerge me. *Ahh. This is just what I need to wake myself up.* Cupping a handful of water, I brush my fingers through my hair, every muscle and nerve growing calm. This feels surreal but a good kind of surreal. I can't believe a vampire has run me a bath and is making me breakfast! I keep wanting to pinch myself, expecting to wake up and find that this has all been a dream.

When I've finished bathing, I towel myself down, brush my teeth and return to the bedroom, where I find a beautiful blue dress and fresh underwear laid out on the bed. My heart flutters at the sight of them. *How sweet and thoughtful of Nick.* The dress is *so* me and has little pictures of Minnie Mouse printed all over the material. Oh, and he got my size right too. The thought of him going out to buy me clothes makes me sort of teary. *Wow, could this man be any more perfect?*

Lovingly, I run my fingers over the lacy black underwear and balk when I see how skimpy the thong is. *Good God.* I don't normally wear this type of stuff but hey, if Nick wants to see me in a thong then I'm not about to argue.

Cutting short my morning make-up ritual, I dress quickly, apply only a bit of lipstick and mascara, then make my way downstairs. As soon as I enter the kitchen, my nostrils are greeted by the glorious scent of freshly-ground coffee.

"Did you have a nice bath?" Nick asks, taking a pan off the cooker and shaking the contents onto a plate.

"Yes, it was great. I feel so refreshed. Oh, and thanks for the dress. I absolutely love it."

"Yes, it looks very sexy on you. Right, I hope you're feeling hungry because I've made us a proper feast: eggs, bacon, sausage, the works."

"Mmm, I can see that. It looks delicious." Smoothing down my dress, I take a seat on one of the chrome-plated stools by the island. My pulse races as I remember what took place here last night. Nick's cleaned up everything so good, you'd never know we'd had rampant sex here only a few hours ago.

He laughs softly as if reading my mind. "Are you still thinking about yesterday?"

I blush crimson. "No."

"Liar. I bet you were."

I join in the fun. "Okay, maybe just a little. It's not something I can easily forget, is it? Oh, and by the way, I must commend your cleaning skills. You've made this place look like a palace."

"Why thank you. I do try." He places a plate of food before me and pours me a coffee.

"Wow, this looks good," I grin. "There's only one problem: I'm not sure I should be eating it."

"Why not?"

"My mother thinks I'm fat. She says I need to go on a diet."

"Your mother needs her eyes tested."

My heart melts at the compliment. "Do you think so?"

"I know so. Carly, you're perfect just the way you are. I love your body; every single curve of it. If your mother thinks you're fat then she needs her head as well as her eyes examined. Put it this way: if you lose any more weight, you'll have me to answer to. I don't want you becoming a bag of bones and losing that gorgeous derriere of yours. Speaking of which—did you put on the underwear I bought for you?"

"Of course."

"Prove it."

Rolling my eyes, I slide off the stool, flip up my dress and give him a little wiggle and a flash of my thong.

"Very, very nice," he murmurs.

Lowering my lashes, I sit back down and shovel a forkful of bacon in my mouth. This guy could charm the knickers off a nun.

Smiling sweetly, Nick dishes out the rest of the food, and then he pulls up a chair and sits beside me at the island. As he picks up his fork, I shoot him a look. "You don't have to do this, you know."

He raises his eyebrows. "Do what?"

"Pretend to eat. I know you're only humouring me, but really, you don't need to. I know it's not enjoyable, so just... *don't*. I'm perfectly happy to eat on my own."

Slowly, Nick puts the fork down. "Okay, if you're sure. But I honestly don't mind."

I shake my head and take another mouthful of bacon. "I just want you to be yourself around me."

We both fall silent as I launch a savage assault on my plate, clearing off three pieces of bread and butter in quick succession.

"What?" I ask, wiping my mouth.

"Nothing," Nick smirks. "I told you before; I just love watching you eat."

"I bet you think I'm a right pig."

"Not at all. I love a woman with a healthy appetite."

I smile and shake my head. Nick is incorrigible.

When I've finished eating breakfast, he clears away the dishes and begins washing up. Hopping down from my stool, I grab my handbag and head towards the door. "I'm just popping out for some fresh air."

"Okay."

I step into the hall and stride through the conservatory to an immaculately pruned private garden. For a second, I stall on the steps relishing a crisp breeze on my face. The sky is grey and powdery-looking. Glancing back toward the conservatory door, I double-check that Nick hasn't followed me. Then, when I'm certain the coast is clear, I quickly rummage through my bag and pull out a cigarette. It takes me a few seconds to light because the wind keeps blowing out the flame. Finally, I succeed and take a few shallow puffs, closing my eyes as the nicotine whips through my system. *God, this feels good.* I've been absolutely dying for a cigarette all morning.

Hastily, I take a couple more puffs, then I stamp out the butt and reach inside my handbag for my compact mirror. I grimace at my reflection. Somehow, I've managed to get lipstick on my teeth—*again*. As I try to rub it off, I see Nick reflected in the mirror. He's standing at the conservatory door, watching me and frowning.

With a little shriek, I drop the mirror and clutch my chest like I've just had a seizure. "Oh my God! Nick, you frightened me. You really shouldn't creep up on me like that." Stooping down, I pick up the mirror from the grass. *Dammit. The glass is cracked.* "Well," I continue, "at least I know the myth about vampires casting no reflection is rubbish. I just saw you clear as day."

Nick doesn't see the funny side. It looks as if I've been rumbled.

CHAPTER TWENTY-FOUR

Icy

"**I** SEE YOU'VE started smoking again," Nick says icily. My eyes stray from his, my cheeks burning with embarrassment. "Y-yes. I'm sorry. I just couldn't help myself."

"Yes, you could. We both know that you did this on purpose. You wilfully disobeyed me because you wanted to break my hold over you to give you some independence. I'm right, aren't I?"

"Yes. Are you angry with me?"

He doesn't answer. Slowly, he walks toward me and stops just a few inches from my face. For a second, he towers over me like some kind of dark angel. Then he slips his finger under my chin and tilts my face upwards so that he can see my eyes.

"No, I'm not angry with you," he says softly. "If you want to smoke and it genuinely makes you feel good, then do it. I'm not going to stop you. I've always said you're free to do exactly as you please. I want you to be your own woman, Carly. But let's get one thing straight, okay? Just now, you told me to be myself; well, so should you. There's no point hiding anything from me, because I'll always find you out." He releases my face, slides his hand down my shoulder and reaches inside my bag. Pulling out a cigarette, he places it between my lips. Then he takes out my matches and lights it for me.

"Thanks," I say.

There's a tense silence. He continues to stare, his eyes transfixed on my mouth as I suck hard on the cigarette and blow smoke through my nostrils. It's pretty clear what he's thinking, and my sex slickens at the thought of what he'd like to do to me. Right now, I want nothing more than to take this upstairs, but I hold back because I enjoy teasing him. The hungrier he is for me, the better; it means that when I'm ready to submit, he'll give it to me rough, just the way I like it.

"You really know how to turn me on," he whispers.

"Do I?"

With a low growl, he grabs my free hand and presses it against the throbbing bulge in his dressing gown. My nipples harden and I have to squeeze my thighs together to keep under control. Grinning broadly, I ease my hand away.

"You're a monumental tease," he rasps.

"So I see. And it looks like you've got something pretty monumental going on down there." I laugh at my own joke.

Nick doesn't see the funny side. His face continues to smoulder, and he looks almost in pain. *My God, he's really getting me wet. This has a stop.*

After a few more puffs, I extinguish the cigarette and run my fingers through my hair. "Listen, I should probably go. It's getting late and I promised to pick my father up from the hospital."

"No problem. Just give me a second to cool off and I'll drive you." With a loud sigh, Nick slinks away and goes back upstairs to get changed. A short while later he returns to the living room dressed in jeans and a T-shirt. Fleetingly, my eyes travel over his body, focusing on the way the clothes cling to every inch of his muscular frame. A wave of excitement shoots to my crotch. *Good Lord, the man is a god.*

"What?" Nick smiles. "Why are you looking at me like that?"

"Oh, nothing," I grin. "I've just never seen you dressed so casually before. It makes a nice change."

"Glad you like it." He shrugs on his jacket and then pats down his pockets to check that he's got everything. "All right, darling. Ready to go?"

"Yes." Buttoning up my coat, I follow Nick out the house into the street. The sky has darkened and the wind is blowing pieces of dirt and grit all over the pavement. Shivering a little, I walk up to the Jaguar and get in. Almost instantly, we're on the move, heading in the direction of south London.

"Let's have some music." Nicks turns up the stereo on "Talk to Me, Talk to Me," by Little Willie John, and for the rest of the journey, he serenades me to a succession of slushy '50s love ballads.

Around three o'clock, we arrive in Tooting. Once we've parked up, I lead Nick into Queen Victoria Hospital and we take the elevator to the Churchill Ward on the third floor. As soon as the doors open, I head straight for the reception, where I find Issey and a male nurse deep in conversation. Clearly, something has set the cat among the pigeons and I just hope it isn't my dad.

"Hi, Issey, good to see you again. I'm here to collect Steve Singleton."

Issey throws up her hands despairingly. "Oh my goodness, I'm so glad you're here. Steve has been a nightmare. I can't tell you how much disturbance he's caused today. We've been trying to contact you all morning but your phone was off."

"Sorry, my battery died. What exactly has he done?"

Issey sucks her teeth. "More like what *hasn't* he. Steve's been screaming to go home all day and he's hurled abuse at every single member of staff, including Dr Noble. He's also broken a door and two wheelchairs. No word of a lie, if you hadn't come, we would have had no choice but to call the police. He can't be allowed to upset the other patients like this. There's people here recovering from strokes and it just isn't fair for them to be exposed to this kind of drama."

Nick and I exchange worried glances. "I'm so sorry," I stammer. "Where is he? Can I see him?"

"Of course. Maybe you'll be able to talk some sense into him."

Hurriedly, we follow Issey through the long corridor to the breakout area where we find Dad eating biscuits and watching TV with a group of sour-faced old men. I can't believe my eyes. He looks even younger than he did last night and right now, I'd say he could easily pass for forty. His skin looks so fresh and rejuvenated, and he even appears to have put on some weight, giving him fuller, more rounded features.

I gasp. My father hasn't looked this good since... well, since forever.

"Carly!" he shouts, pushing back his chair and standing up to greet me. "Thank God, you're here. These idiots have been trying to keep me a prisoner, but I knew you'd come and rescue me. Now, please, please, just sign their bloody consent forms so that I can leave here as soon as possible. I'm telling you, if I spend another second here, I'll go crazy." Tilting his head, he glances beyond me and starts waving frantically. "Hello Nick, good to see you again. We've got a lot to talk about. My positive affirmations have finally worked! Look,

I've healed myself through the power of thought."

"You have indeed," Nick agrees.

"Isn't it wonderful?" Dad beams. "The next novel I write is going to be a belter. I've even thought of a title: *The Path to Healing Mark Two: How I Cured Myself in Seven Days And Then Got Totally Plastered.*" Throwing down his chair, he begins dancing around the room, waving his arms and singing "Gimme Shelter" at the top of his voice.

Nick snickers. He seems to find my father terribly amusing. I, however, fail to see the funny side.

"Stop encouraging him, Nick," I scold. "You'll only make it worse."

"Oh, don't be such a spoilsport. Let your dad have his fun. I promise it will wear off soon, so don't worry."

"Ahem," interrupts a deep voice. I turn around and find Dr Noble standing behind us. His face looks grim. "Carly, could I have a quick word with you in my office?" He throws a glance in Nick's direction and adds, *"Alone."*

Nick frowns at me and I mouth, "Don't worry, I've got this."

Puffing air through my cheeks, I follow Dr Noble into his office and take a seat at his desk. Clasping my hands, I wait nervously for him to leaf through various files and documents.

At last, he lets out a sigh, takes off his glasses and rubs his eyes. He looks as if he hasn't slept for about a week. Running his fingers through his hair, he forces a smile and says, "Listen, I'll level with you, Carly. It's a Sunday, and I don't normally work on Sundays, but Annie told me it was important, so I came in anyway. To be frank with you, your father's recovery is nothing short of miraculous and, with your permission, I'd like to detain him here for a couple more days. I need to run some tests and write a full report about what took place here."

I clear my throat. "I'm sorry, but I don't think that will be possible. My father has expressed very vocally that he wants to leave here. Issey says he's caused a lot of trouble on the ward today and it's clear he doesn't like hospitals. Plus, from what I can see, he's fit and healthy, so there's no reason for him to stay."

Dr Noble laughs stiffly and wipes the corners of his mouth. Beneath the surface, I can sense a volcano about to erupt. "I don't think you quite understand the magnitude of what we are dealing with, Carly. Steve has not only recovered from the stroke, he's also displaying some truly phenomenal capabilities."

"Such as?"

"Well, he came to the hospital a frail old man, but he's leaving as some sort of... some sort of *Hercules*. For crying out loud, he snapped a door off its hinges today and ripped the wheels off a wheelchair without even breaking into a sweat. I've never seen anything like it. And then there's his face: his skin appears so much younger than it did when he arrived, almost like he's aging in reverse." Dr Noble says the last part in a whisper.

I giggle nervously, desperate to quash this line of questioning. "Oh come on, doctor; listen to yourself. Do you seriously expect me to believe that my father is some kind of superhero? Really! He looks just the same as he did yesterday. Perhaps you're taking this thing far too—"

"Do not mock me," Dr Noble hisses, finally beginning to lose his cool. "You and I both know what's happening with your father isn't normal and warrants further investigation. I simply cannot authorise his release today."

"What do you mean?" I'm shouting now. "If my dad is fit and of sound mind, then you have no grounds for keeping him here. Look, I'll sign any consent form you want; just please let him leave here today. I won't allow you to use him as some sort of human guinea pig."

Dr Noble opens his mouth to speak but is interrupted by a knock at the door. "Come in," he shouts, clearly irritated.

The door opens and Nick enters the room. Placing one hand on the back of my chair, he reaches across the table and shakes Dr Noble's hand. "Hi! I'm Nick Craven, Carly's boyfriend. I heard raised voices and wondered if everything's okay in here?"

"Everything's fine," the doctor snaps. "We were just discussing what's best for Steve—" The sentence dies as he attempts to pull his hand away, but Nick refuses to let go. Staring intently at him, Nick fixes Dr Noble with a hypnotic glare that makes his posture slacken, like he's suddenly gone drowsy. Shoulders slouched, the doctor slowly sits back down, his eyes vacant as a mannequin.

"That's right," Nick purrs, releasing his hand. "Close your eyes and take a deep breath. Good...empty your mind completely, relax every part of your body and just focus on my voice. You're falling deeper and deeper into trance. Deeper and deeper..."

Obediently, Dr Noble shuts his eyes.

Nick continues to stare at him, his hold over the physician as potent as a cobra about to strike. "When I will you to do a thing, it shall be done. From this moment on, my will is your will, and you shall cross land and sea to do my bidding. Do you understand?"

"Yes," Dr Noble whispers. Slowly, he opens his eyes again and blinks a few times. Then a broad smile spreads across his face. "What was I saying? Oh yes. So Carly, if you'll just sign these consent forms, I can let your father go home today. He's made a phenomenal recovery, so I see no need to keep him here any longer."

"Great!" I take the paperwork from him and hastily sign everything off.

Nick hovers by the door, grinning. "We'd like to thank you and your staff for taking such good care of Steve, Dr Noble. We'll be forever grateful."

"Well, that's what we're here for," the doctor says cheerily. "All done?"

"Yes." I hand him back his pen and the consent forms.

"Fantastic. Okay, that's everything done. Steve is free to go home."

"Excellent, thanks again," Nick smiles. "Have a wonderful afternoon."

"And you."

"Darling, you were absolutely magnificent," I gush when we're alone in the corridor. "I honestly don't know how you get away with it!"

Nick laughs conceitedly. "Thank you, but let's not get too comfortable. Remember, we're not quite out of the woods yet. We've still got to get past all those nurses. Let's save the celebrations for when we're back in the car."

I nod excitedly. *God, I love him.*

CHAPTER TWENTY-FIVE

Imagination

SOMETIME AROUND SIX, Nick guns the Jag back into our street and parks across the road from my house. The recent shower has calmed to a drizzle, dotting the windscreen with miniscule specks of water. I sigh with relief. *Thank heaven that's over.*

My father unclips his seatbelt. "Home sweet home," he laughs. "Hey Nick, are you sure you don't want to come inside for a coffee? We've still got loads of stuff to talk about. Did I ever tell you about the time I met Sai Baba?"

"Thanks, but I'll have to decline," Nick replies. "I've got an early start tomorrow, so I really should be heading home. But we'll definitely catch up soon. Your stories about India are fascinating."

"Trust me, you haven't heard the half of it. There's stuff that's happened to me that will make your hair stand on end!"

I smile and shake my head. It's been a crazy, crazy drive. Ever since we left the hospital, my father has behaved like a problem child. He's talked non-stop without once taking a breath, and keeps fidgeting and laughing to himself, like there's some private joke we're not in on. At one point, he even leaned out the window and challenged another driver to a race, before Nick intervened. Ar first, I'd found Dad's wild behaviour amusing, but now the joke has worn thin and I just want him to shut up. He's starting to give me a headache.

"Okay," I sigh. "I guess we'd better be going. Oh, Nick, what's the plan for tomorrow?"

"I'll pick you up after work and we'll take it from there," he smiles.

"Great!"

"Have you done your Christmas shopping yet?" Dad asks.

I slap my hand across my forehead. "Oh gosh, it's Christmas on Wednesday! I totally forgot. So much has happened, I've completely lost track of everything."

"Not to worry," Nick winks. "I'm sure we'll sort something out. It's Christmas; not the end of the world."

Laughing maniacally, my father pushes open his door and jumps unceremoniously onto the pavement. Mumbling to himself, he races across the street to our house.

I shoot Nick a look. "I hope to God you're right that this wears off soon. This is utterly exhausting, and I don't know how much more I can take. He's like the bloody Duracell Bunny."

Nick chuckles wickedly. "Will you stop worrying? Like I said, give it a couple of hours and he'll be back to normal, I promise. This is just a phase. It won't last forever." Tenderly, he strokes my cheek with his thumb, his gaze so penetrating I'm forced to avert my eyes. Then his lips find mine and he's eating me out with an intensity that makes my head swim.

After what seems forever, I pull away, breathing pretty hard. "So, I'll see you tomorrow?"

"Definitely."

"I can't wait."

"Me neither."

I get out the car and for a second, I stand by the curb, watching Nick reverse the Jag out of the parking space. He winds down the window, waves at me, and then he's gone.

With a happy sigh, I turn around and follow Dad back into the house.

As soon as I get inside, I run upstairs to charge my mobile. The battery's been dead since morning and I suspect my mother has been trying to contact me. Sure enough, the moment I switch the phone on, a series of voicemails and texts appear. Without bothering to read them, I dial her number.

"Oh my gosh, I've been trying to get through to you for ages."

"Sorry," I reply sheepishly. "My battery died."

"What the hell's going on? Mike and I are at the hospital and the nurses just told us your father's been discharged."

"Yes, that's right. We just got home now."

"But, I don't understand—"

I rub my temples. Now *she's* starting to give me a headache. "Listen, maybe it's best you come down to see us. It's kind of a long story and probably better we talk face to face."

"Okay sweetheart. We'll start coming down now."

"Great. See you soon." I hang up. Collapsing on the bed, I take a few seconds to get my head together. I'm physically and mentally exhausted and could do with some sleep, but I know I need to square things with my mother first.

After a while, I sit up and rub my eyes, trying to keep awake. Throwing on my dressing gown, I go down to the living room, where I find Dad tapping away furiously on his laptop. It seems he's really got his mojo back. Smiling, I head to the kitchen and make us both a cup of tea. About an hour later, the doorbell goes. Bracing myself, I hurry through the hall to answer it.

"Darling, we've been so worried," Mum squeals, kissing

both my cheeks Italian style. "Where's Steve? Is he okay?"

"He's fine," I say. "He's in the living room." I wrinkle my nose. She absolutely stinks of booze.

"Hello, sweetheart," Michael smiles, wiping his boots on the mat. "I hear a celebration is in order."

"Yes, I suppose it is," I grin. Tightening the belt on my dressing gown, I lead them through to the living room.

Mum gasps and covers her mouth in shock. "Good gracious! Steve, what in the world—"

Dad smirks and closes his laptop. "Hello, Katherine. Surprised?"

"Surprised doesn't even come close…" Her voice trails off and she shakes her head incredulously. "What's happened to you?"

He doesn't answer, just keeps grinning.

"Wow, Steve, you look incredible!" Michael gasps. "I hardly recognise you. What the hell did they do to you at the hospital?"

Dad taps the side of his head. "Ah, but it wasn't the hospital, was it? No, it was me. I did this. Through the Laws of Attraction, I healed myself."

Michael frowns. "The Laws of what?"

"New Age mumbo jumbo," Mum snaps. "Honestly, Steve, do you seriously expect us to believe that you did this all by yourself? You look like you're wearing fake tan and had Botox."

He shrugs. "Think what you like, but it's the truth; take it or leave it. I'm living proof that positive affirmations work, and I'm going to share my knowledge with the world. The next book I write is going to focus on how to heal yourself spiritually."

Michael gives a crazy laugh. "I just can't get my head

around this. I don't know what you've done, but whatever you're taking, I want some."

My father laughs and I detect a dangerous fire in his eyes. This is starting to get scary.

Flexing my knuckles, I tilt my head from side to side. I'm like a coiled-up spring. I need to get out of here before I lose it. "Hey, do you guys want some tea? You don't take sugar, Mum, do you?" Before she can respond, I'm already out the door and heading for the kitchen.

"I think I'll need something a lot stronger than tea," she murmurs, following me. "Have you got any Jack Daniels?"

"Nope."

"Oh come on; you must have something even mildly alcoholic."

"I don't think we do." And it's true. Neither my father nor I are big drinkers so we rarely ever keep alcohol in the house. However, on reflection, I do seem to remember having a bottle of Lambrusco somewhere; an unwanted birthday present from someone at work.

Crouching down, I open the cupboard below the sink, pull out the dusty bottle and wipe it clean with a towel.

"Oooh, lovely, you've found something." She rubs her hands together.

Placing the bottle on the sideboard, I go in search of a corkscrew while Mum peruses the cupboards for some wine glasses. She's left bitterly disappointed. We don't have any of those either. Finally, she settles for a chipped red mug from the drying rack.

"Sweetheart, this cup's absolutely filthy," she grumbles. "You never were very good at washing up, were you? You do know you're supposed to use hot water to get all the bits off?"

I ignore the jibe and put the kettle on.

Muttering to herself, my mother turns on the taps and rinses out the mug thoroughly. I smile grimly. For once, her alcoholic tendencies might actually be helping the situation. Given the bizarre circumstances, she's coping remarkably well, and I reckon we have the booze to thank for that. Had my mother been sober, I'm certain this whole thing with Dad would be freaking her out a lot more than it is.

Turning away, I rummage through the bottom drawers and find a bottle opener. I hand it to her. "So, what are we doing for Christmas?" I ask as she fills her cup with the sickly-sweet Lambrusco. "Are we still supposed to be coming up to yours?"

"Of course," she replies. "If the plan had changed, I would have told you. Although, with everything that's happened, I expect it's going to be a rather strange Christmas. Everything's changing and I sense something odd in the atmosphere."

"What do you mean by odd?"

Cup in hand, Mum leans against the sink despondently. "Oh, I don't know. I've just been feeling strange lately. I've been finding it very hard to sleep and I keep having bad dreams."

A shiver courses through me but I don't say anything. The kettle finishes boiling. Silently, I spoon some coffee into my mug and pour the water in. "What sort of dreams?" I ask, not looking at her.

She sighs. "Oh, I don't know. You'll probably think I'm being silly."

"Try me."

"Well, one of them was about you, actually."

"About me?"

"Yes. I dreamt that you were running away from something: a horrendous creature with no face. It was chasing you through an endless corridor and you kept shouting for help but no one was listening. I don't usually take my dreams seriously, but this one was pretty disturbing." She sips her wine and shakes her head dismissively. "Look, please ignore me. I'm feeling groggy. It's probably nothing."

Slowly, I stir the spoon in my coffee. "What did the creature look like?" I ask quietly. "Was it some kind of monster?"

"I don't know what it was. I told you, it didn't have a face, but the whole thing was horrible. I felt like you were in danger, but from what, I couldn't say."

My shoulders stiffen. This is spooky. *Has she got some kind of sixth sense?*

Pushing the thought from my mind, I switch the conversation back to Christmas. For a few minutes, we talk about inconsequential things. I try to keep the mood light and not think too much.

"Actually," I say, "there *is* something I've been meaning to discuss with you." She lifts her brows enquiringly. I take a deep breath. "Is it all right if I bring someone to spend Christmas with us?"

She stares at me a second, her face as blank as a sheet of paper. "What, do you mean like a friend? Ronan?"

I flounder. "No, not Ronan. I mean, like as in a boyfriend."

Her eyes narrow. Hastily, she downs the last of her wine and slams the cup on the sideboard. "Boyfriend? Carly, have you started seeing someone and forgotten to tell me?"

My cheeks burn. "Uh, no. Of course not. I-I wanted to tell you ages ago, but there's been so much going on and, well… we've only been seeing each other a few weeks. You know I'm not that big on… well, you know, making a fuss about things." I pause. "But so far, everything's going great. He's wonderful and I can't wait for you to meet him."

Mum continues to look mortally wounded. "But who is he? Where did you meet him? Is he someone from work?"

"No. His name's Nick and he's a hypnotherapist. We met when I went to him for help to quit smoking and we just hit it off. He's a really lovely guy."

"Well, lovely he may be, but he can't be a very good hypnotist."

"Why?"

"Because you're still smoking like a chimney."

I shrug. "So, anyway, as I was saying; is it all right if Nick spends Christmas day with us? All his family live abroad and I don't want him to spend it alone."

"Darling, of course you can bring him. In fact, I insist. It's about time I met this mystery man of yours."

"Great, I'll let him know. Nick will be over the moon. He's been really looking forward to meeting you."

She smiles but it doesn't reach her eyes. Turning away, she pours herself another glass of Lambrusco and downs it in three gulps.

Suddenly, there's a loud cry from the living room.

Startled, we both look at each other. Then I put down my cup and race out the kitchen to find Dad and Michael having an arm wrestle on the coffee table. Clearly, Dad's getting the upper hand and looks as if he's about to snap off Michael's wrist.

"Hey, hey, break it up!" I shout, lunging between them. "Enough of that!"

"Hold your horses," Dad chuckles. "We were only larking about. No harm done."

"Wow, that's some powerful grip you've got there,"

Michael gasps, rubbing his wrist reproachfully. "I think you may have broken my arm."

"Oh no!" I shout. "He hasn't, has he? Please tell me you're okay?"

Michael continues to rub his arm, prolonging the suspense, then he breaks into a roguish grin. "No, I think everything's present and accounted for. No broken bones today."

I breathe a huge sigh. Then I glare at my father. He doesn't say anything, just sits on the sofa watching us like a mischievous child. I don't know how much longer I can take this. Counting to ten, I run my fingers down my nose and squeeze my eyes shut.

"Listen," I say, turning to my mother. "Maybe it's best we call it a day. Dad's only just come out of hospital and he really should be resting. He shouldn't be arm wrestling—"

"But we only just got here," she interjects. "Why are you kicking us out?"

"Please Mum, don't make this difficult. Of course, I'd love you guys to stay, but I'm just thinking about what's best for Dad. He needs to rest, and I've got to get up early for work tomorrow."

"Carly's right," Michael agrees, putting his hand on her shoulder. "Perhaps we *should* go. It's Christmas Eve on Tuesday, so we'll be seeing them anyway. Plus, if we leave now, we might be able to beat the traffic."

Grudgingly, Mum agrees. As soon as they're gone, I race upstairs and collapse on my bed. Taking ragged breaths, I loosen up and start to see straight again. *Hold it together. Hold it together.*

I roll over on my side and stare at the dolls on my dresser. Judd Nelson and Molly Ringwald gaze down at me from *The*

Breakfast Club poster, their expressions comforting and tender.

Rubbing my temples, I shake my head ruefully. Am I making a mistake letting Nick meet my mother? In the past, she's never got on with any of my boyfriends and I doubt he will be the exception. And then, there's the small matter of him being a vampire... *Oh God.* What if it's a total disaster?

Then I think about how good Nick and I are together, and how he's the love of my life, and my optimism returns. Closing my eyes, I tell myself to stay strong. Of course Nick must meet my mother. *Of course.* For this relationship to work, we need to act like any other normal couple—and normal couples spend Christmas with the in-laws.

Sitting up, I reach down the side of the bed and fish out my box of Marlboros. Then, with a sigh, I walk over to the window and throw it open. Cupping my hands around a match, I light a cigarette and it tastes good. For a moment I stand there, staring out into the dark night, relishing a cool breeze on my face.

As I crush out the cigarette, my gaze falls on a shadowy figure hovering behind a tree in the garden. Shrinking back, I dive beneath the windowsill, heart pounding like a machine gun. Fuck! *What the hell was that?* Even the swift glance I threw was enough to freeze the blood in my veins. Whatever it was didn't look human. Slowly, slowly, I count to ten, pull back the window curtain and stare down at the spot where the creature had been standing.

My breath comes thickly.

There's no one there. *Thank goodness.* It must have been my imagination.

That's what I tell myself, anyway.

CHAPTER TWENTY-SIX

Quickie

THE NEXT MORNING, I get another nasty surprise. As I head through the hall on the way to work, something tells me to check the living room. Peering round the door, I find a young woman lounging on the sofa in one of Dad's old T-shirts, drinking coffee and flicking through one of my gossip mags. Her pink lipstick is smeared, and her nails are all chewed out. She doesn't look a day over twenty; worse still, from the waist down, she's wearing just her knickers.

I'm slack-jawed. "What in the…?"

Instantly, she throws down the magazine and scrambles to her feet. "I-I'm so sorry," she stammers. "Steve never mentioned that he lived with anyone."

"I'm his daughter. Who are you?"

"Sheila." She smiles shyly and looks down at her feet.

"What are you doing here?"

"Your dad… Steve invited me," she replies timidly. "We met at the pub last night and he asked me round. I-I didn't know he lived with anyone. If I did, I wouldn't have come."

In a rage, I storm to my father's room and shake him awake. "Dad, there's a strange girl in the living room. Can you explain?"

"What girl?" he mumbles, burying his face in the pillow. "I don't know what you're talking about."

"Yes you do. You've brought a strange girl back to the house and I want answers—*now!*"

"You must be hallucinating. There isn't any girl..." He breaks off, then a broad grin spreads across his face and I fight the urge to slap him. "Oh yeah, now I remember. I *did* meet a girl at the pub last night. Shelley or Sheba was her name."

"Sheila, her name is Sheila!" I snap. "Or were you so off your face you don't even remember the name of who you picked up? I'm telling you, you've got some serious explaining to do. For Christ's sake, Dad, she's old enough to be your grand-daughter! And what's this about a trip to the pub? You were in bed the last time I saw you."

"I know, but I decided to go back out again. I was buzzing so much I just couldn't sleep. I wanted a bit of fun, so I went to the Brown Hog for a couple of pints. And I'm glad I did. It was truly a great night."

My mouth gapes. I'm totally speechless. There's so much I want to say to him; so much I want to get off my chest, but now is not the time. I'm already late for work so the dressing down will have to wait till I get back.

I jab my finger at him. "Listen," I hiss. "I don't know what you're playing at but I'll tell you one thing: that girl had better be gone by the time I get back. If she isn't, then I'm packing my things and I'm out of here. It's her or me, okay?"

"Oh come on, Carly, you're making too big a deal out of this. Really, it's not as bad as all that. We didn't even have sex. We only—"

I hold up my hands. "For God's sake, spare me the details. I don't want to know. Just make sure she's gone when I get back, okay?"

"Okay. I'm sorry."

"Apology not accepted. Jesus, Dad, don't you think I

already have enough on my plate? What the hell were you thinking?" I glance at my watch and stamp out into the hall. As I pass the living room, I see Sheila gathering up her things, ready to go. When she see me, she flashes a sheepish smile. I scowl at her. Now is not the time for pleasantries.

I step out the front door into a Winter Wonderland. It's snowed overnight and all of the houses are covered in shimmery blankets of white. Everything is silent and serene and despite my anger, I start to get a Christmassy feeling. I stall for a moment, patting down my pockets to check that I haven't forgotten anything. Then I lock up and march down Lavender Hill in the direction of the train station.

With shaky fingers, I light a cigarette and phone Nick for some moral support. He answers after just one ring, and I get the distinct impression he was expecting this call.

"So what's Daddy done now?"

"What are you? Psychic?"

"Mmm, I might be," he teases. "So, tell me, what did he do?"

I raise my eyes heavenward. "Where do I start?" Bitterly, I relay everything that happened with Sheila. Nick punctuates every one of my sentences with a gleeful chuckle, and clearly finds the whole thing hilarious.

"This isn't funny, Nick," I moan. "His behaviour is really starting to frighten me. It feels like I'm living with a child who constantly has to be watched. And—oh God, did I tell you about the arm-wrestling fiasco with Michael yesterday?"

"Arm wrestling?" Nick explodes with laughter. "This gets better and better."

I still don't see the humour. "For crying out loud, it's not funny. He almost broke the poor guy's arm. Seriously, he's a liability."

"Oh go easy on him," Nick soothes. "Remember, this is just a phase. It won't last forever, I promise you. He'll be his old self by the end of the day and then we'll both look back on this and laugh."

"Why do I not believe you?"

"Poor baby. Look, what can I do to cheer you up? Shall I treat you to lunch today?"

My heart melts and I smile despite myself. "I'd never say know to a free meal."

"What time's your lunch break?"

"One-thirty."

"Fine. I'll meet you outside your office at half one and we'll take it from there. Hopefully, I can find a way to put a smile back on your face."

I giggle mischievously. Everything about him is so damn sexy. "Oh, I forgot to say; I spoke to my mother and it's all sorted. You're spending Christmas with us."

"Wonderful. I look forward to it."

"Great! Ooh, I'm so excited. She's expecting us to come down tomorrow for Christmas Eve and spend the night. It's going to be so much fun."

The line goes quiet and for a second, I wonder if Nick's really as happy as he's making out. It bugs me a little, but I put it down to last-minute nerves about meeting Mum.

"Darling, I'd better go. I'm almost at the train station." Taking a final drag on my cigarette, I tell Nick I love him and hang up. Then I fumble through my pockets for my Oyster card and head into the station.

Throughout the journey to work, I keep replaying the events of the morning over and over. I wonder if Sheila's still at the house and if she and Dad swapped numbers. I wonder how old she is and if this is definitely the last I'll see of her. I also wonder what other mischief my father could be getting up to. I stress so much about it, I give myself a headache and spend most of the journey clutching my temples.

When I finally arrive at work, I'm still fuming about everything.

"Men are bloody impossible!" I snipe.

Mark glances up from his *Metro* and grins. "Ooh, sexist! There's some bloody impossible women out there too you know."

I throw down my bag and stamp my foot. "Do you know what my dad did last night?"

"No, but I think you're going to tell me."

Through gritted teeth, I tell him about Sheila, but before I've even finished, he's whooping and clapping like it's the best news he's ever heard. "Brilliant, brilliant! Your dad's a total legend. I just hope I'm still able to pull twenty-year-olds when I'm his age."

"Oh my God, Mark, not you too. Why does everyone find this funny?"

"Because it is. I think you're making a mountain out of a mole hill. He's single, she's single; they're two consenting adults, so I don't see the problem. You need to give your dad a break, Carly. It sounds like he's having fun and you're spoiling the party."

"But what if it was *your* father, huh?"

"I'd give him a high five."

"Oh Mark, you're impossible."

"Is that your new favourite saying or shall I give you a thesaurus?"

Still chuckling, he folds up his paper and throws it down on the desk. "Now, here's the million-dollar question: did you remember to buy my M&M's?"

"Yes, but I'm loathe to give them to you now that I know you're siding with the enemy."

"I'm not siding with anyone. I just tell it like it is."

Reluctantly, I rummage through my bag and hand over the shiny, yellow packet.

"Merci beaucoup."

After I've hung up my coat, we swap positions and I take my place behind reception. Almost immediately, the phone starts ringing. "Hello, reception desk, Carly speaking. Uh-huh, uh-huh. Yes, he's here." I stop the phone against my chest. "Mark, it's Tim. He says—"

"The women's toilet is broken again, and he wants me to reset the password?"

"Um, yes. Sorry."

Mark shakes his head. "Off we go to the third floor again. This is getting tedious, but on the plus side, my legs are getting plenty of exercise."

Placing the receiver back in the cradle, I press the release button and watch him disappear into the elevator.

"Thanks for covering me," I shout. "I really appreciate it."

"Pas de problème."

As soon as he's gone, I fumble through the cleaning box in search of the spray polish. When I find it, I wipe down the desk, arrange the signing-in folders and do a general tidy up. Then I answer some emails and try hard not to think too much. The rest of the morning drags and by lunchtime, I'm bursting to escape the building and see Nick.

Just as I'm heading out the door my phone starts beeping. Excitedly, I flip it open and see a text from Nick: *Take off your knickers and meet me at the front of the building in 5.*

His words cause a monumental swell of desire between my legs. *Oh my gosh, this is so sexy.* Checking that the coast's clear, I hitch up my skirt, step out of my tights and knickers and put them in my coat pocket. Steeling myself, I head through the automatic doors into the street. I glance left and right.

No sign of him.

Did we definitely agree to meet at the front of the building?

Frowning, I open my phone and read the message again. No, it definitely says the front of the building. Just as I'm about to close the phone, another text comes through: *Turn right and keep walking till you get to the stationary shop. You'll see me very soon.*

With a dirty big grin, I tighten my scarf and continue down the street at a steady pace, my stomach turning somersaults at the thought of what is to come. The air is bitterly cold and cuts into my cheeks like piano wire, but I don't care. Nothing can stop me. I'm so excited a tsunami couldn't prevent me from keeping this rendezvous.

I walk for another few minutes but still see no sign of him. Heart racing, I pull out my phone to call him, but before I get the chance, a powerful hand slips into mine and drags me down an alleyway. Pushing me against a wall, Nick throws himself on me, his arms spread-eagled as his body grinds hard against mine. I swoon at his touch, my head spinning with excitement. This feels like a dream, a crazy dream I never want to wake up from.

His hands are everywhere, pawing my skin, tearing at my clothes and breasts. It feels like an assault, but I absolutely love it. Locking his fingers in my hair, Nick tilts my face upwards to meet his gaze. His eyes burn with longing.

"You make me so crazy," he growls. "It's agony being away from. I've spent all day dreaming of this moment."

Closing my eyes, I moan softly as his powerful arms wrap

around me and lift me up as if I weighed nothing. Lowering his head, his mouth bites and scrapes my lips, eating me out with ravenous urgency. My whole body is on fire. I have no sense of time or space, only a soul-destroying void that needs to be filled.

Roughly, he slips up my skirt and seeks out the scorching-hot wetness there. I gasp as he rubs slow circles around my clit before burying one finger deep inside my pussy, causing an explosion of juices down my thighs.

"Fuck, you're so wet for me," he rasps. "You need a good seeing to and I'm more than happy to oblige." Rapidly, he starts to finger me, while simultaneously covering my face and lips with hungry kisses that rob me of sanity.

Someone rounds the corner and crosses to the other side of the alley. This is getting dangerous.

Whimpering with excitement, I shut my eyes and focus on the wonderful sensation down below. It feels so good having his fingers inside me, but my pussy is longing for something thicker and more substantial. This is a very sexy game we're playing. The idea that we could be seen at anytime turns me on big time.

After a while, Nick withdraws his hand, bites my earlobe and whispers: "Are you ready for me?"

"Uh-huh."

"How much do you want it?"

"So much."

Unbuckling his trousers, he frees his huge throbbing cock and with one mind-blowing thrust, he's inside me, buried so deep it's like he's splitting me in two. Back and forth he slams, stretching me beyond the point of no return. To outsiders, we have the appearance of lovers locked in an embrace, and it thrills me to know I'm secretly getting fucked in front of strangers.

With a low sigh of pleasure, I drop my head onto Nick's chest as his huge throbbing shaft pounds into to me again and again. I'm completely full and loving every single minute. The bricks feel hard and rough against my spine but I don't care. I feel alive, *so bloody alive*. With frightening strength, Nick fucks me harder, deeper, banging me so ferociously I'm seeing stars. I am dying in ecstasy, lost in a whirlwind of lust I never want to end.

At last, a nourishing warmth ripples through my body as Nick increases his thrusts, working me up into a crescendo of sparking fireworks. Bursts of juice coat his dick as I finally orgasm. I bite back a scream and he explodes inside of me. Still, he continues fucking through the tightness, elongating my climax longer than I've ever experienced.

Then, with a loud gasp, he falls away from me. Dazed and breathless, I slide my knickers and tights back on and smooth down my crumpled skirt. I'm completely and totally spent.

Smiling warmly, Nick wraps me in his coat and tenderly kisses my forehead. "I'm sorry baby, I'm going to have to love you and leave you. I've got an important meeting this afternoon so I'll need to get back to the office. But I'll see you back here at five and we'll go Christmas shopping."

"Yes," I murmur, trying to keep my balance. "I'll see you then."

"I love you."

"Love you too. So, so much."

Taking my hand, he walks me back to my office.

CHAPTER TWENTY-SEVEN

Shopping in Bond Street

A T FIVE PAST five, I pull on my coat, say goodbye to Mark and step out into the snow-covered street. Instantly, Nick catches me in his arms and crushes his lips against mine, consuming me with a heat that makes my knees tremble. After what seems forever, he releases me and tenderly strokes my cheek with his thumb.

"Ready?" he whispers.

"Uh-huh." Feeling light-headed, I take his arm and he leads me through hoards of late-night shoppers and tourists in the direction of Bond Street. Everything looks like Santa's Grotto: coloured lights and seasonal store displays. Rubbing my arms against the cold, I stamp my feet in an effort to keep warm. My eyelashes are frozen and I can't feel my legs, but I don't care. With Nick beside me I feel like I'm walking on air. Everything is so wonderfully Christmassy, it's like I'm a child again.

We walk at a steady pace, blending flawlessly with all the other couples out for Monday night in search of a last-minute bargain. I feel so proud to be on his arm, yet at the same time it's also a little weird; a mixture of excitement and apprehension. I wonder what all of these people would say if they knew Nick is a vampire. I whisper my fears to him, but he just laughs it off with a shrug. He says he likes the danger; likes the fact that we have this big secret that no one else is in on.

I have to agree it is sort of fun and a little scary.

Around six o'clock, we reach Selfridges and fight our way through the crowds to peruse the designer shelves. Clutching my hand, Nick takes me up the escalators to the second floor where he buys my mother a gorgeous Chloé shoulder bag, a Rolex watch for Dad and a set of gold cufflinks for Michael. Then he asks me what I want for Christmas and tells me I can have anything in the shop.

I shake my head and give his hand a little squeeze. "That's sweet of you, but I don't want anything."

"Are you sure? I told you, you can have anything. No expense spared."

"No, I've already got what I want. Nick, you're the best present a girl could wish for."

He smiles down at me warmly, his expression filled with love. "Do you have any other shopping to do? Have you bought your mum and dad their presents yet?"

"No, I already crotched their gifts months ago. I made Dad and Michael reindeer sweaters and Mum a new scarf."

"That sounds great. You're so creative, my darling."

I beam at the compliment. For a moment, I forget all of the darkness and dare to dream of leading an ordinary life with him. Golden moments like these are what it's all about.

After Nick's paid for his stuff, we head back to find the car, which is parked in one of the turnings off Harley Street. As we walk, I ask him if he ever has any problems with religious symbols, especially at this time of year. Surely, I reason, his adverse reaction to crucifixes means he must steer clear of all objects associated with Jesus? Okay, so churches are easy enough to avoid but what, for example, would happen if he saw someone wearing a crucifix in the street? Or saw a crucifix on TV? Or in a shop window? Would that cause an immediate reaction or does the crucifix have to have direct contact with his skin?

"It doesn't work like that," Nick smiles. "Inanimate religious objects are not enough to produce a reaction in me—it is the *belief system* behind them that affects me." He pauses as he takes out his car keys and unlocks the doors to his Jag. "On its own, a crucifix is nothing but a scrap of metal, but if the person wearing it truly believes in Christ, then it affects me."

He laughs bitterly. "Luckily for me, a recent survey showed that only 25 per cent of the British public actually believe in God, as opposed 50 per cent who definitely don't. What this means is that there are far more atheists out there than you think, despite England being described as a 'Christian country.' For most people, Christmas is a time to stuff their faces; for greetings card companies and supermarkets to milk the masses and quadruple their sales of turkey. Very few people actually care about what this time of year originally represented and in the wake of terrorism, the majority now view religion as the cause of more harm than good in the world."

Nodding silently, I open the door and slip into the passenger seat. Nick loads up the car boot with his purchases. *This is starting to get very interesting.*

"So," I say. "That must mean I believe in God."

Nick doesn't answer straight away. Quietly, he gets in the car and fastens up his seatbelt. Then he looks at me and says, "Yes, I suppose it does. For me to have had that awful reaction when you gave me the crucifix, I would say it most certainly points to that."

My brows furrow. "But I didn't think I did... *not really.* Neither of my parents is particularly religious. Okay, so my mother's a non-practicing Catholic and Dad's obsessed with all that New Age stuff, but no one ever forced me to go to church. Of course, I did go to a Catholic girls school, but since then I've only ever been to church a couple of times over the years, and that's just for funerals and weddings."

"Well, for whatever reason, you must have an unwavering faith, despite what you say. Sometimes our true beliefs are buried deep in our subconscious and only manifest at times of great urgency."

My heart soars with hope. "So, God exists? Is that what you're trying to tell me? All that stuff about Jesus and the Christmas story is real?"

He makes a non-committal sound. "Hey look, we're running low on fuel. Keep an eye out for a petrol garage."

"Please answer the question."

He laughs good-humouredly. "My lips are sealed."

I bounce up and down, barely able to contain my excitement. "But Nick, for vampires to hate crucifixes, that must mean that Jesus was real. It means he was the son of God!"

Nick snickers and covers my mouth to shush me. "Sssh, not so loud. Do you want the whole street to hear our conversation?"

"Just answer yes or no. Did Jesus exist?"

Shaking his head, Nick starts the engine and carefully steers the car onto the main road and heads in the direction of south London. Throughout the journey, he refuses to answer any of my questions, saying that when the time is right, he'll reopen this discussion. But for now, he just wants us to enjoy the drive.

Playfully, I agree to drop the subject but make a mental note to revisit this another time. There's no way he's getting off that easily.

At quarter past nine, we arrive back in my street. Nick parks up and for a moment, we sit in semi-darkness, our faces illuminated by the green light from the dashboard.

"So…" he sighs.

"So…" I sigh. "What's the plan for tomorrow?"

"Are you going to work? It's Christmas Eve and I thought most people had the day off?"

"No such luck. My manager Tim wants everyone in, but he's letting us go early, so that's at least some consolation. Tomorrow I should be finished around three o'clock."

"Great, well, why don't you head straight home, and I'll pick you and your father up at six? Your mother lives in Purley, right?"

"Yes."

"Fine, then that's settled. I'll pick you up at six."

"Hey, remember to bring your overnight gear. Oh, and a toothbrush."

He smiles indulgently. "You're so cute."

"Cute? What happened to sexy?"

"That goes without saying."

There's a moment of blissful silence. I can feel his eyes on me, probing me deep. Reaching out, he softly strokes the sensitive skin behind my ear, something that always made me go crazy. I squeeze my thighs together and privately count to ten. Nick smiles seductively. He knows exactly what buttons to push. Gently, he continues to stroke my face, making me moan with pleasure, then slowly, he moves his hand down my shoulder, rests his fingers on my thigh, and traces invisible circles.

I catch my breath and tilt my head back with my eyes closed. "Damn that feels so good."

Soothingly, his hand continues its journey into my skirt

and up my thigh, stroking, teasing, sending me out of my mind. Then abruptly, he pulls away, grabs both of my hands and kisses them passionately.

"Carly, I have something important to say." I open my eyes and look at him, my heart thudding against my ribcage. "You know how much I love you, don't you?" I nod. "And you still want to marry me?" I nod again. "Okay," he says quietly.

Releasing my hand, he opens up the glove compartment and retrieves a small, black box. Deftly, he flips it open to reveal a stunning engagement ring with a magnificent diamond in its centre.

I cup one hand over my mouth. "Oh my God Nick, it's beautiful!"

Silently, he takes out the ring and slides it onto my engagement finger. I squint at it. The stone is absolutely breathtaking.

He clears his throat. "Carly, you know I've already accepted your marriage proposal, and I want nothing more than to be the perfect husband for you, but it's only right that I return the gesture to make it truly official. Will you take my hand and walk through life next to me forever?"

I fan myself to calm my racing heart. "Yes! Yes, a thousand times!"

Never in my wildest dreams did I ever imagine someone proposing to me in such a romantic way. It feels like a fairy tale, like I'm Snow White or Cinderella, living the dream in one of my favourite Disney movies. I never, ever want this to end.

Taking me in his arms, Nick kisses my nose, my forehead, and then my lips. When he tries to loosen his grip, I continue to cling to him, not wanting to let go. Finally, he pulls away and whispers, "You'd better go inside now and get some sleep, darling. I'll see you tomorrow."

"Promise?"

"I promise."

After a final, lingering kiss, I unclip my seatbelt and step out onto the pavement.

"Love you!" he shouts through the window.

"Love you more!" I shout back. Then I blow him a kiss and he pretends to catch it. We both laugh. Waving a final goodbye, I turn around and race toward my house. My heart swells with joy; it feels like I'm walking on air.

As soon as I get inside, I head straight for the living room where I find Dad eating a sandwich and watching a game show. He flashes a sheepish grin and switches off the TV. Tucking his shirt into his trousers, he gets to his feet and walks over to me. His face has lost much of its youthful glow and I'm relieved to see that the effects of Nick's blood are starting to wear off.

"Hello, my dear, did you have a good day?"

"Yeah, it was great. I just got back from shopping with Nick." I glance around the room. "Where's Sheila?"

"Oh, I sent her packing ages ago. I paid for her taxi home." He hesitates, choosing his words carefully. "Listen Carly, I just wanted to apologise again for what happened last night. It was totally unacceptable and I honestly don't know what came over me. But you can rest assured it won't happen again. Your old dad isn't going to do anything else embarrassing, I promise you."

"Apology accepted. Hey, look at this…" I flash my engagement ring. His eyes widen.

"Is that what I think it is?"

I nod silently, eyes shining.

Dad throws his arms around me. "Oh my dear, that's wonderful! I'm so happy for you. I'm assuming Nick's the lucky guy?"

"Who else?"

"Great, just great. I couldn't ask for a better son-in-law."

"You don't think it's too soon?"

"Of course not. If you both feel the time is right, then why wait? Why put off to tomorrow what you can do today?" He hugs me again, and I sense that his delight is genuine. "No really my dear, this is the best news I've heard in ages. Let's see the ring again." I hold it up to him. He smiles and shakes his head. "That's one killer stone. Nick has really outdone himself."

I smile magnanimously. It feels so good to have my father's approval.

CHAPTER TWENTY-EIGHT

Dinner

A T TWENTY TO eight the next evening, we arrive outside my mother's large mock Tudor house on a pretty, tree-lined street near Purley train station. As Nick pulls over, he tells me and my father to go on up to the house while he fetches our bags from the car boot.

Taking my arm, Dad leads me up the drive toward the grand entrance door. I let out a long slow breath. My mother has really gone to town with the fake snow and Christmas lights, and for some strange reason, seeing it gives me butterflies. I don't know what the night will bring, but I hope I've made the right decision bringing Nick here.

Dad rings the bell. Almost instantly, Mum appears on the doorstep wearing the snowman sweater I made for her last year and sparkling antlers on her head.

"Come in, come in," she trills. "You must both be freezing."

I stomp the snow off my boots. "How are you, Mum?"

"I'm fine. I've just put the potatoes in."

"Oh, so that's what smells so good," Dad grins. "What's on the menu tonight?"

"Only beef. Nothing too fancy." She gives him a hug and pecks me on the cheek. Smiling, I present her with the bottle of Château Begadan Cru Artisan Médoc Nick bought for her.

"Very, very nice," she observes. "Your boyfriend obviously has expensive taste."

I giggle coquettishly.

"Do I hear voices?" Michael appears from a side door and Dad goes through to the hall to greet him. I remain on the doorstep with Mum, waiting for Nick to return with the bags. As he crosses the street, he smiles and waves happily at us. For a brief second, a peculiar expression crosses my mother's face; a mixture of excitement and unease. Then she wipes it away with a smile and waves back to him.

"Is that Nick?" she says through gritted teeth.

"Yes, that's him."

As he gets closer, her gaze slips over his body, devouring every piece of him with hungry eyes. The sexual attraction is instant, and I find myself mesmerised by the awfulness of the unfolding debacle.

Oh no. This is not good.

"Hello Katherine, it's so lovely to finally meet you." Nick offers her his hand and she shakes it stiffly. She keeps patting her hair and licking her lips, her eyes transfixed by the scar on his face. She's like putty in his hands.

"Carly's told me so much about you," he continues.

"That's odd," she says. "I've heard very little about you. Until yesterday, I didn't even know you existed. But I'm sure we'll redress the balance tonight."

"Indeed we will."

There's a short, uncomfortable silence. My mother doesn't seem to know what to do with herself. Then at last, she steps aside for him to enter. Nick remains on the doorstep, holding the bags like an expectant concierge. He flicks a glance in my direction and I suddenly realise his dilemma.

Shit! Crossing the threshold, crossing the threshold…

"Is that a formal invitation?" Nick asks softly.

"Of course!" Mum replies. "Come inside before we all freeze to death."

Grinning broadly, Nick finally enters and I breathe a huge sigh of relief. *That was close.*

"Oh, you can drop the bags in the hall," Mum says. "Michael will take them upstairs in a minute."

"Thanks."

Silently, we follow her through the glittering entrance lobby into a large sitting room where an enormous Christmas tree sits before a brick and tile fireplace. Double doors lead to the open plan dining room and bi-folding doors leading to the rear garden.

"Hello, hello," Michael booms. "Nick, I presume?"

"Yes, and you must be Michael."

"Mike."

"Mike! Okay."

They shake hands warmly. "Is that your Jag outside?"

"Yes."

"What a beauty. What does she top out at?"

"One-seventy."

Michael gives a low whistle. As they launch into a conversation about cars, Mum pulls me to one side.

"Well, what do you think?" I whisper. "Do you like him?"

"What's this?" She grabs my hand and scrutinises my engagement ring.

My cheeks flame. "You know what it is," I stammer.

Mum releases my hand, her eyes wide and incredulous. "Steve, have you seen this?"

The three men turn in our direction. Dad nods his head excitedly. "Yes, Carly told me yesterday. It's marvellous, isn't it?"

"What's marvellous?" Michael frowns. I flash the ring at him and his face lights up. "Oh my God, you're engaged? That's fantastic! Have you set a date?"

"Not yet," I smile. "But soon. The sooner the better."

"Wow, then we're really going to have to celebrate. Time to crack open the Moet methinks." Beaming, Michael slaps Nick on the back. "Congratulations!"

Nick doesn't answer. His eyes are fixed on my mother, trying to gauge her response to the news. It's hard to tell what he's thinking.

"Katherine," Dad frowns. "Aren't you going to congratulate Carly on her wonderful news?"

I lift my brows questioningly. "Mum?"

Reluctantly, she reaches out and gives me a stiff, one-armed hug. "Congratulations, sweetheart. I'm so thrilled for you both." Her lips barely move like it's paining her to be civil.

"Katherine!" Michael prods. "What the hell's wrong with you? Your daughter is getting married. This is an engagement party not a funeral."

"I know," she says coldly. "I guess I'm just a little miffed to be presented with a fait accompli, but whatever, I'm happy for you both." Forcing a grin, she hugs me again. She can't bring herself to do the same to Nick. "Well, now that's over, I guess I'll continue making dinner. I'd give it about another forty minutes."

Without another word, she hurries off to the kitchen. I'm dumbfounded by her rudeness, but know there's more to this than meets the eye.

"Sorry about that," Michael says quietly. "I don't know what's got into her."

"One too many vodkas, probably," my father says cheerfully. "Don't worry; a couple more should set her straight."

There's another awkward pause. "Hey, let me take you upstairs and show you guys your rooms so you can get settled."

"Thanks, Michael," I smile.

We follow him upstairs to the first-floor landing. Nick and I have been given the guest room next to the study and Dad has been put in Michael's son's old room a few doors down. Our room is sparse and white with a large double bed and en-suite bathroom. The air is heavy with the scent of roses.

"Right," Michael says, "I'll leave you guys to freshen up. If you need anything, just give me a shout, okay?"

"Thanks," Nick smiles. "You're too kind."

"Are you okay?" I ask when we're alone. "I must apologise for my mother's stinking behaviour. I guess I should have expected this. It's a lot for her to take in. I mean, she only just met you today and then she hears we're getting married. It must have knocked her for six, but I guess that's how most mothers would react. But I'm sure she'll come around eventually."

Nick doesn't reply. Silently, he starts to unpack our clothes, laying everything out neatly on the bed. I watch him for a few seconds. "Darling, please say something," I implore. "At least let me know what you're thinking."

He glances at me with hurt eyes, but continues to remain silent. His expression breaks my heart.

"Nick, please! Just... *say something.*"

"She hates my guts," he says quietly. "The moment she laid eyes on me, she hated me. I felt it."

"No, she doesn't. She's just scared of change, that's all. Once she's got to know you better, she'll be fine. You can charm her, Nick. I know you can. I've seen you do a hundred times. Don't tell me you can't charm her."

He laughs bitterly. "You really think it's that simple? We're dealing with a mother's intuition here."

"Oh, come on, I thought you were stronger than this. No one ever said this was going to be easy. Just give it some time and everything will be fine."

"No, it won't. You saw the way she looked at me. Don't try to deny it, Carly. I know you did! First, she felt the attraction, that was obvious; it's in my genetic makeup, part of my lethal design." He pauses, takes a ragged breath. "She felt the attraction, but then she hated herself for it, and then the feeling became a heavy stone of hatred in her stomach. She sensed something abnormal about me; it practically reeks from every pore of my being, and she sensed it. She knows something's up and it's bugging her big time."

"So what if she does?" I retort. "She'll never guess the truth in a million years. Look, if we just play it cool we can—"

"I think maybe it was a mistake to come here." He rakes his fingers through his hair. "I don't want to cause any rifts between you and your mother."

"I don't care what rift it causes. If she can't be happy for me, then that's her problem. She'll just have to deal with it. We made a pact, Nick; we agreed to stick together no matter what. You're the one I love, the one I want to be with. If she can't deal with that, then tough! We're in this together Nick. Please don't let me down now."

He turns away and walks over to the window. The sky outside is black as a vampire's tomb. We stay like that for a while, motionless—our breathing the only sound in the room. Then I come up behind him and softly stroke his back, his shoulders, his arms, trying to calm him, trying to soothe him.

Instantly, I sense all his tension melt beneath my fingers, and he lets out a low, frustrated sigh.

"I'm sorry darling," I whisper. "I know how hard this is, but we've just got to face it. Let's give this one final go, okay? Perhaps we can win her over, but even if we don't, who cares? At least we can say we gave it a try."

"Okay," he replies. "Let's do this." Turning around, he grabs my hand and presses it roughly to his cheek. "I love you."

"I love you too."

We return downstairs and find the cutlery laid out for us in the dinning room. My father is already seated, stuffing his face with bread rolls and lashings of butter. "You look beautiful, my dear."

I glace down at my Minnie Mouse dress. "Thanks, Dad. You don't look too bad yourself."

"Make yourself comfortable, guys," Michael beams, opening the Château Begadan Cru Artisan Médoc.

Nick and I take a seat at opposite sides of the table. At that moment, my mother enters the room brandishing a tray of roast parsnips. She places it in the centre of the table. "A word of caution, all the plates are hot. Touch them at your peril."

Without making eye contact with any of us, she sweeps back to the kitchen. I roll my eyes. *Okay, so we're playing that game, are we? Bring. It. On.*

"Hey Nick, did I ever tell you about my time at the Tibetan monastery?"

"No Steve, but I'd love to hear it."

"You spent time at a monastery?" Michael enthuses, coming around to my side of the table.

"Yes, back in '93. Just after I returned from Singapore."

"Tell me when, Carly," Michael says. He's about to pour the wine when I place my hand over the glass.

"Er, no thanks. I think I'll stick with water tonight."

"It's Christmas. Surely you can have at least one glass?"

I release my hand and let him pour. "Okay, just one, but that's it."

"There's a girl."

Placing the bottle on the table, he takes a seat next to Nick and the two of them listen to dad's hair-raising stories of Tibet. Ten minutes later Mum returns with the beef and we all settle down to eat. Every now and then I glance up at her to check if she's softened at all. Nope. She still looks like somebody's died. *Oh give me a break!*

I raise my eyes heavenward. This is getting unbearable.

"So, what do you do, Mike?" Nick asks, breaking the ice.

"I work in construction," Michael replies.

"Construction? That sounds interesting. What sort of construction?"

"Oh, new builds, renovations, that sort of thing." Happy to be holding court, Michael tells a story I've heard dozens of times before, the one about how he left school at sixteen and went straight into an apprenticeship before starting up his own company, Hilltop Construction at the tender age of twenty. The rest, as they say, is history.

"My big break came when I got a contract with Croydon Council," he boasts. "That's where the money is, council contracts. If you have friends in the Town Hall, then you're sorted. Are you familiar with the Mansfield Estate, the one near East Croydon train station?"

Nick nods vaguely. "Yes, I think I passed it on the way down."

"Well, that estate was one of our first big jobs. Once we

got it, everything else just fell into place. Like I said, once you've got a foot in the Town Hall, you're head and shoulders above the competition. It guarantees a steady stream of work and over the years, they've become our biggest client. I've also just been very lucky. If I was starting over today, it might not be so easy."

"Oh, don't be so modest," Nick laughs. "I'm sure you worked very hard to make your 'luck' happen. I congratulate you on your success, it must feel good to have finally achieved your dreams."

"It certainly does." Michaels pauses and takes a sip of his wine. He is clearly enjoying Nick's compliments.

"Whatever Mike wants, Mike gets," Dad says with a touch of steeliness to his voice. "Take this house for instance. I remember we used to pass it every day on the way to school, and Mike used to say, "one day I'll have that house." All the other kids laughed and thought it was a pipe dream, but now look, here we are fifty years later, sitting in it. I mean, isn't that something?"

"It most definitely is," Nick agrees.

"Positive affirmations go a long way to getting what you want." Dad hesitates, weighing up his next words. My mother shoots him a withering look. We all know where this is heading, but Dad just can't help himself. "It even works when you apply it to your love life. It can get you any woman you want, even if that woman is already taken."

"Please, Steve," Michael begs. "We're just trying to have a nice evening. Give it a rest, huh?"

"But it's true," my father says innocently. "You've got everything you want: the house, the wife, the career. I take my hat off to you. I don't know a better example of a self-made man."

Michael throws down his napkin in exasperation. "All right Steve, if you want to punish someone, then fine, punish me. But please bear in mind that there are other people present who don't deserve to have their Christmas ruined by two squabbling old men. Now look, you've just survived a stroke, and your lovely daughter here is getting married. You should be on top of the world. In fact, I can't think of any reason for any of us to be unhappy right now. Getting you out of hospital is the best Christmas present we could ask for. Sure, we've all had some shit to deal, but for once, can everybody please just agree to get along?" He glances around the table. "Agreed?"

The room goes quiet for a beat. Mum stabs a carrot onto her fork and chews it like she's chewing leather.

"Agreed?" Michael repeats more forcefully.

"Agreed," we all bleat.

"Could you be a dear and pass me the bread knife?" Mum asks. I hand it to her, and she proceeds to cut the wholemeal loaf into meticulous slices.

Nick clears his throat. "So, Michael, I take it you and Steve grew up around here?"

"Yes," Michael says. "We used to live next door to each other. Our old primary school is a couple of streets down from here."

"Nice."

Michael begins eating again. "So, what about you, Nick? Katherine tells me you're a hypnotist."

"Hypnotherapist," Nick corrects.

"What's the difference?" my mother says flippantly. "Surely they're one and the same?"

"Not exactly," Nick replies. "Anyone can learn to put someone into trance to perform a parlour trick, but just giving suggestions on a superficial level does not resolve the deeper issues; it only stops the problem for a short period of time. Now, a *hypnotherapist* goes much deeper. For instance, when treating addictions, we're talking about very complex issues that require years of professional training and an understanding of how the mind works to successfully treat underlying behavioural patterns."

"In other words, there's a method to the madness," Mum says.

"Exactly," Nick agrees. "A hypnotherapist will always know his boundaries. When a patient agrees to undergo hypnosis, it involves a great deal of trust and so should only be carried out by a consummate professional."

"And are you?" my mother asks sweetly.

"Am I what?"

"A consummate professional?"

"Of course."

"I beg to differ."

Nick struggles to keep his composure. "How so?"

She flicks a sly glance in my direction. "Well, having a romantic affair with one of your patients is surely not the most professional conduct, is it? If you were a medical doctor, that could get you struck off for impropriety." There's a moment of loaded silence. Michael looks like he wants the ground to swallow him up. I have to bite my tongue.

Nick puts down his fork and looks her squarely in the eye. "I can assure you, nothing inappropriate occurred between Carly and I while she was still my patient. And for the record, I am no longer treating her so we are not in breach of anything."

Michael glares at his wife. "You don't have to explain yourself, Nick. It's Katherine's rather odd attempt at humour which sadly often misses the mark. You were only joking, weren't you Katherine?"

All eyes are now on her. She laughs gently. "Yes, of course. What do I know anyway? You're both consenting adults so what you do is your business. You're not the first couple to break the doctor/patient boundaries and I'm sure you won't be the last."

"What's on TV tonight?" Dad pipes up. "I fancy watching an old movie. Maybe *It's a Wonderful Life*."

I take a large gulp of wine to calm my nerves. *Jesus, I just want this fucking night to be over.*

CHAPTER TWENTY-NINE

Desire in the Night

"MY GOD, SHE'S impossible," I grumble. Brushing my teeth furiously, I run the tap continuously as I spit out water and toothpaste. "She's absolutely bloody impossible." I stare angrily at my reflection. "Impossible, impossible!"

"What was that, baby?" Nick shouts from the bedroom. "I can't hear a word you're saying."

I turn off the tap. "I *said* my mother's impossible!"

"All right, no need to shout; I can hear you loud and clear."

Buttoning up my night dress, I switch off the bathroom light and head into the bedroom where I find Nick already under the duvet, waiting for me. He looks irresistible, but right now, my mind can't focus on anything sexual. Irately, I march over to the dresser and open a tub of peach-scented face cream. Rubbing lotion into my skin, I continue to rant. "I mean, honestly, she's completely spoiled Christmas. That lovely present you bought for her from Selfridges; she doesn't deserve it. Now I just can't wait for tomorrow to be over so we can go home and never come back."

"You don't mean that."

"Oh, yes I do. She's completely ruined the atmosphere; all those nasty, spiteful digs she made during dinner. It took every ounce of strength for me not to lunge at her."

"Calm down, baby," Nick soothes. "You're getting too worked up over this. We both know why she's behaving this way. It's a reaction to me, she can't help herself. I told you, my genetic makeup—"

"No, Nick, I'm not letting her off that easily. This isn't about you; it's about me. She's never approved of any of my boyfriends. Not you, not Andrew, not anyone. It's like she doesn't want me to ever be happy."

"I'm sure that isn't true. Every mother wants their child to be happy."

"Well, maybe I'm the exception." I gesture wildly. "Every time it looks like I'm getting my life together, she puts a spanner in the works. It's like she doesn't want my life to ever move forward; like she wants me to stay in this nice little box where she can pick me up and play with me and put me away again when she's done." I jab my finger at him. "I swear to you, if she doesn't change her attitude, she's not coming to the wedding. No way. I won't have bad vibes on my big day. I just won't stand for it."

He shoots me a smouldering look. "Why don't you come to bed and forget about this for a while? Things will be better in the morning, I promise."

"I wouldn't bet on it," I say darkly. "Trust me; this is just the start of the war."

Nick raises himself on one elbow and studies me hard. Then, with a seductive grin, he throws back the duvet to reveal he's completely stark naked. My breath catches. *Fucking hell. Now* he's got my full and undivided attention. I moisten my lips in anticipation of what is to come. Then I remember where we are and my heart sinks. *No nookie tonight.* Not in this house; not with my parents sleeping just a few doors away.

Miserably, I switch off the lights and dive on the bed,

pulling the covers right up to my chin. Nick gives a low snicker and reaches out for me. I roll away from him and perch at the very edge of the mattress, pretending to be tired.

"Night," I say. "Sleep well."

"Hey, what's all this about?" he laughs, grabbing me and snuggling me into his chest. I want to pull away but, as usual, my body isn't following instruction. *Shit, this feels too good.*

"I'm tired, Nick. We need to sleep."

"Don't you want to make love?"

"I-I do. But..." I gesture toward the ceiling. "These walls are like paper. You can hear everything. It wouldn't feel right."

"What doesn't feel right is being next to your delectable body and not getting to ravish you."

I smile despite myself. He knows exactly what buttons to push. "I know, but we just can't."

"Can't or won't?"

"Both."

"Don't I at least get some relief? You've got me all worked up here with nowhere to go." Without warning, his arm moves down my night dress and he thrusts his hand into my soaking wet knickers. "My God Carly," he whispers, "I can feel how much you want me. Please let me fuck you."

I brush his hand away. "No. Sleep!"

"You're such a prick tease."

"I am not."

"Yes, you are."

"Okay, okay, I'll give you a little release. But that's it. We can't go all the way."

"Whatever you're offering, I'll take it."

Rolling on top of him, I bury my face in his neck and softly start to lick and suck him, milking quiet moans of pleasure from his lips. Immediately, I cover his mouth with my hand. "Ssssh! This can only work if you're absolutely silent, okay? No talking."

He nods obediently. With a sexy smile, I resume my sweet assault, licking and sucking, tracing the letters of the alphabet over his silky-smooth chest. Working my way down, Nick hisses as I run my tongue over his rock-hard abdomen, before lightly scratching his thighs with my nails. Hungrily, my lips continue travelling down, touching and teasing, giving him a little taste of what is to come. Then, with considered slowness, I lower my head and swamp my mouth around his dick, probing his little sensitive hole with my tongue.

"Don't stop," Nick gasps. "That feels fucking amazing."

I reach up and cover his mouth again. "I said no talking," I hiss.

He lets his breath out slowly. I can tell he likes this game; likes me in the dominant role, and he the submissive. Releasing my hand, I lower my head again and return to the task at hand. Greedily, I continue to kiss and suck his cock, licking and caressing every last remnant of tangy pre-cum. Then moving lower, I swirl my tongue around his balls, relishing his sour-sweet taste.

I glance up at him with hungry eyes. "Do you like that?" I whisper.

Nick grits his teeth.

Seductively, I devour his entire shaft again, forcing it down as deep as it will go, shoving it till it reaches the back of my throat. He whimpers quietly. *Oh, my God, I need him inside me* now. Slowly, I withdraw, licking and suckling the underside of his cock with loving relish, then I take each of his balls into my mouth, and suck them like I'm starving.

"Oh, my God, you're killing me," Nick rasps.

His words spur me to suck even harder. My jaw aches but I don't care; I'm absolutely loving the danger and excitement of the situation. We're like a pair of naughty teenagers getting up to no good.

After several frenzied minutes, Nick lets out a loud gasp and shoots his creamy load down my throat.

"Mmmmm," I smile, licking and sucking his shaft until I've consumed every last drop. "Delicious." I wipe my mouth with my hand and stick out my tongue to show him I've taken it all in.

"Did you enjoy that, baby?" he whispers. "Did you like how I tasted?"

"Mmmm, so good."

"My God, you're amazing."

Pulling me up against his chest, he wraps his strong arms around me and tells me that he loves me. Then, with a contented sigh, I snuggle into him, ready to sleep.

Only, I can't. He's got me so wound up, sleep is no longer an option. I'm like a coiled up spring, waiting for release. I need to orgasm or I'll go crazy. Discreetly, I reach down into my knickers and slowly start to masturbate.

Immediately, Nick senses the movement, and before I know it, his hands are in there too, guiding my fingers up and down my clit.

"Fuck, you turn me on so much," he growls. "You're getting me hard again." With painful need, he rolls on top of me and with one swift movement, tears off my knickers. Within seconds, his cock is deep inside me. He's a little soft at first, but as his pelvic thrusts gain momentum, he's soon back to his glorious best. Back and forth he slams, stretching out my tight hole like an elastic band. The mattress jerks and creaks as I quietly beg him to fuck me harder. *Oh my gosh.* Right now, I couldn't care less who hears us. I need this. I need to vent my frustration, and dear Lord, I need to come.

Suddenly, out of nowhere, a crazy thought pops into my head. *I'm having unprotected sex with a vampire.* What if I get pregnant?

No, the doctors said that was impossible.

But…what if they got it wrong?

"Are you okay, baby?" Nick whispers. "You don't really seem into it."

"What if I get pregnant?" I blurt.

He stops pumping and his body tenses. "But I thought you said you were on the pill?" I can hear the fear in his voice. "You said we had protection, Carly."

"I-I am on the pill. But, well, you never know, do you? Sometimes these things don't work the way they're supposed to."

Moodily, he slides off me and turns onto his side, facing away from me. I can feel anger radiating from him like an electric current. "Tell me the truth, Carly. Are you definitely on the pill? Think hard now. This is important, so please, please don't lie to me."

"I'm not lying. I-I just got scared, that's all."

"Are you sure?"

"Yes!"

We both fall silent, each lost in our private thoughts. When Nick speaks again, his tone is softer; more sympathetic. "If it bothers you all that much, then we'll go back to using condoms from tomorrow. I don't want you to do anything you're not comfortable with."

"Are you mad at me?"

"No, I'm not mad at you. I just wish you'd be honest and

tell me what's really on your mind."

"What do you mean? I *have* been honest with you."

He hesitates. "Is it really the fear of getting pregnant that bothers you, or is it something else?"

"What else could it be?"

"Oh, I don't know. Maybe you think I've got toxic vampire germs or something."

"Don't be silly, Nick. Of course it's not that. I just swallowed you, didn't I?"

He makes a noncommittal sound. I can tell that I've hurt him deeply.

"Darling, I'm sorry. I hope I haven't offended you? Nick, please…" I reach out my hand and touch his shoulder. He shrugs me off.

"Let's just sleep."

"Okay. I love you."

He doesn't respond. For long moments, I lie awake, blinking in the darkness with a great lump of misery sitting in my belly. I want him so much it hurts. I need to feel his cock inside me. I need him to fuck me hard and make me come, but that can't happen now. Not after all the things I just said to him.

Truth be told, I don't want to go back to using condoms. Sex is so much better without them, but what can I do? I can't risk getting pregnant.

But the doctors said it's impossible. Less than a one per cent chance, they said.

Yes, but what if they're wrong? Doctors get things wrong all the time. Oh God, I'm so fucking confused.

Suddenly, my mind is made up. *To hell with it.*

Reaching out, I gently touch Nicks shoulder again. This time he doesn't shrug me off and I know I've got him where I want him. Emboldened, I press up against him and feel my way down to his cock. I gasp. He's still rock hard for me.

"Please, fuck me," I breathe.

"Uh-uh. You said you didn't want to."

"Forget what I said. Just fuck me."

Nick remains still, his breathing growing shallow as my hand travels up and down his throbbing shaft. Finally, with a low groan, he rolls onto his back and roughly lowers me onto his penis. I clench my teeth to force back a silent scream as he starts to impale me with deep, delicious thrusts. Again and again, he pounds into me, hitting my G-spot every time. The room spins around me. Nothing is real, nothing makes sense. There's nothing but him and me on this planet.

Whimpering with delight, I grind up and down furiously, taking him as far as I can go, gasping each time he stretches me out just a little bit more. After a few moments, I reach back my arms and spread my buttocks, opening myself up so that he can get all the way to the hilt.

"Shit," he whispers. "You're killing me."

Suddenly, I stop jerking and throw my head back, crying out as waves of intense pleasure crash through me.

"That's right, baby. Give it all to me."

I shut my eyes and grit my teeth. Jesus, I need a few seconds.

But Nick's not ready to stop. He continues pounding and pounding till I feel an eruption of liquid inside of me. With a throaty gasp, I lurch forward onto his stomach, my whole body bucking and twitching with sparks of euphoria. I've taken him all in; every last drop. And it feels good. Right at this moment, I'm closer to him than I've ever been before.

"I'm never letting you go," he pants. "Not ever. I love you."

"I love you too."

CHAPTER THIRTY

Good Advice

WHEN I WAKE up the next day, the room is bathed in bright sunlight. Milky shards of warmth filter through the blinds, casting strange, exotic shapes across Nick's sleeping form. I blink a couple of times, feeling a little disorientated. Then I remember that it's Christmas day, and a thrill of excitement courses through me. Despite all that's happened, I'm hopeful that the day can be salvaged. Perhaps Mum will start behaving herself and we can put what happened yesterday behind us.

Propping myself up on one elbow, I study Nick's face, still trying to convince myself that I haven't dreamed the past few weeks. Am I really lying next to a vampire? For a reality check, I lean over and softly stroke his cheek. He looks so beautiful asleep. I love everything about this man: his face, his body, his scar. *Everything.*

Suddenly, Nick opens his eyes and looks at me. He smiles a big, beautiful smile that melts my heart. Then with a stifled yawn, he raises himself up on his elbows and looks round the room.

"Darling, what time is it?"

"I don't know. Early, I guess." I reach over to the dresser and pick up my *Kermit the Frog* watch. "Nine twenty-five. Time to be getting up."

Nick flops back down on the mattress and buries his head in the pillow. "Last night was amazing," he grins.

My cheeks flush. "Yes, it was."

"Fancy a sequel?"

"Yes, but if we start that we'll end up spending the whole day in bed."

He chuckles darkly. *Damn, everything he does is so sexy.*

Throwing back the duvet, I go to the wardrobe and slip on a dressing gown. "I'm absolutely starving. I think I can smell toast, so I'd better go down and see what's cooking." I'm about to ask him what he wants for breakfast, when I catch myself. Of course! Vampires don't eat breakfast. Well, not the bacon and egg variety, anyway.

Fastening the belt on my gown, I kiss him goodbye and make my way downstairs. As I pass the sitting room, my heart warms at the sight of the brightly-coloured Christmas tree laden with presents.

Life feels good again.

I enter the kitchen and find my mother washing dishes at the sink. The kettle is boiling for tea and two pieces of toast are laid out on a plate.

"Morning Mum," I say. "Did you have a good sleep?"

"It was okay," she replies sourly.

I shake my head. *Okay, not off to the best start.*

Moistening my lips, I join her at the sink and ask her if she needs any help with the dishes. She coldly declines.

Why can't she look at me? Just what the hell is her problem?

The kettle finishes boiling, and I ask her where the tea bags are kept. Silently, she points to one of the top cupboards. Following her instructions, I fetch a box of Red Label and finish making the tea.

"Where's Dad and Michael?"

"Probably still sleeping."

The tension is getting unbearable. I want to ask her outright, but my pride prevents me. If she wants to play games then fine, I'll play.

"So," I say, sipping my tea, "what's the plan for today? Are we going to exchange presents before or after lunch?"

Woodenly, she turns off the taps and looks at me. "Sex isn't the be all and end all, you know."

"What do you mean?"

"I mean, just because a man is good in bed, it doesn't mean he'll make a good husband."

My mouth gapes. "Oh my God, were you listening outside our room last night?"

She drops her gaze to the floor, suddenly flustered. "No, of course not. I just mean that I can tell by looking at Nick, what the primary attraction is. I'm warning you: relationships built on lust alone are doomed to failure. Get out while you still can."

I slam down my cup on the sideboard. "That's pretty rich coming from the lady who ended a twenty-year marriage because she couldn't keep her knickers on."

"How dare you!"

"*How dare I?* Excuse me, but do you really think I'd take relationship advice from a heartless witch who broke my father's heart? Do you know how much your affair with Michael destroyed him? He still hasn't gotten over you, even after all these years."

"Now you're not being fair. This isn't about your father and me. This is about preventing you from making the biggest mistake of your life. That *creature* you're going to marry is evil. The way he looks at you... it scares the hell out of me. It's like he wants to eat you. I don't know what kind of spell he's put on you, but you'd better snap out of it pretty damn quickly. If you don't get out now, he'll destroy you."

I bite down on my fist to stifle a sob. I can't take this anymore. She's gone too far this time. Tearfully, I storm out of the kitchen and march up to our bedroom. "Pack your bags, we're leaving."

Nick pops his head out the bathroom, his lips covered with toothpaste. "Baby, what's wrong?"

"She's a disgrace," I spit. "A complete and utter disgrace. The bile that just came out of her mouth… I've never heard anything like it. We need to leave here right now and never come back."

"But darling, what exactly…"

I hold up my hand. "Please. I don't want to talk about it. I just want to get as far away from here as possible."

There's a quiet knock at the door and my father enters. "What on earth was all that screaming about?"

"I'm sorry Dad, but we have to go. She's fucked everything up as usual. I've tried and tried to make things work between us, but she'll never change, I see that now. I'm better off without her. As long as she's in my life, I'll never be happy."

"Jesus, what has she done this time?"

"She wants me to break up with Nick." I run my finger down my nose. "Look, I can't really talk about this. You should start packing too, Dad. Nick can give you a lift home."

"But I can't just up and leave. It's Christmas, Carly. Isn't there any way you could work things out with your mother? Maybe talk things through?"

"Nope, she's gone too far this time. Look, if you want to stay here, that's fine, but I refuse to spend another minute in a house where my fiancé isn't welcome."

Dad and Nick exchange helpless glances. "All right, I'll start packing," Nick says quietly.

By the time we get back to Pimlico, it's well past eleven. We had an easy drive back because all the roads were virtually traffic free. Nick hits the brakes and pulls the Jaguar to the curb. Above looms his tall, Regency-style house with a white stucco facade and a black entrance door framed by two huge columns.

"Are you okay?" he asks.

I shrug. "Not really, but what can you do? You can't choose your parents."

He reaches out and gently strokes my knee. "Just give it some time, huh? Perhaps she'll come around."

"No, she won't. I told you, I'm through with her. There's no going back." Unclipping my seatbelt, I clamber out the car and follow him through the snow to the steps of his house. Taking my hand, Nick unlocks the door and leads me inside. He switches on the lights, then we go to the living room and crash out on the sofa. I'm physically and mentally exhausted. All I want to do is sleep. Blinking twice, I wipe the sides of my mouth and tell him I'm going to the garden to smoke a cigarette. He kisses me and tells me not to be long.

I grab my handbag and head towards the door. "I promise I'll be back in five," I say.

"Okay." The sadness on Nick's face tears me up. I can tell this whole business with Mum has really affected him.

I step out into the hall and stride through the conservatory to the garden. As I step onto the steps, I almost have a heart attack.

There's a stranger in the garden; a woman standing under the snow-covered Chestnut tree. Dressed in robes of scarlet and black, she is hands down the most monstrous thing I've ever seen. She is standing very still, almost like a statue. Her skin is chalk-white, her lips parched and cracked, with blood red eyes that are sunken back in her head like a corpse. Cuts and bruises cover her cheeks and forehead, and a revolting purple liquid oozes from a scab above her right brow. Her fingers, if you can call them that, are more like talons, ready to scratch your eyes out at the slightest provocation.

In a daze of horror, I stare at her, my limbs completely paralysed with fear. I want to run but my legs are too weak to move.

And then she flashes a demonic grin, showing two sets of razor-sharp teeth, and I fall into vortex of darkness. Worse than her decaying flesh and horrendous face is the sense of pure evil emanating off her; an intense, black hatred that sucks everything good out of me.

I gasp and clutch my throat. It's like I can't breathe, like an invisible rope is being pulled tighter and tighter, strangling the air from my lungs.

With a shrill cry, I finally find my feet, bolt back inside the house and race to the living room to find Nick.

"Carly, what's the matter?"

I collapse in his arms, hysterical. "Oh my gosh, it was so awful. I-I saw this h-horrible creature in the garden. She has these horrible red eyes like a devil and… oh gosh, it was just so awful, and those claws!" His body stiffens and he holds onto me more tightly. I look up at him, my eyes imploring him to believe me. "Please Nick, just go to the garden and see for yourself. I'm not imagining it. There's really something there!"

Calmly, he releases me, sits me down on the couch and slowly walks into the hall.

"Be careful!" I shout.

He doesn't answer.

Numb with apprehension, I sit on the edge of the sofa,

clasping and unclasping my hands. I try to keep my head clear and not think about his progression through the conservatory to the garden. A whole five minutes pass and the house remains as silent as the grave. I start to grow restless.

What the hell is going on? Why hasn't he come back yet?

Finally, Nick returns and I get to my feet expectantly.

"Well?"

His face remains placid.

"Did you see anything?"

Nick shakes his head, but his expression looks troubled. "No, there's no one there."

"But I'm telling you, I saw someone! She was as real as you."

"Oh, I don't doubt for one second that you saw something."

"Then you believe me?"

"Yes, I believe you." Silently, he steps across to the window, draws back the curtains and stares out at the bleak grey sky. His face is deeply pained, contorted by some private torment I cannot fathom.

"Nick?"

He glances at me, then back out the window. He continues to remain silent.

"Please can you just tell me what's going on?"

"So, it's true," he murmurs. "I didn't want to believe it, hoped that I'd laid the past to rest, but now I see that no good deed goes unpunished."

I slam my fist on the armrest. "Can you please stop talking in riddles and just tell me what's going on? What do you mean you thought you'd laid the past to rest? Who or *what* was that creature out there?"

Chewing his lip, Nick turns and fixes me with burning eyes. "That creature is my wife."

CHAPTER THIRTY-ONE

Nightshade

A COLD PARALYSIS creeps up my neck. I can't believe what I'm hearing. "Your wife?" I stammer.

"Yes," Nick replies calmly. "Although technically, we are no longer married."

"What do you mean technically? Are you married to her or not?"

"When we took our marriage vows, we said till death do us part. Then I died and became a vampire, and that broke the bond of marriage. Don't you see? Death parted us, so in the eyes of God, we are no longer man and wife."

I slump down on the sofa, my head spinning with confusion. I try to focus on inhaling and exhaling. That's all I can do to stop myself from completely breaking. The floor has dropped out from under me and every part of my body feels numb. I can't get my head around the enormity of this revelation and what it means in the bigger scheme of things. It's just too much to comprehend.

Nick's married?

I shake my head, not wanting to believe it.

"And when exactly were you planning to tell me this?" I ask icily. "On our wedding night?"

He looks at me with hurt eyes. "Of course not. I was planning to tell you. It just never seemed the right time, but I promise you, I would have told you eventually."

"Oh really? Just how many other secrets are you keeping from me? You know what, it's about time we had this conversation. I've let you get away with too much secrecy for far too long. I don't know a single thing about your past, and that's dangerous. I've been patient enough. No way am I letting you off this time, so you'd better start talking."

Smothering a sigh, he strides over to the window and stands there a while, staring out at the falling snow.

Tears welling in my eyes, I draw myself into a sitting position. "You'd better start explaining, and this time I want the truth. No more games, no more riddles, the whole truth. I need to know everything or we can't move forward with this relationship. I need to know exactly what I'm dealing with so that I know how to protect myself." I pause and take a deep breath. "I want to see the paintings."

"What paintings?"

"The paintings you removed from the walls of this room. I'm not stupid. Did you think I wouldn't notice? I know you took the pictures down because you're hiding something. I want you to bring them from the attic now and show them to me."

For a second we lock eyes, like two bulls ready to fight. Neither of us wants to back down. Finally, it's Nick who relents. With another deep sigh, he leaves the room and goes upstairs to retrieve the requested items. He returns a few moments later, carrying a large wooden crate containing numerous portraits in heavy gilt frames. Setting them on the floor, he straightens up and shoots me a warning glance.

"Are you really sure you want to know?" he asks quietly.

"Yes!"

Like a man resigned to his fate, he slowly reaches down

into the box and pulls out the first picture. Without showing it to me, he strides across the room to the far wall and carefully fixes it back in position.

I cover my mouth with my hand. The painting shows Nick sitting in what appears to be a dimly-lit parlour. He looks about twenty and is dressed in dark Victorian-style clothing. Standing beside him is a tall, grey-haired man with a kind face and piercing green eyes.

"That's my father," Nick says. "Dr William Craven."

Silently, he returns to the crate and pulls out another painting and attaches it to the wall opposite me. This one shows Nick standing beside a stunningly beautiful woman with black hair and peach-coloured skin. She too is dressed in dark Victorian attire.

"My wife, Veda," he says softly.

My eyes widen. The gorgeous woman in the painting bears no resemblance to the horrific creature I just saw in the garden. I look to Nick for clarity, but he ignores me and continues rummaging through the crate.

At last, he pulls out the final painting and attaches it to the wall above the fireplace. This one shows a pretty girl of perhaps five or six years old, wearing a black frilly dress under a white pinafore. She's sitting on a chair, holding a large porcelain doll. Instantly, I see the resemblance and before he says anything, I already know who she is.

"My daughter, Coppélia." His voice is almost a whisper and his eyes are moist with tears. My heart breaks for him. I know the tale which follows will not be good.

Wordlessly, he steps back to the window and stares out at the bleak grey sky, his face is the picture of disquietude.

"Nick?"

He flicks a glance in my direction, then looks back out the

window. When he speaks again, his voice is low and hushed. He tells me he was born in 1860, an only son to loving, doting parents. He grew up in Belgravia in a beautiful townhouse surrounded by cherry trees. For the most part, his childhood was a happy one, full of joy and laughter. His father, Dr William Craven, was a prominent statesman during the reign of Queen Victoria.

Well-liked by his peers, William appeared the picture of respectability, but behind closed doors, he nurtured a deep-rooted obsession with the occult. In his youth, he travelled the world in search of strange things that could not be explained by scientific logic. It was during this time that he first encountered vampires in Eastern Europe, and witnessed first-hand the devastation caused by their evil. Tormented, William swore to rid the world of them and so, for want of a better word, he became a vampire hunter.

Between age nineteen to thirty, Nick worked as his father's assistant and travelled across Europe with him, hunting down vampires in an attempt to rid Mankind of their evil. For a while, things went well and the two men gained a fierce reputation as the most effective vampire hunters in the world. However, events took a terrifying turn on a trip to Romania when they visited a deserted village. The place was over-run with rats and the stench of death lay heavy in the air. After searching each cottage, they found that almost every man, woman and child had been killed in what Nick described as the worst mass slaughter he'd ever seen.

The perpetrators, they soon discovered, were seven beautiful women—the wives of a German nobleman named Count Karlock, who lived in a hilltop castle above the village. Karlock was well-known in those parts as an evil man, a rumoured Satanist and a vampire who had sold his soul to the

Devil.

Survivors from the village, led by William and Nick, invaded Karlock's castle and found an underground tomb where the seven vampire brides lay sleeping. After a great battle, in which several men were killed, Nick and his father succeeded in driving wooden stakes through each of the brides' hearts. They then searched the castle for Karlock but could find no trace of him.

Weary from fighting, father and son returned home to England where William suggested Nick settle down and find himself a wife. William was getting old and Nick had no desire to spend the rest of his life hunting vampires, so the two opted for a life of domesticity in London.

"I had known Veda since we were children," Nick explains softly. "Her parents and my parents were great friends and they'd always hoped that one day we would marry. Up until then, my father's exploits had prevented that from happening…" He hesitates and looks wistfully into the distance. "Veda was the most beautiful woman I'd ever seen—the kindest, sweetest person imaginable. As soon as I returned to England, I proposed and we were married that Spring. A year later, Coppélia came along and our lives were complete."

My breath comes thickly. *The most beautiful woman he'd ever seen*. The words pierce my heart and I'm consumed by a colossal wave of jealousy. I glance up at the painting on the wall and imagine him kissing her, making love to her, and it's almost too much to bear. My hands are shaking; inside I'm coming apart, but somehow, I manage to hold it together. I need to stay strong so that I can hear this.

"So, what went wrong?" I ask in a choked voice.

"What do you mean?"

"Well, it sounds like you had it made: the perfect wife, the perfect daughter…" I break off. I don't mean to sound bitter but I simply cannot help myself. The thought of Nick loving someone else and having a family tears me up inside. Knowing that Veda was able to give him a child, something that I will likely never experience, is completely soul-destroying.

"Are you okay?" he asks.

"I'm fine," I lie. "Tell me what went wrong."

"Are you definitely sure you want to hear this?"

"Yes. Whatever it is, I can handle it."

He pauses and looks me over very carefully, taking his time about it. I wonder what he's thinking. For a long moment, we stare at each other, the air thick with tension. I fold my arms protectively across my chest. I need answers *now*.

Finally, Nick resumes: "For five years, my life was blissfully uneventful. I took a job at a law firm and hoped to put the past behind me. Then one day, my father received a very strange letter. It was written in German…" He wets his lips.

"Go on," I say.

"The letter was from Count Karlock, telling my father that he would be seeing us both very soon. He said he despised us and wouldn't rest until he'd avenged the murder of his seven wives in Romania. He told us to prepare for a bloody retribution."

I gasp. "Oh my God! What did you do?"

"What could we do but watch and wait? I kept Veda and Coppélia close to me at all times; we rarely ever left the house and had to have all of our amenities delivered. For two weeks, we sat on tenterhooks, waiting for something to happen, but nothing did. Then I received a telegram from my father asking me to meet him in Bishop's Park. The message didn't say why, just that it was very urgent." Nick shakes his head and draws in a sharp breath. He speaks so quietly I can barely hear him.

"At midnight, I reached Bishop's Park and found my father waiting for me on a bench. The instant I saw him I knew something wasn't right. There was something feral about him; wild, almost deranged. I sat beside him and he calmly informed me that my mother was dead. She'd been raped and someone had… *torn* her throat out."

My blood runs cold. "Jesus!"

"I was beside myself with grief," Nick continues. "I think I started crying, and my father… well, he put his arms around me to comfort me. And that's when I saw the blood on his hands, and I knew, I just *knew* he was the one that did it. I knew he had murdered my mother."

I get a sickish feeling in my throat. "Oh my gosh!"

Shaking his head, he walks slowly over to the sofa and sits down next to me. His whole body is trembling. Gently, I reach out and slip my hand into his. He gives me a small, weak smile. I can't begin to imagine how hard this is for him.

Quietly, he resumes his story. "I told my father I knew he'd murdered my mother, and he didn't even try to deny it. Then he started laughing at me; I'll never forget it. He laughed and laughed and laughed. Called me a fool. Then he pulled off his scarf to reveal two puncture wounds in his neck, and I realised then that it was too late—Karlock had already got to him." I cover my mouth with shock. "I tried to fight him off, but he was too strong for me, Carly. The last thing I remember is an excruciating pain in my neck, and then I must have blacked out."

"You mean you died?"

Nick swallows and licks his lips. "Yes. I don't know who found my body or anything about the funeral. Everything just went... *blank*. The next thing I know I'm waking up in a coffin, buried six feet under."

"Jesus!"

"It was horrific. I think I must have gone crazy down there. I felt so claustrophobic... I just needed to breathe fresh air again. Eventually, I punched a hole through the coffin and clawed my way back to the surface. My father was waiting for me in the cemetery. He was laughing, smiling, like it was all a big joke. He told me I was now a vampire, like him, and that London was ours for the taking. He took me to Soho, to the opium dens, and we fed recklessly. I'm not proud of what I did that night, but you must understand that this was all new to me, so I didn't know how to control my urges."

There's a long, dark silence.

"Did you kill anyone that night?" I whisper.

"I don't remember," he admits. "I might have done, I don't fucking know. Everything we did that night was a terrible blur and the next morning I woke up in a strange woman's bed, despising myself for what I'd become. I decided then and there that I couldn't live with myself. I didn't want to be a vampire and realised that there was really only one ultimatum: I had to kill my father to stop him spreading this terrible plague."

I squeeze his hand tightly. "What did you do?"

Fighting back tears, Nick sucks air through his teeth and focuses on the floor. "For the next two days, I played along with him; made him think I enjoyed what we were doing. Then I got two stakes and hid them in my coat—one for him, one for me. I went back to the opium den and found my father in one of the upper rooms. He was in bed, asleep with a prostitute. I took out one of the stakes and prepared to strike, but he woke up just in time. A terrible fight ensued…" Nick breaks off and points to the scar on his face. "That's when this happened."

"Fucking hell," I gasp.

"Eventually, I got the better of him. I pierced his heart with the stake and watched him die a slow and painful death. I was inconsolable. Despite everything, I still loved my father and didn't blame him for the evil things he'd done. No, I laid the blame firmly at Count Karlock's door." He hesitates. "After I'd killed him, I planned to take the other stake from my coat and end my own miserable existence, but one thing prevented me: I needed to see Veda and Coppélia one last time before I died, just to say goodbye properly. It was biggest mistake of my life."

CHAPTER THIRTY-TWO

Confession

S ILENCE PULSATES THROUGH the room. "What happened when you went back home?" I whisper.

Nick chews his knuckles, his face twisted with pain. "Veda was beside herself. She was absolutely terrified of me. Remember, my funeral had taken place only a few days earlier, and everyone thought I was dead. She couldn't understand what had happened. She had no idea about vampires because I'd always kept that side of my life a secret from her." He hesitates, his eyes straying from mine. "Once she got over the shock, Veda wanted to make love to me. And I… let's just say I couldn't resist. I needed to feel wanted, so I gave into my urges, and damn the consequences. I fed on her. *My God*, I fed and fed, sucked her completely dry. It was the worst thing I've ever done."

My arms go rigid. I can't believe what I'm hearing.

"Do you hate me?" Nick whispers.

"No, I don't hate you. You… couldn't help yourself." I pause. "Tell me what happened next."

He rubs his eye with one knuckle. "For a few moments, I held Veda's body…wept for her like a lost child. I was in complete and utter hell. Eventually, I lay her down on the bed and went to get the stake from my coat. I knew if I didn't do this now, her soul would be forever damned and she would rise again as a vampire. I didn't want Veda to share my misery, so to spare her, I positioned the stake against her chest, preparing to end it all, when suddenly, my dear little Coppélia appears at the door. "Please don't hurt Mummy," she says. "Can't you see Mummy's sleeping? Don't ever hurt her, Daddy. I love you.""

Tears collect in Nick's eyes. "And I couldn't go through with it. I couldn't let my darling daughter see me hurt her mother. So I put Coppélia back to bed and left the house. The next day, Veda's body was found and her family held a funeral shortly afterwards. Coppélia was taken to live in the country with Veda's sister Emily, which suited me just fine. I wanted my daughter as far away from London as possible. With her out of harm's way, the only thing left was to go to the cemetery and wait for Veda to rise."

I stare at him, awestruck. My throat has gone dry, my body weak with horror. On autopilot, I listen to the rest of the story, my mind a torrent of agony. He tells me of the night Veda returned to life and went crazy when she realised she was a vampire. He tells me of the torment they felt at having to step away from their beloved daughter. Both Nick and Veda were dead to their family and friends, and could not continue living in London without drawing attention to themselves. To avoid detection, they were forced to assume new identities and move to Austria to start again, but they never forgot about Coppélia.

Nick wipes away a tear with the back of his hand. "Every year on Coppélia's birthday, Veda and I returned to England to check up on her. We would go to the gate at the bottom of Emily's garden, and just stand there, hoping to catch a glimpse of her through the windows. We could only watch from a distance, but it was so wonderful watching her grow up, safe from all the darkness. Veda found it very hard to handle; she always wanted to go in and speak to Coppélia, to hold her and tell her that we still loved her; and I had to fight so hard to stop that from happening. I couldn't allow Veda to blow our cover, and she slowly grew to hate me for it. She said I was keeping her from our daughter. Still, as time went on, Coppélia started coming to the bottom of the garden all by herself, almost like she knew we were out there, watching her. Deep down, I think she knew that we were still alive. I like to think so, anyway."

He pauses. "For the next fifty years, we kept up that routine. We led a hobo's existence, travelling from place to place, never settling down to avoid detection, and every 1st of July for Coppélia's birthday, we paid a brief visit to England. We watched our daughter age, while we stayed forever young. I can't begin to describe how devastating it is to see your child grow from a baby into a beautiful young woman, and then succumb to the curse of aging. To make matters worse, Coppélia's life wasn't a happy one. She grew very reclusive, never married and suffered bouts of severe depression. The traumas of her early childhood prevented her from having any lasting relationships and she died a lonely spinster."

"Coppélia died?"

"Yes," he replies. "Of cancer. She was in her late seventies. Veda and I were at the hospital the day it happened." He breaks off, his voice twisted with sadness. "I'm sorry, I think that will be all for today. I don't want to talk about this anymore. It's just too painful."

I nod silently. I try to extract my hand, but Nick refuses to let go. His mournful gaze runs up and down my body, and the vulnerability in his face kills me.

"Look me in the eyes and tell me that you hate me," he rasps.

I can't. *How could I ever hate him?*

"Say it. Tell me that I'm a bad husband, a failure as a father and a murderer, and that you despise me."

Finally, I lift my head and look at him. I continue to remain silent. *How could I ever despise him?* If anything, I love him more than ever. It must have taken great strength to overcome the horrendous cards life dealt him.

Wordlessly, I run my hand over his face, trying to reach beneath the surface and see what's in his heart. Then he collapses in my arms and clings to me like his life depends on it.

"Oh my darling, my darling," he sobs. "What would I do without you?" That's all he keeps saying, and I keep stroking his back, soothingly, lovingly, like a parent consoling a child. We stay like that for ages, feeding off each other, trying to ward off all the darkness.

"I love you so much," I whisper.

"I don't know what I'd do without you. I can't begin to tell you what a relief it is to finally be able to tell you all this. I've never spoken to anyone about this before."

My heart bleeds for him—all the pain and suffering he went through—it's almost too much to bear. I wish I could erase his past and make everything all right again. I wish I could wave a magic wand and bring Coppélia back to him. But I know I can't. Life doesn't work like that.

Oh what a cruel and wicked world we live in.

At last, I pull away and gently kiss his forehead. Then I get to my feet and walk slowly towards the door.

"Where are you going?"

"Home," I reply. "I need to be alone for a while; I need

time to get my head together."

"But you can't go!" Nick's voice sounds desperate. "I just bared my soul to you. Right now, I need you more than ever. Please don't do this to me."

I shake my head sadly. "I'm sorry darling; I just need to be alone for a couple of hours. This is a lot to take in and… well, I need time to think about what I want to do."

"But it's Christmas! There's no transport. How will you get home?"

"I-I don't know. Maybe I'll call a cab or something." The sentence dies and I suddenly feel very stupid. He's right. What the hell am I thinking? And how do I know Veda isn't still lurking out there somewhere, waiting to pounce on me?

I exhale sharply in an attempt to psych myself up. I'm desperate not to show any weakness. "My heart weeps for you, Nick. What you just told me tears me up and I can't believe what you've been through. I want to be strong and loving, and all of these things you want me to be, but right now I just can't. I'm only human."

"What's that supposed to mean?"

I can't look at him. *Veda was the most beautiful woman he'd ever seen—the kindest, sweetest person imaginable.* Jealousy ignites in my belly and licks me all over. I imagine Nick kissing her, banging her, making her moan, and it's all I can do to keep standing. Yes it's childish to feel this way, but I can't help myself.

"Do you think I don't see what's going on in that brain of yours?" Nick snaps. "You're jealous, and you're letting it get in the way of us."

"I don't know what you're talking about. I'm not jealous of anyone."

"Yes you are. This is because I said Veda was beautiful,

isn't it? You can't handle my honesty. Well, I'm sorry, but I'm not going to apologise. She was my wife, Carly, and she *was* beautiful. I can't change the past, but whatever I've been through, good and bad, has made me the person I am today; *the person you fell in love with.*" His tone darkens. "Look at me when I'm talking to you!"

Startled, I do as he says. My hands are shaking. He's never shouted at me before and the dominance in his voice turns me on. *Finally*, he's taking control.

He stares at me a second, then he stands to his full height and walks swiftly towards me. Instinctively, I back away in an effort to maintain some distance between us. The fury on his face makes my knees weak. In an instant, he has me up against the door, his body pressed hard against mine.

"Please, let me go," I whimper.

Roughly, he cups my face in his hands, forcing me to meet his gaze. "Calm down. I know you're angry, but just hear me out, okay? I love you. I love you so fucking much, I think I'll go mad from it. Yes, Veda was beautiful; yes I loved her. Why wouldn't I? She was the mother of my child. But what I feel for you, I've never felt for anyone. The things I've done with you sexually… I've never done with anyone. I'm not as experienced as you might think. You've shown me a whole new way to live and love and brought a peace to me I never thought possible. You're my best friend, my everything. You're absolutely vital to my existence."

I tilt my head away from him. His words have moved me, but jealousy continues to eat at my heart. "Can I *please* just go home?"

"You're not going anywhere!" Nick bellows. "Stop behaving like a spoiled child." Releasing my face, he slams his fist through the door, making me quake with excitement.

Shaking, he retracts his bleeding hand and digs his fingers into my shoulder. Splinters of wood cascade around us. "You're going to stay here and do exactly as I tell you," he growls. "You're not going to walk out on me again. You're going to be very quiet and listen to everything I have to say, okay?"

"Okay," I gulp.

Catching me round the waist, he carries me back to the sofa and sits me down on his lap.

"Why are you behaving like this?" He buries his face in my neck. "Why must you always be so difficult? Do you seriously think I prefer Veda to you?"

"I-I don't know. I don't want to feel this way, but I do. I keep thinking about the two of you together and it kills me. All right, you've got what you want, Nick. A full confession. I'm jealous and I don't care. I want you all to myself. It's as simple as that."

His soft lips tease the hairs on my neck. "So you *do* love me?"

"Of course I bloody love you."

His hands are all over me now, tracing the outline of my breasts through the flimsy material of my dress. I squirm, giving out little moans of pleasure I couldn't control. For a while I let it happen, then suddenly, I come back to my senses.

"Take your hands off me!" Wrenching myself from his grip, I jump up and make a run for the door, but he's too quick for me. With a cry of rage, Nick throws himself on me and brings me down to the floor. Pinning both arms above my head, he holds me there until I have no more fight left. His tears fall slowly, bitterly.

"You are seriously testing my patience," he says through gritted teeth. "You pursued me relentlessly. You told me you'd do anything to be with me. Well, now you've got me, what are you going to do with me? Every single piece of my heart belongs to you, so don't fucking play with it, okay? You know how weak I am for you; you know I'd do anything for you, and you use it to your advantage. Well, no more, I tell you. It looks like I'm going to have to make you see sense."

CHAPTER THIRTY-THREE

Lust

B REATHING HEAVILY, NICK slowly releases my arms and I gasp with relief. The strength of him is terrifying and I tremble at the thought of what is to come.

"What do you want me to do?" I demand.

"First of all, I don't like that tone of voice. Change it *now.*"

I shiver with longing. My knickers are completely soaked. The anger radiating from him is such a turn on it takes all of my will power not to drop to me knees.

"Okay, what do you want me to do?" I repeat in a softer tone.

Without warning, he silences me with his lips, kissing me so deep I find it hard to breathe. Excitement shoots straight to my crotch. My head goes dizzy and I have no sense of time or space. This is beautiful, wonderful madness. For what seems forever, our tongues glide together in a flurry of unrelenting lust. Then, when he's finished feasting on my lips, he flips me over and pushes me down onto the bear-skin rug. The floor feels hard against my breasts but I'm too excited to care. Roughly, Nick unbuttons the back of my dress, milking soft cries from my lips. Then, with frightening strength, he tears off my knickers with his teeth. His fingers burn into my skin, infusing me with a deep sense of relief, as if I've been in pain my whole life and have just been healed.

Burying his face in my hair, Nick breathes in my scent like it's a bed of roses. "My God, Carly, I want to fuck you every single minute of every single day. I want to fuck you in the morning, I want to fuck you in the evening, in every single orifice."

My legs go weak as my diaphragm contracts and an explosion of euphoria bursts from my abdomen to my upper body. *Lord have mercy.* His words have given me my first spontaneous orgasm!

"I felt that," he whispers. "You just came, didn't you?"

"Mmmm…" I have no come back. Words have deserted me.

Lowering his head, Nick runs his hot tongue up and down my spine, biting and scraping my skin with his teeth. I squeal with pleasure. It's like he can't get enough, like he wants to devour every piece of me. Then, tearing open the bottom part of my dress, he licks and sucks the backs of my thighs with such ferocity, I know there will be bruises tomorrow. But I don't mind. In fact, I love it. *I want him to mark his territory.* Gradually, he works his way down to my calves, my ankles, and then back up again, biting, teasing, sending me out of my mind. I shudder with delight and have to hold my screams inside.

Out of nowhere, he grips my hips and raises me up onto my hands and knees. Pulling his shirt over his head, he throws it across the room and positions himself behind me. Moving his hands down the small of my back, Nick roughly slaps and squeezes my buttocks. Then he lowers his head and sinks his teeth into my left rump, pulling on the skin like it's a juicy piece of meat. I shut my eyes in rapture. *Fucking hell, this is just too good.* With a satisfied growl, he lowers his face further and buries his tongue deep inside my pussy, licking, sucking, eating me out with an intensity that leaves me breathless.

Gasping loudly, I jerk forward and sink my teeth into the rug. *Jesus, this more than I can bear.* Nick continues lapping and sucking, pushing me to the brink of insanity, then he spreads my buttocks and licks a long, slow stroke up and down my crack. My moans grow more frantic, and he knows then that he's hit my sweet spot.

"You like that, don't you?" he whispers. "You like it nasty. Admit it. You do, don't you?"

"Y-yes," I gasp. "I love it so much."

"Do you still want to go home?"

"No."

"Tell me how much you want to stay."

"I-I want to stay here with you, Nick."

"Tell me you'll never think of leaving me again."

"I'll never, ever leave you."

"Do you still want to marry me?"

"Yes!"

Running his large, strong hands down my back, he pushes me forward a little, then with reckless abandon, plunges deep inside my butt-hole, licking me out like he's licking an ice-cream cone. I close my eyes and grit my teeth. *Holy hell.* As his tongue goes even deeper, Nick slides two fingers inside my dripping wet slit.

"More," I whimper. "More, more!"

Rapidly, he starts to finger me while his tongue sides up and down my butt, taking me to seventh heaven. My knees shake uncontrollably. I don't want this to ever end.

Fuck!

Soon, I'm feeling the fireworks and I cry out as a second orgasm hits me. But still Nick doesn't stop. No, he's only just getting warmed up. Removing his fingers, he resumes his former position and presses himself against my wet slit, making my juices trickle down my thighs like a tap that won't stop. He's playing with me, making me wait. Oh my gosh, I just want him to shove his cock in and fuck me senseless.

"Do you love me?" he breathes.

"You know I do."

"I want to hear you say it."

"I love you so goddamn much."

"You'd better not be playing games with me, Carly. My heart wouldn't recover if you were."

"I promise, I'm not."

"Then you really *do* love me? You're not bored with me?"

"Please… I'm dying here. I need to be fucked *now*."

Silently, Nick slips down his boxers to free his big, beautiful cock. With one swift thrust, he pushes inside. For a second, I'm paralysed; then, as he continues to ease himself in, pain gives way to pleasure and I start to enjoy it. Inch by inch, Nick's enormous shaft burrows deeper and deeper into my soaking wet slit, bumping and stroking every part of my tight hole. Back and forth he slams until finally, he's all the way to the hilt.

I whimper quietly. *Holy shit, it hurts so good.*

"Do you like that?" Nick demands. "Do you like how well I fuck you?"

"Ohhhhh!" I push back against him, grinding my hips furiously. He grabs my hair and rides me like a stallion. I clench my teeth and beg him to fuck me harder. The wooden floor shakes beneath us, creaking in time to every single one of his potent thrusts. My knees ache but I don't care; he's taken control of my body and it feels fucking beautiful.

Once more, a fire ignites in my belly and I come for the

third time, but still he isn't through with me. Groaning loudly, Nick pulls out his cock and turns me over onto my back. I moisten my lips and moan softly as he runs his hands down the backs of my thighs, scratching the skin with his nails. Then, looping my legs over his powerful shoulders, he slowly starts to re-enter me.

"Still want to go home?" he breathes.

"No…"

"Don't ever think of trying to leave me. You had your chance, but now it's too late. You made me love you, sent me half-crazy with desire, and now this is how it's going to be forever. Just you and me. No one else. Understand?"

"Y-yes."

Moving his hips in slow, steady thrusts, Nick groans softly as each delicious nudge of his cock buries him deeper inside, stretching me out with his hugeness. "Look at me, Carly," he growls.

I open my eyes. His face is consumed by lust, his lips gleaming and shimmering with my juices. I glance down and see my breasts bouncing up and down in time his savage thrusts. The sight of it makes me even wetter. I've never felt so good in my life. Right now, in my head, there are no vampires, no dark clouds on the horizon; there is only Nick and me and the merging of two souls as one.

"Open up for me," he breathes. "Let me fuck you properly." Tilting my head back, I allow him to lift my legs higher for better penetration. "That's good. I can feel every part of you now. Do you want to come again?"

"Y-yes."

"How much?"

I whimper softly. "So goddamn much."

"I love you."

412

"I-I love you too."

Nick grips my waist and pounds into me as hard as he can, till he too is crying out with pleasure. We yell in unison, and he explodes inside me as I climax for the fourth time.

It's over.

It's all... *over.*

Flushed and pouring with sweat, Nick slides off me and rolls onto his back. I'm shaking all over; right now I'm incapable of speaking. For a while, we just lie on the living room floor, staring up at the ceiling, recovering. Eventually, Nick gets up and sweeps me into a fireman's lift. "Let's go and rest."

I nod mutely.

Effortlessly, he carries me through the hall to the staircase and begins to ascend, two steps at a time. I shriek with delight; it's wonderful having his big strong arms around me. Within seconds, we're on the first-floor landing, surrounded by doors on either side. Kicking open the nearest one, Nick takes me into his lavish bedroom. Throwing back the duvet covers, he gently lays me down on the mattress. Then he climbs in beside me, takes me in his arms and runs his fingers through my hair, over and over again to soothe me.

"Merry Christmas, baby," he whispers. "You're not still thinking of leaving?"

"No."

"Are you sure?"

"Yes! I love you. This is where I belong."

Pleased, he nuzzles my face into his chest. I shut my eyes and focus on my breathing. *In and out, in and out.* Every part of my body is sore but I love it. I try to focus on good things, happy things, like sex and getting married. I don't want to think about the horrors Nick endured in his past. I don't want to think about Veda or Count Karlock or vampires taking over London. I just want to be in the ever present now. For a what seems forever, we lie wrapped in each other's arms, soaking up the serenity of the moment. Harsh winds rattle the window, creating a rhythmic soundtrack to our breathing.

"I want you to move in with me."

I open one eye. "What?"

"I want you to come and live with me," Nick repeats. "I can't bear to be away from you any longer. I need you to move in with me today."

I raise my head from the pillow. Now I'm fully awake. "But I can't."

"Why not? We're getting married, I love you, it makes perfect sense. Why delay the inevitable?"

A thrill courses through me as I briefly imagine a life of domestic bliss with him. Then I come crashing back to Earth. "But what about my dad?"

"What about him? Carly, you're thirty-six years old. Surely you don't want to live at home forever?"

"Of course not, but…" I hesitate. "I have commitments."

"Such as?"

"Well, for one, I help pay my father's mortgage. If I move out, how will he survive?"

"How much is his home worth?"

"I-I don't know." I do a quick mental calculation. "Dad bought it back in the nineties, so if I hazard a guess, I'd say he owes the bank around a hundred grand. I don't know, I'd have to check. It was an interest only mortgage too, so I doubt he's paid much of the capital off. He's terrible with money."

"No problem. If it means I can have you all to myself, then I'll happily pay off his mortgage."

My eyes widen. "What? The whole hundred grand?"

"Yes. It's a small price to pay for your freedom."

"Oh my gosh Nick, that's so lovely of you, but really, I can't let you do that. It wouldn't feel right."

"Why not?"

"It's too much money. I mean, come on, a hundred grand!"

"Carly, he's my future father-in-law. He's virtually family. Really, it's no big deal and money is no object. If it means taking away that financial burden, then I'll do it, no problem. In fact, I insist, so no more arguments, okay? I'll transfer the money as soon as the banks are open."

My lips make a tight smile. "Thank you, I don't know what to say."

"Just tell me that you're going to move in with me and I'll be happy."

I drop my face onto his chest. I can feel his heart beating.

"Is that a yes?" Nick pushes.

"Yes," I say.

"Fantastic! Then that's settled. We'll go to your house tomorrow and pick up your things. Oh, my darling, I'm so happy. This is the start of a whole new life for us."

I nod my head slowly. I should be happy as well, but there are too many things bothering me. Images of Veda's demonic face keep popping into my head and the thought of seeing her again makes me ill.

"Why do you think she came back?" I ask timidly.

"Who?"

"Veda."

Nick's body stiffens and I can sense his mind ticking over. "To catch up, I suppose. Veda lives in Austria, but every couple of years, she returns to London and pays me a visit for old times' sake. I don't exactly look forward to those encounters, for obvious reasons. Usually, we meet in my garden and reminisce about Coppélia, and well, that's about it."

"What sort of relationship do you have with her?"

"We don't really have one. The affection we once had died long ago. Now we're more like acquaintances, but we do still have a mutual respect for each other. Given our shared history, how could we not?" He pauses, weighing up his words. "Please don't be scared of Veda. I know she looks fearsome, but she would never, ever hurt you. She knows that you're mine, and we made a pact long ago, never to tread on each other's territory."

My brows snap together. "I'm not sure I can believe that," I say.

"Why not?"

"It's hard to describe."

"Try."

"When I saw Veda in the garden, it was like there was an evil energy pouring out of her, like pure hatred. I don't know if it was directed at me, but it was absolutely terrifying."

Nick falls silent for a while. "Nevertheless, she isn't a threat to you," he insists. "Believe me Carly, I know. Veda and I have an understanding."

"What sort of understanding?"

"She never harms the people I care about."

I drum my fingers on his chest. "Then who does she harm?"

"What?"

"Who does she feed on? You said you adhere to a strict code of conduct. You said you never drink from the same person twice, that you only take the bare minimum you need to survive. Is Veda so charitable?"

He flounders, and I sense that he's hiding something. "I don't know what Veda gets up to these days, but when she was with me, she followed the exact same code of conduct. She respected human life. What she does now is no business of mine. I told you, we no longer have that type of relationship. We lead completely separate lives."

"Before today, when was the last time you saw her?" I ask.

"Oh, five or six years ago. Veda doesn't frequent London often. It holds too many painful memories for her."

I hesitate. "Why does she look so bad? I mean, she's a vampire, right? Why doesn't she look normal like you do? She used to be beautiful. Why is she…so monstrous-looking?"

"Bitterness," Nick says simply. "After Coppélia died, Veda went mad with grief and she never got over it. Over the years, her bitterness has manifested on her face, and now it's etched there forever."

I close my eyes and try not to think of Veda. I can't believe how calmly he talks about her, like she's a normal person. The evil I saw in her eyes is something I'll never forget, and no matter what Nick says, I'm still afraid of her and know there's things he's hiding from me. There was something he said earlier that bugged me, something about hoping he'd laid the past to rest, and how no good deed goes unpunished. What exactly did he mean by that? And what about Count Karlock? Is he still lurking about somewhere, attacking people and spreading misery? There's so much I want to ask, so much I want to know, but now is not the time. It's already taken a lot to get this much out of him, so for now, I'll drop the subject.

CHAPTER THIRTY-FOUR

New Beginning

A LITTLE AFTER two pm the next day, we pull up outside my house. The snow has stopped, but the air still retains an icy chill. For a moment, I sit silently in the passenger seat, my hands folded in my lap. Nick kills the engine and looks at me.

"Are you ready?" he asks softly.

"Ready as I'll ever be."

He reaches over and squeezes my hand. "Thank you for agreeing to do this. I know we're doing the right thing."

I smile warmly. Nick's right, of course. This has been a long time coming. I'm a grown woman of thirty-six and it's about time I started behaving like it. Even so, I'm a bag of nerves as we make our way up the drive towards my front door. *Am I really going to say goodbye to this place forever?* Silently, I let us in the house and head straight to my bedroom. Nick remains downstairs and starts assembling the flat-pack boxes.

Biting my thumbnail, I collapse on my bed, feeling kind of emotional about everything. Numbly, I gaze around my bedroom one last time, taking in every last little detail. Pink and pristine, nothing much has changed in twenty years. Stacks of books and DVDs line the walls, as do expensive display cabinets containing my precious Disney memorabilia.

Stuffed toys from the *Muppet Show* dominate the bed. Judd Nelson and Molly Ringwald's eternally youthful faces gaze down at me from *The Breakfast Club* poster, along with images from all of my favourite movies: *The Goonies*, *Princess Bride*, *Labyrinth*, and *The Never-ending Story*.

I let out a low sigh of anguish. This room has been my whole world for so long, it's difficult to imagine leaving it behind and starting again elsewhere. For what seems ages, I sit frozen on the bed, my mind racing over all the good times I've had here. Then, with a lump in my throat, I pull out my phone and dial my dad's number.

"Hello, my dear. Did you have a good Christmas?"

"Yeah, it okay." I tuck a hair behind my ear. "Um, listen, Dad, when are you coming back home?"

"Mike's planning to drive me back tomorrow. Why?"

"There are a few things I'd like to discuss with you." I flounder, trying to find the words. *Sod it!* "Okay, so basically, I'm moving in with Nick."

The line goes quiet. I can hear my mother's voice in the background, asking to speak to me. Dad ignores her. "That's wonderful news!" he crows. "I knew this would have to happen one day. So my baby's all grown up and getting married, and this is the obvious next step. When are you moving out?"

"Today, actually," I reply sheepishly. "We're at the house now, clearing out my room." I pause, my throat clogged with tears. "But listen, I'm still going to support you financially. Nick has got this great idea that we'd like to run by you tomorrow."

"My dear, I'm old enough to take care of myself. Please don't worry about me. Just enjoy this new chapter in your life and—"

"No, Dad. I *want* to do this. You've always been there for me every step of the way, and now I want to be there for you. Now, we have a proposal that we'd like to discuss with you, so we'd like to take you out to dinner tomorrow. Please say yes."

"All right, yes."

"Brilliant! Can't wait to see you. I'll text you the restaurant details later." I hang up and run my fingers through my hair. I don't know why I'm getting so emotional. Maybe it's because this feels like the end of an era; the start of something new and scary. But at the same time, I find it greatly liberating. Finally, at the ripe old age of thirty-six, I'm going out into the world to stand on my own two feet.

There's a quiet knock at the door and Nick enters the room carrying a large box. He sets it down on the floor and smiles at me. "Everything sorted?"

I put on a brave face. "Uh-huh. Dad's agreed to meet us tomorrow."

"Fantastic. You see? I told you things would come together eventually." He glances around the room. "Right, where shall we start?"

For the next two hours, we work together, packing up everything into boxes until we've stripped the place bare. Sometime around four-thirty, we head out to the car and put as much as we can in the boot. It doesn't all fit of course, but Nick says we can come back tomorrow to pick up the rest. Then he kisses my hand, starts up the engine and steers us onto the main road. Within seconds, we're moving through the snowy streets, heading towards Pimlico. I feel so restless and excited, like I'm doing something I shouldn't be.

For a while, we drive in silence. Then Nick asks me how I'm feeling.

"A little emotional," I admit. "This is a big step for me and to be honest, I'm finding it kind of scary. But it's also very exciting. The idea of waking up everyday with you is amazing."

"I understand," he says sweetly. "But trust me Carly; you're doing the right thing. I promise I'll take care of you."

I don't reply. I just keep my eyes on the road, watching the wipers dance back and forth.

"Are you looking forward to getting home?" he asks.

"Home?"

"I mean your new home—*with me.*"

"Oh yes, of course. Which room will I be having?"

He steals a quick glance at me. "What do you mean? You're going to be sharing my room, of course."

"Oh. Okay! I wasn't sure, you know..." My voice trails off and I laugh nervously.

We stall at a set of traffic lights. I can feel his eyes on me, watching, studying.

"I can't wait to get you home," he whispers. "I've been thinking up new ways to explore your body."

My cheeks flush. *Not again!* The man is insatiable. We've made love three times today already, and I feel so weak, so sore, I don't think I can take any more. My God, he wants it in the morning, he wants it in the evening... I really don't know how long I'll be able to cope with this level of intensity. Still, as Nick continues to whisper exactly what he'd like to do to me and how, I can't help getting wet. His silky voice, the way he enunciates the words gives me an indescribable thrill and I'm like putty in his hands.

As soon as we get back to Pimlico, he's on me in the hall, pawing at my clothes, wanting to fuck me right then and there. He's coming on so strong I find it kind of frightening.

His sex drive is relentless, out of control, and I wonder how on Earth I will cope if every day is going to be like this. Playfully, I manage to fight him off and tell him I'll need something to eat first. Reluctantly, he goes back to the car and brings in the boxes, while I fix myself coffee and a sandwich.

Sitting on the living room sofa, eating, I find it hard to believe that this is my new home. Every room of Nick's house is fitted out with Persian rugs and antique furniture; every available surface covered with priceless porcelains, urns and crystals vases. Why, the contents of this room alone must be worth about at least a million. It all feels so surreal, I almost feel like pinching myself.

Carly Singleton, you've really moved up in the world.

"Right, that's all your boxes put away in the attic," Nick says, collapsing next to me on the sofa. "I've put some of your clothes in the top drawers, but I think we should leave the rest of the unpacking till tomorrow."

"I agree. I don't have the energy."

There's an awkward pause. I glance out the corner of my eye and catch Nick watching me like a hungry wolf.

"What?" I smile.

He doesn't answer. Taking my hand, he sets down my drink, pulls me onto his lap and kisses me with an urgency that takes my breath away. I stifle a gasp as his long, agile tongue plunges down my throat, eating me out like he wants to consume every piece of me. I find the depth of his love stifling. At last, I come up for air, breathing pretty hard.

"Let's take this upstairs," he whispers.

I shake my head vehemently. "Darling, listen...I don't think I've got the energy for this."

"Yes, you do. You've got to. I need to be inside you, Carly. I need it now or I'll go mad."

"But we've already done it three times!"

Nick looks at me like I'm crazy. "Do you really think that's enough to satisfy me? I want you every single minute of every single day."

I roll my eyes. He's incorrigible. Bowing my head, I allow him to lead me upstairs to the bedroom. Lost in a whirlwind of desire, he throws me down on the mattress and hungrily consumes my face with hot, passionate kisses. Lust spreads under my skin and burns me all over. Tired as I am, when he gets down to it, I find it very hard to say no to him.

Tearing open my dress, Nick pushes up my bra and licks a trail from my breasts to my abdomen. Then, working his way back up, he licks and sucks each of my nipples, before blowing hot air over them. I squeeze my eyes shut. *Lord, this is too much to handle.*

Seconds pass. Minutes. The room spins around me and I can't think straight, can't see straight. As Nick continues to work his way down, I purse my lips and open my thighs to let his hands seek out the scorching-hot wetness there. Pulling my knickers to one side, I let his fingers tinker with my clit, caressing and teasing till I'm numb with excitement.

Suddenly, everything stops.

Nick scrutinises my face. "What's wrong, darling? You're not making any noise. Am I doing something wrong? Tell me how you like it."

"No, no. It feels great. I'm just so *tired*. My body hurts all over and I don't think I can take another heavy session."

"Baby, don't do this to me. Don't you know how hard I am for you?"

"I know but…"

"No buts. I need to be inside you *now*."

God, this is getting exhausting.

With a sudden burst of adrenaline, I roll on top of him and tear at his shirt like a she-cat. His eyes widen in surprise. He wasn't expecting that. It's time for me to take control of things. Hopefully, he'll be happy with just a blow-job.

Moistening my lips, I unbuckle his belt and slide down his trousers to reveal powerfully built thighs with an enormous erection nestled between them. I glance up at him, and flash a sexy smile.

"You're so fucking beautiful," he whispers.

I don't answer. Slowly, slowly, I slip down his boxers to free his big, beautiful cock.

"Shit, Carly, you really know how to turn me on."

Wordlessly, I bend down and take his cock in my mouth, swallowing him all the way to the hilt, almost choking myself. The muscles in his body tense and he moans quietly at the sensation. "Fuck, that feels so good."

Up and down I go, licking and sucking his huge shaft, each time taking him a step closer to ecstasy. It feels so good having him in my throat, knowing I'm the one making him whimper like that.

With a low groan, Nick reaches down and digs his fingers into my hair, goading me to take it all the way. I'm more than happy to oblige. Gently, I run my nails up and down his balls, and then squeeze on them hard. I can tell he likes that. Without words, I know exactly what Nick wants, where to touch him, how to touch him. It's like we have a telepathic connection.

After several frenzied minutes of licking and sucking, he grabs my head and pulls his dick out of my mouth. "I can't take anymore. I need to be inside you." His voice is thick with longing.

"Please let me finish you off," I beg. "Honestly, I can't

take more sex."

"Yes, you can."

"I'm too sore!"

For a second he looks at me, his eyes dancing with amusement. Then, with a hard smile, he reaches up and gently strokes my cheek. "You know what I'm hungry for," he whispers. "And when I'm hungry for it, nothing else will do. Bring that sweet pussy here."

Shaking irrepressibly, I roll off him and allow him to guide me down onto the mattress. Pulling me to the edge of the bed, he tears off my knickers, spreads my legs wide and softly starts to kiss the sensitive skin of my inner thighs.

"Tell me where it's sore and I'll make it better," he breathes. "There?" He kisses the edge of my pussy. "Or is it there?" His tongue licks a long, slow stroke up my clit. "Is that where it hurts, baby?"

"Yes... God, yes!"

I shudder with delight. My limbs go rigid, and my nerve endings are ablaze. *Fuck, this is just too sexy.*

For a few seconds, Nick continues teasing me, licking and sucking all around my opening. Then he buries his face in my slit and eats me out with an intensity that sends me slightly crazy.

"You taste so good," he growls. "I can't get enough."

"Mmmmm..." I moan.

Ravenously, he swirls his tongue up and down my clit, before moving deep inside my wet hole, slurping and savouring every last drop of my juices. Taking ragged breaths, I gaze up at the ceiling, my heart beating so fast it feels like it will explode. As I surrender to the force of his need, I realise that I want something more substantial than his tongue inside me.

As if sensing my thoughts, Nick stops licking and raises his head to look at me. "Are you ready to be fucked?"

"Uh-huh."

"Good girl."

Trembling with longing, he pushes me back a little and hooks my legs over his shoulders: his new favourite position. I bite back a gasp as he slowly starts to ease himself in. I close my eyes and beg my knees to stop shaking. "That's it baby, take it all in. Ah, you're so hot and tight for me."

Soon, he's all the way to the hilt and I'm absolutely loving it. Slowly, he pulls out until only his tip is inside, then he slams back into me like an animal, demolishing me with deep, delicious thrusts that make me scream down the house.

"Don't stop!" I cry. "Harder, harder!"

Nick's more than happy to oblige and soon his dick is causing a whirlwind of euphoria inside me, pushing towards the point of no return. Reaching down, he starts to rub my clit to help speed up my orgasm.

"I'm going to come," he warns. "Tell me when you're there."

I shake my head, breathless. This feels too good to stop now.

Abruptly, Nick withdraws and holds his dick in his hand. "I'm sorry, I need a few seconds, then I'll be ready to go again."

I squeeze my eyes shut and lick my lips. Every part of me is throbbing.

Without warning, Nick flips me over onto my hands and knees and positions me at the edge of the bed. Crouching down, he parts my buttocks and begins licking me out, whetting my appetite for what is to come. A ripple of fear courses through me. *Dear Lord, this is definitely going to hurt.*

"I'm ready to go again," he rasps.

"Please go easy on me," I beg.

"I will my darling. I will."

Silently, he bends me over and slides his dick up and down my pussy to get his tip nice and wet. Then, very slowly, he pushes into my butt-hole.

"Too fast!" I gasp.

"Don't be afraid," he soothes, reaching down and rubbing my clit again. "I'll be gentle as a kitten."

Bowing my head, I clench my teeth as I allow his cock to enter me. He's barely more than a few inches in when my head goes dizzy and a great wave of bliss sweeps through me. I cry out. *Loudly.* Every part of my body shakes convulsively. There's a final explosion, and then the world goes dark around me.

CHAPTER THIRTY-FIVE

The Visitors

L ATER THAT EVENING, I awake to find the space next to
me empty. Nick has left the bed and the whole room is
shrouded in darkness. With a happy sigh, I roll onto my back
and gaze up at the ceiling, my heart beating like a drum. I'm
still consumed by the effects of the orgasm and my head is
high as a kite. *Wow, that was one amazing sex session.*

Sitting up on my elbows, I reach down the side of the bed
and pull out a box of Marlboros. Then, throwing back the
duvet covers, I walk over to the window. Cupping my hands
around a match, I light a cigarette and it tastes good. For a
moment I stand there, staring out into the black night,
looking at the silhouettes of trees outside the window. *I
wonder what time it is.*

As I finish the cigarette, I cast my gaze over the garden
and my heart almost stops beating. Nick is down there with
Veda. They're standing under a tree, talking in hushed tones. I
can't hear what they're saying, but Nick seems absolutely
furious. And then suddenly he's shouting at her and jabbing
his finger in an accusatory fashion. Shockingly, Veda looks
terrified of him and keeps cowering back, as if expecting a
blow.

Fearfully, I dart behind the curtain. I've seen enough. No
way in hell do I want Veda seeing me and fixing me with

those burning, hateful eyes. Crouching down, I pick up the cigarette butt from the floor. I find the whole thing with Veda deeply disturbing. What on Earth is Nick so angry about? Is he telling her to clear out and stay away from us for good?

Dear God, I hope so.

Feeling sick and shaky, I step away from the window and flop down on the bed, clutching my temples. I feel a headache coming. With trembling hands, I light another cigarette. I need to keep cool; keep calm, but it isn't easy. Even at this distance, Veda's evil aura is permeating my senses.

Ten minutes later, I hear a door slam and the sound of heavy footsteps in the downstairs hall. Nick's back from the garden. Throwing on a dressing gown, I head hurriedly out the bedroom into the dark landing. I call out his name three times.

No answer.

Gripping the banister, I walk slowly down the stairs to the hall. I find Nick hanging up his coat on the clothes rack. He looks a little flustered, but quickly smooths it away with a smile.

"Baby, you're awake," he beams. "Did you have a good sleep?"

"The best. Where have you been?"

"I just came in from the garden. I needed a bit of fresh air."

I hesitate, wondering if I should ask him about Veda. I try to find the words, but the moment passes.

He flings his arms wide and I step into his embrace. Instantly, all of my misgivings fade away to be replaced by the wild beating of my heart. "Are you feeling hungry?" he asks. "I was going to make spaghetti."

I force a laugh. "That sounds lovely."

Pushing thoughts of Veda from my mind, I follow Nick into the kitchen. After dinner, he takes me upstairs and tells me what he wants to do to me. Needless to say, we don't get much sleep.

The next morning, I'm sitting at the kitchen island, eating my breakfast, when the doorbell goes.

"Darling, do you want me to get that?" I shout.

"Yes, please," Nick replies from somewhere upstairs. "I'm not sure who it could be, though. I'm not expecting any visitors."

Frowning, I put down my cup and head into the entry hall. Unlatching the door, I find a man and a woman dressed in dark clothing standing on the steps.

The man, an overweight guy in his forties with black hair, smiles at me. "Good morning, sorry to trouble you; is this the home of Dr Nick Craven?"

"Yes, it is," I reply.

"I'm Detective Chief Inspector Philip Holmes of the Metropolitan Police. And this is Detective Sergeant Tina Ashford. May we come in, please?"

"Of course." I step aside for them to enter.

Instantly, Nick appears behind me and flashes a winning smile. "Hello, hello, I'm Nick Craven. How can I help?"

Holmes explains who they are and Nick shakes each of the detective's hands warmly. "Holmes, eh? As in Sherlock Holmes?"

"Yes," Holmes laughs. "But my first name is Philip and I don't live in Baker Street." Nick chuckles and it seems the visit is off to a good start. Even so, my stomach churns as he leads the detectives into the living room and gestures for them to be seated.

Just what the hell is this about?

Fighting hard to keep my feelings in check, I take the armchair opposite the police officers and cross my legs. Nick follows suit and gives me a reassuring grin. Ashford's eyes dart from left to right, scrutinising everything in meticulous detail. For a second, her gaze rests on the hole Nick punched in the door last night, and I wonder what she's thinking.

"What a beautiful room," she says finally.

"Thanks," Nick replies. "Would either of you like a drink? Tea, coffee?"

"No thanks," Holmes replies. "We only just had breakfast."

There's a brief silence. "So, what can I do for you both?" Nick pushes. His smile is starting to get a little strained.

Ashford steals a quick glance at me, and Holmes gives a business-like cough. "If you please, we'd much rather discuss this with you in private. The matter is a little... *sensitive.*"

Nick laughs good-humouredly and places his arm on the headrest behind me. "I'm perfectly happy for Carly to stay. Anything you wish to discuss can be done in front of my fiancée."

Ashford raises an eyebrow. "The two of you are engaged?"

I flash my ring at her. "Yes."

"Congratulations," Holmes grins.

"Thank you."

Ashford reaches into her bag and pulls out a tatty-looking notebook. "You said your name is Carly? Could I have your last name please?"

Nick holds up his hand. "Whoa, whoa, wait a minute; before we go down that road, perhaps you'd like to tell us what this is all about?"

Holmes wipes the corners of his mouth. "Now there's no

cause for alarm, sir. We just want to ask you a few questions, that's all." He pauses for dramatic effect. "Look, I'll cut to the chase, Dr Craven—"

"*Please*, call me Nick."

"Okay, Nick. We're here about Jessica Kemp-Barton."

I cast my eyes downward; my pulse is booming in my ears. *Shit!* Looking up at the ceiling, I take in a lot of air to calm my racing heart.

"Terrible, terrible business," Nick says, shaking his head sadly. "That poor girl. My heart goes out to her family, really it does. Have you had any luck apprehending her killer yet?"

Holmes and Ashford exchange glances. "We're not at liberty to comment," Holmes replies, "but suffice to say, we are still exploring several lines of enquiry."

"I see."

Ashford starts writing in her notebook while Holmes continues: "I think we should start by establishing the nature of your relationship with the deceased. Exactly how long did you know Jessica Kemp-Barton?"

"Let's see, she was my patient for about, oh, let me think, about a month."

Ashford looks up from her notebook. "What were you treating her for?"

"I'm afraid patient confidentiality prevents me from revealing that sort of information."

"That's quite all right," Holmes says. "We have other ways to verify that without compromising your professionalism. So, what kind of a relationship did you have with her?"

"I don't know if you could describe it as a relationship," Nick replies. "My association with Jessica was very brief: our time together equates to a total of three one-hour sessions at my office in Harley Street, during which she revealed very little about herself. Oh, I knew the basics, of course—that she was mother to a four-year-old girl, that she was an actress—that sort of thing. But nothing too personal."

As Nick speaks, Ashford stares at his lips and she keeps crossing and uncrossing her legs. I can tell she's getting wet. There's a hunger on her face I know all too well; the same hunger I saw on my mother's face the first day she met him. That same crazy magnetism that seems to pull every women to him. The question is, will Ashford's attraction to Nick help or hinder the interrogation?

"Anything else?" Holmes presses.

"No," Nick replies airily.

"Did Jessica ever mention anything to you about her boyfriend, Benedict Lewis?"

"No. Like I said, we never spoke about anything personal." Nick pauses. "Look, I don't know what else you want me to say. Jessica was my patient, I saw her for a total of three hours, and that's about it."

"Was her treatment successful?" Ashford asks.

"Not really," Nick admits. "I decided to end Jessica's treatment early because we weren't making much progress and there didn't seem any point wasting her money."

"Who's decision was it to end the treatment?" Holmes prods. "Yours or Jessica's?"

"It was a mutual decision. We both decided that there was nothing further I could do for her."

There's short, uncomfortable silence.

Holmes stares intently at Nick. It's like he's trying to read him, work him out. "Are you sure there isn't anything else you want to add?"

Nick shakes his head. "No. I think that's about everything."

"Just for the record, what *were* your whereabouts on the 24th November, round about midnight?"

Nick looks at the floor. "Wow, let me think. The 24th was a Tuesday, right?"

"That's right," Holmes nods.

Nick flexes his shoulders and takes a few calming breaths. In a show of solidarity, I reach over and hold his hand. His skin feels as cold as ice.

"So," Holmes pushes, "where were you?"

"Um, I'll have to check my diary, but I'm pretty sure I was at a house party in North London. In fact, I'm certain of it."

"Who's house party?" Ashford probes. "Do you have a name?"

"Yes," Nick smiles. "It was my receptionist Tara's birthday party. She and her husband had a small gathering at their flat in Crouch End. There must have been, oh, about twenty people there I'd say."

"So, there are witnesses who can verify your whereabouts on that night?" Holmes asks.

"Yes, of course," Nick nods.

"And what time did you leave the house party?"

"About three in the morning."

"What did you do after that?"

"I drove straight home."

"Is there anyone else who could verify that?"

"Yes," I say quickly. "I was at the house when Nick got back. I'm happy for you to put that down on record."

"Okay, good." Holmes shoots a sly glance at Ashford. "Oh, and just for the record, do you have your receptionist's full name and telephone number so that we can talk to her directly?"

"Yes, certainly," Nick grins. "But I don't understand why. Surely I'm not under investigation?"

"No, this is purely just routine. No cause for alarm." Holmes scratches the side of his mouth and looks a little uncomfortable. Then he leans back in his chair and presses his fingertips together. "Were you aware that Jessica kept a diary?"

Nick frowns. "No."

"Well, she did. One of my officers picked it up from her dressing table when we searched her flat. Would it surprise you to learn that you featured quite prominently in Jessica's diary in the weeks leading up to her death?"

My body stiffens and I look to Nick for clarity. *I don't like the sound of this...*

Nick wets his lips, his expression suddenly grim. "No, this is all news to me."

"Some of her diary entries were very, very interesting," Holmes continues. "It appears Jessica was besotted with you. In fact, I would go a step further and call it boarder-line obsession. One incident in particular comes to mind; a very embarrassing incident..."

I squeeze Nick's hand. "Darling, what's he talking about?"

Holmes gives a mirthless smile. "It seems that Jessica harboured unrequited feelings for Nick. According to her diary, she bombarded him with phone calls and emails on a daily basis declaring her undying love for him, and his frequent rebuttals were the cause of much anguish to her. Some diary entries even spoke of her feeling suicidal." He hesitates, waiting for his bombshell to sink in. Then, addressing Nick again, he says, "On her final visit to your Harley Street office, Jessica describes an incident when she, ahem, exposed herself to you."

My eyes widen. "Exposed? What does that mean?"

"It means she took off her clothes," Ashford clarifies. "She went to Nick's office wearing only her coat with nothing underneath and flashed him."

"Jesus!" I bury my head in my hands.

Holmes fixes his gaze on Nick. "Is what Jessica said in her diary true? Is that the real reason you terminated her treatment early?"

"Yes," Nick answers quietly. "It didn't seem right for us to continue. Her attachment to me was getting unhealthy."

"How did you feel about Jessica's behaviour?" Ashford asks. "Did you find it very stressful?"

"I admit I found her a bit challenging at times but as I said, I made the decision not to continue treating her. That was my solution to the problem."

Holmes looks at the floor a second, then back at Nick. "And did she ever mention her boyfriend acting violently towards her?"

"No," Nick replies. "Why?"

Holmes wags his head from side to side. "It seems her boyfriend, this Benedict Lewis, found some of the emails Jessica sent you on her computer and went totally ballistic. Neighbours say they heard constant arguments in the days leading up to her death."

I bite my thumbnail. "Surely you don't think Jessica's boyfriend did it?"

"We don't have any conclusions yet," Ashford interjects quickly. "We are simply trying to gather the facts, establish a timeline of events and the whereabouts of all those concerned."

The interrogation continues for another twenty minutes or so, but they don't get much more out of him. Nick's got his alibi and he's sticking to it.

"Thanks again for your time," Holmes says as we see them out onto the doorstep. "Listen, Nick, would you be available to come by the station tomorrow to sign a statement?"

"Certainly," Nick smiles. "I'll pass by around two-thirty?"

"Perfect. I'll see you then."

As we close the door on the detectives, I grimace. Nick has got some serious explaining to do.

CHAPTER THIRTY-SIX

The Truth

"**W**HY DIDN'T YOU tell me about Jessica?" I hiss, following Nick through the hall into the living room. "Why didn't you tell me she was obsessed with you?"

"I didn't think it was relevant," he replies sheepishly.

"Of course, it's relevant!"

"Come on; the poor woman is dead. No good ever comes of speaking ill of the dead."

"Yes, but you could at least have told me she was stalking you. I had a right to know."

"She wasn't stalking me. She was just a little... *over-excited*."

"That's putting it mildly. Bombarding you with emails twenty-four-seven and then dropping her knickers for you... oh, I think I'd call that stalking."

"As I recall, Jessica's behaviour was not too dissimilar to a certain other person I know. Only in that case, the attention I received was very much wanted."

My cheeks flush as I realise he's talking about me. *Jesus, he's right*. My own conduct was pretty obsessive in those first few weeks of meeting him. That wild, crazy love that drove me to the brink of insanity. Suddenly, I put myself in Jessica's shoes and feel desperately sorry for her. I imagine her sprawled out on a bed, her pale face twisted and caked with blood. It's so horrible it doesn't bear thinking about.

Shaking my head, I collapse on the sofa, clutching my temples. "My God, the police think Jessica's boyfriend killed her. They're planning to send an innocent man to prison."

"But how do we know he's innocent?"

"Because we know it was a vampire."

"Correction. We *think* it was a vampire, we don't know for certain."

"But if it was, and an innocent man gets blamed for it, that would be so terrible. I mean, if Benedict goes to prison, Jessica's daughter would be left without a father. I refuse to let that happen. We have to do something."

"What do you expect me to do?" Nick explodes. "Call the police and say, hey, I'm a vampire and I think one of my kind may have been responsible for Jessica's murder?"

I fall silent. I have no comeback. Seething, he strides over to the window, his face the picture of disquietude.

"I feel like you're hiding something from me," I say quietly.

"I'm not hiding anything," Nick snaps.

"I think you are." I pause, picking words. "I saw you talking to Veda in the garden. What was all that about?"

He shakes his head. "It was nothing."

"Don't tell me it was nothing. The two of you were having a full blown argument. What were you saying to her?"

"I was telling her to stay away from us. I can't have her dropping by anytime she feels like it and scaring you. I want a fresh start Carly, and that means putting the past behind us once and for all."

"And has she agreed to stay away?"

"Yes."

"I don't believe you."

"Well, start believing. It's the truth."

Raking his fingers through his hair, Nick stamps over to the sofa and looms over me. For a moment we stare at each other. Tension crackles in the air like electricity.

"Darling, I know you're innocent," I whisper. "I know you didn't harm Jessica, but I still think you know more than you're saying. Was it Veda?"

He hesitates. "No."

"Are you sure? You wouldn't lie to me?"

"No!"

"Did you ask her?"

"No."

"Then how do you know she didn't do it?"

"Because Veda wouldn't do something like that."

"Then was it Count Karlock?"

"Good God, how the hell would I know? I haven't seen him in over a hundred years."

"But the murder has to be connected to you somehow. You're a vampire, and Jessica's body was drained of blood. Was it someone trying to frame you or settle some kind of score?"

"You're asking questions I don't know the answers to. Remember, we still don't know for sure it *was* a vampire killing."

"But she was drained of blood, Nick. That's more than a coincidence, don't you think?"

"I agree, I agree." He sighs. "Look, I'll think of something, okay? Give me some time. I'll do some digging and see what I come up with, but I promise you, if it really was a vampire, than I'll make sure Jessica's boyfriend is completely vindicated. I won't let a innocent man take the rap." His voice softens. "Listen darling, I don't want us to fight about this. We're supposed to be a team, and you need to remember that I'm on your side here. I want to get to the bottom of Jessica's death as much as you do, but can't we just put it aside for today? Can't we focus on happy things, just for today?"

I nod silently. Tenderly, he reaches down and strokes my cheek, causing a small sigh from my lips.

"I love you," I whisper.

"I love you too."

"I'm scared."

"Don't be. Everything will work out, I promise." He pulls me to my feet. "Come on. Let's go and finish unpacking your things."

I follow him upstairs and we spend the rest of the afternoon trying to keep busy. Sometime around six, we head to West End to meet my father at a little Italian restaurant off Regent Street.

As soon as we enter the brightly lit foyer, a moustachioed waiter sidles up and asks for our names to check whose party we've come with.

"Nick Craven plus two, seven-thirty."

The waiter scans his list of bookings and ticks our names off. "Great, I've got you down here." Tucking two menus under his arm, the man then leads us through the crowded restaurant to a table for three at the back.

"Oh, Dad's not here yet," I groan, placing my handbag on the table. "I hope he hasn't stood us up."

"Don't panic, it's only seven-thirty-five," Nick says, glancing at his watch. "Give him some more time. Perhaps the trains were delayed."

Glumly, I sit down and nibble on a bread stick. Nick orders us some wine and I scan the menu to get an idea of what I might like to eat. To be honest, I don't feel particularly hungry. There are too many questions playing on my mind, and I'm sure I can feel Veda's dark presence in the air. Or perhaps I'm just being paranoid.

Nick reaches across the table and strokes my hand. "Are you okay, baby?"

"Yes."

"Good. I want you to be happy. *Always.*"

He smiles warmly and my heart flutters with love. Despite all the evil around us, when he looks at me like that, I know this relationship is worth fighting for.

"So sorry I'm late. There were delays to the Northern Line again." We both look up and see my father standing over us. His face is red and puffy, like he's just run a marathon to get here.

"Hi, Dad," I smile, getting up and pecking him on the cheek. Nick shakes his hand.

"Did you bring the paperwork?" he asks.

"Yes," my father replies, patting his big fat briefcase. He's about to open it when Nick stops him.

"No rush, there's plenty of time to talk business. Why don't we relax for a bit and enjoy a bite to eat? I've ordered wine. I hope you like red?"

"Yes, red's great." Dad sits down and pats back his lank, grey hair.

"So, how was Christmas at Mum's?" I ask tentatively.

He rolls his eyes theatrically. "Quiet."

"Really?"

"Really."

"Pull the other one, Dad. I bet she was bitching about me no end."

"Actually, she wasn't."

"Don't try to cover for her. I know what mum's like."

"No seriously, your mother was actually quite subdued after you left. I think she's slowly coming to terms with it."

"Well, I don't give a toss if she hasn't. I'm marrying Nick with or without her consent. I refuse to let her control my life."

Nick clears his throat. "Perhaps we should drop the subject. I thought we agreed to keep the mood light tonight?"

I smile thinly. "Okay, just this once, I'll keep my mouth shut."

"Sounds like a plan," Dad chuckles. "Hey, can I take a look at that menu?"

The rest of the evening passes quickly. The food is nice, the company great, and a few times I even manage to crack a genuine smile. My father is like a ray of sunshine and it's so good to have something to take my mind off all the darkness. Towards the end of the evening, Nick goes through Dad's mortgage papers and after much toing and froing, they reach an agreement that Dad is comfortable with. I'm astounded by Nick's generosity and can't help feeling guilty about it; that he would go to such lengths to keep me happy makes me feel awfully indebted to him.

Finally, Nick swallows the last of his wine and glances at his watch. "Well, Steve, it's just gone ten to ten. I think I'll ask for the bill."

"Good idea," Dad nods.

Raising his hand, Nick signals to the waiter who comes over quickly to clear away the plates. As he does so, Nick asks for the bill, and when it comes, he gives it the onceover before placing a platinum credit card on the table. Dad reaches for his wallet to make a contribution but Nick bats it away.

"This one's on me," he smiles.

"Oh, come on, Nick, you've already done too much for me. Please let me pay for this."

The two of them argue playfully before Nick finally relents and allows Dad to pay. Despite bailing him out over the mortgage, he knows my father needs to be allowed at least some dignity.

"Okay," I say, standing up and smoothing down my jacket. "Time to get going. How are you getting home, Dad?"

"Oh, I think I'll just Tube it back."

"I can give you a lift," Nick offers. "My car's parked just around the corner."

"Oh no, I'm fine," Dad laughs. "I've already bought a day travel card so I may as well make use of it. I hate wasting money."

"Okay. Well, if you change your mind, the offer's there."

Nick shrugs on his coat and, waving goodbye to the waiter, the three of us head out the restaurant into the street. Immediately, we head in the direction of Oxford Circus Tube station. Once outside, we quickly exchange hugs and then I watch my father disappear down the steps into the Underground.

"All right, let's go pick up the car," Nick grins. "Gosh Carly, your hands are freezing. Have you forgotten to bring your gloves again?"

"Yeah. I keep losing them."

He squeezes my hand to help warm my fingers. I sigh. *He's such a sweetheart, I don't know what I'd do without him.*

"Overall, I think that went rather well," he comments as we turn off into a side street.

I nod my head. "I can't thank you enough for all you've done for me and my family. Words can't begin to describe how grateful I am..." I break off, starting to get a little emotional.

"Hey, hey, what are the tears for? Remember, we're family now. Nothing is too much for my beautiful bride-to-be."

I smile. I don't need words. My expression says it all.

We pick up the Jag and after we've been driving for a few minutes, Nick tells me that he wants to take a detour to North London.

"Why?" I frown. "I'm knackered. I thought we were going straight home?"

"I'm sorry, but I promised Tara we'd swing by her place for a bit. She's having a post Christmas get-together and I said we'd show our faces."

My neck stiffens. "I don't really fancy going to a party. I'm so tired and—"

"It's not really a party," Nick interjects. "Just a few friends and a bit of music. Nothing too heavy." He steals a quick glance at me and then returns his gaze to the traffic. "Please do this for me. I know it's a pain, but I've been dying to show off your ring to everyone. And remember, these are some of the people who will be coming to our wedding, so it's a good chance for you to get to know them before the big day." I make a non-committal sound and he laughs. "Honestly, Tara's husband is great. I think you'll really like him. It won't be as bad as all that."

I pull a face. "Okay," I pout. "I suppose we could drop by for half an hour, but please promise me it won't be an all-nighter."

"Don't worry; it won't."

For a short time, we drive in silence. Then a sudden thought hits me. "Does Tara know you're a vampire?"

"Of course not. Why do you ask?"

"I don't know. I guess it's the first time I ever really thought about it."

"Well, she doesn't. She's just a regular human being, like you. She doesn't believe in vampires, or witches, or warlocks."

"But hasn't she ever suspected any strange about you?"

"No, never."

"Really?"

"I've got news for you Carly: no matter how strange things get, most people don't suspect their boss of being a vampire." He laughs to himself but I fail to see the funny side. "Oh, come on, don't be so serious. I'm just playing with you. Show me that beautiful smile I love."

I try desperately to remain stony-faced but know I'm fighting a losing battle. Eventually, I have to crack a smile and Nick playfully pinches my cheek. He knows I can never stay mad at him for long.

CHAPTER THIRTY-SEVEN

Ravish

I OPEN MY eyes and for a moment, it's like I'm seeing double. Slowly, I return to the current moment and focus on the car's sleek black interior.

"Rise and shine, beautiful," Nick smiles. "We're here."

"Where?"

"Tara's."

"Already?" Turning my head, I peer out the window at the dark street. We seem to be parked opposite a dead end.

Nick laughs softly. "Don't worry, I haven't brought you out to the middle of nowhere. Tara's house is just behind us. You drifted off and you looked so cute sleeping, I didn't want to wake you."

Wordlessly, I reach into my bag and pull out my mirror to check that my make-up isn't smudged. Goddammit, I look so washed out. *I really need to start going to bed earlier.*

Nick grins angelically. "Darling, stop that. You look absolutely gorgeous. There's nothing to fix. Now come on, let's get this over with so that I can get you home and ravish you."

"Is there any chance we could skip the party and just go straight home?"

"Oh, don't be like that. Remember, you promised." Still smiling, he reaches out and softly runs his fingers down my cheek. "Don't worry, it won't be all that bad. We'll just say hi to everyone, have one drink and then go."

My stomach tightens and I'm consumed by uncontrollable longing. "My God, I want you so much."

"And you will have me. Once we've got this over with."

Suddenly, I bolt forward, grab him around the neck and devour his lips with hot, hungry kisses. When he tries to loosen his grip, I continue to cling onto him, not wanting to let go. Finally, he manages to pull away. "You're such a tease. I know exactly what you're doing. You're trying to get me so worked up I won't want to go inside."

"How did you guess?" I giggle.

"All I'll say is this: when we get home, you'd better be ready for me, because right now I could eat you alive."

I shoot him a smouldering look. "Oh, I think that can be arranged." I lean over and give him a final, lingering kiss, then I unclip my seatbelt and step out onto the pavement. "Okay, let's do this."

Nick locks up the car and leads me across the street towards a pretty Victorian house with a contemporary exterior and large bay windows. Even before we reach the front door, I can hear the sound of muffled chatter and Adele's "Rolling In The Deep" playing at full blast.

I get a sudden rush of butterflies. *Jesus, I hate meeting new people.*

We ring the bell twice before a harassed-looking man answers. "You made it!" he grins, shaking Nick's hand. "And you must be, Carly. Congratulations on your engagement. I'm Barry, Tara's husband. Lovely to see you both! I hope you didn't have any trouble finding the place this time?"

"No, no," Nick laughs. "I remembered the way."

Barry steps aside for us to enter. "Please, please come in. Rebecca and Liz have just arrived and everyone else is having drinks in the lounge.'

We wipe our shoes on the welcome mat and follow him through a dingy entry hall to a flight of stairs that lead to the first-floor flats. Unlocking a scuffed green door, he takes us into a large, brightly coloured living room, where Tara is busy serving drinks to the other guests. She looks stunning in red lipstick and a black off-the-shoulder dress that compliments her figure perfectly. When she smiles her teeth are so white, she looks like she's wearing dental veneers.

"Oh Nick, you made it, how wonderful!" she trills.

She bounds over and embraces him warmly, and then gives me a little kiss on the cheek. "Wow, you look divine, Carly. That dress is so cute on you. Now...let me see this famous engagement ring."

Blushing, I hold out my hand and Tara scrutinises the diamond with genuine glee. "Hey ladies, come over and look at this monster! Aren't you all so jealous?"

"What is it?" someone asks.

"A ring? Oh goody, can I see it?"

I groan as six strangers surround me like a group of mother hens. It's my worst nightmare. I've always hated being the centre of attention and all this fuss makes me feel like a bit of a circus freak.

After all the cooing and clucking is finally over, Tara proceeds to introduce me to everyone. Then she promptly shoves a champagne flute in my hand and disappears off to mingle. Proudly, Nick kisses my nose and wraps his arm protectively around my waist.

"Are you okay, baby?" he whispers.

"Yes," I reply. "Never been better."

"You see, it wasn't so bad, was it? Let's give it another twenty minutes, then we'll call it a day."

I nod stiffly.

"Are you definitely sure you're okay?"

"I just feel a bit… hot in here."

"Do you want to go outside for some fresh air?"

"Yes, please!"

Gripping my hand tightly, Nick leads me through the swathes of bodies to a set of glass doors that open out onto a spacious balcony. Setting down his glass, Nick sits on one of the plastic chairs and pulls me in close. The air feels so cold my teeth start to chatter.

With a wicked smile, he moves his hands along the bottom of my thighs, touching and caressing, before working his way up into my dress. I moan quietly as he slowly pulls down my knickers and helps me step out of them.

Shit! What is he doing?

Nervously, I glance back inside the house to check that no-one is watching. "I can't believe you just did that," I whisper.

"Relax," Nick purrs. "I've got everything under control." With a sexy smirk, he rolls my knickers up into a ball and puts them in his coat pocket.

Dear Lord. What does he have planned for me?

Softly, soothingly, he pulls me forward and starts to kiss the tops of my thighs, his hot lips sending a trail of goosebumps up my skin. I wince. This is more than I can bear. I'm completely breathless and need those lips to be kissing me somewhere else.

"I want so much to fuck you," he growls. "I've a mind to bend you over and have my wicked way with you right here, right now."

"Then why don't you?"

"Because I like the chase."

His words send a quiver up my spine and I go from wet to soaking. I'm crying silently for his fingers to reach up a little higher and bless me with their warmth. As if sensing my thoughts, he moves up my dress to my wet slit and begins to rub slow circles around my clit.

"Do you like that?" he breathes, looking up at me. "Like how that feels?"

"Uh-huh."

"Do you want me to stop?"

"Don't you dare."

"You're so wet for me. I can tell your pussy's hungry; let me feed her." Parting my thighs, he buries two fingers deep inside my burning hole.

I shut my eyes and try to think of England. "Shit, don't stop."

For long moments, I'm frozen with pleasure as he continues thrusting in and out, sending me out of my mind. Then abruptly, everything stops.

I open my eyes, my cheeks all hot and flustered. "What's going on?"

"I think you need a top-up," Nick drawls, taking my half empty glass.

"Where are you going?" I ask desperately. "You can't just leave me hanging like this."

"I need to go inside for some more champagne. Wait here. Don't worry, I promise I won't be long." Within seconds, he's gone.

Smoothing down my dress, I collapse on a chair and try to calm down. Dammit, Nick really knows how to pick his moments. An inferno of longing burns between my legs and I want him so badly it hurts. It was cruel of him to get me so worked up, especially in a public place. Desperately, I try to push sexy thoughts from my head, but it isn't easy. He's like an addiction I can't control.

Five minutes later, I start to grow restless. It's not nice sitting out here on my own and my legs are feeling very cold. Craning my neck, I squint through the glass partition. *Where on Earth is he?*

Irritably, I stand up and march back inside the house. Instantly, I spy Nick huddled in a corner, talking earnestly with Tara. She's leaning in close with a sombre expression on her face. Nick's whispering something in her ear, to which she nods and mouths the words: "Don't worry; you can count on me."

I get a sick feeling in my stomach. *Of course!* Why didn't I see this before? Now everything is falling into place. It was no accident that Nick brought me here today. It's quite obvious that he came to warn Tara about the police enquiry and brief her on what to say so that they can both get their stories straight.

Cold fear pours through my veins. *Shit!*

In a panic, I work my way across the room and sidle up to Barry who's piling up his plate at the snack table.

"Enjoying yourself?" he asks cheerfully.

"Yes, I'm having a great time," I lie. "I absolutely love Adele."

"So do I! I can't wait for her to release another album. It's been too long."

I smile weakly. "So, how was Tara's birthday party?"

Barry raises his eyebrows. "What birthday party?"

"Nick told me you guys had a party here a few weeks ago for Tara's birthday. He said it went on until three in the morning."

"There must be some mistake. Sure, it was Tara's birthday, but we didn't throw any party. She just wanted a quiet one so I took her out to a Chinese restaurant. Maybe Nick got confused?"

I give a fake laugh. "My apologies. Perhaps I misheard or I'm getting the dates mixed up. Silly me; forget I ever said anything."

"No harm done. It was nice of you to ask. Well, now that you're here, why don't you have another drink?"

Before I can refuse, he plonks a glass of wine in my hand. "Thanks," I croak.

My head is spinning and my throat has gone all dry. *Jesus, so Nick lied to the police.* He wasn't with Tara the night of Jessica's murder so…what the hell does this mean?

CHAPTER THIRTY-EIGHT

Falling

I N A FEVER of agitation, I race across the room and tap Nick's shoulder. He spins around and flashes a loving smile. "Carly, my darling, I was just about to come and get you. It's time to go home."

"Oh no, you're not leaving already?" Tara pouts. "You only just got here." She's being playful but her eyes betray hostility.

Emboldened, I grab Nick's arm and pull him roughly towards the door. "Can we please just go?" I hiss. "I need to speak with you urgently."

"Sorry Tara," he grins, "I'm afraid the wife has spoken, so we'll have to get going, but I'll phone you tomorrow, okay?"

"Okay. Thanks both of you for coming and have a safe journey home. Oh, and good luck with the engagement. I look forward to receiving my invite."

Laughing pleasantly, Nick waves a final goodbye to everyone and follows me out into the landing. Slipping his finger under my chin, he tilts my face upwards so he can see my eyes. "What's gotten into you? Has someone upset you?"

"I can't talk here. Please, can we just go to the car and I'll explain everything."

"Your wish is my command."

Releasing my face, he wraps his arms around my waist

and pulls me into the street. Taking out his car keys, he presses a button on the chain and unlocks the doors of the Jaguar. Hastily, I slip in the passenger side and wait nervously for him to join me. As he gets in the driver's seat, I squeeze my eyes shut to psych myself up. I don't know how much more stress I can take and secretly wish I hadn't thrown away the Thurlax.

For a few moments, the two of us sit in silence, listening to the sound of our breathing.

Nick's the first to break the deadlock. "Baby, what's this all about? I'm really worried about you."

"You lied to the police. You told them you were with Tara the night Jessica died, but you weren't. Barry just told me there *was* no birthday party on that night." Nick doesn't say anything. I continue: "Why did you lie? Is there something you want to tell me?"

"No."

"Then why lie to the police about your whereabouts? If you haven't got anything to hide, why pretend you were out with Tara? Look at me, Nick." He looks at me. "Be honest and tell me where you were that night. I promise I won't be angry, just tell me the truth."

"I was at home asleep."

"Don't give me that!"

"It's the truth. I only gave Tara as an alibi to ensure I was safe from further interrogation. Yes, I could have told the police the truth, but that would have left me wide open. Can't you see that I did this for us?"

"Yeah, right."

"It's true. I'll do anything to protect our life together, so if it means telling a little white lie now and again, I'll gladly do it."

"But this isn't a little lie, it's a big lie. One that makes me question your sincerity."

He slams his fist on the dashboard. "Oh my God, are you insinuating that I murdered Jessica? Do you have that little faith in me? You honestly think I would do something that despicable?"

I run my fingers through my hair. "I don't know, I don't know. I don't want to believe it but, well… it's not looking good, is it?"

"We're supposed to be a team. I thought you loved me?"

"I do love you."

"Then how the hell could you think I murdered Jessica?"

I fall silent. The truth is, I *am* starting to have doubts again. Deep down, I want to believe that Nick's innocent, but all these lies he's telling are beginning to take their toll on me. If he truly has nothing to hide, then why does he keep lying?

"Nick, listen—"

He holds up his hand for silence and I realise that I've pushed him too far this time. Moodily, he starts up the engine, sets the Jag in motion, and the sudden jerk throws me against him.

"Put on your bloody seatbelt," he growls.

Hastily, I strap myself in. The anger in his voice is scary.

With a melancholic expression, he turns on the heater and a blast of warmth fills the car. Carefully, he steers the Jaguar onto the main road and within seconds, we're moving through the dark north London streets, heading in the direction of Pimlico. Trembling, I lean back against the headrest, my skin prickling with nervous energy. I ask no questions. I just keep my eyes on the road, watching the wipers dance back and forth across the windscreen. I can tell Nick's furious with me and in all honesty, who can blame him? Okay, so he lied about his alibi, but that doesn't make him a killer. I can completely understand why he's hurt. I think about how good he's been to both me and my father and I know that he doesn't deserve to be treated this way. Desperately, I wrack my brain to find a way to make amends and get back on his good side.

We arrive back in Pimlico around midnight. As soon as we get inside the house, Nick heads straight upstairs to the bedroom. It's clear he's in a foul mood and nothing I say can lift his spirits. He hasn't said a word to me since we left Tara's, and I think this time, my rash behaviour has cut him deeply. Oh how I wish I could turn back the clock and not said all those hurtful things.

Sheepishly, I kick off my shoes in the hall and follow Nick upstairs. When I get to the bedroom, I find him standing by the four-poster, looking all stiff and agitated. I hover in the doorway, staring at him. The air is thick with tension.

He stands there like he doesn't know what to do with himself, then, slowly, he takes off his jacket and his shirt and lays them in a neat pile on the chair. I catch my breath. The ripped body beneath those clothes is enough to give a girl heart failure, and as he slides down his trousers and boxers, my stomach starts doing crazy things. His cock is already stiff and despite his anger, I am in no doubt that he wants me.

He's doing this on purpose. Why the heck is he naked? He knows damn well the effect he has on me and he's milking it for all it's worth.

Without making eye contact with me, Nick climbs in the bed, rolls onto his side and makes a point of moving as far away to the edge as possible.

"I'm so sorry," I whisper. "Please can we talk about this?"

"There's nothing to talk about," he snaps. "You think I

killed Jessica. You think I'm some kind of a monster, and maybe you're right. Perhaps all this time I've been deluding myself. Perhaps you never truly loved me."

"How can you say that?" I counter. "Of course, I love you. I want to marry you!"

"Well, you don't act like it. Every time there's the slightest hitch, you accuse me of being a killer." He shakes his head. I can't see his face, but I can tell by his voice that he's very emotional. "Perhaps this is karma," he murmurs. "Perhaps I don't deserve to ever be happy. Do you know how long I've waited to meet someone like you? Before you came into my life, I'd been celibate for over ninety years because I couldn't bear to share my heart with anyone."

My mouth gapes. "You were celibate? But I don't understand. Surely you could have had any woman you wanted?"

"I could have," he agrees. "Being a vampire means I can cast a spell over anyone I choose, but exploitation is not in my nature. I have never abused my power in that way and I have never taken anything from a woman that wasn't given freely. When I make love, I need to know that the woman truly wants me for me." He swallows. "I need to know that the woman truly loves Nick the man, not Nick the vampire."

I wet my lips and take a step forward, my heart beating so fast it feels like it will explode. "But remaining celibate for all those years must have been so difficult."

"It was. Some days I wanted sex so bad, I felt like killing myself. But eventually, I trained myself not to want it. Even when it was offered to me on a plate, I resisted temptation because I promised myself only to ever give my body to one special woman – a woman who truly loved me." He pauses. "The first day you came into my office… I wanted you so bad it made me physically ill. I couldn't sleep, couldn't concentrate on anything. I had never felt a desire like that before and when you started to pursue me, oh God, it was the happiest time of my existence. Never in my wildest dreams did I believe that you could actually feel the same way that I felt about you. That's why I relinquished my hold over you, because I had to be sure that your attraction to me was genuine."

"Of course it was genuine!" I shout. "You know how much I love you. How many times do you want me to say it before it gets through to you?"

"Actions speak louder than words. If you really loved me, then you wouldn't keep accusing me of killing Jessica. When you love someone, that's something you just don't do. I mean, what is a relationship without trust?"

"I agree, but I refuse to take all of the blame. If you'd just be straight with me and stop telling lies and half-truths all the time, perhaps I *would* be able to trust you." I fold my arms across my chest. "Think how difficult this is for me. In the past two days alone, you've sprung a monstrous ex-wife on me, told me that London is crawling with vampires and lied to the police about your whereabouts on the night of a murder. Put yourself in my shoes and then tell me I've behaved badly. Considering the circumstances, I think I've coped pretty damn well."

"Look, I don't want to talk about this anymore," he growls. "If you want to go on thinking that I'm a killer, fine. I can't change that. Now do you want to switch off the light or should I?"

Cursing under my breath, I walk over to the switch by the door, and plunge the room into darkness. Quickly, I strip off my clothes, clamber into the bed and face away from him, my shoulders hunched defensively. Now the only light in the room is the golden embers of the fire in the grate.

For long moments, I lie awake, blinking in the darkness with a great lump of misery sitting in my chest. I need to feel his cock inside me. I need him to fuck me hard and make me scream, but right now, that seems highly unlikely. Not after all the things I just said to him.

Finally, I can bear it no longer. With trembling fingers, I reach out my hand and touch his shoulder. He coldly shrugs me off.

"Go to sleep," he barks.

"Darling, please! Can't we at least talk?"

"I told you, there's nothing to talk about."

"But I love you."

"No, you don't. You think I'm a killer."

"I don't! Please stop saying that."

With a grim expression, I plump up my pillow before resting my head on my elbow and facing towards him. He's still turned away from me and my pussy gets hot as I ogle his beautifully sculpted back. Leisurely, my eyes travel down the length of his body, openly salivating at the delectable feast on display. *Dear Lord*, I want his cock so badly I can almost taste it, but I need to take my time to break down his barriers.

Softly, I reach out again and stroke his shoulder. This time, he doesn't shrug me off, and I sense that I'm starting to win him over. Moving forward, I cautiously run my fingers down his spine, lightly scratching the surface of his skin with my nails; he shudders with repressed longing and I can tell he's trying mighty hard to stay mad at me, but fooling no one. I own this body and he knows it. When it comes down to it, he can never, ever say no to me.

Licking my lips, I gently turn him onto his front and straddle him. He puts up no resistance and I know then that

I've got him hook, line and sinker. Working my way down, he moans quietly as I run my tongue over his spine, relishing the sweet taste of his warm olive skin.

I love him so much.

Moving lower, I softly lick the cheeks of his buttocks, swirling my hot tongue in slow, sensuous circles that make him gasp, then I press my lips to his left rump. He sucks air through his teeth. *God, he tastes so good.*

Slowly, teasingly, I work my way across, kissing a trail from his left buttock to his right, before burying my tongue deep inside the crease. Taking my time, I lick him up and down some more, my warm mouth eager to explore his darkest regions.

"Stop it," Nick moans. "Why are you doing this? You don't love me. You don't want me. Stop pretending..."

I raise my head. "I'll show you just how much I want you." Eagerly, I return to his butt and plunge my tongue deep inside, making him crazy with excitement. Fuck, I love those whimpering sounds; love knowing how much power I have over him.

Moving down from his delectable bottom, I gently lick and suck the backs of his thighs, his calves, his feet, then I gradually work my way back up again. His moaning grows harder, more urgent.

"Turn around," I whisper. "I want to taste you some more."

Obediently, he rolls onto his back and I get an eyeful of his huge throbbing cock. Oh my, all I want is to sit on it, but I have to control myself, tease him some more. I stop to catch my breath. My hair is damp; my skin glistening with sweat.

"You're so cruel," he breathes.

"Why am I cruel?"

"You know how weak I am for you; you know how much I love you, and you're abusing your privileged position."

"Well, if I am, then I'm only doing what you taught me. I've got to admit, you're a pretty good teacher, Nick. You've got me wrapped around your little finger and now it's payback time."

With a sexy smile, I walk my fingers down his thighs and rest them on his balls. For a second, I hold them in my hands, teasing them, caressing them. Then I lower my head, join my hand and mouth together and suck on him in a slow, steady rhythm that makes his whole body tremble.

"Oh, my God!" he rasps.

I sing inwardly, knowing that I've finally got him where I want him. Hungrily, I swallow his shaft all the way, almost making myself gag, but I don't care. It's what needs to be done to show him just how much I love him.

Succumbing to my carnal urges, I release his dick and work my wet lips from his navel to his chest, tracing invisible shapes with my tongue. Then I bury my face in his neck and softly bite his earlobe. "How much do you want to fuck me?" I demand.

He doesn't answer. He's so turned on, he has no words.

Silently, Nick grips my hips and guides me down onto his dick, pushing through my tightness like a red-hot nail. I clench my teeth to force back a scream. I can't believe how good it feels to have him back where he belongs. Roughly, he impales me again and again and again, stretching me out with deep, delicious thrusts that make my head spin. Fuck. *I never want this to end.*

"Open up for me, baby," he breathes. "I know I can go deeper."

"Ahhhhh!" I moan. My pussy tightens around his cock as I come, but still he continues thrusting into me, pushing through the tightness, sending me beyond the point of no return.

"That's just how you like it, huh?" he whispers. "Rough and deep."

"Yes! Oh Yes!"

With a gasp, I push myself up and down, grinding my clit furiously into his pelvis each time I reach the hilt. I can feel his dick stiffening and I whimper as he hits my sweet spot for the second time. The room spins around me in a vortex of darkness. Monsters, vampires, I don't care. All I want is for him to fuck me senseless. Break me in two. I can't think straight, can't see straight. There's only him and me and this exhilarating feeling.

"Are you ready to come?" he pants.

"Yes."

"Good. Wait for me."

With a loud cry of joy, Nick explodes inside of me and I drop my face onto his sweat-drenched chest. Every part of my body feels numb. Shaking, he releases me and the two of us roll onto our backs, gazing up at the ceiling, drawing our breath in deep gulps. Reaching over, he grips hold of my hand, and for a second, we are connected: two souls merged as one.

Suddenly, he rolls on top of me and starts kissing my neck again. Lord, it feels so good that I put up no resistance; I love what he's doing and don't want it to stop.

"Want to come again?" he murmurs, nuzzling his face in my chest.

"Oh my gosh, I don't know if I can take more."

"Yes you can. You've got to."

With painful need, he moves down and sucks and kisses my breasts, stroking the nipples between his fingers before biting on them like a cherry. I moan loudly. This man is a god. He's sending me to the moon and back.

Stroking my thighs with his palms, Nick circles my clit with his tongue then, moving lower, he plunges deep inside my burning hole, flicking his tongue in and out, making me crazy with his scorching wet heat. I close my eyes and grit my teeth. *Oh, my God. This is sooo good.* Spurred on by my desire, he inserts a finger in my pussy as his tongue continues to play with my clit, taking me to Seventh Heaven.

At last, a fire sparks through me and a satisfying warmth ripples through every one of my nerve-endings.

Nick quits licking and rolls onto his back. With a happy sigh, I fall against his chest and shiver with delight as he wraps me in a bear hug that makes me feel safe and protected. My pulse is all over the place.

"That was amazing," I whisper. "I love you so much."

"I love you, too."

For a while, we lie peacefully in each other's arms, listening to the sound of the wind blowing through the trees. My heart is filled with love. *I've never felt so good.*

"You make me so happy," he sighs, stroking my hair. "When I'm with you, I hold the whole world in my embrace."

"Oh Nick, you're so romantic."

"But it's true.

"How much do you love me?"

"So much."

"Really and truly?"

"You know I'd do anything for you."

"*Anything?*"

"That's what I said."

He hesitates, mulling this over. Then he kisses my forehead. "I've waited so long to find you, Carly. I'm completely obsessed with you and I'm never letting you go, *ever*." He pauses again, and I sense there's something on his mind.

"Darling, what's wrong?" I probe.

"It's nothing."

"Don't give me that. I know every inch of you, and something's wrong, I can feel it."

"No, really, I'm fine."

"No you're not. Talk to me. Tell me what's on your mind."

Nick's breathing grows shallow and his muscles tense. "I have a confession to make," he whispers.

"What is it?"

He swallows hard and licks his lips. "I don't quite know how to say this."

"Just say it."

He hesitates. Fear grips me and refuses to let go. "Please just say it. Don't keep me in suspense."

A minute passes before he's ready to talk. Gently, he grips hold of my hand and says, "I haven't been completely honest with you. You said we shouldn't keep secrets from each other, so...the truth is, I know who killed Jessica."

My eyes widen with horror. "Oh my God..."

"Veda did it."

"Your wife?"

"Yes."

"But why?"

Tears fall slowly down his cheeks. "Because she's evil, Carly. Her own life was destroyed so she cannot bear to ever see anyone else happy. She murdered Jessica because she resented the bond Jessica had with her daughter, Molly. And it kills me, because I feel responsible. I feel like I could have prevented it. I should never have allowed Veda to get as strong as she's become. But I didn't ever confront her behaviour because I felt so guilty about the past we share. After all, I was the one who made Veda the monster she is. So many times over the years, I've had the opportunity to put her out of her misery. I could have driven a stake through her heart long ago and protected humanity from her evil. But I never laid a finger on Veda because I didn't want to go back on the promise I made to my darling Coppélia all those years ago, never to harm her mother."

"You can't blame yourself," I whisper, squeezing his hand reassuringly. "You are as much of a victim as Veda, except that you choose to do good with your life. You didn't ask to become a vampire. It was a cruel card life dealt you. You were in an impossible situation and you simply cannot hold yourself responsible for the wicked path Veda has chosen to take."

He smiles weakly. "You can't imagine how much that means to me. I've wanted to tell you the truth for ages, but I was so scared of how you would react. I thought if I told you the truth about how dangerous Veda is, you wouldn't want to be with me. I thought you would leave, and to be without you was unthinkable." He pauses, momentarily overcome with emotion. "That's why I've told so many lies... just to keep you close to me. I am so sorry, my darling. Can you ever forgive me? I acted selfishly and should have been honest with you from the start so that you knew exactly what you were letting yourself in for. But I promise I'll make things right. Tomorrow I'll talk to the police and find a way to get Jessica's boyfriend off the hook. I won't let an innocent man go to prison for what Veda did. If only I could—"

Nick's sentence dies. His mouth drops open as his gaze rests on the large sash window beyond me. Eyes bulging with terror, he shouts: "Carly, look out!"

In a panic, I turn around to see what he is looking at and gasp. Veda's wasted face is pressed against the window, her foul breath steaming up the glass, her lips pulled back in a horrendous leer. Screeching like a banshee, she smashes open the window and lunges for me. Within seconds, she's got me in a stranglehold, her cold, sharp fingers pressing into my throat, tighter and tighter, squeezing the life out of me.

"Get off her!" Nick roars, but it's like Veda cannot hear him. In one swift movement, he grabs her around the waist and rips her off of me, throwing her to the ground as if she weighs nothing. Veda flails and rolls around like a demented beetle that has been turned on its back.

There's no time to lose.

Racing over to the dressing table, Nick picks up a chair and breaks one of the legs off. Then, with a loud cry of anguish, he storms across to Veda's prone body, raises the chair leg high above his head, and plunges it straight through her heart, impaling her to the floor.

Blood spurts everywhere and Veda lets out a loud shriek of pain that reverberates throughout the entire house. And then something miraculous happens. Veda's cruel, twisted face begins to fade and is replaced by the stunningly beautiful countenance she once had. She twitches a couple more times, and then her body goes completely still. Her eyes close like she's in a deep dreamless sleep. And then... silence.

Total silence.

The vampire curse has been lifted and Veda is finally at peace.

"Oh my God, Nick!" I gasp, falling onto him, sobbing

uncontrollably.

He wraps his warm, strong arms around me and pulls me into an embrace I never want to end.

"It's over, baby," he soothes, stroking me gently. "The nightmare is over. Veda will never darken our lives again and I promise to keep you safe forever. I won't ever let anyone or anything harm you again."

I breathe a huge sigh of relief. Veda is gone and I know finally that I am safe to be with my sweet vampire forever.

CHAPTER THIRTY-NINE

Bonus Novel From Nick's Point Of View

A note to the reader

I want to take this moment to thank all the wonderful fans who have been so supportive of me over the past few months. I cannot begin to tell you how much each of you means to me. After an incredibly busy couple of weeks, I have finally completed the book you hold in your hands: Nick's Story. Before you begin reading, I want to quickly explain what this book is about.

Due to popular demand, I have written this novella as a companion piece to My Sweet Vampire. It is not a direct continuation of the events that take place in the book – rather, Nick's Story is a stand-alone piece written entirely from Nick's perspective and covers several key events that happened in My Sweet Vampire. It also provides fresh information regarding Jessica's murder that will leave you in no doubt of who the killer is. Hopefully this fragment will give my readers further insight into Nick's head and add a new dimension to Carly's story. That's what inspired me to write it in the first place.

I hope you enjoy reading Nick's Story as much as I enjoyed writing it.

Love Arabella

CHAPTER FORTY

First Meeting

HARD, WET RAIN drums against my office windows, transforming the London skyline into a mosaic of water colours. I glance at my watch: *six twenty-five*. Thank God the day's almost over. My session with Jessica today was exhausting and I'm seriously beginning to question her sanity. The things she said to me today are unrepeatable, and if she continues behaving this way, I will have no choice but to sever all contact, which would be a shame, as I hate giving up on people.

When I first met the vivacious redhead a few weeks ago, I was convinced I could help her beat her demons, but now it seems my presence is doing more harm than good. The truth is, hypnosis doesn't work for everyone; some patients just can't be cured, no matter what you do, and they are destined to self-destruct. I fear that Jessica is one such case.

Stifling a yawn, I push my chair forward and open my *Outlook* calendar to see my final appointment is with someone called Carly Singleton. My eyes narrow. *Hmm*. Tara hasn't said much about this one; usually Tara's notes are long enough to give Tolstoy a run for his money, but this time she's pretty brief—all Carly wants to do is quit smoking.

Thank goodness for that.

After Jessica's crazy outbursts and the complexities of

Body Dysmorphic Disorder, I anticipate this should be a relatively painless affair.

Suddenly, I hear the sound of footsteps in the corridor. Getting up, I step away from my desk, sink back into the shadows and make myself invisible. I always do this with new patients to catch them off guard. It's a way for me to read them to help me decide whether or not I want to treat them. When presented with my seemingly empty office, most people can't resist poking around, and the shock on their faces when I finally reveal myself is priceless.

With bated breath, I wait in the shadows for this Carly Singleton to appear. There's a strange electricity in the air and time seems to stand still.

Slowly, the door opens, and a young woman enters the room. She looks about twenty-five, with white-blonde hair, lightly tanned skin and the most gorgeous brown eyes I have ever seen. She's wearing a bright purple jacket with a long-tasselled skirt and green ankle boots. My gaze runs admiringly over her body and my dick begins to stir like an out-of-control horse. *Dear God.* She's a complete and utter goddess: sturdy and full-bodied with curves in all the right places, just the way I like it.

Wiping my brow, I loosen up my collar and pray for my head to stop spinning. Suddenly, the room feels very hot.

Awestruck, I watch as this beautiful creature strolls around my office, scrutinising everything in meticulous detail. She looks so sweet it takes all of my will power not to spring forward and kiss that cute little frown. For two or three minutes, I allow her inspection of my belongings to continue. My breath catches and my knees go weak. For the first time in sixty years, I can actually feel my heart beating. For the first time in sixty years, every single part of my body feels alive.

471

And it's all because of *her*.

Finally, I can bear it no longer. I decide it's time to make an appearance.

Feeling drunk and light-headed, I step from the shadows and walk swiftly towards her.

"Carly Singleton?" My voice sounds stiff and unnatural.

She freezes.

Even before she turns around, I can tell that I'm affecting her. I can sense her breathing quicken; hear her pulse booming in my ears like a Jack hammer. Slowly, slowly, she turns around and rewards me with a smile—the most beautiful smile I've ever seen. *Fucking hell, that mouth!* So full and inviting, so perfect. God help me, I could spend years just feasting on her lips.

"Hello, Carly, I'm Dr Nick Craven." I slip my hand into hers and the soft touch of her skin sends a bolt of heat straight to my throbbing dick. It feels like I'm drowning, like I'm at the bottom of a well and can't get up. Fuck, I'm behaving like a muddled school boy. This has to stop.

"I hope you haven't been waiting long?" I choke. *I wonder if she can tell that my hands are shaking?*

"No," she replies in the sweetest voice I've ever heard. "I-I haven't been waiting long at all. Good to meet you, Doctor Craven."

"Please, call me Nick." For a second-long eternity, I stare into her beautifully angelic face. All I can think about is what those lips would taste like and how they'd feel wrapped around my cock. *Shit, I'm a complete mess. This wasn't supposed to happen.*

Once again, I find my voice. "Can I take your coat?" I ask.

"No! I mean… yes, of course." She laughs gently and tilts her head back, exposing her creamy white neck to me. My eyes home in on a particularly prominent vein and I can feel her blood calling out to me, begging me to sink my teeth in and drain every last drop. Excitement grips me and I start to perspire. *My God, can she tell how much I'm drooling?*

For a second, I envisage her naked but I manage to shake the thought from my head. *Hold it together, you idiot!*

She flicks a glance at me with those bewitching brown eyes and I'm a slave to her next instruction. My cock is hard enough to drive nails and it's actually getting quite painful to walk. Slowly, she unbuttons her coat. I bolt forward a little too eagerly. She looks startled by my sudden movement, but I don't care; I just have to touch her. If I don't, I'll go mad.

With trembling fingers, I place my hands on her shoulders and pull off her jacket. I sense her body stiffen and I know she's getting wet for me. Fuck, this is absolute torture. I can tell that she wants me. It's written all over her face. Then again, why should that be a surprise? All women are attracted to me, and truth be told, if I really wanted to, I could have Carly right here, right now. But that's not how I operate. I like to take my time with these things.

I've never abused the dark power the Devil has given me to sate my carnal urges.

Using the black arts to get my wicked way with Carly would be far to easy. No, I want to take my time with this one; see how it plays out, because I feel that this woman is special. From the moment I laid eyes on her, I felt an unexplainable connection that I'm simply dying to explore further.

I study the silken fall of her hair and get a whiff of her gorgeous scent: lavender soap. Freshly washed body. My senses have reacted to her in ways I cannot control, like I'm the slave and she's the master. There's something so sweet about her, something so adorable, I cannot help but put her up on a pedestal to worship her. She is so many miles out of my league, I shouldn't even be considering making her mine. But I've always been a dreamer, and one can only hope that I find a way to charm her.

For a split-second, I close my eyes. All I want is throw her down and lick every inch of her body. I feel completely intoxicated. *Damn you, Lucifer!* No woman has ever had this effect on me.

"You're wet," I blurt. *Fuck! Where the hell did that come from?*

Carly's cheeks blush a pretty shade of pink and my heart melts.

"W-what?" she stutters.

"Your clothes," I say, hastily trying to salvage the situation. "They're absolutely drenched. Not a very pleasant day. Did you come by car?"

"No, I walked here."

Turning away to hide my erection, I pad over to the rack and hang up her coat. Then I close the door and shut the blinds. "That's better," I say jovially. "We don't want any distractions. Right, let's make a start." I gesture to one of the big, padded chairs in the middle of the room. "Please take a seat, Carly."

"Thanks."

We sit opposite each other, and she tries her best to get comfortable, but I can tell she's painfully shy. For a moment, my eyes linger over her, reading her body like a map waiting to be explored. Mentally, I'm undressing her, and it's driving me nuts. I imagine running my tongue all over those soft, bountiful breasts that look so ripe for the taking. I imagine spreading her legs and gorging myself on what will no doubt be the sweetest pussy I've ever tasted. I want to make her moan, want her to call out my name in the throes of an explosive orgasm.

God help me. This wasn't supposed to happen. I'm in a constant state of arousal and it's killing me. I want to bend her over the desk right here, right now. Hitch up that skirt and fuck her till she screams down the building.

Yes, I could have Carly if I wanted to. And make no mistake, I find the idea extremely tempting. It wouldn't be hard at all. With one snap of my fingers, I could have her on her knees performing acts of unspeakable lust on the office floor. But I won't, because it would be a hollow victory.

I've always liked the thrill of the chase and believe the fruit always tastes sweeter when you've gone through such pain to get it. When I take a woman, I need to feel that she genuinely wants me, and I refuse to resort to cheap parlour tricks.

"So, Carly, tell me a bit about yourself," I purr.

"What do you want to know?" She bites her lip. I love it when she does that.

"Oh, just the basics: how old you are, where you grew up, that sort of thing."

"I already filled out the questionnaire at reception."

Covertly, I glance at her left hand and note that she isn't wearing a wedding ring. *Good.*

Straightening up, I lick my lips and continue: "This isn't an interview. I don't make notes, so nothing you say will be recorded. All I want is an informal chat with you. Before I start a course of treatment, I like to first build a picture of my patient: gauge your dreams, your fears, and your aspirations. In short, before I agree to take you on, I need to first clarify that we will be a suitable fit for each other."

"You mean you might not be able to help me?"

I laugh softly and explain that hypnosis doesn't work for everyone. When I finish my speech, I ask if I've answered her question.

"Yes," she grins. *Fuck, she gets more beautiful by the second.*

I clear my throat. "So, Carly, give me a brief history of *you.*"

She places her hands in her lap and looks a little uncomfortable. "I'm thirty-six years old. I grew up in Fulham but now I live in Battersea. I currently work as a receptionist for a media company in Charlotte Street."

I raise an eyebrow. "Charlotte Street? That's not far from here."

"Yes," she beams. "It's literally around the corner."

Knowing the answer already, I ask her if she's married.

"No," she replies. "I live with my dad."

"Any children?"

"No." *Wonderful!*

"And your mother?"

"My parents are divorced. My mother remarried and now lives in Purley with her new husband." *This just gets better and better.*

"How do you feel about that?"

She bites her lip again and gives the most adorable little shrug. "I don't know. It happened such a long time ago, I'm pretty much over it."

Inwardly, I'm singing. So far, Carly sounds like the perfect candidate. No husband, no children, no family ties. No loose ends to tie up when I sink my teeth into that delectable little throat… oh wait, but I'm getting ahead of myself.

Slow down, idiot. Do you want to scare her off?

CHAPTER FORTY-ONE

Hot And Sweet

DRAWING IN A sharp breath, I decide to change the subject. "Tell me three of your favourite things."

"What?" Carly looks startled again.

"Tell me three things you like."

She scratches the side of her neck and I start to feel light-headed. My mouth is salivating to taste her cunt.

"Three things?" she frowns. "Um…cream-coloured ponies and crisp apple strudels, doorbells and sleigh bells and schnitzel with noodles."

"*The Sound of Music*," I chuckle. "Great film. But I asked for three and you gave me five."

She throws her head back and laughs; a sweet laugh that makes my balls tingle. "Sorry, I don't know where that came from. The song just popped into my head—"

"Let's try that again," I say gently. "This time I want you to relax. I can tell you're nervous, but there's really no need to be. I don't bite, Carly. We have all the time in the world, so just take it easy, okay?"

"Okay." She giggles hysterically and she looks so good, it takes all my strength not to pounce on her. "Right," she smiles, "three things I like are: fruit salads, Mickey Mouse and sunny days."

"And three things you hate?"

"Mushrooms, spiders, politicians."

"Do you like your job at the media company?"

"Yes."

"And why do you want to quit smoking?"

"Because I don't like it."

"Why don't you like it?"

"Because… because it's bad for me, and it makes my clothes stink and I think it will give me lung cancer. And… and it makes me feel weak."

"Do you like being in control?"

She blinks at me. "What do you mean?"

Oh, don't play innocent with me. You know damn well what I'm talking about. I can just see you in knee-high boots, dominating me with a whip, ordering me to submit to your every demand.

I smile wryly, shaking the thought from my head. "You said smoking makes you feel weak, so does that mean you like being in control?"

"Um, I suppose so," she replies. "All I know is when I smoke a cigarette, I feel terrible afterwards." Carly then tells me about her father's health problems, and my heart goes out to her. She looks so distressed, I can tell it's obviously affecting her deeply. I wish I could do something to take away her pain.

After she's finished speaking, there's a short silence. My protectiveness kicks in and I fight mighty hard not to throw my arms around her. I want to comfort her, wrap her in cotton wool, be her knight in shining armour.

At last, I resume: "When did you first start smoking? How old were you?"

"I don't remember."

"You must have some vague idea. Were you still at school? Did you sneak behind the bike shed for a clandestine smoke?"

"No, it was much later than that. I started smoking after I finished university, so I would have been in my early twenties."

"Interesting."

"Why?"

"Thought association," I explain. "If I can take your subconscious back to the first time you smoked, it may help to kick the addiction."

"I'm sorry, Nick, I don't remember the exact day I started."

"That's absolutely fine. There are still plenty of avenues for us to explore."

She grins like an adorable little pixie. "Does that mean you've agreed to take me on?"

"What do you think?" I pause to prolong the suspense. "Yes, Carly. I believe you're an ideal candidate for me."

"Phew!" She wipes her brow and appears genuinely pleased. "Thank God for that."

We both laugh, and for a second, I'm transfixed by her lips. *She's so fucking sexy.* Lord, I can just imagine that mouth around my cock, licking, sucking, making me moan, sending me out of my mind. I imagine how soft she must feel and start to fall apart inside.

Fucking hell, pull it together fool!

With great difficulty, I manage to compose myself. "Before we begin, do you have any other questions?"

"Yes. I won't do anything stupid, will I?"

Oh dear lady, if only you knew what I am capable of…

"Of course not," I smile. "Another popular myth is surrendering of your will. A lot of people think that when you go into trance, you lose your sense of self. This is completely untrue. When you undergo hypnosis with me, at all times, you will be in complete control of your behaviour, meaning you will not embarrass yourself, reveal secrets or do anything you wouldn't normally do in a waking state. Hypnosis is not about surrendering your free will. It is similar to a daydream and merely facilitates helping you learn to control unwanted behavioural patterns." I smile magnanimously. "Does that put your mind at rest?"

"Yes," Carly replies. "Thanks for explaining it so thoroughly."

My heart turns somersaults. *I can sense that I've gained her trust.*

"Good," I say. "Okay, let's get comfortable. Loosen up and relax. Take off your shoes."

"What?"

"Take off your shoes."

Embarrassed, she bends down and unlaces her boots. I can tell I'm affecting her again. Her fingers are trembling like a leaf.

"Do you need any help?" I ask, trying not to smile.

"No, no, I'm fine."

"Wiggle your toes."

"Are you serious?" she laughs. *Oh, how I adore that laugh!*

"Try it," I say. "I think you'll find it relaxing."

She follows my orders and her obedience makes my legs weak with excitement. My hold over her is growing stronger by the second, and soon she will be in the palm of my hand.

My joy doesn't last for long, however. Her eyes fix on my scar and she looks a little uncomfortable. All at once, my confidence evaporates and I'm riddled with insecurities about my appearance. *Damn it, I had forgotten how ugly I am.*

Fighting to keep my emotions in check, I force a playful

smile. "That's right, Carly. Shake those toes. Doesn't that feel better?"

She nods happily. "Yes, but I do feel a bit silly."

"That's good. Feeling silly is good." Chewing my bottom lip, I fold my arms and sit up straight. I pray that she can't see my erection. "All right. Close your eyes and take a deep breath."

She follows my instructions and I get aroused as her body becomes a toy for me to play with. Her limbs go floppy; her head tilts to one side like a benign rag doll. Within seconds, I'm deep inside her head, two minds merging as one.

"That's right, Carly," I whisper. "Empty your head completely. Relax every part of your body, don't think about anything, just focus on my voice. Let all of your worries fade away to nothing, and just breathe. *Breathe.* Inhale deeply and exhale slowly through your mouth. That's right; you're falling deeper and deeper into trance. Deeper and deeper…"

For ten minutes, I stare at her silently, watching her eyelids flicker like she's in the grip of some terrible nightmare. I worry where her thoughts have taken her.

"Help me," she moans. "For God's sake, someone help me."

Fuck, what I would give to be the one making her whimper like that. Her mouth looks so inviting it makes me want to do things…

I glance at my watch and decide to give it another fifteen minutes or so. The times passes quickly. *Too quickly.*

At last, lowering my voice, I whisper, "When I will you to do a thing, it shall be done. From this moment on, my will is your will, and you shall cross land and sea to do my bidding. Do you understand?"

She nods obediently. "Yes, oh yes!"

Shit, this is absolute torture. I need to bend her over and fuck her.

Leaning forward, I snap my fingers in her face. "Hold for the count of five, four, three, two, one. And now you're awake."

Slowly, Carly opens those beautiful brown eyes and blinks a couple of times. She appears disorientated.

Locking my hands behind my back, I stand up and stride across to the window. The storm has calmed to a gentle murmur.

"How do you feel?" I ask softly.

She spins around and I can feel her eyes burning into my back. I hope she likes what she sees.

"How do you feel?" I ask again.

"I feel… great," she replies.

My shoulders sag with relief. There's so much I'd like to say to her, but now is not the time. I'm too crazy, too out of control.

Hurriedly, I glance at my Rolex. "All right, I think we should call it a day. Overall, I'm very pleased with the progress we've made so far. If you continue responding in this way, this promises to be a very successful treatment."

Stooping down, she laces up her boots and asks me how many more sessions she will need.

"Oh, four or five usually does it," I reply nonchalantly. "Then again, it depends on the individual. But you've made a phenomenal start, Carly, and I'm confident if we continue this way, we will definitely beat your addiction."

I bring over her coat and I can tell from her expression that she's disappointed our session is over. My God, she's so beautiful I can barely look at her.

I need some relief before I do something stupid!

Hastily, I walk her to the door. For a second, we stare at

each other, and I can sense how wet she is. I know how much she wants me and it's killing me I can't have her. I'm so turned on I'm almost in pain.

"Well, Carly, it's been a pleasure," I say. "Shall we say the same time next week?"

"Yes, definitely." Her eyes shine like two chocolate stars.

"Excellent. See Tara on your way out and she'll book your next appointment. Have a safe journey home."

As soon as the door is closed, I exhale loudly and collapse against a wall, my whole body shaking with sparks of excitement. Trembling, I unbuckle my trousers and grab hold of my throbbing cock. Closing my eyes, I listen to the sound of rain hitting the window as I masturbate to thoughts of Carly.

My God, I want her so much. I need to be inside her. Need to taste her blood. Fuck, I can just imagine how hot and sweet she'll be.

I imagine Carly dropping to her knees, taking my cock in her mouth, and I come almost instantly.

CHAPTER FORTY-TWO

Innocent

O N THE WAY home, I'm still so jittery from our encounter, I almost crash my car. My head is so full of Carly, I'm behaving like a complete and utter lunatic. No woman has ever had this effect on me and my weakness for her terrifying.

I'm so disappointed in myself.

For ninety years, I've managed to remain celibate and harden my heart to all things love related. For years I've avoided relationships and wilfully abstained from sex because no woman deserves to be brought into this nightmare of mine.

But as always with me, nothing ever goes according to plan.

Out of nowhere, Carly's come into my life and turned everything upside down. She's forced me to re-evaluate everything I thought I believed in.

I think of my past—all the bad things I've done, all the darkness I've endured, and part of me thinks I don't deserve to be with someone so pure and innocent. Yet, at the same time, she has awoken a hunger in me that refuses to sleep. Her sweet, sensual aura has brought me back from the dead and made me wonder how I've gone so long without the warm caress of another human being.

Carly's hold over me is something supernatural; a magnetism stronger than anything else I've ever experienced. She's all I can think about and I just have to, *need to* make her mine if it's the last thing I do.

As soon as I get home, I take a long cold shower. I need to cool off and gain some perspective on things. Freezing jets of water spill around me, helping to heal my troubled mind.

After I've finished drying off, I wrap a towel round my waist and go downstairs to the living room. Picking up my phone from the table, I call Tony Strickland, my private investigator. I've worked with Tony loads of times, and favour his services over all the others because I know he's always discreet.

A frisson of nerves pass through me as I pace up and down the room, cursing the ceiling and begging him to fucking answer.

On the fourth ring, he finally picks up. "All right, Boss? Long time no hear."

"Are you alone?" I hiss. *Screw the pleasantries.*

"Yeah. I'm at home, watching telly. What can I do for you?"

"I need you to run a check on a woman named Carly Singleton. She's thirty-six years old and lives in Battersea"

I hear the rustle of paper as Strickland takes out his trusty old notepad. "Hmm... Singleton, eh?"

"Yes," I nod. "Carly Singleton. I want you to find out everything you can about her: who she lives with, who her friends are, where she works, where she went to school, any boyfriends, who she's currently seeing. I want all of this information by tomorrow night, do you understand?"

"Loud and clear, Boss." He crunches something hard and I wince. *He's eating those damn cough sweets again.*

Holding the receiver away from my ear, I continue: "If you can promise to have all of this for me by tomorrow night, I'll pay you double your usual fee."

"Wow, that's generous," Strickland quips. "You must be psychic. My car needs a new gear box so that money will come in handy. However, for the turnaround time you're asking, I'll need a bit more information about Carly. Have you got anything else for me other than just her name?"

"Hold that thought." Reaching for the table, I pull out Tara's questionnaire and reel off everything I know so far, including her address and medical history.

"Okay great, that will do for starters," Strickland says when I've finished. "I'll get on the case tonight and have something for you by tomorrow, I promise."

"Brilliant. I look forward to it."

I hang up the phone and catch my breath. I glance around the room furtively. Everything looks different: the marble-mantled fireplace, the oak flooring, the sash windows fitted with Venetian blinds. I feel as if I have been reborn. For the first time in ages, I have something to look forward to.

What the hell has Carly done to me?

In a daze, I step into the corridor and head for my study. For a moment, I stand in the doorway, my mind consumed by loving thoughts. Then, tightening my towel, I stride across the room to the full-length mirror and stare at my reflection. I'm not exactly handsome—far from it in fact. My nose is far too large, my face scarred by a lifetime of angst and grief. My eyes are dark and murderous-looking.

I look like a fucking killer.

Raising my arms, I study my broad shoulders, bulging biceps and rock-solid six-pack. Despite my many short-comings, I've got to admit that my body is damn near perfect.

I can't imagine Carly having any objection to what I see before me.

Slowly, I let the towel drop to the floor. Even flaccid, my cock looks huge.

With a grim smile, my mind drifts back to my childhood. On the whole, my formative years were happy ones. Growing up in Victorian London, I lived the kind of affluent lifestyle many can only dream of. My parents had a big house and gave me all the luxury money can buy. Even so, I never felt happy with my appearance. At school, the other children teased me mercilessly, calling me the 'Little Hunchback.' Back then, I never stood up for myself and allowed their cruel taunts to knock my confidence into the ground.

As a result, I spent my first nineteen years convinced that no woman would ever love me. I truly believed my ugliness prevented me from ever finding *the one*.

That all changed on my twentieth birthday when a group of friends took me to Soho and arranged for a prostitute to 'make a man of me.'

I'll never forget my first sexual encounter. Franny Ward was her name. She was very much older than me, perhaps in her forties, but at the time I thought she was beautiful.

Today when I call to mind her bad skin and heavily made-up face, I suspect most of it was smoke and mirrors, but nonetheless, I'll always remember her as being beautiful.

After all, Franny was my first.

I can remember it like it was yesterday—entering her squalid chambers in Soho, wondering if I was doing the right thing. I remember vividly the Turkish rugs and the orange glow of candles.

I remember Franny's eyes scrutinising me inch by inch, making me feel like a horse at an auction house. I remember her stripping me naked and studying me methodically, before telling me bluntly: "Your face is a disappointment, but your cock is an asset to be treasured. What you have between your legs is so magnificent you will never be short of female company. With the proper training, I can show you how to bring great pleasure to women."

We spent one night together, promising each other our passion would only last a day. But it turned out not to be enough—*for either of us*. Franny just couldn't get enough of me, and taught me things I didn't dream were possible. With gentle encouragement, she taught me how to go down on a woman, how to use my lips and my tongue to bring the most exquisite pleasure imaginable. She taught me how to make a woman climax just by saying the right words, in the right tone of voice. Most of all, she taught me how to fuck properly, how to use my dick as an extension of my desire; how to hold back and control my reflexes in order to bring as much satisfaction as possible.

By the time Franny was through with me, I truly felt I had become a man.

Shaking my head, I push the past from my mind and return to the current moment.

Picking up my towel, I return upstairs and spend the rest of the evening in a gentle haze of euphoria. I think about Carly every second of every minute. I don't know how I'm going to endure a week without seeing her.

Sometime around twelve, I turn in for the night and try my best to sleep, but it's no good. She's taken complete possession of me.

Finally, I can bear it no longer.

Dressing quickly, I grab my coat and keys, jump in my car and head straight for Battersea. Even if I can't see her, I figure

I can at least be near to her. I need to be close to her to retain my sanity.

Around two in the morning, I arrive on Carly's street and park across the road from her house. It's a modest place—a nondescript semi with a blue door and messy front garden. All of the lights are off, and I wonder which bedroom is hers. Instinctively, I suspect it's probably at the back of the house.

Closing my eyes, I lean against the headrest and imagine holding Carly in my arms, caressing her sweet face, keeping her safe and warm. I imagine kissing those delectable lips, running my tongue all over her body, and it's all I can do to keep from exploding.

My God, I simply have to see her again.

I stay outside the house till daybreak before reluctantly returning home.

The next day is a total blur. I go into autopilot, lost in a stupor of sweet daydreams. I see all of my regular clients, behave impeccably, but deep down I feel completely detached from everything. I think of Carly constantly and wonder how she's spending her day. I wonder if she's thinking about me. Wonder if she's yearning for me. Dear God, when will this torture be over? I'm literally counting down the seconds until our next meeting.

When I get home from work, I pray I'll have some news from Strickland soon. It's agony waiting for the phone to ring and I find I can't focus on anything. Finally, at around eight-thirty, I receive a text message telling me he's parked downstairs.

Elated, I throw on my coat and head outside. It's stopped raining and the street is ominously quiet. Instantly, I spy his battered red Ford parked a few blocks up. Rubbing my hands together, I race up the street to the car, open the passenger door and get in.

"All right, Boss?" Strickland grins, licking icing off his fingers. He's still as fat as ever, his huge gut poking out of his shirt like an overstuffed sausage. The floor of the car is covered with doughnut crumbs and a crumpled box of *Krispy Kreme's* lies near the brake pedals.

"So, what do you have for me?" I ask.

Wordlessly, Strickland reaches in the glove compartment and pulls out a clear plastic folder. He hands it to me and flashes a broad smile. I try not to laugh. He's got bits of doughnut stuck to his teeth.

"Carly's father is a writer called Steve Singleton. Ever heard of him?"

"No," I reply, leafing through the folder. "What does he write about?"

"He's sort of a New Age writer," Strickland explains. "In 1994 he wrote a book about Transcendental Meditation called *Path to Enlightenment: Six Ways to Change Your Life*. He and Carly share a house together. That's him, right there." Strickland points to a picture of a man with John Lennon specs, high cheekbones, and locks of lank, grey hair swept back in a ponytail. For a second I stare at the photo, seeing little resemblance between this person and my angel. Regardless, I privately thank him for bringing Carly into the world.

I leaf through a few more papers then, frowning, I lean forward and scrutinise Steve's picture in more detail. "Hey, you got this from Wikipedia!"

Strickland laughs. "Don't knock it. Some of the most accurate information I've ever had is from Wikipedia. It's the 21st century Encyclopaedia Britannica." Reaching in the glove compartment again, he takes out a copy of *Path to Enlighten-*

ment and gives it to me. "I picked that up from Waterstones's, just in case you wanted some bedtime reading."

"How thoughtful of you. Okay, so what else?"

"Carly grew up in Fulham—an only child, no brothers or sisters. She attended a Catholic girl's school called Christchurch, before studying Textile Design at Luton University. It seems she quit before she finished her foundation course."

"Do we know why she quit?"

"Search me. Maybe she got bored. You know what kids today are like. Since then, she's worked as a receptionist for Midas Media, a company based in Charlotte Street. Her best friend is a guy called Ronan Hewitt. Don't worry, he's gay so I don't see him as much of a threat. Apart from that, Carly doesn't appear to have any other close friends. Her last serious relationship was with a guy called Andrew Saunders, but they broke up over five years ago."

"Interesting," I murmur. "Anything else?"

"No, nothing else of note." He pauses. "Oh, but here's a bit of trivia for you. At university, Carly was classmates with Dylan Daniels."

"Who's that?"

Strickland looks at me like I'm from outer space. "Come on; don't tell me you don't know Dylan Daniels, the Radio One presenter? He's only the highest paid DJ in the country. You can't open a magazine without seeing his smug face plastered everywhere."

I shake my head. "Sorry, I just can't picture him. Perhaps I'll look him up on Wikipedia."

Strickland chuckles. "Well, it's not majorly important. As far as I know, he's not in contact with her anymore, but I just thought it was a nice piece of trivia for you."

"I like how thorough you are."

Silently, I reach in my coat and pull out a manila envelope stuffed with bank notes. "Here," I say, handing it to him. "You've done a great job, as always."

"That's why they call me Mr Impossible," Strickland grins. "Because I make the impossible possible."

We shake hands and I get out of the car, clutching Steve's book like my life depends on it. Thoughtfully, I make my way back to my house.

CHAPTER FORTY-THREE

Blood Lust

O N MONDAY AFTERNOON, I'm just about to go to lunch when there's a quiet knock at my office door.

"Come in!" I shout.

The door opens and Tara enters. "Hi Nick, I hope I'm not disturbing you?"

"Of course not," I smile. "What's up?"

"I just got a call from Carly Singleton."

My back stiffens. "Oh?"

"She says she's terminating her treatment as of today."

My throat tightens. I can't believe what I'm hearing.

How can this be? No, no, no! My angel is slipping away from me.

"Did she say why?" I ask in a weak voice.

"No," Tara replies, "but I got the feeling it may have been something to do with money. Oh well, I guess that's the last we'll see of her. Shame. She seemed liked such a nice girl."

"That she did," I agree. Then, forcing a smile, I add, "Thanks for letting me know, Tara."

"No worries."

"Oh, by the way, I was just about to run over to Tesco's. Do you want anything?"

"A packet of crisps would be nice. Cheese and onion flavour."

"One packet of crisps coming up."

Turning on her heel, Tara sweeps out the room, leaving me in a state of utter confusion. *Carly's cancelled on me? What the fuck?*

The thought of never seeing her again sends me half crazy. Why the hell is this happening? Is it some kind of judgment from God? A warning for me to stay away from her?

Numbly, I study my reflection in the glass panelled bookcase. The eyes that stare back are red and watery with tears.

Perhaps it's just as well. I mean, what good would have come of it anyway? What sort of life would we have had together? I'm a vampire for fuck's sake. In the long run, it would have only ended in heartbreak.

Miserably, I pick up a glass tumbler from my desk and crush it to pieces. Shards of glass cascade to the floor, tearing my hand to ribbons. Blood is everywhere but I don't care. Right now, I can't even feel pain. *All I can think about is her.*

Life has played a very nasty trick on me. It presented me with my soul mate, but just as soon as she was offered up, she was taken away from me. Something out there must really hate me, I am sure of it.

Trembling, I grab a wad of Kleenex and blot the blood from my hand. The wound won't take long to heal, thank God.

Breathing raggedly, I tilt my head back and close my eyes, consumed by a fog of misery. Visions of Carly flash before me.

My God, I've got to have her. I don't care about the consequences. I don't care if I'm damned to hell for all eternity. Even if it's just for one night, I've simply got to!

I open my eyes and stare at the ceiling, focusing on my

breathing. In and out, in and out…

Okay, okay, pull yourself together. Just calm the fuck down. It's not the end of the bloody world. You'll think of something. You always do.

With shaky fingers, I pick up my mobile, scroll through the list of contacts and dial her number. Nervously, I run my hand through my hair, waiting for the call to connect.

As soon as Carly answers, my heart skips a beat. *Fuck, I want her so bad.*

"Hello?" She sounds a little scared.

"Carly, it's Nick Craven." There's a short pause. "Carly, are you there?"

"Y-yes, Nick, I'm here."

"Tara told me you don't want to continue with your treatment. May I ask why?"

"There were unforeseen circumstances."

"Such as?" I lick my lips and try my best to sound natural. She hesitates, and I wonder what she's thinking. "Is it for financial reasons?" I push.

"Yes," she answers quietly.

"I thought so. Now listen, I think we can come to an arrangement."

"What sort of arrangement?"

"In June, I'll be attending a hypnotherapy convention in Toronto," I lie. "In the lead up, I plan to write a paper about the effects of hypnosis on smokers, and I will present my findings to the National Healthcare Trust. With your consent, I'd be happy to waive my fee if you'd agree to be my case study."

"You mean you'll treat me for free?"

"Exactly."

"Wow, I don't know what to say."

"Say yes."

"All right, *yes*. A thousand times, yes! And thank you. Your kindness is overwhelming."

She laughs and my heart starts to sing. "So, I'll see you this Friday, as arranged?"

"Yes. I'll be there."

I hang up, too choked to speak.

Punching the air, I spin my chair around, my face the picture of pure joy. Carly sounded so sweet on the phone, and I could tell from her voice that she was genuinely delighted to hear from me. Despite all of the darkness, this gives me hope that perhaps there is something worth fighting for.

I may as well admit it—I am completely and utterly besotted with her.

Suddenly, my limbs slacken and my chest gets tight. It's like a heavy weight is dragging me down. I know this feeling all too well—the hunger for blood is taking over.

The walls of the room seem to be closing in on me. My throat feels dry. In agony, I double over as a great wave of pain strikes me to the core. I won't be right again till my thirst has been quenched.

Somehow, I manage to pick up my phone and dial Ahmet's number. He's the only one who can help, the only one who understands my predicament.

Dr Ahmet Khan runs a hospital in Cambridge which gives him unlimited access to blood supplies. As a result, he has created a lucrative business supplying all the vampires in England with blood.

Whenever I ask, Ahmet is always on hand to send me down a fresh supply by courier. He makes an absolute fortune, but if I'm honest, I only use him when I absolutely have to. Donated blood is all well and fine, but it doesn't taste half as good as blood taken directly from the vein.

Still, as my stomach continues to lurch with pain, I realise that beggars can't be choosers. I need blood, and I need it *now*. If not, I'm likely to do something stupid.

Taking deep breaths to calm myself, I hold the receiver to my ear, the room weaving around me in a kaleidoscope of colours.

"Hello, Nick," Ahmet greets warmly. "To what do I owe this pleasure?"

"Please," I gasp. "Can you get some gear to me tonight?"

"Of course; I'll send Dennis over now. It should be with you by sundown."

"Thanks."

"Are you sure you're okay? You don't sound too great."

"I'm just feeling a little weak."

"I know the feeling. Are you at work?"

"Y-yes."

"Maybe you should take the afternoon off. Go home to rest. You work too hard anyway. Now look, don't worry; Dennis will be with you very soon. Okay?"

"Okay. Thank you, Ahmet." I hang up. Perhaps he's right. Perhaps I *should* go home.

On shaky feet, I get up and walk over to the coat rack. Slipping on my jacket, I lock up and head out the office.

CHAPTER FORTY-FOUR

Sexy Games

I SPEND THE rest of the week counting down the days until I see Carly again. When six o'clock on Friday finally arrives, I can barely contain myself. Glancing at my watch, I keep telling myself to play it cool. *The last thing I want to do is scare her off.*

As she enters the room, I position myself by the window with my back to her. I fix my eyes on the view outside. I can't look at her. I need time to compose myself and soak in her aura.

"Hello, Nick," she whispers.

Smiling, I turn around and can't help ogling that magnificent body. She's even more beautiful than I remembered, and I'm so enthralled I can barely speak.

"Hello, Carly," I say. "Good to see you again."

"It's good to see you, too." She giggles and my cock begins to stir.

Down boy, down!

Walking towards her, I ask for her coat. Before she can refuse, my hands are on her shoulders, spinning her around very slowly. In one swift movement, I have her coat off. She moans lightly, and heat floods my cheeks. *My God, she turns me on so much.*

Turning away, I take her coat and hang it up on the rack.

I shut my eyes and bite my lip. *If only she knew what I'd like to do to her...*

"Hey, I brought you something," she says brightly. I can hear the smile in her voice.

"Oh?" I raise my eyebrows.

Excitedly, Carly passes me a bright purple bag. I take it from her and study it for a second. What on Earth is this? I glance back at her. Her eyes are shining, and she looks so adorable I want to hug her.

Carefully, I pull out a neatly wrapped package.

I wonder what this could be?

Giddy with anticipation, I tear off the paper to reveal a grey-and-black scarf made from the softest wool I've ever felt. I study it a moment, caressing the material with my fingers. I feel so emotional, I want to cry. I'm deeply touched that Carly would take the time to make something so lovely for me.

Raising my head, I look at her with a placid expression, fighting hard to keep my feelings in check.

"Thank you," I whisper. "It's been so long since anyone bought me a present."

The most gorgeous smile spreads across her face. "I made it myself," she says shyly.

"Wow, then that makes it even more special. I promise to cherish it always." And I mean it. This scarf will be my most treasured possession. "Who taught you to crochet?" I ask.

"My mother."

"How quaint. It's nice to know that the younger generation is still keeping the old pastimes alive." I pause. "So, I take it you like creating things."

"Oh, yes," Carly enthuses. "Ever since I was little, I've loved making presents for people."

I laugh. "What did you study at university?"

"Textile Design."

"So, you're a qualified designer?"

Carly shuffles her feet and looks at the floor like a lost child. Suddenly, I remember the conversation I had with Strickland, about her dropping out in the first year of university. Something about this bothers me, something that I can't quite put my finger on. I decide to probe further in the hope of getting more information.

"Then shouldn't you be doing something that exploits your creativity? Why are you working as a receptionist and not following your dreams?"

"Because I never actually finished my degree," she blurts.

"Oh." I hesitate, weighing up my words. *Play it cool, play it cool.* Of course, I'm dying to know what happened, but I also need to tread carefully. This matter requires the utmost sensitivity.

"Why didn't you finish your degree?" I ask finally.

Carly blushes and turns away from me. "I-I don't know…" There's a short silence. "Look, Nick, I'm sorry. That came out wrong. What I really meant was, I don't want to talk about it. It's kind of a long story, and not one I enjoy telling, if I'm honest."

"That's quite all right. If you don't feel comfortable talking about it, that's absolutely fine." Wrapping the scarf around my neck, I point towards the padded chairs. "Shall we?"

Smiling again, Carly takes a seat opposite me and kicks off her shoes, ready to begin the session.

"I think the treatment's working," she beams. "Since last week, I haven't once craved a cigarette."

I laugh inwardly. *Like hell you didn't.*

"Really?" I grin. "Not even once?"

"Well…" She breaks off and laughs hysterically. *Wow, I can really see I'm affecting her.* "Okay," she admits, "if I'm being completely honest, I *do* still have cravings, but something stops me from acting on them." She hitches up her skirt and I get a glimpse of her stocking-clad thigh. I start to get hot under the collar. *Holy Mother of God, how I long to run my tongue all over that soft, creamy body and explore the sweetness below her navel.*

I scratch the side of my mouth. "Tell me your thought processes. Tell me what prevents you from smoking; what goes through your mind at the point of rejection."

Carly frowns and I'm dying to kiss the cute little spot between her brows. "It's kind of weird," she says. "When I crave a cigarette, it's like I can hear your voice in my head, telling me not to. And then I can't go through with it. It's like you're inside of me."

"I think I know what you mean," I murmur. *Shit, she's pushing me to breaking point.* My God, I need to tear her clothes off, right here, right now. I need to be inside her and feel her sweet juices wrapped around my cock.

Slow down, you fool. Do you want to scare her off? All in good time, all in good time…

Leaning back, I press my fingertips together in an effort to look suave and sophisticated. "Okay, Carly, close your eyes and take a deep breath. That's right… empty your mind completely. Relax every part of your body and just focus on my voice."

Carly closes her eyes and swiftly drifts into unconsciousness. She looks so beautiful lying there, it takes all of my strength not to pounce on her and rip her clothes off. She's so delectable, so ripe for the taking, it's like torture to watch her.

I study her smooth white neck, the gentle rise and fall of

her breasts through her blouse and my dick gets so hard I want to erupt.

I can't take much more of this…

Suddenly, she lurches forward with a look of anguish on her face. "Make it stop!" she shouts. "Make it stop, make it stop!" It sounds as if she was having some sort of nightmare.

"Enough!" I boom. I snap my fingers in her face. "Now hold for the count of five, four, three, two, one. And now you're awake."

Carly opens her eyes and stares at me like she's never seen me before. Her face is white as a sheet.

Jesus, what the hell just happened?

"It's not real," she murmurs. "It's all in the past…the past."

"Are you okay?" I ask worriedly. "You seem a little disorientated."

She looks up at me. "I-I'm fine. Wow, that was pretty intense." She tries to smile but I can sense that she's hiding something.

"What happened while you were in trance?" I probe. "What did you see?"

She tells me again about the green fields and the hot air balloon, but I know it's just a ruse. There's plenty she's not telling me.

"Is that definitely all you saw?"

She nods, smiling. "There's nothing else. Only what I told you—the field, the hot air balloon, and that's it."

I shake my head. *We both know there's a lot more, and I intend to find out what. But now is not the time. I need to handle this as delicately as possible.*

Feigning nonchalance, I glance at my watch. "Right, that's about it for today. You've done very well, Carly. I think we're making real progress, and I feel privileged to be working with someone of your caliber. Your response to me has been phenomenal."

She blushes and thanks me. Emotion flickers in her eyes as she fiddles with her collar. "Listen, Nick…" She breaks off, her blush deepening. *My God, she's gorgeous.* "What are you doing tomorrow night?"

I play it coy. "Nothing. Why?"

"I just wondered…" She can't meet my gaze. *Sweet Jesus, she's so fucking adorable.* "Well, you see, it's like this: my friend was supposed to come to the theatre, but she's cancelled at the last minute, so I have this spare ticket going. I was wondering… I was wondering if you'd like to come?"

My heart almost stops beating. *Is Carly asking me out on a date?* For a second, I'm so overcome I can barely speak.

There's a tense silence. She looks at the floor. "Of course, if it's against protocol, I understand. I know I'm your patient and that you might not want—"

"Carly, I'd *love* to," I grin.

"What did you say?"

"I said yes. What time and where?"

Her whole face lights up. "Oh, my gosh! Okay, well, the show starts at seven-thirty. It's at the Arts Theatre near Leicester Square, and the show's called *Ghost Stories.* I don't know much about it, but the poster looks good."

"Sounds great. Would you like us to meet beforehand, maybe go for a coffee or something?"

"That would be wonderful! Shall we say six o'clock to-morrow at Leicester Square station, Cambridge Circus exit?"

I flash a broad smile. "Perfect. I'll be there."

We say our goodbyes and as I close the door, I can barely believe what just happened. Carly asked me out on a date. *She wants me! My God, she wants me.*

I'm shaking so much I need to sit down.

Closing my eyes, I take out her scarf and breathe in her glorious aroma. The wool feels soft and silky against my cheek.

Carly, what have you done to me?

CHAPTER FORTY-FIVE

Tingle

I GLANCE AT my Rolex: *ten past seven*. So far, Carly's over an hour late. Weak with anxiety, I run my fingers through my hair.

I'm standing outside Leicester Square Tube station in the freezing cold, waiting for my angel to arrive. The weather is dismal, but I barely notice. All I can think about is *her*; I wonder whether she's stood me up or if perhaps she got cold feet at the last minute. Perhaps I scared her off.

Dammit, this is worse than torture.

Biting my cheek, I reach in my pocket and pull out my phone. *No messages.* I shake my head ruefully.

This doesn't look good.

No! I refuse to believe that she would have stood me up. I remember the excitement on her face, the joy in her eyes as I said yes to this meeting, and I know something must have happened to delay her. She's still coming, I can feel it.

I put my hands in my pockets. Glance up and down the street. I'm looking pretty good if I do say so myself: black shirt, waistcoat, expensive Italian brogues. I've even had my hair cut especially. It took me hours to decide what to wear. Every single second of the day was spent building up to this moment and I cannot, will not, give up on her.

I'll wait hours if that's what it takes.

I look at my watch again: *seven-fifteen on the dot.*

Tightening my scarf, I glance towards the station entrance and that's when I see her—a vision in leopard print. The most perfect make-up. *Fuck, she's even more beautiful than I remember.*

Bubbling with excitement, I watch Carly glance left and right with a worried frown on her face. After a few seconds, she huddles in a doorway, clearly distressed by my absence. My heart starts to sing.

Excitedly, I race forward, and grab hold of her hand. For a moment, we stand in a haze of delirium, smiling at each other.

"I'm so sorry I'm late," she stammers. "I lost my phone and then I—"

"Sssh…" I whisper. "You don't need to explain. All that matters is you're here now."

My grip tightens, and I thank God I'm wearing a big jacket. It helps to hide my near-constant erection.

"We'd better hurry," she says. "The show's due to start in ten minutes."

"Fine. You lead the way." I take her arm and we head briskly in the direction of the theatre. I'm so happy it feels like I'm floating.

Carly is still fretting. "I still feel so bad for making you wait. I promise I'll make it up to you. Perhaps I can take you for a coffee after the theatre."

I don't say anything. Her beauty has left me too choked to speak.

We reach a Zebra crossing and wait for the lights to change. As we approach the Arts Theatre, I see a small crowd gathered outside and men in baseball caps handing out flyers. We enter the foyer. To our left is a bar with a long queue of people waiting to buy refreshments, and to our right is the box office.

Carly pulls out a receipt. "I'll pick up our tickets," she says with a cheeky grin.

Suddenly, I remember my manners and ask her if she wants a drink.

"Yes, but I don't think we have time," she replies. "The show's due to start any minute."

Carly heads towards the box office. Discreetly, my eyes travel down the length of her back, taking in the dip and swell of her perfectly round bottom. I imagine bending her over and sliding my tongue deep inside the crease. I imagine making her nice and wet just before I...

But wait.

I shake my head.

Stop dreaming, you nasty bastard. You're getting ahead of yourself again.

Heat travels up my neck and I realise I'm blushing. I shake my head again, trying to force the images from my head.

Very soon, Carly returns with our tickets and the ushers lead us to the auditorium. As we are finding our seats, a loud voice announces that the show is about to start. Then the lights go dim and I take Carly's hand in mine. Heat surges through me. Jesus, her skin feels so soft I can't get enough of it. She is like a drug to me.

"Do you like being frightened?" I whisper.

She giggles and shakes her head. Fucking hell, even her laughter makes my dick throb. *My God, I want her so badly it hurts.*

And then the curtain rises and the show begins. Over the next two hours, the story that unfolds on stage is filled with surprises. However, I couldn't tell you what it was about because I can't focus on anything but Carly. All throughout the show, my eyes are focused on her neck, fighting the urge to sink my teeth in. Inside there is a violent conflict of insatiable hunger and sexual longing. It's like I'm constantly thirsty; like I need to totally consume her before I go mad.

I look at those beautiful eyes, those full, rosebud lips, and all I can think about is having her up against a wall and fucking her hard and deep. I know it's wrong to have such thoughts, but I can't help it. Carly Singleton is quite simply *irresistible*.

When the show's over, the actors take their bows to rapturous applause. The play has been a huge success.

"That was fantastic," Carly beams.

"Pure genius," I lie. *How would I know? I haven't exactly been concentrating!*

"Excuse me," shouts a lady further down the aisle. "Could the two of you please move along? We need to get out."

"I think that's our cue." I help my angel to her feet. "Do you fancy going somewhere for a bite to eat?"

"Yes, please. I'm famished."

I take her to the Corinthia, my favourite hotel. Unbeknown to her, I've already booked a room—the best room in the whole place. If things go according to plan, this promises to be the best night ever.

Taking my angel's hand, I lead her into a vast lobby with high ceilings and Grey Marquino flooring. A massive Baccarat chandelier dominates the sweeping circular staircase and off to the left, glass doors lead to a maple-lined courtyard.

Carly is awestruck. "Wow," she gasps.

"Do you like it?"

"Like it? I *love* it!"

My mouth waters with anticipation. Just a few hours to go before...

No. You're getting ahead of yourself again.

A concierge in a top hat takes us to the restaurant and settles us in. Then a waiter comes over and hands us two oversized menus. Carly seems a little out of her depth so I take control and order us a bottle of Château Begadan Cru Artisan Médoc—the finest wine they have. Tonight, no expense shall be spared.

"Have you decided what you want for a starter?" I ask. Carly tells me she wants onion soup and I sense she's trying to be a cheap date. "Are you sure that's definitely all you want?" I push. "I thought you said you were famished?"

"I know, but I seem to have lost my appetite."

"Carly, humour me a little, eh? Have soup for starters but eat something proper for your mains. I won't have you starving yourself to save me a few pennies."

She bites her lip and I wish to God I'd worn loose-fitting trousers. I'm so hard it's getting painful. The way that dress clings to every curve of her delectable frame, the way it cups her breasts is just so... *Fuck! I can't take this teasing.*

"How is it?" I ask, trying to keep my voice calm.

"Huh?" Carly looks confused.

"The wine. Does it taste good?"

"Oh, yes, it's lovely. Very rich." She laughs that sweet, sing-song laugh and I lose all feeling in my legs. Trying to keep my composure, I continue: "By the way, Carly, I haven't told you how stunning you look tonight. That dress really compliments your figure."

She grins and shrinks down in her seat. "Oh, this old thing? Ha! It's just something I threw together at the last minute. But I'm glad you like it. You look really good, too. I-I love that shirt on you."

She loves my shirt?

Fuck me, if she loves the shirt, wait till she sees what lies beneath.

"Are you ready for your starters?" the waiter asks.

"Yes," I reply. I place our order.

"So, what made you want to be a hypnotherapist?" Carly asks when he's gone. "Was it something you always wanted to do?"

"Not at first," I say. "I come from a long line of medical doctors. Before my father died, he enjoyed a distinguished career as a heart surgeon; so naturally, my family assumed I would follow in his footsteps. However," I add, twirling the stem of my wine glass, "my interests have always leaned toward more sociological pursuits. The human mind fascinates me, and I've made it my mission to find out what makes people tick."

Carly nods excitedly. "Your website mentioned you've worked with lots of famous people. Anyone I might have heard of?"

I glance down at my knuckles. "Sure, but confidentially prevents me from naming names. However, I will say that I once treated a Premiere League football player for a chronic gambling addiction that saw him blow half a million pounds in a single weekend. Then there was the TV chef with a sex addiction that tore his whole family apart. I'm pleased to say I cured both men and they're now living happy, fulfilled lives."

"That must be so satisfying for you," she smiles. "To know that you're able to make a difference."

"It is. I wouldn't change what I do for the world. Helping people is a way of life. It really is a vocation for me, and I'm constantly humbled by all of the wonderful letters I receive from patients whose lives I've transformed. They are very uplifting." I sip my wine and try not to wince at how tasteless it is. "So, tell me about your job at the media company."

She suddenly looks uncomfortable. "There's nothing much to tell. What I do isn't very interesting."

"Let me be the judge of that."

"Er, well… what exactly do you want to know?"

"Tell me about the people you work with. Do you get along with them?"

"Oh, yes, everyone there is lovely. I have no complaints in that department."

"Do you socialise much?"

"Not really. But now that you mention it, I did go out the other day for my friend Jill's fortieth. It was a bit of a disaster."

"How so?"

"Do you really want me to tell you?"

"Yes. I'm intrigued."

Carly lowers her gaze. "Okay, I was wearing these false eyelashes—"

"False eyelashes?"

"Yes."

"Are you wearing them now?"

"No way; once was enough. But as I was saying, I wore these false eyelashes, and I didn't glue them on properly. So halfway through the meal, one of them came off and got stuck to my cheek, but I didn't notice till I went to the bathroom. And then, oh, my God, it was so embarrassing, I looked like I had a spider stuck to my face!"

I chuckle softly. "That's funny."

"No, wait, it gets worse," Carly continues. "On the way out the restaurant, I tripped over and fell into this guy. Actually, he was Jill's brother, but I didn't find that out till later. And then he…" She stops to catch her breath. "So, um, yeah, it was really embarrassing. Not a night I want to repeat anytime soon."

I stare at her a second, trying not to laugh. "You're so funny."

"Funny? Funny in a good way, I hope?"

"Oh, yes. You're really quite beguiling." *I wince inwardly. Am I coming on too strong?*

At that moment, our food arrives, and we drop the topic to focus on our plates. For a long while, we eat in silence, smiling every so often at each other across the table. My mind races back to Strickland's report about Carly's love life. He assured me there were no other men in the picture, but how can I be sure?

"So, Carly," I ask. "Is there anyone else in the picture?"

"What do you mean?"

Smiling, I lay down my fork and fold my arms. "Is there a secret boyfriend lurking around somewhere that I don't know about?"

"Oh, no," she laughs. "Trust me, I'm definitely single."

My heart races. "Exactly how long have you been single?" I ask.

"Let's just say it's been a while," she replies. There's a naughty gleam in her eyes.

My gaze drops to her succulent lips and it's a struggle to control the carnal thoughts in my mind.

"It's been a while for me, too," I whisper.

She falls silent. The lust in her face is all too apparent. *Shit, just a little more and I'm in there, I know I am.*

The waiter returns with dessert and the two of us tuck into a delicious chocolate and coconut mousse sprinkled with pineapples.

"This tastes so good," I say with a teasing smirk. "I could

do with seconds." Slowly, I withdraw the spoon from my mouth, turn it over and lick the metal clean. Carly's eyes soak in every gentle flick of my tongue and I know damn well what she's thinking. She's wondering what my tongue would feel like between her legs, licking her out till she screams for me to stop. She's imagining how good it will feel and to be honest, so am I.

So. Am. I.

There's a tense silence. Then the waiter returns to clear away the plates, and I ask for the bill. Carly offers to pay half, but I flat out refuse. There's no way my angel is going to pay for anything.

"Thanks," she grins. "I don't know what to say."

My God, she's just too beautiful.

The waiter brings the portable card reader and takes the payment. As he hands me my receipt, I start to get butterflies.

It's now or never...

"I've booked us a room," I say.

"Huh?" Carly's eyes widen. For a second, the world freezes around me as I await her decision.

Please say yes. Please say yes!

"I said I've booked us a room," I repeat.

"Oh," she says.

And then she starts laughing, and so do I, because it's the only thing I can do.

Please say yes. Please say yes...

She shoots me a sidelong glance. "I think you're taking a hell of a lot for granted," she says humorously.

I arch an eyebrow. "Am I?"

Carly doesn't answer.

"So, are you up for it?" I push.

"Yes. I'm up for it," she whispers.

My balls begin to tingle.

CHAPTER FORTY-SIX

Hard and Deep

I TAKE CARLY up to our suite on the second floor. The room is amazing with a king-size bed, leather-panelled walls, plasma-screen TV and a panoramic view of the River Thames.

As we enter the room, I can tell by her face that's she's impressed. How could she not be? I've pulled out all the stops to make this the most perfect night ever.

I can't stop my hands from shaking. My limbs feel like marble and my dick is hard enough to break concrete. I've never been so nervous. I can't believe we're finally alone. I can't believe she's here with me. She looks trusting; so ripe for the taking so... so innocent. She has no idea what's about to hit her.

"I'm sorry," she whispers. "I don't think I can do this." She turns to go, but before she reaches the door, I lunge forward, barring the exit.

I slip my finger under her chin. *Jesus, those eyes!*

"Please, don't go," I whisper, trying not to show my desperation. "Nothing's going to happen if you don't want it to. We can just sit here and talk, or watch a movie. I don't want this night to be over. Please, stay. Is that too much to ask?"

We hold each other's gaze for a minute. I wonder what

she's thinking. Then she releases a heavy sigh.

"All right, I'll stay," she says in a small voice. Bowing her head, Carly allows me to lead her over to the bed, and for what seems like forever, the two of us sit side by side, looking away from each other. Her arms are folded protectively across her chest, and I can see that she's scared.

Please don't be scared of me, baby. I'll be gentle as a kitten.

"So, do you come here often?" Carly asks, breaking the silence.

"You mean to this hotel?"

"Mmm."

"Yes, I stay here a couple of times a year. It's one of my favourite hotels."

She gives a low whistle. "Sounds like you're a pretty busy guy."

"What's that supposed to mean?"

"Nothing."

"If you're implying that I bring women regularly to the Corinthia, I'm afraid you're very much mistaken. My business here is purely professional. Sometimes clients fly over from abroad, and I'm obliged to stay in the same hotel as a show of hospitality."

"How nice for you."

"Do I detect a note of sarcasm?"

"No," she giggles. "Definitely not."

There's another silence.

"By the way, Nick, I never asked you how old you are."

"How old do I look?"

"Oh, I don't know, thirty-five?"

I decide to play with her a little. "I'm one-hundred and fifty-five years old."

"Yeah, right. Pull the other one."

I laugh inwardly. *If only she knew.* "I'm not pulling anything. It's true."

"Okay, I'll say this. If you really are over a century old, then you must use a bloody-good moisturiser. I must get the name of your supplier." We both chuckle and then she adds, "No, but seriously Nick, how old are you *really?*"

"I just turned thirty-eight in September."

She smiles and my balls start to tingle again. *Dammit, sometimes I forget to breathe.* I glance down at my hands. They're shaking like a leaf.

All right. It's now or never…

"You're so beautiful." I whisper. "Can I touch you?"

I hear her catch her breath, then she nods slowly.

Nervously, I reach out and tenderly caress her cheek with the back of my hand. Oh my God, her skin is even softer than I imagined.

Calm down. Remember to take it slow.

Swallowing hard, I lower my hand and gently stroke her hair with my fingers. I can't stop trembling. I want her so much, it's like I'm going to have a seizure.

"Does that feel good?" I breathe.

"Yes," she replies, and I can hear the desire in her voice. This turns me on no end.

Emboldened, my hand travels down the side of her face, then down to her neck, and lightly caresses the warm base of her throat. *Fuck this is heaven.*

"Shall I take off your jacket?" I whisper.

"Y-yes."

With intentional slowness, I ease off her coat and drop it to the floor. My gaze rests on the outline of her nipples and I fight the urge to tear her blouse off with my teeth.

Slow down fool. One step at a time…

Tentatively, I take off my jacket and sit back down next to her. Her beauty is making my head spin.

"You're trembling," I observe. Carly drops her hands into her lap. "Don't be afraid…" I reach out and softly touch her lips, her nose, her eyelids. She arches her back and moans as my hand slithers down her waist and pulls her closer to me.

"Can I kiss you?" I gasp.

She bites her lip and nods.

Cautiously, I press my mouth against her cheek and inhale her glorious scent. She smells of strawberries and lavender. Fuck, this is torture. I want to consume every last piece of her.

One step at a time remember?

Gently, I kiss her mouth, her neck and run my tongue in and out of her ear hole, pantomime fucking her. From the way she's moaning, I can tell that she likes it. Hungrily, I kiss her hard on the mouth. I kiss her so hard, it's like I'm choking. The desire she ignites in me borders on murderous.

For what seems forever, our tongues glide together in a frantic waltz of lust. Her lips taste of wine—the sweetest wine I've ever tasted. Each kiss takes me deeper into her and I fear I'm falling to a place I cannot come up from.

At last, we pause for air. The room is quiet except for the sound of our heavy breathing. I stare down at her, awestruck. I can feel her blood calling out to me, begging me to taste her, but somehow, I manage to fight to urge.

For fuck's sake, pull yourself together!

"It's been so long," I murmur. "So very long…"

I can bear it no longer. I need to taste her now. Excitedly, my hand runs down her back and lowers the zipper of her dress. Carly whimpers as I bring my face level with hers.

"I promise I won't go too crazy," I lie.

She smiles a small, tight smile. I can see the lust in her eyes and it turns me on no end.

She wants me. *She fucking wants me.*

Silently, I guide Carly to her feet and take off her dress. I catch my breath. Her body is even more perfect than I imagined: all creamy white skin and curves as soft as silk...

Carefully, I unbuckle her Kermit the Frog watch and lay it down on the table.

Then I crouch down and take off her boots, leaving her standing in just her tights and knickers. She looks so gorgeous I can barely contain myself.

"Take off your bra," I command.

Obediently, she follows my orders. Once she's undressed, I push her down on the mattress and take a few seconds to worship her like she deserves.

Slowly, sensuously, I strip down to my boxer shorts.

Carly's eyes widen with shock when she sees the size of my erection. Inside, I'm singing. This is just the reaction I was hoping for.

A tad shyly, I peel down my shorts and toss them to the floor. I'm now completely naked.

Carly's mouth drops open. It's like she's never seen a dick before, and I love it. *I absolutely fucking love it.*

Holding her gaze, I walk slowly over to the bed and slide in beside her. For a moment, we face each other, listening to the steady rise and fall of our breathing. I don't know how much longer I will be able to control myself.

"You're absolutely perfect," I whisper.

"I don't believe you," Carly smiles.

"You should start believing. I don't think you realise how gorgeous you are."

She dips her head and lowers her lashes. I don't feel I have the right to touch her. I don't feel I have the right to sully such perfection. But I must touch her. I need to touch her. I simply cannot help myself. I have to have her. I have to or I'll go crazy.

Trembling with longing, I lunge forward and trail my tongue from her neck to her collarbone, before burying my face deep between her breasts. Coming up for air, I lick and suck each nipple, relishing the flavour of her silky-smooth skin.

"I'll do anything," I whisper. "Just say the word and I'll do it."

"This feels... fine," Carly gasps. "I like what you're doing now."

I roll my tongue over her left breast, making her whole body shudder. "This is all I've ever wanted," I breathe. "From the first moment I laid eyes on you."

She shuts her eyes and whimpers with delight as my lips circle her navel and continue working their way down. As I slide off her knickers, her body goes rigid.

I look up at her. "What's wrong?" I inquire softly.

"I, that is, I don't feel comfortable," she replies.

"Why not?"

"I don't know."

I will her to submit to me. "Open up for me, darling. I need to taste your sweetness."

Carly hesitates. Closing her eyes, she leans back and finally allows me to take control. Carefully, I spread her legs wide and swirl my tongue up and down her inner thighs. She tastes so fucking good; it's a struggle to control myself. I want to sink my teeth deep into her flesh. I want to taste her blood, but I manage to hold back.

Softly, I lick and suck every last inch of her body. From

the sounds she's making, I can tell she likes what I'm doing to her. My heart sings. Soon I'll be inside her, stretching her out, hitting her G-spot, making her scream, and then there will be no going back for either of us. Once Carly lets me fuck her the way she needs to be fucked, she'll be mine forever. No woman has ever had a taste of my cock and not wanted more.

Slowly, teasingly, I suck each of her toes in turn, then I lick the soles of her feet. She shivers with delight. Lowering my head, I run my tongue up and down her legs, my mouth edging closer to her special place. I'm taking my time with her, savouring every last inch of her delectable body. Carly squeals with excitement.

Dammit why does she have to be so sexy?

"You're going to be doing a lot more screaming," I rasp.

With gentle persuasion, I push her knees against her chest and bury my face deep between her thighs. I'm like a man possessed. Ravenously, I lick all around her opening, then I plunge my tongue deep inside her soaking wet hole. My head starts to spin. Her pussy is so delicious it gives me chills; her juices are thick and sweet as honey.

"Mmmmm," I moan rapturously. "I've never tasted anything so good."

A gentle smile plays on her lips.

Softly, I dance my tongue all over her clit, making her whimper with pleasure. Shit! I can't get enough. This is like a dream I never want to wake up from. I never want this to end. I never want to come up for air; all I want is her glorious pussy in my mouth forever.

"Shit, you're so wet for me," I breathe.

Carly doesn't answer. Her face is contorted with ecstasy.

Slowly, I slide one finger inside her burning hole. The flesh of her pussy is hot and slippery. Then, lowering my head, I circle my tongue around her clit, making her knees tremble. I shiver. The sight of that warm pink slit is so mouth-watering; I just have to get another taste.

With reckless abandon, I bury my face between her thighs again.

"More," she whimpers. "More, more! Holy shit, don't stop!"

I can feel how turned on she is, and I love it. I absolutely love it.

Then, just as she's about to come, I withdraw my hand and lick her juices off my fingers. *Fuck!* The smell of her turns me on so much it's hard to see straight.

I take a few seconds to catch my breath. Then I'm ready to go again.

Pinning her legs back, I kiss the nub of her clit, working the skin between my lips. Then, moving lower, I spread her buttocks and lick a slow line down her crack.

She whimpers quietly. I can see this is getting too much for her.

"Do you like that?" I whisper. "Do you want me to continue?"

"Mmm."

"How much do you want it?"

"So much."

I flash a sexy smile. My God, her butt tastes as divine as her pussy. Could this woman get any more perfect?

Running my hands up her legs, I push her back a little, spread her buttocks wide and plunge my tongue deep inside her hot, tight hole. Carly thrashes about and closes her eyes in rapture. She looks so divine.

"Does that feel good?" I ask, looking up at her.

"Yes, so good."

Little by little, I'm teasing out the bad girl in her, and I absolutely love it. The way she responds to me is phenomenal.

When I've finished licking her out, I reach for my coat in search of my condoms. The last time I had sex, most people didn't use protection, so I've had no experience of how to put one on. I detest the idea of using them, but feel I have no choice. There's no way I can take any chances. I can't run the risk of getting Carly pregnant. It wouldn't be fair to her.

She smiles a small, encouraging smile. Her face is consumed by lust.

Don't worry baby, I promise you're going to like this.

I rip open one of the foil packets with my teeth and try to put it on. There's a sharp popping sound. *Dammit!* The condom's burst.

Mortification floods me.

"Lucky these things come in threes," I grin, trying to salvage the situation.

Carly doesn't say anything. She looks sort of terrified.

Don't worry baby, I promise I'll be gentle.

Cautiously, I open another condom and this time it works a treat. Trembling with longing, I push her back onto the bed and spread her legs wide.

This is it. She's really going to let me fuck her. Oh my God…

Feeling light-headed, I rub my dick up and down her pussy to get the tip nice and wet.

"Do you want this cock inside you?" I murmur. I'm so excited I can barely breathe.

"Yes."

"How deep do you want it?"

"So goddamn deep."

Shit, this woman is just too sexy. I need to make her come hard.

Hesitantly, I lower myself between her thighs and slowly ease my cock in, one inch at a time.

Carly cries out with pain, and I stop immediately.

"Am I moving too fast?"

"Please... don't stop," she gasps.

God I love her.

Spreading her legs further apart, I resume feeding my cock into her sweet, tight pussy. Shit, she's so hot for me.

Carly bites back a scream and I'm so fucking proud of her. My angel is taking every inch of me without complaint. Soon, I'm all the way to the hilt, and it feels so good, I almost pass out. I've never had pussy this good. The way it wraps around my dick... I've never felt anything like it. She's so tight, so sweet, it's a struggle not to come immediately.

Very, very slowly, I start to withdraw. Then I slam back in, completely demolishing her with huge deep thrusts that make her scream down the hotel.

I love the way she pushes back on me. I love that she doesn't just lie there and make me do all of the work. We are in a partnership, she and I, our bodies melding together like two hot pieces of clay.

For long moments, I slam into her again and again, stretching her out, giving her my all, making her shriek with ecstasy. It's the best feeling ever. My one regret is that I have to wear this fucking condom. I hate the fact that we're not flesh to flesh, as it spoils some of the intimacy. I'm just longing to fuck her bareback and bathe my dick in her heavenly juices, but I care about her too much to take that kind of risk. *Life can be a bitch.*

"Do you like that baby?" I breathe. "Like how well I fuck you?"

"Uhhhhh! So much."

Then suddenly, everything comes to a standstill.

"Is that all you've got?" Carly chokes.

I gaze down at her, incredulous. "What did you say?"

"I want more. I need more. I want you to fuck me sense-less."

This woman is an animal. I love it!

Sweeping her off the bed, I slam her against the ward-robe. I have to be careful. I don't want any broken bones, but I've just got to let her know what I'm capable of.

Back and forth, I fuck her up against the wardrobe; fuck her till the wood starts to splinter. Jesus, the feeling is electrifying.

Finally, Carly's pussy starts to tighten, and I know she's ready to come. Eagerly, I increase my thrusts until at last we both explode.

Fuck, fuck, fuck.

I've never felt such euphoria. My legs have turned to water and it feels like I'm floating outside of my body.

My God. I think I am in love.

Breathing heavily, I slip the condom off my throbbing penis. Carefully, I take it to the bathroom to dispose of it. When I return to the bedroom, I find Carly collapsed against the wardrobe. Gently, I take her hand and help her back to her feet. Her face is flushed and dripping with sweat.

Silently, I examine the cut on her shoulder.

"You're bleeding," I say sombrely.

She turns and looks at the graze. "Oops! That doesn't look too good," she laughs.

"I'll get you some cloths from the bathroom." Hurriedly, I race to the bathroom in search of a flannel. This is an emergency. I need to get that blood cleaned up before I do something stupid.

"I'm sorry I hurt you," I say, wiping down her shoulder. "I got carried away and didn't mean to be so rough. Will you forgive me?"

Carly grins wickedly. "Nick, there's nothing to forgive. I loved every minute of it." She hesitates. "But what are we going to do about the wardrobe? I don't think the hotel will be too pleased when they see what we've done. That furniture must cost a fortune to replace."

"Don't worry. The manager is an old friend of mine. I'll write him a cheque, and that will be the end of it."

"Are you sure?"

"Yes. Now please, stop worrying."

She falls silent.

When she's finally stopped bleeding, I look her over very carefully from head to foot. Then, gently, I take her hand and kiss her fingers, warming them with my lips. I can tell she likes that. Keeping my eyes on her, I place her middle finger in my mouth and suck on it deeply.

Carly shuts her eyes in rapture.

"Are you sure you're okay?" I whisper.

"Yes," she grins. "I've never felt better."

My stomach clenches. *I'm really starting to fall for this woman.*

Gripping her waist tightly, I pull her back to the bed, throw back the duvet and guide her in. Plumping up the pillows, I make her comfortable, switch off the lamp and plunge the room into darkness. With a loving smile, I wrap my arms around her and drift into a deep, dreamless sleep.

I've never felt so at peace.

The next morning, I take a long hot shower while Carly eats breakfast in bed. When I've finished dressing, I find it hard to meet her gaze, knowing that soon we'll have to say goodbye. This is the painful part. The thought of leaving her makes me feel physically sick, but what choice do I have? I'm a vampire with a very complicated life and a million and one skeletons in the closet. I need to think long and hard about where Carly fits into it all, before I make any definite commitments to her.

"So, what have you got planned for today?" Carly asks, eyeing me intently.

"I have a meeting with a client at one o'clock," I lie. "When we leave here, I'll be going straight to Shepherd's Bush."

"Oh." She looks so disappointed my heart bleeds for her. I hate treating her like this but feel I have no choice. I need some time to reflect on everything and get my head together.

Adjusting my cufflinks, I ask her what she's doing for the rest of the day.

"Oh, I'll probably just go home," she replies weakly. "I've got lots to do, plus I don't fancy walking around West End in the same clothes from yesterday."

I force a laugh. "That's true. Pity me then. I've got to get through a whole meeting before I can go home and get changed."

"Where do you live?"

"Pimlico."

"Very posh."

"Oh, not really. The best thing about it is the transport links. It's a doddle for me to get to work in the mornings."

There's an uncomfortable pause.

Carly downs the last of her orange juice and races to the bathroom to shower. When she's finished washing and dressing, she returns to the bedroom to find me sitting on the bed, watching the highlights from a football game on TV.

"Are you ready to go, darling?" I ask.

"Yes, I think so," she replies flatly. Her face looks so sad I want to throw my arms around her and hug her.

Smiling sweetly, I pick up the remote and switch off the TV. Shrugging on my coat, I take one last look around the room. "Have we definitely got everything?"

She pats down her pockets. "I think so."

"Ah ha!" I snatch her Kermit watch from the dresser and dangle it before her. "We almost forgot this little treasure."

Carly laughs but I can tell it isn't genuine.

Smiling again, I walk over and put the watch back on her wrist. As I finish strapping it up, our eyes meet, and I sense that she requires some sort of explanation. She wants to know if she'll ever see me again after today, but right now, I don't have the answers. I need more time to think about where to go from here.

Linking my arm through hers, I finish locking up, then I lead her out into the corridor. We take the elevator down to the lobby and drop off our keys at reception. As promised, I mention the broken wardrobe to the concierge and a phone call is made. Minutes later, my old friend Luigi appears and takes me to one side for a chat. In no time at all, an agreement is struck.

"So, I'll post you the cheque on Monday?" I grin.

"Yes, sir," Luigi replies. "Whatever's most convenient for you."

We shake hands—a gentleman's agreement. Then I take Carly's arm and lead her out of the building.

A harsh breeze is blowing, and she turns up her collar to fend off the morning chill. Instinctively, I reach in my pocket and roll out the scarf she made for me. Releasing her arm, I tie the scarf around my neck and look around us to get my bearings. "Right, where do I need to take you? The nearest station is Charing Cross. Five minutes in that direction."

"Charing Cross will be fine," she shrugs.

We start walking and in no time at all, we're standing at the entrance to the Underground.

"So, you'll be all right getting home?" I ask earnestly.

Carly nods and forces a grin. "Of course." The silence seems to last forever.

"Aren't you getting the Tube, too? I thought you said you were going to Shepherd's Bush?"

"That's right," I reply, "but I might have a browse of the shops first. I've still got some time to kill before the meeting."

That's a lie. And a not very good one. I wonder if she can tell?

She tucks a hair behind her ear and shifts her weight awkwardly. Inside, I'm dying. I hate behaving like such a bastard.

Lovingly, I wrap my arm around her waist and draw her close. Softly, I kiss her cheek. Fuck, she smells delectable. "Safe journey, darling. I'll call you when I get out of the meeting."

Her face perks up. "Do you promise?"

"I promise."

"Thanks for a wonderful night. It was simply… *awesome*."

For a second, I'm too choked to speak. Wordlessly, I give her a final squeeze, wave goodbye and leave her at the Underground. I dare not look back.

If I do, I know I'll have a breakdown.

When I get back to Pimlico, I collapse on the couch, laughing hysterically. I'm both happy and sad; feel like dancing, feel like crying all at once. My head is so mixed up, I don't know what to do with myself.

I feel like this could be the start of something special, yet at the same time, I'm riddled with severe misgivings about what the future holds for us should I decide to pursue this relationship. I have no doubt that Carly is my soul mate. She totally completes me—the yin to my yang. The joy I feel when I'm with her is indescribable, and I crave our next meeting like a junkie craves heroin. But is it wise for me to feel this way, knowing what terrible dangers may lurk on the horizon? My head is telling me one thing, my heart something else, and I'm completely torn over what to do.

For a while, I sit in my study, contemplating all that has happened in the past few hours. Then, out of nowhere, I sense that I am not alone.

It's the smell that hits me first: an awful odour of death and decay that makes my stomach lurch.

Fearfully, I glance towards the study door. Slowly, it opens, and a dark shape appears before me like some kind of recurring nightmare—a hideous figure I know all too well. Every part of my body goes cold.

My wife Veda, looming over me—a She-Devil returning from the fiery depths of hell.

She smiles a horrendous smile, showing rows of cracked teeth, and I wither a little inside. It kills me to know that I am the architect of that cruel, hate-filled face. I took something beautiful and made it evil. We are cut from the same cloth, Veda and I, united by a history of tragedy and depravity. The things we have seen, no human should ever have to see. The terrible things we have done, we can never undo.

For a silent eternity, I lock eyes with the wife I once thought beautiful. Dressed in deepest black, her face is pale and gaunt, making her look a victim of starvation. Her fingers are talons, and her expression is contorted with pure black hatred.

An expression that I created.

Slowly, I get to my feet and force a half-cordial smile. "Hello, Veda."

Veda remains silent, her eyes burning into me with deranged intensity.

"Hello," I repeat.

"Hello," she replies. Her lips barely move.

"What brings you here?"

"You." She smiles that demented smile. "Always you. Aren't you glad to see me?"

"Of course, I am. You know you are always welcome here."

I swallow and look away from her. I can't stand the guilt, can't stand to look at the goodness and beauty I destroyed. A minute passes. The room throbs with tension. Fighting my revulsion, I manage to continue: "Did you receive the blood Ahmet sent you?"

"Yes," Veda nods. "You have been very generous to me. I can't thank you enough."

"Good, good. Glad to hear it. So... so what else brings you here?"

She tilts her head from side-to-side, then spreads her hands. "I just needed to talk to you. I needed to share something with you."

I sigh. My patience is starting to wane. "What is it you want to share?"

"I followed a girl today. One of your patients; a flame-haired goddess with dimples."

My eyes narrow. "Are you talking about Jessica? You followed Jessica Kemp-Barton, my patient?"

"Yes. I followed her to the park. She has the most delightful daughter. A little girl called Molly. They looked so happy together playing on the swings. It was an absolute joy to watch."

My blood runs cold at the thought. "I want you to stay away from her. I mean it, Veda. Jessica is one of my patients. Can you imagine what would happen if somebody saw you following her? Can you imagine what harm it could do? For God's sake, think about what you're saying. How could you be so careless? You had no right to—"

"What's wrong with just looking?" Veda counters. "Surely I am allowed at least a few moments of joy in this miserable existence of mine? An existence you condemned me to?"

"You know damn well what's wrong with it!" I shout. "What if someone saw you?"

"I don't care. Watching Jessica with her daughter… it was the most wonderful feeling. Seeing them together reminded me of how we once were. When Coppelia was alive."

"Coppelia is gone, Veda," I bellow. "We both know she's never coming back. Now look, we've cried our tears, said our prayers, and now it's time for both of us to move on. You know we can't resurrect the past."

Veda's tone darkens. "Well, if I can't resurrect it, then I will destroy it."

"Don't you dare! If you lay one finger on Jessica or her daughter, I will kill you with my bare hands. I promise you, Veda. I'll do it. You know I'm not bluffing. You've seen what I'm capable of…."

"Oh, believe me, I know what you're capable of. But I'm not afraid of you anymore, Nick. I am my own woman and I'll do whatever I—"

"No, you won't! It's not like you need the blood, Veda. Ahmet has sent you everything you need. There's no need for you to—"

She laughs contemptuously. "If Ahmet's imitation blood is so good, then why don't you drink it? I'll tell you why, Nick. Because deep down, you know there is nothing sweeter than the taste of fresh human blood. Don't even try to deny it. We both know that crap you send me is a pale imitation."

"That may well be so," I concede, "but you'll take what you're given or I'll sever ties with you completely. And stay the hell away from Jessica."

Veda holds my gaze, doesn't even flinch. "Perhaps," she replies noncommittally.

"I don't care what you do in Austria. I don't care who or what you feed on, but understand this: when you are in London, you'll play by my rules or we won't play at all. Understand?"

With an evil smile, Veda turns and glides out the door. "Perhaps."

"There is no perhaps, Veda. I repeat: stay the fuck away from Jessica, and stay the fuck away from me."

The door closes and she's gone.

I bury my face in my hands. How could I ever have been so stupid? How could I ever even contemplate bringing Carly into this horrible mess? I'm a vampire, for Christ's sake! Am I so deluded, so drunk on love that I would risk endangering the life of the woman I love?

It's then that I realise I will have to give her up. There is simply no way I can allow my relationship with Carly to continue. The idea of extending our dalliance beyond a one-night stand is complete and utter madness.

With a cry of rage, I pick up the table and smash it against a wall. Then I claw down the crystal chandelier from the ceiling and throw it to the ground. Roaring like an animal, I tear the mirror off the wall and fling it across the room, scattering shards of glass everywhere.

I have destroyed the room my ancestors so carefully built, but I don't care.

I can't have Carly, and the pain is worse than a stake in the heart.

CHAPTER FORTY-SEVEN

Weak

I PULL BACK the office curtains and gaze forlornly at the rain. It's almost a week since I last saw Carly, and I've been going out of my mind. I want her so much it hurts, but I have to be strong for both our sakes. My heart breaks to treat her like this, but I feel I have no choice. I can't risk exposing her to the dangers of my secret life.

Since Saturday, she's bombarded me with constant phone calls, trying in vain to break through my wall of silence, but I've avoided her at every opportunity. Much as I long to be with her, I know I have to be strong and resist the temptation to answer her calls.

There's a knock on my office door.

"Come in," I shout.

Tara appears. "Ready to go?"

"Yes," I reply.

I gather my things, lock up the room and follow her out into the dark street. For a second, we huddle together on the doorstep of my office, uncertain of our next move. Neither of us has an umbrella. Eventually, we say goodbye and part ways, Tara heading in the direction of Oxford Circus.

As I head in the direction of my car, I hear someone calling out my name. I turn around and see Carly running towards me. Every part of my body freezes. I can't believe what I'm seeing. Is this real or some sort of crazy hallucination?

"Carly! What the hell are you doing here? You're absolutely soaked."

"I don't care," she hisses. "I need to speak to you. You won't take my calls, so what else am I supposed to do?"

Furtively, I glance around the street to check that no one's watching. "All right, we'll talk, but not here. We'll both catch pneumonia if we stand in the rain. I'm parked just around the corner. Let's go."

Taking her umbrella so it shelters us both, I lead her to the quiet, residential street where my car is parked. Closing the umbrella, Carly slips in the passenger side and waits for me to join her. As I get in the driver's seat, my stomach lurches with apprehension.

Oh, my God! I never thought I'd ever be this close to her again.

For a long time, we sit in silence, listening to the sound of our breathing and the rain pummelling the roof and windscreen.

"So…" I sigh. "What is it you wanted to talk about?"

"Why haven't you returned my calls?" she demands. "Why are you treating me like this?"

I remain silent. I have nothing to say in my defence.

"What you did was pretty low," she continues coldly. "Did you really have to get Tara involved to do your dirty work? What did you tell her? That I'm some kind of crazy stalker?"

"I admit I could have handled things better," I say quietly.

"That's the understatement of the century! I want an explanation, Nick. I need to know why you're treating me like this. What have I done wrong?"

I close my eyes and release a heavy sigh. "All I can say is

I'm sorry. You're right. I've behaved like a coward and what I've done is completely reprehensible, but you've got to believe, I didn't mean to hurt you."

Carly laughs bitterly. "Last Saturday was the best night of my life. To me, it wasn't just making love; it was like we had a real connection: something deep, something spiritual. Since that night, all I can think about is you. Talking to you, being near you, holding you…"

My throat gets tight and I'm finding it hard to breathe. This is getting too much.

She stares at me for a long time. "What I'm trying to say is, I don't want this to be over between us."

I turn my head and focus on the rain-speckled windscreen; I can't look at her right now. I'm feeling too emotional. "I enjoyed Saturday, too," I admit finally. "We had a lot of fun and I found it very entertaining, but I've taken this as far as I want it to go."

Carly is now close to tears. "You planned this from the start, didn't you? You must get a sick thrill out of tormenting people. Is it just me, or do you sleep with all of your patients?"

"Now don't go too far, I'm warning you. Remember, it was you who asked me out. I didn't exactly put a gun to your head."

"And it was you who badgered me to take part in your bloody case study," she hisses. "You offered me free treatment. You booked us a hotel room. What was I supposed to think?"

There's a long, seething silence. I'm in a terrible position. For the first time ever, I don't know what to do. Then she starts to cry, and once she's started, she can't stop. My heart breaks. I'm dying to put my arms around her to comfort her but something prevents me. It's like I'm frozen.

"Why don't you want me?" she sobs. "Wasn't I—wasn't I good?"

"It's not that," I reply.

"Then what is it?"

I look at the dashboard. "I just don't think it would be a good idea. We're simply not compatible, and it would only end in tears."

"Is there someone else?"

"No."

"Are you married?"

"No."

"Then what?"

I stare at her for a long time. "This is insane," I whisper. "We barely know each other."

"How can you say that after what we did at the hotel?" Carly shouts. "Sex isn't a handshake, Nick. It isn't something impersonal you can just erase like… like it never happened. People have feelings you know. I opened up to you, I gave you everything, we did the most intimate thing two people can do, and still, you treat me like a stranger. What have I done to deserve this?" She pauses and wipes mascara from her eyes. "I guess I only have myself to blame. I should have known this would happen. I won't bore you with the details, but let's just say my life up to this point hasn't been great. It's one big disappointment after another. But you know what's funny? Even after all that's happened, I always clung to the hope of a happy ending. I deluded myself that one day a person's luck can change for the better. Well, let me tell you something; you've completely destroyed even that one last shred of hope."

I start to tremble.

Fuck, Carly, don't do this to me.

Silently, I look straight ahead. Words have deserted me.

Carly leans forward and forces a smile. "Listen, Nick, I understand if you don't want anything serious, but what about something casual?"

"What? You mean just sex?"

"Yes. Friends with benefits."

"Would you really be happy with something casual?"

"Yes. If it meant I still got to see you, then yes, I-I think I would."

"Too bad I'm not prepared to do that."

She rubs her face with her hand. "Right, I give up. Why won't you give me a chance? Just tell me what your problem is."

"You really want to know?"

"Yes!"

"The problem is I'm in love with you, Carly. And I'm fucking scared. This wasn't supposed to happen."

The car goes quiet. Taking ragged breaths, I reach down and locks my fingers through hers. After a few seconds, I'm ready to talk again. "That feeling you described, that connection between us, I felt it from the first moment I saw you. I've never believed in love at first sight, but it's the only rational explanation." I pause to catch my breath. "Last Saturday was insane. The second we left the hotel and I said goodbye to you at the station, it felt like my life was going into freefall. I didn't want to let you go, but I knew I had to."

"Why?"

"Self-preservation. I knew if I didn't let you go then, I never would. And then there'd be no going back. I didn't want to fall in love with you. I tried so hard to fight it, tried so hard to keep things professional between us, but you've gotten to me in a way no one else ever has. Your kindness, your sweetness, it hits me right here." I take her hand and press it against my heart.

"But I don't understand," Carly whispers. "Why would you want to prevent yourself from being happy? Why is loving me so bad?"

I stare into my lap. "Because I'm not right for you."

"What are you talking about? Nick, you're the best thing that's ever happened to me! Don't you think I should be allowed to decide what's right for me?"

"I am not good enough, not worthy enough," I say. "I don't deserve you. There's so much you don't know about me."

"Yeah, and there's a lot you don't know about me," she counters. "I'm ready to swap notes whenever you are."

I throw my head back and laugh. "Your naivety is endearing."

Carly doesn't see the funny side. "But isn't that how all relationships start? With neither person knowing much about the other? That's what makes it fun. I was living half a life before I met you; I was drifting through darkness, numb to everything. It wasn't a life; it was just existing, waiting for that day when the light is finally put out. And then I had that one night with you, that one perfect night, and everything brightened. Please, don't send me back to that dark place."

Oh my God. I've waited a lifetime to hear those words.

Shaking with emotion, I bite down on my fist to help steady myself. This is all too much. None of this was supposed to happen. My defenses are down and I've never felt so vulnerable in my life.

Carly reaches across and softly strokes the side of my face, caressing the raised bumps of my scar. My balls start to tingle. She knows how to turn me on and has me wrapped around her little finger.

"Please give me a chance," she whispers seductively. "I know I can make you happy. Please, don't shut me out. If you let me in, I promise I won't put a foot wrong. Okay, so you've got secrets. Haven't we all? I don't care about that. All I care about is you, being with you; please... I just need to have you in my life."

"Are you sure this is definitely what you want?" I ask dubiously.

"Yes!"

I stare at her, deliberating. I've never felt so torn. *What to do, what to do...*

Finally, I come to a decision. "Okay, if it's sure to make you happy, we'll give this relationship a chance. I can't bear to see you so upset, and knowing I'm the cause tears me up inside."

Carly's face glows with joy. *Jesus, I love her so much.*

Softly, I kiss her hand and steer the Jaguar back onto the main road. Within seconds, we're moving through the rainy streets, heading in the direction of Pimlico. I don't say a word. I just keep my eyes on the road, watching the wipers dance back and forth across the windscreen.

I don't know what the future holds for us but one thing I know is this: tonight, I am going to eat Carly alive.

Nick and Carly's story continues…

If you would like to join my exclusive VIP Reader Club

GO HERE **and be the first to know when the next book in the "My Sweet Vampire" series is available!**

eepurl.com/hiHqEP

Thank You!

Thanks so much for reading this book and trusting me to entertain you for a couple of hours. If you enjoyed any of my books, I would be so grateful if you could take a moment to post a review on Amazon, Goodreads or elsewhere. Reviews are so important to authors, and your help makes a big difference. I love connecting with readers so please feel free to contact me on Instagram: @aholmesauthor or email me at arabellaholmes402020@outlook.com.

Love,

Arabella Holmes

Printed in Great Britain
by Amazon